THE PARADISE WALTZ

THE PARADISE WALTZ

Jessica Stirling

WINDSOR
PARAGON

First published 2009
by Hodder & Stoughton
This Large Print edition published 2010
by BBC Audiobooks Ltd
by arrangement with
Hodder & Stoughton

Hardcover   ISBN: 978 1 408 48778 5
Softcover   ISBN: 978 1 408 48779 2

British Library Cataloguing in Publication Data available

To Gillian
(The One and Only)
With Love

Printed and bound in Great Britain by
CPI Antony Rowe, Chippenham and Eastbourne

CONTENTS

PART ONE

A Very Long Weekend

CHAPTER ONE

She knew without glancing at the wall clock or slipping her watch from her pocket that it was close to half past three and that the working week was almost over. John Thomas had begun to bounce up and down in his seat and, taking their cue from the biggest boy in class, the five- and six-year-olds scrambled to find their schoolbags and scoop up their books and pencils.

'Still,' said Christine evenly. 'Sit absolutely still.'

The little ones froze obediently but the rebels in the back row muttered and, for some incomprehensible reason, kicked the iron stanchions of their desks as if, Christine thought, they were contemplating mutiny just to avoid five more minutes of confinement.

At the beginning of the winter term Mr McKay—Freddy—had finally persuaded the Board of Rural Education that an electrically operated bell was essential to the welfare of the thirty-four pupils in his charge and that failure to install such a device would seriously damage their chances of going on to university. The fact that Greenhill Primary had promoted only three pupils into advanced education in the past ten years cut no ice with Freddy, who regarded every labourer's son and farmer's daughter as a bud just waiting to flower.

'Times are changing, Chris, my love,' Freddy informed her. 'Out of the peasant class will spring the leaders that this country of ours—Scotland, I mean—so desperately needs. Observe the poor wee morsels, hungry for knowledge and parched of ambition. What do they know of the great wide world or the changes the twentieth century will foist upon them? Believe me, before long every ploughman and cowherd will be obliged to present a diploma in science to find any sort of employment at all.'

Christine suspected that Freddy had pitched a similar argument to members of the Board who, to shut him up, had sent two men to fit a cable, a battery, a bell and a button and relegate the heavy brass-tongued 'clanger' to the cupboard. She rather missed the old wooden-handled bell. The button for the new electrical system was hidden beneath Mr McKay's desk in his classroom across the hall and she, like her restless charges, was obliged to await the headmaster's pleasure, which was not always as prompt as it should be.

'Miss, miss, Charley's out there again.'

'Charley,' Christine said, 'has been out there all afternoon.'

'Aye, miss, but now he's at the fence.'

In Christine's opinion there was nothing remarkable about Charley Noonan who, perched on the skinny metal seat of the Wallis tractor, peeped into the classroom and gave his juvenile admirers a friendly wave.

'I see he's put the studs on,' one eight-year-old remarked.

'Aye, no' before time,' said another. 'It rained heavy last night.'

Nine years ago, when the big American-made Wallis had been new, the boys would have raced to the window and pressed their noses to the glass, for Noonan's tractor had been the first of its kind in the parish. Now, in 1932, several other tractors had appeared, lighter, faster and more economical than Noonan's old puffer with its upright exhaust and smelly paraffin engine.

The boys were no longer impressed.

The girls had no interest in Mr Noonan's agricultural equipment. They signalled to Charley in hectic semaphore and darted sly glances at Miss Summers as if they expected her to dissolve into jelly at the mere mention of the farmer's name.

'Oh, miss, he's waitin' for you, miss.'

'See, miss, he's wavin' at you.'

For the past four days Charley had been preparing the field behind the school for potato planting. It had been a wet winter and Charley, like most Stirlingshire farmers, was running behind. Running behind, or not, he still found time to anchor his tractor by the fence shortly before the bell was due to ring.

'If you're goin' t'marry Mr Noonan,' one six-year-old piped up, 'can I be a flower girl, miss?'

'Can I be a flower girl, too, Miss Summers?'

'Me too, miss. Me too.'

'If ever I do decide to get married you can all be flower girls,' Christine said, 'but right now I'm not engaged to Mr Noonan—or to anyone else.'

'Is he not your sweetheart then?'

In her day, not so long ago, whether you were five or fourteen, talking out of turn inevitably brought a taste of the tawse, that thin black snake of a strap that lay coiled in every teacher's pocket ready to be drawn across a small, trembling palm at the first sign of familiarity. It was still much used, she supposed, in city schools or rural institutions that didn't have an 'enlightened' head

5

like Frederick McKay who believed that freedom of expression was a keystone of learning.

'No, Joyce, Mr Noonan is definitely not my sweetheart.'

'Why not, but?'

'Because he—' Christine began.

Then the bell buzzed, like a bee in a bottle.

And the class exploded.

*   *   *

Greenhill Primary lay on the high road between Ottershaw and Kennart. Although traffic was rarely heavy at that hour of the afternoon, there were perils enough in the countryside to threaten small children. Infants were released a half-hour before Juniors, an inconvenient arrangement that obliged Christine to hang about to ensure that every child under seven had a brother, sister or trusted friend from the Junior class to accompany them to the road-end or farm gate where, in an ideal world, mother would be waiting to greet them.

Johnny Thomas and his little sister made for the village where their father, a blacksmith, had his forge. The two mechanically minded experts, still arguing about fly-wheels, magnetos and studs, set off for the row of workers' cottages on the Balnesmoor Estate. Christine ushered six little stragglers into the playground. They ran at once to the fence, drawn by the brown paper bag of wine gums that Charley had fished from his pocket.

There was nothing sinister in Charley Noonan's liking for children. Whatever his faults—and they were many—he had an impeccable reputation as a

6

Sunday school superintendent and an officer in the Boys' Brigade. He had enough respect for convention to wait for Christine's nod before he began lobbing sweets over the fence, like a zoo-keeper feeding fish to seals.

Chris hung back until every child had a wine gum stuck in his or her cheek then, with a sigh, she wandered over to confront the burly young farmer.

'You really shouldn't do that, Charley.'

'Do what, darlin'? It's only a few sweeties.'

'Stop at the window, I mean, wave to them.'

'I wasn't wavin' to them. I was wavin' to you,' Charley said. 'Any roads, what harm does it do?'

'It gives the children the wrong idea.'

'Aye, aye,' said Charley. 'You mean they think I'm your sweetheart.'

'Which you're not.'

'It's not for want o' tryin', is it?' Charley laughed.

Four little girls had formed a half circle behind the teacher and, sucking noisily on their sweets, were listening raptly to Mr Noonan's attempt to woo her.

'Don't be so nosy,' Chris told them sharply. 'Go over there and play,' and, to her relief, saw them scamper off.

'Fancy a wine gum?' Charley said. 'Plenty left.'

'No,' Christine said. 'Thank you all the same.'

'Cigarette then?'

'I don't smoke,' Chris reminded him, 'on school property.'

'Aye,' Charley said, 'you're a model o' propriety, right enough.'

She ignored the back-handed compliment. 'When will you finish here?'

'If the rain stays away we'll be finished by Wednesday, like as not.'

'Good.'

'Can't wait to get rid o' me, eh?'

'I don't like you bothering me in front of the children.'

'Is it such a bother to snatch a bit o' conversation?'

'It's not the conversation,' Christine said, 'it's where the conversation leads that bothers me.'

Charley leaned on the steering wheel. 'An' where might that be?'

'I'll tell you where it's not,' Christine answered. 'It's not to the Young Farmers' dance tomorrow night.'

'What have you got against farmers?'

'Not a thing,' said Christine.

'What have you got against me then?'

She shook her head. 'I like you, Charley, I just don't want to . . .'

'To what?'

'Encourage you.'

'It's a bit late for that,' he said. 'I've been courtin' you for years, in case you haven't noticed?'

'Oh, I've noticed,' Christine said. 'How could I not notice? Why won't you take no for an answer?'

' 'Cause I'm just as stubborn as you are,' he said cheerfully. 'Now, what do you say? Stick on your glad-rags, powder your nose, I'll pick you up at seven o'clock tomorrow an' we'll dance the night away.'

'In Kennart church hall,' Christine said, 'with a midnight curfew?'

'Half past eleven,' Charley corrected her. 'It's always the same wi' Saturday dances, in case

8

you've forgotten.'

It had been eight years since she had last been to a dance in Kennart or, for that matter, in any of the villages in the neighbourhood. It was not that she did not like dancing, even the obstreperous jumping about that passed for dancing among young farmers. She could not bring herself to tell Charley Noonan that he was the reason she no longer went anywhere. Ever since she had arrived in Kennart and had passed three terms seated in front of him in what had then been the old parish schoolhouse he had been making up to her with a determination that most young women would have found flattering.

Charley had never been cruel, had never bullied her, had never tugged her pigtails, dripped ink on her jotter or slipped grasshoppers down the neck of her dress. Indeed, he had protected her when other boys and girls had tormented her because of her unfamiliar accent and the fact that she lived with the Brigadier at Preaching Friar, which rendered her, in their eyes, 'posh'.

There was no reason for her not to like Charley, in spite of his bitten fingernails and coarse brown hair. Perhaps it was the shape of him, as broad as he was tall, that put her off, or the barely contained vitality that made him the life and soul of every party. But now, approaching thirty, she was almost ready to admit that she was well and truly 'on the shelf' and that if she did not marry soon she would not marry at all. A new generation was springing up and Christine suspected that if she showed her face at the dance in Kennart she would be surrounded by fertile young things of eighteen, nineteen or twenty who would dismiss her as far too old to be considered a rival for any man's attention, even Charley's.

She nursed a gloomy feeling that being plain, with no figure to speak of and no other suitor on the horizon, she might eventually be daft enough to marry Charley Noonan, who, with all that energy spilling out of him, would drag her off to Ottershaw and fill her up with one baby after another until, in ten or fifteen years, she would be a worn-out hag. Besides, she was not cut out to be a farmer's wife, but that did not seem to matter to Charley.

'If I promise to keep my hands to myself an' deliver you back to your mammy by midnight, will you consider it?' Charley said. 'Anyhow, it's hardly the weather for lyin' about in the heather, is it?'

He was trying to make a joke of it but Christine remained wary. He had kissed her once, long ago, had held her so close that she could hardly breathe and although she had thrust him violently away, she had not forgotten the brief, lurid loss of control that his kiss had occasioned.

As if he had read her thoughts, Charley went on, 'I was too young to know better, Christine. It was a bloody long time ago, anyway.'

'It's not that, Charley,' she told him.

'What is it then?'

'I just don't want to give you any false hopes.'

'Hopes?'

'I'm not the marrying kind, Charley.'

'Why? Don't you like men?'

'I like men well enough.'

'But not this man, eh, not me?' There was, it seemed, a limit to his patience. He adjusted his broad hips to the metal seat and reached for the

10

starter switch. 'Damn it, it's only a dance, Chris, only another dance.'

'Charley, I'm sorry.'

'Not as sorry as I am,' he said and, when the engine sputtered into life, fisted the wheel, steered the tractor round in a half circle and drove away up the side of the field without looking back.

CHAPTER TWO

It had been a good day, a very good day. He had thought of Marion hardly at all. He had called for an early surgery and had been at the table by eight with a varied slate to keep him occupied.

First he had removed six large grey polyps from the nose of a five-year-old, a brave wee lad, who had shed not a single tear even when his nose was being cocainised. He would have preferred to put a patient of that age under but Josie Carmichael, his anaesthetist, was reluctant to use gas for what was, on the surface, a minor operation. He had let her have her way.

Fifteen minutes with the cold wire snare and broad-bladed forceps had done the trick. The child had been so well-behaved that he had even taken time to pick off the tags and ensure that there were no other nasal deformities. It had all been perfectly simple, an easy tune-up for the more complicated operations that lay ahead. Perfectly easy save for the fact that the little boy had kept his eyes open all the time, big, brown eyes without a trace of fear in them, only a dog-like trust that he, the surgeon, would do him no harm.

Compassion had not translated into self-pity, though, and for the rest of the morning he had been so absorbed in his work that Marion might never have existed, let alone have died.

'Popping off early, old man?' said a voice behind him.

He balanced his coffee cup on the brass-topped table of the railway refreshment bar and looked round.

McEwan was chief dispensary physician at the South Side Infirmary. He leaned on the bar, nursing a whisky and puffing on a shiny black cheroot. His overcoat was thrown open, scarf trailing, his hat, a squashed fedora, pushed back from his brow. He had been in the running for the Martindale Chair of Clinical Medicine at one time but rumours concerning his fondness for drink and fondling young nurses, though never confirmed, had put paid to his chances.

Alan let out a muffled groan as McEwan eased over to his table.

'Heard about the old lady, Kelso. Sorry.'

'Thank you.'

'Not sudden, though?'

'No, not sudden.'

'Best part of a year, was it?'

'I'd hardly call it the best part,' Alan Kelso said.

'No, of course not.'

McEwan pulled out a chair and, without invitation, plonked himself down at the table. He drew on the cheroot. 'Cancer?'

'Yes.'

'Where?'

'Colon.'

'Nasty,' McEwan said. 'Very nasty.' He shrugged

12

as if, duty done, it was time to step off the eggshells. 'So where are you off to for the weekend? Somewhere exciting, I trust.'

'Home,' Alan told him.

'Stirling, is it?'

'Ottershaw.'

'That's it, that's it,' McEwan said. 'I believe I did hear you'd become a lord of the manor. How long have you been out there?'

'Five years.'

'Really! I had no idea. Not awfully convenient for the factory, is it?'

'Not awfully,' Alan agreed.

'How do you cope with early surgery, let alone ward rounds?'

'I put up at the Caledonian overnight.'

'Ah, yes, the jolly old Caledonian. I was blackballed out of the Caledonian, you know, back in the twenties.'

'No, I didn't know.'

'Anyway, 'nuff said about that. What are you drinking?'

'Coffee.'

'Coffee—on a Friday afternoon? Let me stand you a stiff one.'

'No, thanks,' Alan said. 'I'll have to be off in a minute or two.'

The hand on the sleeve, that confiding tone again: 'Big house, is it?'

'Big enough.'

'Big *empty* house these days, I'll bet.'

'Yes.'

'Housekeeper?'

'I've a woman—'

'Thought as much—though I didn't like to pry.'

'. . . a woman who comes in every day.'

'And every night? Sorry, sorry. Tactless thing to say.' McEwan's apology lacked conviction. 'It's just that if it were me, if I was your age—what age are you, Kelso, about forty?'

'Forty-six.'

'Well, if I was your age and, heaven forbid, my Doris gave up the ghost I'd be far too miserable to live on my own for long. I mean, how *do* you manage without a lady to look after you on the— shall we say—the domestic front?'

'I keep busy,' said Alan thinly.

'Work, the great healer, yes. Still, all work and no play . . .'

Alan got to his feet. 'My train leaves in five minutes.'

McEwan rose too. He glanced at the clock that dominated the concourse. 'God! Is that the hour?' He swallowed the remains of his whisky and dropped the butt of the cheroot, still burning, to the floor. He punched Alan softly on the upper arm. 'Talking of ladies, I'm off to Aberdeen to fish the Don with a rather attractive peeress of a certain age. No names, no pack drill.'

'And Doris?'

'Gone south to visit the grandchildren.' McEwan chuckled. 'What the missus doesn't know won't kill her, will it?'

'No,' Alan Kelso said, 'I don't suppose it will.'

Then, hefting up his briefcase, he wished McEwan a brusque goodnight, and headed for the faraway platform and the shabby two-coach train that would carry him home to Ottershaw.

*　　　*　　　*

14

Bruce began barking as soon as she entered the house. She could hear the Scottie scratching frantically at the door of the sitting-room and, a moment later, the Brigadier calling out, 'Christine, if that's you, will you do something about this blasted dog, please, before I wring his neck.'

Dumping her satchel on the chest beneath the window, Chris crossed the hall to the sitting-room and mischievously rattled the ornate knob for a moment or two before she opened the door and, kneeling, let the stumpy little terrier leap into her arms.

Bruce was four years old and had not yet acquired the dour character common to all Scotch terriers. He spent most of the day lying on the Brigadier's lap in one room or another or, if the Brigadier was busy with letters or trying to read a newspaper, snoozing at his master's feet. But the instant Christine arrived home, he changed from a passive, if annoying, lap dog into a noisy, tail-wagging bundle of energy. Officially, Bruce was the Brigadier's pet but it was Christine who fed him, Christine who took him walking and, the Brigadier grumbled, it was obvious to whom the deceitful little devil, like all pot-lickers, gave his true allegiance.

The only member of the Brigadier's household who Bruce did not take to, and who did not take to him, was Christine's mother, Maude, but although she might grouse at the Scottie and now and then give him a nudge with the side of her foot, she knew better than to abuse him.

The Brigadier twisted round in his high-backed armchair. 'There,' he said, 'she's home at last. Are

15

you happy now, you rascal?'

Puffing a little, for Bruce was no light weight, Christine carried the dog into the sitting-room where a coal fire burned in the grate and a standard lamp in the corner had already been lighted. 'I'll take him out, shall I?'

'Have tea first,' the Brigadier suggested.

He tweaked the threadbare tassel that some long-dead tyrant, probably his grandfather, had installed to keep the servants on their toes. Maude Summers arrived with the tea tray before the echo died away.

Tipping the dog on to the carpet, Christine brought a little kidney-shaped table from the corner and placed it by the old man's chair. Her mother set the tray upon it, removed the muslin cover from a plate of toasted teacakes and poured two cups of tea.

'Aren't you joining us, Maude?' the Brigadier asked.

'I'm in the middle of making dinner.'

The old man reached for a teacake. Maude slid a plate on to his lap and Christine tucked a napkin into the neck of his cardigan.

The Brigadier frowned but did not complain. In the past few months, he had become reconciled to the debilitating infirmities of old age and no longer chided the women for 'babying' him.

Bruce put his paws on the arm of the chair and cocked his head.

'Now what could you possibly want?' the Brigadier said as he tore off a piece of teacake with his crooked fingers and fed it to the dog.

'I do wish you wouldn't do that,' Maude Summers said. 'It's small wonder the creature has no manners.'

'Manners?' the Brigadier said. 'He's a dog, for heaven's sake.'

'And should be treated as such.'

'Madam,' the Brigadier said, 'don't you have something to do in the kitchen?'

'Yes,' Maude Summers said. 'I do.'

'Then scamper off and do it,' the Brigadier told her, not at all sternly, while Bruce, having gobbled down the titbit, squatted at Christine's feet and placed a pathetic paw on her knee.

'Mum does have a point, you know,' she said. 'Bruce is getting rather fat.'

'A good run about will pare him down,' the old man said. 'It'll soon be time for you to dig out the bicycle and race the little blighter from here to Ottershaw. If I were ten years younger, I'd do it myself.' He bit into the teacake, chewed and swallowed. 'I used to run the legs off poor old Bracken when she was alive.'

'You used to run the legs off me, too.'

'Oh, you were more than up to it in those days.'

'I still am,' Christine reminded him.

'Of course, of course you are.' He lifted his teacup and, holding it close to his chest, sipped. 'Why, when I was your age, I was . . .' He paused. 'Where was I?'

'In the Transvaal,' Christine told him.

'So I was, so, indeed, I was.' He looked up. 'By gum, child, you know my history better than I know it myself. You've heard it rather too often, I suppose. Well, I'll not bore you with more of the same—at least not today.'

Christine had been brought to Preaching Friar in 1915, a few months after her father had been

17

killed in the March offensive at Neuve Chapelle. The Brigadier had been wounded in the same battle and, much to his disgust, put out to pasture. He had retreated to Preaching Friar, the big, old ancestral house in which he had spent no more than a handful of months in the course of a long military career.

He claimed not to have known Christine's father, a lowly private, and his reason for contacting Maude out of the blue had never been made clear. He had written to Mrs Summers to offer her a position as his housekeeper, the child being, it seemed, no impediment. With nothing but a scrap of pension to support her, Maude Summers had jumped at the offer.

The Brigadier sat up. 'Here,' he said, 'what time is it?'

'Just after five,' Christine answered.

'Switch it on then, girl, switch it on.'

Carefully wiping her fingers on a napkin, Christine crossed to the breast-high walnut cabinet that housed the radiogram. She switched on the set and thumbed the Bakelite knob until a faint whine changed to a fierce crackle through which the strains of a dance band emerged.

'Who is it tonight?' she asked.

'Jack Payne,' the Brigadier told her.

Five o'clock marked the beginning of the BBC's evening programme of light entertainment and brought Brigadier Sandy Crockett's dreary afternoon to an end. Newspapers excepted, he had no stomach for reading nowadays but revelled in the sweet, swinging music that the wireless provided. He knew all the orchestras and band-leaders by name and, to Christine's amusement, would croon the sentimental love songs without so much as a blush.

During the long winter evenings they sat, all three, by the fire in the sitting-room and listened to one programme after another or, if the broadcast turned pompous, played records on the gramophone. Before his legs became too weak to support him the Brigadier would dance, sedately, with her mother. Even now, half crippled, he would hoist himself from the armchair and sway in time to the music as if the rhythms remained, youthful and clamouring, in the marrow of his bones.

The band-leader's signature tune emerged loud and clear from the cavernous cloth-covered speaker.

The Brigadier let out a sigh and, closing his eyes, sank back in his chair.

'Happy now?' Christine asked.

'Quite happy, thank you,' the Brigadier answered and hardly seemed to notice when she cleared the tea things and, with the Scottie trotting at her heels, carried the tray out into the hall.

*　　　*　　　*

If there was one thing Alan hated it was riding home in the dark and the long, stumbling walk following the beam of his pocket torch up the country road from Ottershaw Halt to Moss House. He gazed, thoughtfully, from the window as the train rattled through the small, smoky towns on the outskirts of Glasgow and jogged at length on to the line that skirted the hills.

'Rain before morning, I fear.'

19

'Yes,' Alan agreed, 'another wet weekend in store by the look of it.'

Weather was the sole topic of conversation between the two men who shared the first class compartment. Alan did not even know the chap's name, only that he smoked scented tobacco in a blackened briar pipe, wore pale grey spats and pored over the *Scotsman* with grim concentration.

He did not get off at Ottershaw but rode on, with nothing more than a nod by way of farewell; rode on to where, Alan wondered: to Kennart or Harlwood or all the way out to the junction and beyond?

One word to Marion and she would have unearthed everything there was to know about the fellow but he had never mentioned his mysterious travelling companion to Marion, and it was too late now.

He watched the hills slide away as the track looped along the plain.

The river, the Kennart, trailed the embankment for a mile or two. He caught the glint of fading daylight on the water before the river vanished into the trees above the salmon pool. Marion and her friend Mrs Waddell had often toddled down there in the autumn months and had come back full of tales of spate and spray and the courage of the spawning fish. Marion had revelled in the wonders of the natural world, wonders that he had long ago put behind him.

He spotted a tractor, big and square like a water tank, rolling along the highway in the gathering dusk, and on the back road that climbed from the river a dung-cart drawn by a Clydesdale and, a little further on, a girl and a dog.

20

He craned forward to watch her wave her scarf at the passing train, as a child might do. For a moment he was tempted to wave back but before he could obey the impulse the curve of the track blocked her from view.

The gentleman lowered his newspaper an inch or two and regarded him with the trace of a smile.

'Sandy Crockett's girl,' he said.

'Sandy Crockett?' Alan said.

'The Brigadier.'

'His daughter?'

'His housekeeper's daughter.'

'I didn't know we had a Brigadier in these parts. What regiment?'

'Gordon Highlanders. Retired,' the gentleman said, and retreated behind his newspaper once more.

CHAPTER THREE

'For God's sake, Charley,' Beatty McCall said, 'if you're going to hang about like a soul in torment, the least you can do is make yourself useful.'

'What do you want me to do?'

'Give me a hand with this tree branch for one thing.'

'What are you burnin' that for, Beatty? It's good firewood.'

'It is not good firewood. It's green rubbish that'll make my chimney smoke. I've more than enough firewood to see me through the spring, as well as a coal pile the size of Ben Lomond. Here, grab hold.'

She gave him a thump with her shoulder to spur

him on.

Between them, they dragged the huge broken branch to the bonfire and, on Beatty's count, lifted it and swung it on to the blaze. A shower of sparks rose into the air and rode gleefully off to flicker into oblivion halfway across the pasture.

Beatty planted her hands on her hips and watched the flames eat into the smooth grey bark. She looked handsome in that pose, Charley thought. She was taller than he was, and older. She wore a patched ankle-length skirt and a faded flannel shirt and her features had a lean, almost masculine cast. When she lifted her shoulders and stuck out her chest, though, there was no mistaking her for a man.

'What are you burnin', anyway?' Charley said. 'You've no bracken on your patch, have you?'

'Keep your mind off my patch, Charley Noonan, or I'll tell your mother on you.' She clapped a grubby hand to his shoulder. 'What do you want? I've no spare ponies if that's what you're after and if you're looking for an extra hand to help plant your spuds—forget it.'

'It's not that.' His Adam's apple bobbed. 'It's—ah—the dance.'

'What dance?'

'Young Farmers—at Kennart—on Saturday.'

'What about it?'

'Would you—I mean, do you fancy a dive out there, Beatty?'

She stared at him for five long seconds then threw back her head and laughed. 'Dear God, Charley, if I didn't know you better I'd think you'd been at the booze. I mean, I don't clap eyes on you for weeks then you turn up to invite me out for a

22

spot of the old ballroom with a bunch of kiddies.'

'They're not all kiddies.'

'Aye, but they are,' Beatty said. 'When you reach my age everyone's a kiddie—even you, Charley Noonan.' She nudged him with her shoulder and steered him towards the long, low hut that nestled near the pillar of the railway bridge. 'Come on, sonny, out with it. What do you really want? It can't be to invite me to a dance? For God's sake, I'm old enough to be your mother.'

'No, you're not, nowhere near.'

'Well, no, actually, I don't suppose I am,' Beatty admitted. 'But in this part of the world if you're still single at twenty you're past it and if you're female and fast approaching forty they think you've one bloody foot in the grave.'

'You're not past it, Beatty.'

'Aye, but I am.'

'You don't look it.'

She grunted, more amused than flattered, and pushed him on to the step that led up to the open door of the hut.

For a moment Charley thought she might be about to drag him inside, as she'd done once before, ten years ago. She'd been tipsy on beer that night and he'd been too dumb to know what she wanted with him until it was all over. He did not regret it—far from it—but when, a week or two later, he'd come sniffing round looking for more of the same she'd sent him off with a flea in his ear and had never let him near her again.

Beatty seated herself on the step beside him. She fished a crushed paper packet of Woodbine from the pocket of her shirt and offered him a cigarette.

He took it, straightened it carefully, and, digging out his matches, lit her cigarette and his from the same match while cupping his hand over hers; something he'd seen Maurice Chevalier do in *The Playboy of Paris* and had being dying to try ever since.

'If it's romance you're after, Charley'—Beatty removed her hand from his—'why don't you go solo? I'll bet there's a dozen young girls who'd be more than willing to be led astray by a fine handsome guy like you.'

'I'm not interested in young girls.'

Beatty blew a plume of smoke into the night air. 'It's the teacher, isn't it? You're hoping to make the teacher jealous. You want to shuffle into the hall with a woman on your arm and let it leak back to her. What's wrong, Charley? Will she still not give you the time of day?'

'Nah, she won't.'

'Then she's not the one for you.'

'She is,' said Charley sourly. 'She just doesn't know it yet.'

'You mean, she's not desperate enough.'

He drew on the cigarette and slumped forward with his arms on his knees. 'I'm not lookin' for a bit o' fluff, Beatty. I want to marry her.'

'How long have you been courting Miss—what's her name again?'

'Christine Summers: ten years, give or take.'

'And you're not getting any younger, right?'

'I'm damned near thirty-two.'

'Lucky you!' said Beatty. 'Is there someone else?'

'No, Christine's the only one for me.'

'I mean does *she* have someone else, someone

on the side?'

Charley sat up. 'I never thought o' that.' He shook his head. 'Nah, I'd have heard if there was someone else.'

'Then she's waiting for him.'

'For who?'

'Prince Charming.'

'Geeze!' said Charley. 'She'll wait long enough for one o' them.'

It was almost full dark now and the wind was cold. He stared at the bonfire and watched the elm branch sag and another dense shower of sparks fly upward. The woman beside him was warm—he could feel the heat of her body through her clothes—but he had no desire for her now, or not much.

Out in the pasture pressing against the sagging wire fence that he had put up for her a year or two back he saw eight or ten ponies huddled together in a shaggy bunch, their eyes glistening in the firelight.

'What'll I do, Beatty? What can I do?'

'Find someone else, Charley,' Beatty McCall told him, 'someone young enough not to have any illusions.'

'What does that mean?'

She rose suddenly to her feet, flipped away the shreds of her cigarette, offered him her hand and when he took it yanked him upright.

'You're still a fine catch, Mr Noonan. Go and find a girl who has her head screwed on the right way, one who knows a good thing when she sees it and who's willing to learn to be a farmer's wife. You've a thriving farm and a big farmhouse and while you might not be six foot two with eyes of blue you're not the Hunchback of Notre Dame either.'

'The what?' said Charley.

'Never mind,' said Beatty. 'It's one thing to love, Charley, quite another to be loved. If you're desperate enough to contemplate asking me to the Kennart hop then it's high time you learned to tell the difference.'

'So it's not on?'

'No,' said Beatty firmly, 'it's not on, Charley. It's definitely not on.'

'Oh well,' he said, 'you can't blame me for tryin', can you?'

'I never blame anyone for trying,' Beatty said.

She watched him clump off towards the tractor parked at the field gate and then, with a little shrug, went back to tending her bonfire.

*   *   *

Cooking had never been his forte. He could, of course, bone a chicken or fillet a piece of fish—anything less would have been a joke—but when it came to chopping vegetables and gauging the temperature of the iron stove or the electric hot-plate he was all at sea.

In twenty years of marriage he had never been called upon to lift a finger in the kitchen. Marion had seen to all that. Before Marion, his mother had prepared his meals and a maid had served them and all he'd had to do was turn up at table and eat what was put before him. Even during his four years of service in Egypt there had been a batman or orderly to ensure that he was fed and watered. It had come as something of a shock, therefore, to realise how much time and effort was involved in preparing a decent breakfast or a simple three-course dinner.

His erratic schedule made planning difficult for his part-time housekeeper, Mrs Mackintosh. There was no telephone in the house and she rarely had any idea when he would return from the hospital, or if he would return at all.

The poor woman did her best to see that he did not starve by leaving cold cuts, meat pies or bowls of stew under plates in the larder and vegetables peeled in the basin by the sink. She had recently taken to scrawling notes on odd scraps of paper instructing him how to boil potatoes or fry chops. He might have been tempted to replace Mrs Mackintosh with a resident housekeeper if the woman had not proved so invaluable during the last months of Marion's illness.

Mrs Mackintosh lived with her husband, a slater, in a tiny rented cottage on the outskirts of Ottershaw and clung so tenaciously to her independence that he did not have the heart to suggest that she move into Moss House to look after him.

Besides, he had a notion that one day soon he might sell up and move back to Glasgow which, in all respects, would be the sensible thing to do.

The move to Moss House had been Marion's idea. She had never much cared for the city. To please her, he had sold the flat in Glasgow and acquired a lease on the square, grey sandstone house that looked out to the hills above Loch Lomond. For three years Marion had been happy here, pottering about in the garden, fitting into village life, trading news and gossip, making friends. And then she had fallen ill. And then she had died. And everything he had done for her, every trifling sacrifice had seemed like too little, too late.

The stove had been stoked, the fire in the sitting-room set, the electrical lamp in the hall left burning. He couldn't have missed Mrs Mackintosh by more than ten or fifteen minutes.

Putting down his briefcase and peeling off his overcoat, he leaned over the table and read the instructions she had left for him. His appetite waned as he read the note. The effort involved in feeding himself hardly seemed worth while.

The empty house, all six silent rooms, weighed heavily upon him.

Peering through the window above the sink he saw the shrubs thrashing madly in the wind and beyond them, dark against the sky, the larch at the corner of the garden bowed almost double. He thought of the folk who were out on the road in this nasty weather and, for no logical reason, of the girl with the dog on the back road to Kennart.

He wondered if she was still there, waving her scarf at passing trains.

He let out a rueful snort, headed across the hall to the library and poured himself a drink from the bottle of Black & White he kept in the desk. Then, sipping whisky as he went, he ambled from room to room, checking window catches and bolting doors to secure the house against the wild March weather and settle in for what promised to be a very long weekend.

CHAPTER FOUR

Cleavers was expected at half past nine and would bring his list of 'requirements' with him. The list was a joke, of course. Any healthy stallion close to four years old was fair game for the horse dealer.

To Beatty's credit Bob Cleavers had never quite got the better of her even in these hard times. Her sturdy miniature ponies remained in demand in the tight-seamed pits of Lanarkshire and West Lothian. Cleavers was well aware that however indifferent he and his colliery clients might be to bloodlines Beatty McCall's Shetlands were the best that money could buy.

She had four young Shetland stallions ready for sale plus six Highlands, bigger and stronger, on which Cleavers would surely bid. Her stable at Picton—she resisted calling it a stud—was close enough to Cleavers's 'ranch'—his term—on the outskirts of Glasgow for his purchases to be herded on the hoof, thus saving the mean old devil the cost of rail carriage or the bother of sending a couple of his rickety lorries to collect them.

The high days of the early twenties, when a healthy pony had fetched as much as forty pounds, were long gone. With industry in depression and money scarce Beatty expected no more than nine pounds a mane for the Shetlands and six for each of the Highlands; just enough to pay the wages of her stable hands, the vet's bill and buy fodder until Cleavers came round again in the autumn.

Her property was composed of a grassy paddock fenced off from ten acres of rough grazing on which her ponies ran free for most of the year. The hut under the railway bridge was flanked by a tumbledown barn and a slope-roofed stable within which foaling was done and, in the worst winter weather, the herd was given shelter.

She had lived on the patch since her husband had strolled off to fight the Kaiser, just a month after their wedding, and had died in the mud of the Somme. If it hadn't been for a faded studio photograph propped behind a beer bottle on the shelf above the fireplace she might have forgotten what Andy had looked like, though not the ardour with which he had taken her virginity or his appetite for love-making in the few short nights they had spent together in the creaky bed in the upper floor of the McCalls' farmhouse with Andy's father, mother and sisters listening to every gasp and groan.

Maggie and Todd Thomas had turned up prompt at eight, sloshing through the mud in the apron of ground that passed for a yard.

The girl was a willing worker, fond of the ponies and not at all resentful of the monotonous tasks allotted her. Her brother Todd was a different kettle of fish. At fifteen he was already taller than his blacksmith father; a great ugly brute of a boy who had a gentle way with animals but a fiery temper governed, Beatty reckoned, by the phases of the moon.

She perched on the step at the door of the hut sipping tea from a mug and blearily scanned the pasture. Todd had been delegated to round up the marketable ponies and drive them through the gate into the paddock. He rode bareback on Lavender, her oldest mare, and coaxed the herd to follow him.

Beatty was not unduly impressed. The mare was used to gatherings and might, she thought fancifully, have brought the herd in on her own if she had been left to it. She dashed out the tea dregs, tossed the tin mug behind her into the hut and, lighting a cigarette, paddled through the mud to the fence.

She was not at her glorious best. She had blown three shillings on brown ale yesterday afternoon, lugging the bottles down from the off-licence in Ottershaw in a canvas sack and, after Charley Noonan had sloped off, had drunk the lot in lieu of supper. She felt sluggish and dull-witted this morning; not an ideal state in which to deal with Bob Cleavers.

Leaning on the gate, she puffed out her cheeks and let the wind wash through her like a dose of salts. She watched Todd nudge the recalcitrant ponies into the paddock where, to demonstrate their mettle, they galloped madly round and round as if the paddock were a circus ring.

She was still draped on the gate post when, ten minutes later, Bob Cleavers came hopping across the yard like the toad he was and, being nothing if not bold, placed a hand on that indeterminate region between her kidneys and her bum.

'Top o' the mornin' to ye, Beatty me love,' he crooned in cod Irish.

She rolled round and glanced at the motorcar parked on the shoulder of the road. 'I hope you've brought your money as well as your fancy piece.'

'Do you mean the lady or the vehicle?'

'I mean the lady,' Beatty told him, 'though the vehicle looks pretty fancy, too. I trust you haven't squandered all your cash on it—or on her, for that matter.'

'The lady's name's Theresa. She's very spiritual.'

'Aye, I'm sure,' said Beatty sarcastically. 'And the motorcar?'

'Austin Seven—not new,' he added, 'not straight out of the showroom.'

'What happened to your old lorry?'

'Oh, I still have that, never fear.'

'And your old wife?'

'I'm not parting with her either,' Bob Cleavers said, 'just easing her gently out to pasture.'

'Ah, you're all heart, Bob, all heart.'

He was already eyeing up the ponies that Todd had driven into the paddock. He swung round and waved to the woman in the motorcar which, with the hood down, reminded Beatty of nothing so much as a baby carriage.

The woman, a young, slim brunette, was none too happy at being whisked out into the country at such an ungodly hour on a windy Saturday morning and her answering wave was grumpy, Biddy thought, rather than adoring.

Stripping off his driving gloves, Cleavers said, 'Now, Beatty, what have you got for me by way of horse flesh?'

'Bob,' she sighed, 'just show me your list.'

'Then we'll get down to haggling, I suppose?'

'Yes,' Beatty agreed, 'then we'll get down to haggling.'

*   *   *

Alan woke at six with rain drumming against the window. He rolled on to his back and lay listening to the squall for two or three minutes before he turned on his side and, with the sheet over his head, willed himself to sleep again.

Marion had once remarked that with a sheet wrapped over his ears he bore an uncanny resemblance to Lawrence of Arabia, a comparison he did not take too seriously. In fact, he had acquired the habit in the Mena Camp in Egypt as protection against the furnace blast of the *khamsin*, the wind that blew straight from the desert. He had told Marion little about his 'war years' as she chose, just a little mockingly, to call them. She had continued to believe that by not serving in France he had somehow dodged the worst of the fighting and that she, stuck at home, had suffered just as much as he had which, in spite of her miscarriage, was far wide of the truth.

The smell of frying bacon finally lured him from sleep. Ignoring the scowling alarm clock that he had learned not to trust, he reached out to the bedside table for his wristlet watch.

Half past nine: Mrs Mackintosh had allowed him to sleep late.

He swung his legs from the bed, found his slippers, found his dressing-gown, found his way into the corridor and calling downstairs as he went—'I'm up, Mrs Mack, I'm up'—shot into the tiled bathroom. He washed his hands, drenched his face in cold water, decided that his housekeeper would not be too scandalised if he appeared for breakfast unshaven and, drawn by the appetising odour, leapt down the staircase and across the hall to the kitchen.

On Saturdays Mrs Mackintosh left at noon. He would not see her again until Monday. He seated himself at the table and when the woman put a plate of bacon and eggs before him, smiled and thanked her.

'Coffee, Doctor?'

He nodded.

Marion had tried to correct the woman by explaining that Mr Kelso was not a physician but a surgeon. Mrs Mack would have none of it. In her view anyone who worked in a hospital was either a nurse or a doctor and she was a doctor's housekeeper and, he imagined, gained a few stock points in the community because of it. He had no idea where he was placed in the league table: higher than the minister, lower than the vet, somewhere on a par with Tom Currie, the local GP, perhaps?

Landowners and farmers had their own league table, of course.

Top of that particular list was Sir Maurice Vosper, peer of the realm, whose family owned vast parcels of land in the parish. When he was not whooping it up in Paris or Berlin, Sir Maurice resided in a baronial castle in the heart of the Balnesmoor Estate which was, to all intents and purposes, as far removed from the lives of ordinary mortals as the Hanging Gardens of Babylon.

Alan had no interest in the rural class system or who was who in Kennart, Balnesmoor and Ottershaw, though, as Marion had shrewdly pointed out, it was really not so very different from the back-biting, rumour-ridden enclaves of the medical profession which had its own pecking order, no less rigid and defined.

He shook brown sauce on to the edge of his plate, plunged his fork into the heart of a fried egg

34

and watched the yolk run deliciously over crisp strips of bacon. He tucked a napkin into the collar of his pyjama jacket and set about demolishing his breakfast while Mrs Mackintosh, a small, stout, broad-beamed woman of about sixty, busied herself grinding coffee beans.

'Tell me, Mrs Mack,' Alan said casually, 'who lives in Preaching Friar?'

She glanced over her shoulder. 'The Brigadier. He's lived there for years.'

'I take it he is retired.'

'Aye, he's an old man now.'

'Does he live alone?'

She poured the ground beans into a metal percolator and filled the barrel with boiling water. Alan mopped up egg yolk with a pinch of bread, waiting. He sensed that she did not approve of his questions or, perhaps, that she did not approve of the Brigadier.

'Why are you asking about him, Doctor?'

He couldn't blame her for being suspicious. Until now he had betrayed no interest in what went on in the community apart from a polite enquiry now and then about Mr Mackintosh's health.

He pushed away his plate and sat back. 'Idle curiosity, I suppose.'

The housekeeper rested her beam on the edge of the dresser and folded her arms. 'Well, I'm not one to gossip but he's not the one causes trouble; it's her.'

'His wife?'

'Never had a wife, not official anyway,' said Mrs Mackintosh. 'No sayin' what went on with him in the army when he was off in those foreign parts.'

35

'Who looks after him?'

'Mrs Summers. He fetched her here from Lord knows where about ten minutes after he came home injured from the war; as if there weren't enough ladies in Ottershaw willin' to look after him. Nobody knew her—or the girl.'

'The girl?'

Mrs Mackintosh leaned closer. 'Some say she's his daughter.'

'Is there any reason for supposing that?'

'He dotes on her.'

'Oh! Well, if the girl is his daughter, where's her mother?'

'She's there too. His live-in.'

'The housekeeper, you mean?'

'Call her that if you like.'

'Perhaps she is just his housekeeper,' Alan suggested. 'I assume she arrived with the girl in tow. The girl must have been fairly young at the time. She's not very old now, is she?'

'Old enough to teach at Greenhill School. The Brigadier paid for her year at the training college. Now why would he do that if he didn't have something to hide?'

'Perhaps he's generous by nature.'

'He's rich enough to be generous, I suppose,' Mrs Mackintosh conceded, 'but there was never a man born who gives a woman something for nothing.'

It seemed that his placid little housekeeper had a mean streak after all.

'Is that what the girl does,' Alan said, 'teaches?'

Mrs Mackintosh nodded. 'Nearly thirty years old and still single. We all know what that means.'

'Do we?'

'She's the old man's darlin'. He's not going to let her go.'

The lid of the percolator chugged.

The woman adjusted her apron and returned to the stove.

'I take it,' Alan said cautiously, 'that Mrs Summers and her daughter are not awfully popular in Ottershaw?'

'Keeps herself to herself, the both of them.'

'I see,' said Alan. 'They don't—ah—mingle?'

'Oh no, they're far too grand for the like of us.' Mrs Mackintosh brought the coffee pot to the table and poured a stream of cloudy liquid into his breakfast cup. 'She's had her chances, that girl. Charley Noonan would have had her up the aisle ten years ago but she wouldn't—and she won't—give the poor man the time o' day.'

'Charley Noonan is—what?'

'A farmer, an honest, hard-working, down-to-earth farmer.'

'Of course,' said Alan.

He experienced a ripple of sympathy for the school teacher who, unless he missed his guess, was a victim of rustic snobbery. Salt-of-the-earth farmers might be the epitome of desirability as far as Mrs Mackintosh was concerned, but they were also more than likely to be uncultured and uncouth. He spooned sugar into his cup, added a dash of milk and touched the scalding liquid with the tip of his tongue.

'Careful,' Mrs Mackintosh warned, 'or you'll burn yourself.'

'Yes,' Alan said. 'I think I'll take my coffee into the library to let it cool—if that's all right with you?'

'Why would it not be all right with me?' the housekeeper said stiffly. 'It's your house, Doctor. You can do what you like in it.'

Which, Alan realised with a jolt, was absolutely true.

*   *   *

Beatty was pleased with the way things were panning out. The brunette in the baby carriage was proving an asset. She persisted in bobbing up and down and calling out to 'Bobby' that she was cold and needed to pee. There was a perfectly serviceable chemical toilet behind the hut but Beatty was not about to sacrifice her advantage to some tart's weak bladder.

Todd Thomas sat on the top bar of the gate, grinning.

Maggie lolled beside him, a cigarette dangling from her lips.

Todd might be several pence short of a shilling and Maggie just an innocent country lass but they were both worldly enough to appreciate that Mr Robert Cleavers's impatient companion might cost the dirty old devil more than he had intended to pay. Even with his fancy piece grizzling in the distance, however, Mr Cleavers was not about to dole out a fistful of dough without a struggle.

'They look big to me,' he grumbled. 'That one in particular.'

'He's only thirty-eight inches at the shoulder,' Beatty said. 'For God's sake, Bob, if he was any smaller you could put him in a shoebox and carry him home under your arm.'

'Bobby, Bobby. I need to pee. I need to pee.'

'Who are you buying them for?' said Beatty. 'Is it Duddingston?'

'I haven't found a market yet.'

'You liar!'

'I'm putting them in a parcel, if you must know.'

'What, sending them to Duddingston by mail?'

'Don't be sarky, Beatty. You know as well as I do they have to be bang on.'

'Well, they are bang on,' Beatty said. 'Question is, are they bang on enough for the price I'm asking?'

'Six quid each for the Shelties,' Bob Cleavers stated.

Todd let out a howl that distracted Mr Cleavers still further. Maggie patted her brother on the thigh and passed him half her cigarette to keep him quiet.

'Baloney!' Beatty said calmly. 'I want twelve.'

Cleavers shook his head. 'Can't do it,' he said. 'Seven.'

'Twelve,' said Beatty. 'I'm standing on that, Bob.'

'Bobby, Bobby.'

'Shut your bloody cake-hole,' Mr Cleavers muttered under his breath, then called out loudly, 'Shan't be long, honey, shan't be long. Cross your legs and hold it in for five more minutes, please.'

'Twelve,' Beatty repeated.

'Look, let's talk a package. How much for the Highlands?'

'Eight.'

'I'll give you six.'

'I might consider seven,' Beatty said grudgingly. 'Give me seven per head on the Highlands and I'll put the Shelties in at ten guineas each.'

39

'Guineas?'

'Come on, Bob, you've been around long enough to know what guineas are.'

'What's that for the package then?'

'Twice times forty-two quid,' Beatty told him.

'Make it a straight eighty.'

The offer was higher than she'd anticipated.

She nodded. 'Eighty it is. God, but you're a hard man to bargain with.'

He was already tugging on his driving gloves. 'Not as hard as you, Beatty. You caught me at a weak moment.'

'Well, you shouldn't bring your lady friends on fishing trips.'

He dug into the pocket of his motoring coat and brought out a bundle of banknotes fastened with a rubber band. He deftly extracted four ten pound notes and eight fivers. The money was anything but clean—one of the tenners even had a bloodstain on it—but Beatty was not fastidious. She let the horse trader count the cash into her outstretched hand without complaint.

Todd and his sister watched, hawk-eyed.

'I'll send a lorry round for the Shelties first thing tomorrow,' Bob Cleavers said, 'along with three blokes to herd the rest on the hoof.'

'Those God-fearing Christians won't appreciate a herd o' Highland ponies clattering through their streets on the Sabbath.'

'That's my worry, not yours.'

'You need them in a hurry, don't you?' Beatty said. 'You've sold them in advance, you bugger?'

'Maybe I have,' Bob Cleavers said, 'then again, maybe I haven't.'

'Where are they bound for? Is it Duddingston?'

40

'Maybe it is, then again, maybe it—'

'*Bobby, Bob-eeeeee.*'

'You'd better go before she wets herself,' Beatty told him.

'Aye, an' ruins my upholstery.' He offered his hand, driving glove included. 'See you in September, Mrs McCall.'

'I'll look forward to it, Mr Cleavers.'

She watched him hop away through the mud to placate his latest girlfriend and, most likely, shove her into the nearest clump of gorse to show her where country folk made water.

'Hey, we done good there, Mrs McCall,' said Maggie Thomas.

'We did, dear, we done real good,' said Beatty and shepherded the girl and her brother into the hut to pay them their wages and celebrate with a glass of ginger pop or, just possibly, a beer or two.

*   *   *

Marion's bedroom provided the best view of the loch but Alan rarely went in there now. Marion's clothes were stored out of sight in the big wardrobe, her jewellery and intimate things in the drawers of the dressing-table. One of these days he would get around to selling the clothes or, more likely, give them to the Salvation Army, but laziness as much as sentiment had so far put him off.

The only obvious reminder that his wife had ever occupied the room was the book she'd been reading a few days before her death—Gogol's *Dead Souls*, of all things—which he had left with her reading glasses on the bedside table just where she had put them down.

Marion had always been fond of Russian novels, perhaps because her father, Jake Goodall, had been—still was, Alan supposed—a voluble supporter of the Bolsheviks; a foible that had struck Alan as odd for a man who owned a tannery and dye works and employed upwards of forty hands, few of whom, Alan suspected, shared their employer's views on social revolution.

He loitered by the window in the library—more office than book-room—sipped coffee, smoked a cigarette and stared out at the steely ribbon of water visible between the trees.

It had stopped raining and the wind had eased. Blobs of rainwater still dripped from the eaves and a puddle had formed on the lawn, a grassy pool around which a number of small birds bickered.

Natural history had never been his strong suit. Marion would have rhymed off the names of the birds without hesitation. She had taken great pleasure from her feeding-trays and nesting-boxes and in the almost tame pheasants that strutted about the doorstep awaiting her handouts. He had kept feeding them for a week or two after Marion had gone but had soon lost interest.

On the desk behind him were half a dozen files, case histories on which he would be expected to voice an opinion at the surgeons' meeting on Monday. He had also brought home a copy of his notes on post-operative pulmonary complications which he intended to expand for an informal lecture to his students after ward rounds on Tuesday.

He would spin the work out as long as possible.

Work was the only thing that took his mind off

Marion or, more accurately, from the fact that her passing had left him with too much time on his hands. He did not fish, shoot, play golf or bridge. He did not garden, paint or engage in carpentry. He did not collect stamps or coins, do crosswords or jigsaw puzzles. He read an occasional newspaper and several medical journals but not much else. He had no patience with musical soirées and had never opened the lid of the big new radiogram that had been Marion's pride and joy.

The hospital was his true home, its wards and boardrooms and especially the claustrophobic operating theatres with their glacial electrical lights, antiseptic sheets and astringent smells. From the moment he had slipped a blade into a cadaver in the old anatomy rooms on Gilmorehill twenty-five years ago nothing had gripped him with such tenacity as the study of medicine. Even in Egypt during the war he had endured all the dangers and discomforts without complaint, grateful for the opportunity to advance the range of his surgical skills.

Marion had never grasped that his single-mindedness was not rooted in ambition. His one regret in that respect was that he had let her slip away without trying to explain quite what surgery meant to him.

He turned from the window and riffled the pages of the topmost file: an ischiorectal abscess in a malnourished boy of two, a not uncommon condition in poor Glasgow children. Drugs or surgery? A decision must be made soon. Surgery seemed an obvious choice but he would not jump the gun until he had all the facts at his fingertips.

43

He wondered what McEwan was doing right now. Up to his crotch in cold water or, more likely, crooning words of love to his duchess, if, indeed, she was a duchess. One thing for sure, McEwan would have more on his mind this Saturday morning than hospital business.

He stubbed out his cigarette in the ashtray and carried his empty coffee cup back across the hall to the kitchen.

'Mrs Mackintosh,' he announced to his startled housekeeper, 'I've decided to go for a walk.'

CHAPTER FIVE

The erratic nature of the postal service was the Brigadier's last *bête noir*. Late or early, the cheerful tinkling of Bert Lowden's bicycle bell as he freewheeled down the driveway was enough to bring the old warrior's blood to the boil.

He would hoist himself from his chair and, grabbing his stick, hobble into the hall just as fast as his legs would carry him. If Maude or Christine had already opened the door, he would brace himself against the hatstand and yell, 'What time do you call this, Lowden? What hour is this to be delivering mail?' Bert, already mounted, would call out, 'Good mornin', Brigadier. Grand weather for the time o' year,' and yanking the handlebars, sweep off up the steep incline pedalling for dear life, his sack thumping against his backside.

It was not that the Brigadier did not understand that the scattered nature of the community demanded a degree of compromise in delivery times. It was simply that the postbag was his lifeline to the wide world and his eagerness to have something with which to fill his mornings strained his patience to the limit.

There was no bell, no bicycle and no Bert that Saturday morning, however.

Christine had barely finished breakfast when a shiny new van came shooting down the driveway and in a manoeuvre that would have drawn applause from a Chicago bootlegger, swerved, reversed and squealed to a halt in a shower of damp gravel inches from the front doorstep. Maude was in the washhouse busy stuffing bed sheets into the tub and it was left to Christine to answer the bell.

The man on the doorstep wore Post Office uniform, spanking new. His cap was tipped back at a raffish angle and several strands of blond hair, fine as silk, fluttered flirtatiously in the breeze. He had blue eyes, a firm jaw, a straight nose and, feathering his upper lip, a dashing little moustache that he stroked with his forefinger as he eyed Chris up and down.

'Mrs Crockett?'

'No, I'm—'

'Delivery for Mr Crockett. He at home, love?'

She guessed that she was perhaps two or three years older than the juvenile lead on the doorstep and bridled at his familiarity. 'I'll take it,' she said testily.

'Sorry. No can do. Signature required.'

'I'm Brigadier Crockett's secretary,' Christine lied. 'I'm empowered to receive mail on his behalf.'

'Empowered,' the young man said, 'by who?'

'By me, damn it,' the Brigadier roared with the

45

same sort of authority that had once sent battalions of fighting men rushing into the cannon's mouth. 'Now who the hell are you?'

Bruce crouched by his master's side, growled at the stranger and, rather incongruously, wagged his stump of a tail.

'Postman Woodcock, sir, at your service.'

'Is that your van?'

'Belongs to the Post Office. Test run today to see how it goes. Be in regular service on this route next week, I reckon.'

'Hmm,' said the Brigadier, not much mollified. 'Is that my parcel?'

'It is if you're Mr Crockett.'

'Of course I'm Crockett. Who else would I be?'

'Not for me to say, sir.'

'Good God! Give me the thing.'

Mr Woodcock pressed his elbow against the heavy brown paper parcel, locking it to his hip. He glanced at Christine and raised an eyebrow as if to enquire if he and she might be in cahoots in dealing with the cantankerous old dodderer. 'Is he who he says he is, miss?'

'Of course I'm bloody well who I say I am. Now give me my parcel.'

The prominent yellow label—*Alexander Biggar, Ltd*—indicated that the package contained four gramophone records that the Brigadier had ordered some weeks ago. Mr Woodcock had no way of knowing just what those brittle black discs meant to the elderly toff or that he was dealing with a man who had allegedly presided over firing squads on three continents and had made it a point of honour to deliver the *coups de grâce* personally.

'Here,' said Christine. 'I'll sign your book.'

46

The postman hesitated, then, in response to Christine's sweet smile and her hand on his arm, capitulated.

'All right,' he said. 'I suppose it'll be okay.'

He handed her the parcel, the delivery book and a pencil that, miraculously, had not a tooth mark upon it.

The Brigadier snatched the package, hugged it to his chest and with the stick tucked under his arm, hobbled back into the sitting-room.

'Grumpy old beggar, ain't he?' Mr Woodcock said. 'What's in that parcel he's so keen to get his mitts on?'

'Documents,' said Christine. 'Secret documents from the War Office.'

'The War Office?' said Mr Woodcock. 'You're pullin' my leg.'

'Of course I am,' said Christine. 'Gramophone records, if you must know.'

'Well, I like a bit o' the old toodle-oo myself. It'll be symphonies with his lordship, I suppose, not stuff you can dance to.'

'Yes,' said Christine. 'Symphonies,' and made to step indoors.

'Nice dog,' said Mr Woodcock quickly. 'He bite?'

Bruce growled again and thumped his tail.

'Only postmen,' Christine said. 'Are you new here?'

'Up from Liverpool. Can't you tell?'

'I'm not familiar with regional accents,' said Christine primly. 'What brings you to Scotland, Mr Woodcock?'

'Necessity,' the young man explained. 'Post Office advertised for drivers with mechanical experience, like. Asked if I'd be willin' to work in Scotland. Work anywhere, I told them, just get me off the dole.'

'What did your wife have to say about it?'

'No wife. I send some dough back home to me old mum now and then, otherwise I'm free as a lark or,' he added, 'for a lark.'

'What happened to Bert?'

'Elevated to the sorting office. Were you 'n' him . . .'

'No, me and him were not.'

'Must be slow off the mark then, old Bert. Pretty lady like you.'

'Thank you for the compliment. Goodbye,' Christine said.

She closed the door, then, after a moment's hesitation, skipped into the breakfast-room and peeped from the window at the brand-new van and the brand-new postman who tooted the horn, gunned the engine and shot off up the driveway with one hand poking from the nearside window in a cheeky farewell.

The strains of a saxophone, violins and a muted trumpet came from the sitting-room. Christine found the Brigadier leaning on the radiogram, surrounded by wrapping paper, Bruce quietly worrying a length of string he had dragged beneath the sofa.

Three records, still in paper envelopes, were balanced on the cabinet. The fourth was going round and round on the turntable, stroked by the steely fist of the needle-holder. Christine lingered by the door and listened to a soft androgynous voice adding words to the melody.

'What is that?' Christine said.

'Paradise,' the Brigadier told her and, his ire forgotten, executed four or five waltz steps and one elegant pirouette before he collapsed, exhausted, into his armchair.

*   *   *

Tibial torsion, Alan thought, a very small degree of tibial torsion and slight in-toeing of the feet. He doubted if nutritional neglect had done the damage, if damage it was.

Pigeon toes drew her knees together under her pleated skirt and added a vulnerable quality to her gait. She wore a double-breasted sports coat in a warm blazer-like material with a silky scarf in the collar, a little red hat, like a French beret, and a pair of stout Oxfords with low heels and tasselled laces. If she was a 'kept woman'—which he greatly doubted—someone was keeping her very well.

The tubby little Scottie dog would not afford her much protection, however, if he'd been a middle-aged masher and not a respectable gentleman in trench-coat and soft hat out for a morning stroll on the isolated ridge road.

He shortened his stride, smiled, nodded and, a step or two before their paths crossed, lifted his hat in a casual greeting. 'Better morning.'

'Much better, thank goodness.'

'Rain's not far away, though.'

'Now the wind's gone to the west,' the girl said, 'I expect we'll have another shower before long.'

Weather, a safe topic: 'Is the west wind a wet wind? I didn't know that.'

She was not reluctant to stop and talk. 'You're not from these parts, I think, or you'd know just how wet it can be when the wind shifts.'

'Well,' he said, 'I am from these parts, as it happens, but my job takes me into Glasgow most days in the week. I haven't paid much attention to how the wind blows.'

'Are you Mr Kelso, by any chance?'

Surprised, he said, 'For my sins, I am.'

'Oh, I'm sorry,' the girl said. 'I had no idea. I thought you'd be . . .'

'What? Younger?'

'Older, much older.'

'Now why would you think that?' said Alan.

'Your wife . . .' She reached out and touched his sleeve. 'I'm so sorry.'

'Ah!' Alan said. 'You were acquainted with my wife, were you?'

'My mother knew her. I met her only once. She seemed very nice, very friendly.' She slipped off her glove and offered her hand. 'I'm Christine Summers, by the way.'

He took her hand, gave it a brisk pump. 'Alan Kelso.'

He held his hat down by his side and waited for the inevitable condolences and then the awkward goodbye. No one really seemed to know what to say to a widower, as if the death of a wife were somehow more tragic than the death of a husband. The dog snuffled about in the weeds that lined the verge and appeared to be in no hurry to move on; nor did the young woman.

'We thought you might have gone back to the city,' she said. 'It can't be much fun living in that big house on your own. Do you miss her very much?'

'Of course,' Alan answered. 'Who's "we"?'

'My mother, the Brigadier and me. We're all gossips in this neck of the woods,' Christine informed him. 'I expect you've heard all about us from Mrs Mackintosh.'

'Not all, no,' said Alan guardedly.

'No love lost between my mother and Mrs Mackintosh, I'm afraid,' the young woman went on. 'She thinks we're stuck up.'

'Are you stuck up?'

'Yes, actually, I expect we are a bit.'

'Does the Brigadier set the standard?'

'He's not demanding, if that's what you mean. He's an old man now and too frail to get out and about. He has old-fashioned ideas about how people should behave but he's not in the least fuddy-duddy.'

'You like him, don't you?'

'I do.'

Compared to some of the nurses who tripped about the wards she was quite plain. She had an oval-shaped face and a nose that might fairly be described as snub but her brown eyes were lively and attractive.

'Have you walked far?' she asked.

'Only as far as the crossroad,' he answered. 'How far is that: a half-mile?'

'Rather less.' She paused. 'Are you heading home?'

'Yes, I—I have work to do.'

'Work?' she said. 'What sort of work does a surgeon do at the weekend?'

'Case histories,' he said, 'for review.'

'Ah, I should have thought of that,' she said. 'I'd walk you to the Kennart turn-off but Bruce needs more exercise. The Brigadier thinks he's getting

51

fat—the dog, I mean, not the Brigadier.'

Alan could not be sure whether she was making an excuse to be rid of him or inviting him to accompany her. She was the first female he had talked to in umpteen months who had no fixed place in his life, no rank or status by which she might be defined. He did not know where he stood with her or, perplexingly, where he wanted to stand. 'Well,' he said, 'an extra mile or so won't kill me, even at my advanced age—if, that is, you don't object to my company.'

'On the contrary,' Christine Summers said. 'Bruce and I ran out of conversation long ago.'

Whistling on the dog to follow her, she started out towards the crossroad, still blissfully unaware, Alan thought, that they had not met by chance.

*   *   *

She made nothing of it at first, did not rush in and blurt it out. The gramophone had been replaced by the radio but her mother had turned the volume down to little more than a drone and the Brigadier had fallen asleep in his chair.

She kept Bruce in the kitchen, or, rather, on the step outside where she had filled his feeding bowl with beef and vegetable mash. Through the open door she watched the Scottie's rump wriggle as he ate. He would snooze for the best part of the afternoon, either in the sitting-room or, more likely, in his basket in the corner behind the stove.

'Oh, by the way,' she said nonchalantly, 'you'll never guess who I ran into.'

Her mother was setting a tray for the Brigadier's lunch.

52

She did not even look up. 'Charley Noonan?'

'No,' Christine said, 'Marion Kelso's husband.'

'What? The surgeon?'

'In the flesh. He'd popped out for a breath of fresh air between the showers.'

'Fresh air? What's come over him? From what I gather, he never sticks his nose out of doors. If the Mackintosh woman wasn't still employed up there I'd have said he'd disappeared back to Glasgow.'

'Well, he hasn't,' said Christine. 'He's still living in Moss House.'

'Alone?'

'Apparently.'

Her mother snapped open a spotless linen napkin, rolled it carefully and threaded it into the silver ring that the Brigadier claimed had survived three wars and a tribal uprising. 'Is he as dour as she said he was?'

'As who said he was?'

'His wife.'

'He isn't dour at all,' said Christine. 'I thought he was rather charming.'

'Charming?'

'Pleasant,' Christine said. 'Easy to talk to.'

'Really?' her mother said. 'And what, pray, did you talk about?'

'This and that, nothing much—the weather mainly.'

'You were gone long enough.'

'He walked me over to the crossroad.'

'Did he, indeed?'

'Now, Mama, don't start! He's almost old enough to be my father, though I must say he doesn't look it. Didn't you see him at the church service before the funeral?'

53

'I saw him. Don't you remember, I told you we all thought it odd he had her buried in Ottershaw and not with her folks in Glasgow.'

'She was from Berwick originally.'

'Did he tell you that?'

'He mentioned it in passing.'

'He talked about her then, did he?'

'Hardly at all. He seemed more interested in me.'

'I'll bet he was,' her mother said.

'In teaching, I mean. He teaches, too, on occasions. Medical students. He's interested in children generally. After all he is a paediatrician.'

'I thought he was a surgeon.'

'Oh, Mama, don't be so daft,' Christine said and, before she could be dragged into a long-winded explanation, headed across the hall to waken the Brigadier and tidy him up before lunch.

*   *   *

Nowhere in Ottershaw could one could buy cut flowers at this time of year. In a month or so gardens would be groaning with daffodils and the pretty little yellow things that grew along the edge of the wood—primroses, yes, that was it, primroses. Right now all spring had to offer were snowdrops and a few crocuses and it struck Alan as pointless to lay a bunch of the delicate plants on Marion's grave where they would wither and fall apart before nightfall.

It had been months since his last visit to the 'new' cemetery. It was a pretty enough spot but not well tended, and it lacked the atmosphere of the old graveyard in the heart of the village where space was at a premium and only those and such as those were laid to rest. In time, he supposed, as the village grew and expanded Marion would have more company but as things stood the incomers who were buried here seemed more like outcasts.

It had been Marion's idea to be interred 'just down the road'. She had been astute enough to put it in writing in a letter to her father which, as it turned out, was just as well, otherwise the bullying old Bolshevik would have ridden roughshod over everyone's wishes and had her 'decently' cremated and her ashes scattered from a bridge over the River Tweed.

Marion's mother, brother and sister had been opposed to cremation, a method of disposal too perfunctory for their liking. But, as usual, they had bowed the knee to their lord and master and it had been left to Alan to shape up to the old despot and insist, absolutely insist, that Marion's final request be obeyed to the letter and she be laid to rest here in Ottershaw.

'Damned if I can see the purpose in it,' Jake Goodall had barked. 'Good God, man, what'll happen to her if you move back into Glasgow—or go abroad?'

'I've no intention of going abroad,' Alan had informed him. 'And if I do decide to move back into the city I'll make sure the grave is cared for.'

'But not by you, not by you?'

'Ottershaw's not the ends of the earth, Jake. I can be out here in—'

'Look, look! Tell you what, tell you what, if you won't do the responsible thing and let me organise a cremation then why not ship the body down to Berwick. Her grandfather, her uncles—my brothers—are all buried there. I've a plot already bought and paid for. She'll be happier with her family around her.'

'Jake, she's dead.'

'Of course she is, of course—so what does it matter what we do with her?'

'It mattered to Marion and, therefore, it matters to me.'

'Huh, if only you'd paid as much attention to her wishes when she was alive, she might not be lying in her coffin right now.'

'What's that supposed to mean?'

'If the caps fits, Kelso, if the cap fits.'

The Goodalls had never forgiven him for being in Egypt when Marion's first and only pregnancy had ended in a miscarriage. Perhaps they had never forgiven him for making her pregnant in the first place. They most certainly blamed him, the famous surgeon, for failing to 'cure' the tumour that had made her sick or to subvert the insidious secondary lesions in liver and kidney that had proved too intractable for surgical intervention.

Of course, they had offered no help in nursing Marion through those final terrible months. They had motored up from Berwick only once in the course of her illness and had chosen to pooh-pooh his last-stage warnings that the end was very near. They had squabbled over Marion's will and, before they had finally left, Jake had managed to insult Alan's poor mother who was in no fit state, mentally, to put up with the tanner's insufferable rantings.

Alan hadn't clapped eyes on any of the Goodalls since that sun-drenched August afternoon when they had ridden off back to Berwick in Jake's open-topped Rover. He had received a curt little note from Ellen Goodall in acknowledgement of a few faded photographs and sentimental trinkets that Marion had wished her sister to have, and a card at Christmas—The Tannery Under Snow—but not another word from his in-laws who seemed, thank God, to have written him off.

He pushed open the wrought-iron gate and slipped into the graveyard.

Three new stones had been erected since his last visit and one very raw mound was still awaiting a marker. Unsure what had brought him here, he picked his way along the weedy flagstone path and, removing his hat, peered at the gilded letters on the polished black marble that recorded, without comment, the birth and death of Marion Anne Kelso.

He did not know what to do now, what was appropriate and what was just plain silly. He thought of praying, but he'd never been much of a believer in an afterlife or the transcendent nature of prayer. He certainly had no intention of engaging in an apologetic monologue with an oblong of black marble.

Crouching, he brushed a few wisps of dried grass from the base of the headstone and plucked out a tiny herb that may, or may not, have been a weed.

Then, quite suddenly, quite shockingly, he found himself weeping.

Stooped over, hands clasping his thighs, he let the tears fall for several seconds then rose and looked about him and, to his relief, found not a living soul in sight. He wiped his face with a not-so-clean handkerchief from his trench-coat pocket and felt much better.

'Quite enough of that, Kelso,' he said aloud. 'Quite enough,' and headed briskly for the gate.

CHAPTER SIX

The crime would never be officially solved for the simple reason that the crime was never officially acknowledged. No matter how fond Beatty was of detective stories, she was sensible enough to separate fiction from reality and made no attempt to track down the culprits on her own.

She was embarrassed that she'd been too drunk to defend herself but her main reason for not rushing to the police station in Kennart was that she kept no books and had a holy horror of falling foul of the income tax authorities and being sent to jail like the racehorse owner, Sir Peter Anscombe, whose case had been all over the newspapers a year or two back.

This bit of nonsense trickled through her head as she staggered to her feet and set off up the road with nothing but an old coat thrown over her nightshirt and neither stockings nor shoes on her feet.

She knew that if the big artery in her thigh had been cut she would be lucky to make it as far as the Ottershaw crossroad let alone the telephone box below the railway halt. Even if she did make it as far as the telephone box, who would she call? She didn't have Dr Currie's number and there was no telephone in the Noonans' house. And if she asked the operator for help they would surely send a policeman to investigate and all her crimes would come to light.

Shivering, she stumbled on to the cattle track, a short cut to Ottershaw, in the hope that she might reach Dr Currie's house before she passed out.

*   *   *

Alan had drunk half a bottle of red wine with lunch and had finished it at dinner. He had frittered the afternoon away, dozing on the couch in the parlour and, after dinner, had fallen fast asleep on the rug in front of the fire.

Close to midnight, wide awake and more than a little guilty at having wasted the day, he bathed his face and neck at the cold water tap in the kitchen, brewed coffee and, cup in hand, switched on the outside light and stood on the doorstep in the hope that the night air might clear his head.

The breeze carried the sound of voices from the direction of Kennart, a peculiar cat-like wailing that might have been a saxophone and the chunk, chunk, chunk of a drum that quite suddenly ceased, leaving in its wake a medley of queer little noises that Alan could not identify. He was used to the clamour of the city, the rattle of late-night tramcars, the squeal of buses, drunken quarrelling, and the thump of industry from those shipyards and foundries that still had enough work on their books to justify a night shift, but he did not understand the countryside at all.

Stepping back indoors, he closed the door, bolted it and went straight to the library, determined to wring some profit from what remained of the day or, rather, the night. He lit the desk lamp, laid out cigarettes and matches, a lined notepad, three pencils and a fountain pen then, unbuttoning his cardigan and loosening his necktie, seated himself and pulled down the first of the case histories that required his attention.

He would work until half past two.

Tomorrow, he would rise at half past nine, have breakfast and climb the hill to the village to attend morning service, which was something he hadn't done since Marion had passed away. And after lunch, if the weather held, he might take another stroll along the ridge road in the hope of meeting with the girl again.

'Right,' he said aloud. 'To work, Mr Kelso, to work.'

And flipped open the first of the files.

*   *   *

'Help me,' the woman said. 'Please help me.'

Alan opened the door an inch and peered out at the apparition that swayed on the doorstep. He was, naturally, apprehensive. Who wouldn't be when someone comes knocking on your door at half past two in the morning? He had heard nothing from Mrs Mackintosh about marauders in the neighbourhood but knew from hospital gossip that desperate times had bred desperate men and that armed robberies were rife in the city and its suburbs.

'Please,' the woman said again, 'please, please help me. I'm hurt.'

She swayed once more and might have fallen if Alan hadn't flung open the door and caught her by the arm. He looked past her, peering into the darkness, half expecting two or three burly men to

60

charge out and overpower him, and the woman, the decoy, to spit in his face.

He yanked her into the hall, slammed the door and shot the bolt.

She clung to him, trembling. When he tried to detach her, she pressed her wet hair against his chest. She was remarkably strong for a woman and smelled of damp earth, vegetation and beer.

'What's wrong with you?' he said. 'Are you drunk?'

She pulled back, opened the stained overcoat and showed him her legs, dappled with blood. The nightshirt hid little. Her breasts were heavy; the triangle of hair between her legs was as thick as the hair on her head. Clearly, she was no hysterical adolescent who had allowed her boyfriend to go too far. The thought did cross his mind, though, that he might be dealing with rape or, possibly, a backstreet abortion that had gone horribly wrong.

'I'm cut,' she told him. 'I'm bleeding.'

'Where?'

She peeled up the nightshirt and showed him the wound.

'Who did this? Your husband?'

'I did it to myself.' She shivered so violently that her teeth chattered. 'It was an ack—accident.'

Alan took her arm and helped her into the kitchen. He pulled out a chair and eased her into it. He filled the kettle and put it on the electrical plate, kicked open the door of the stove and shovelled a dozen lumps of coal from the bucket on to the embers. Then he strode across the hall to the library and returned with a bottle of brandy and a glass. He poured a small quantity of brandy into the glass and held it out to her. She tried to take the glass but could not. He held it to her lips and placed his left hand along the side of her jaw to steady her head.

'Drink it,' he said.

She rolled her head back, rolled her eyes and stared up at him.

'Are—are you the—the doctor? The other doctor?'

'Fortunately for you,' Alan said, 'I am.'

'What's your name?'

'Kelso.'

'Can you stitch it up, Dr Kelso?'

'I don't have the proper instruments for stitching.'

'I thought—Charley told me you were a doctor.'

'I'm not a GP like Tom Currie. I work in a hospital.'

She had recovered sufficiently to sip brandy without assistance.

Kneeling, he examined the wound that ran across the large muscle of her thigh and tapered out just on the point of connection with the extensor tendon. He cupped the heel of her bare foot in one hand and carefully manipulated the leg.

'Am I going to die?'

'No,' Alan told her. 'It's a flesh wound. You may need three or four stitches which'—he looked up—'will be Dr Currie's job, not mine. What I can do—what I will do—is clean and dress the wound to stop the bleeding.'

'Is there a telephone here?'

Alan shook his head. 'The line doesn't come down this far. Why? Do you want me to send for someone?'

'Someone?' she said. 'Like who?'

'Your husband, your children,' Alan suggested.

'I've none of those to bother with.'

'The police, perhaps?'

She squirmed and might have jumped up if he hadn't tightened his hold on her calf. The nightshirt—a patched, over-washed garment—did not cover her modesty. Her belly bore no obvious scars or stretch marks. As a paediatric specialist it had been years since he'd examined an adult female. He suddenly became aware of the intimacy of the situation, an unprofessional intimacy at that.

He got to his feet, pulled out another chair and rested her leg upon it.

'Why don't you want me to contact the police?'

'It was an accident, just an accident.'

'An accident with a knife?'

She nodded. 'I fell on it.'

'Come off it,' Alan said. 'This is a gash, not a puncture wound.'

She had stopped shaking and when he lifted her arm and sought for the pulse she did not resist. In all probability she hadn't lost enough blood to be in danger of passing out. Her reactions owed more to emotional than physical trauma. He teased the glass from her fingers, lifted the brandy bottle and headed for the door.

'Where are you going?' she said in alarm. 'You're not going for the—'

'No,' Alan said. 'I'm not going for the police. I'm going in search of my first-aid box.' He paused in the doorway. 'By the way, where do you live?'

'Picton, the stables at Picton.'

'Ah, you're the pony woman.'

'Yes,' she said, with a strange little grimace. 'Beatty McCall, that's me.'

It had been a long, long time since he had been called upon to dress an open wound. He was relieved to discover that he hadn't lost the knack.

'Is that too tight?'

'No, it's fine.'

'Drink your tea. It'll warm you up.'

'Is there no more of that brandy?'

'I think you've had enough alcohol for one night, don't you?' Alan said. 'Now, are you going to tell me what happened?'

She cradled the teacup in both hands, and sighed.

The stove was roaring quietly, the kitchen had grown warm and only the unfamiliar smell of antiseptic—iodine—prevented it from seeming cosy. He did not press her for an answer. Still kneeling by the side of the chair, he split the end of the bandage with a pair of Marion's nail scissors.

The woman had let the coat slide from her shoulders and had no inhibitions about showing off her body. In different circumstances he might have thought she was flirting with him. He tied the bandage with a firm knot and tugged down the hem of her nightshirt.

'What time is it?' she asked.

He had left his watch on the desk in the library and the wooden-faced clock on the wall above the dresser had never been that reliable.

'Probably about three.'

'I'll have to go,' she said.

'Go where?'

'Home.'

'Not in the state you're in,' Alan informed her. 'You're going nowhere until you've got some of your strength back.'

'I'm all right now, really.'

'You are not all right,' said Alan. 'You've lost a fair bit of blood and it would be irresponsible of me just to let you wander off.'

'I'm—I'm expecting company.'

'Company? At this hour of the night?'

'Some men are coming to collect my ponies first thing in the morning.'

'On Sunday?'

'It's a good day to drive a herd. The streets are quiet.'

'Ponies?' Alan shook his head. 'How many?'

'Ten.'

'Don't tell me you intend to travel with them?'

'No, but I have to be there to see them off.'

'And make sure the dealer pays you, I suppose?'

'I've been paid.' The woman handed him the teacup and covered her face with her hands. 'They took all my money. They stole all my money.'

Alan was inclined to comfort her as he would surely have comforted a child. Beatty McCall was no child, though. She was a half-naked woman in her mid-thirties and by no means lacking in physical attractions. The fact that he was conscious of her attractions troubled him. He had long since learned to smother such thoughts at first flicker, as was only right and proper, not to say necessary, for a man who spent his days surrounded by flocks of young women.

'Now,' he murmured. 'Now, now, that's enough of that.'

She rocked in the chair, her elbows tucked into

65

her stomach. There was something pathetic about her distress. She had already impressed him as a proud, independent type, sturdy in spirit as well as body—which, it suddenly occurred to him, was a damned patronising judgement to make on short notice. He slipped behind her and put a hand on her shoulder to administer what Sister Torrance, not without cynicism, referred to as 'the human touch'.

The woman's skin was dry save for a patch at the hair line that remained damp. He cursed himself for his thoughtlessness in not providing a towel and instinctively kneaded the taut muscles of her neck as he had done for Marion when morphine had failed to ease her headache.

'Who stole your money?' he asked.

'They did.'

'The horse dealers?'

'Bob Cleavers might be a rogue but he's not a thief.' She took her hands from her face and caught Alan's arm. 'Doctors aren't allowed to tell the police what they're told by a patient, are they?'

'Well, technically you are my patient, I suppose. You'll feel better if you get it off your chest. I won't tell anyone if you don't want me to.'

'Promise?'

'I promise,' Alan said.

*   *   *

She was sober now, a wee bit too sober for her own good. She could have done with another nip of brandy but she saw his point, him being a doctor and all. Besides, she reckoned she'd fallen on her feet. The tall man with the stooped shoulders

66

might turn out to be a friend in need.

She liked the feeling of his fingers on her neck. It had been over a year since a man had last touched her. That man's touch, unlike the doctor's, had been anything but soothing. She'd picked him up in the Black Bull Inn on a hot June evening and had been just tipsy enough to invite him to accompany her home. He'd been too impatient to undertake the long walk back to Picton, though. He'd pulled her into the ferns at the edge of the Bluebell Wood and had taken her there. He'd pushed his fingers into her to make sure she was ready and had forced her legs apart and mounted her without a kiss or a compliment to smooth the way.

He'd told her his name was Norman and that he travelled in agricultural machinery. He certainly wasn't local but nor was he a tinky-type. He wore Brylcreem, a striped shirt with a collar and a pair of pearly studs in his cuffs. She suspected he might even be wearing suspenders in spite of the hot weather. He took off nothing but his jacket and was on top of her before she'd had a chance to loosen her stockings. He opened her blouse and pushed up her brassiere and squeezed her breasts, not to arouse her but to hold her down.

She'd only struggled when she'd sensed he was close to boiling point and had got him out of her just in the nick of time. He'd been enough of a gentleman to give her his hanky to mop herself off and had offered her a hand to help her up from the grass. He'd walked out of the wood with her as far as the roadside but had told her he had to be up early next morning and couldn't walk her all the way home. Then he'd kissed her and had gone off

67

and, in spite of his promise to 'call again', she'd seen no more of him.

'I clinched a sale this morning and had a few beers to celebrate,' she said. 'I went to bed about half past ten and wakened up in the pitch dark with somebody rummaging about inside my hut.'

'Your hut?'

'My house.'

'I take it there was no forced entry?'

'What?'

'The door wasn't locked?'

'The door's never locked.'

'How many intruders were there?'

'Two,' Beatty answered. 'At first I thought somebody from the dance at Kennart had wandered down to see if I had any beer left.'

'Are you sure it wasn't someone you know?'

'Positive. They were looking for my cash box. When I jumped out of bed and lit my torch one of them was prowling round the fireplace and the other was going through the dresser drawers.'

'So they knew you had cash on the premises?' Dr Kelso said.

'They had a motorcar, a lorry. They probably came out from Glasgow. The horse dealer brought a girlfriend with him this morning. She might have opened her mouth to someone in town.'

'Picton's not that easy to find.'

'Under the railway bridge will find me every time.'

'I take it,' Dr Kelso said, 'you aren't insured.'

'Do I look as if I'm insured?'

'I must admit you don't,' the doctor said. 'But if you've lost all your money why won't you inform the police?'

The bandage was pure white and there was enough dressing under it to ensure that blood didn't seep through. There was a sting in the wound, though, a sharp, exciting sting. She needed the lavatory but was too shy to ask where it was. Funny, she thought, that she could sit here in nothing but a nightshirt before a man she'd met only a half-hour ago yet she couldn't come straight out and ask him to show her the toilet.

She said, 'I don't like the police. I don't trust them.'

'You prefer to sacrifice the cash rather than have the police discover that you were betrayed by a friend; is that it?'

'What if it is?'

'Tell me how you got the knife wound.'

'I was so scared I grabbed a carving knife and went after them with it. They'd found my cash box by that time and they ran like Hades. I had a slash at one of them and got my own leg instead.' She pulled a face. 'I chased them out into the yard and slipped and fell down.'

'Are you sure they rode off in a motor vehicle?'

'Yes, I heard it. It was a lorry, I think, not a car.'

'What brought you here?'

'Charley told me a doctor lived in Moss House.'

'Why didn't you go to Charley for help?'

'I thought I was dying.'

'Well, you're not. The question is, what are we going to do with you now?'

'You're not going to turn me in, are you?'

'Of course not, though I still think—'

'Look'—she made to stand up—'I've got to get home.'

The pain bit into her thigh and zigzagged

69

upward into her belly.

She sat down again, hard.

'See,' the doctor said, 'you're not as tough as you think you are. Unfortunately I don't have a motorcar. But I tell you what we'll do: if you rest for a couple of hours, I'll find you something to wear and a pair of shoes and walk down to Picton with you.'

'I've caused you enough trouble as it is.'

'I'm not giving you a choice, Miss McCall.'

'Mrs McCall. I'm a widow.'

'Well, I'm still not giving you a choice. There's a couch in the parlour and I'll find you a blanket. If you agree to lie down and rest, I'll waken you in ample time to make it to Picton by daybreak. But I am coming with you, like it or not. And tomorrow you must take yourself up to Dr Currie to let him have a look at that wound and change the dressing in case it becomes infected.'

'Can't you do it?'

'I'll be at work.'

'Tomorrow?'

'Today's Sunday; tomorrow's Monday,' he said. 'Here, take my arm and I'll help you through to the parlour.'

She rose cautiously while he supported her. Her head was clear but her legs did not seem to belong to her. The sharp pain in her thigh was no longer exciting. She felt too weak to argue, too weak to worry about what sort of fee he might charge for his services.

She leaned into him. 'Dr Kelso?'

'Hmm?' he said, frowning. 'What's wrong?'

'Dr Kelso,' Beatty whispered, 'I need the toilet.'

70

CHAPTER SEVEN

It was no novelty for Alan to be up and about soon after dawn. He had trudged the stretch of road from Moss House to the railway halt in dark mid-winter and in soft summer sunlight but he had never before had a woman hanging on to his arm; a woman clad in an ancient raincoat, a pink cashmere jumper, a skirt that did not quite reach her knees and a pair of wellington boots that were at least a size too small. Beatty McCall had insisted on taking the short cut along the cattle track where they were obliged to walk in single file, slithering on mud and spattered by droplets from the hedgerows. Alan was relieved to be clear of the high road. He had no convincing explanation to offer Mrs Mackintosh if he happened to be spotted arm-in-arm with a woman whose reputation was almost certainly not in tune with his housekeeper's definition of propriety.

Beatty had washed her face and tidied her hair in his bathroom and had slept for a couple of hours on his couch under a blanket he had taken from the cupboard in Marion's room. He had wakened her at half past five with coffee and toast and had encouraged her to rummage in the armful of clothes he had brought down from the bedroom.

'Are these your wife's things?'

'Yes.'

'Won't she mind me borrowing them?'

'My wife died last year.'

'She had some very nice clothes, didn't she?'

'Yes'—he hadn't thought of it before—'I

suppose she did.'

The hedgerows petered out in the vicinity of the road. He spied the arch of the railway bridge and beyond it, rolling off into the distance, blue-black hills capped by cloud. The woman stopped.

'I can manage from here,' she said. 'I'll see to it you get the clothes back.'

'I'm taking you all the way home.'

'Why? Just to make sure I'm telling the truth?'

'In case some ruffian is hiding behind the door with a knife in his hand.'

'Like Brutus?'

'Yes,' Alan said, surprised. 'Like Brutus.'

*　　　*　　　*

Trust Bob Cleavers's boys to come early. By the look of them, they'd been boozing into the wee small hours and hadn't been to bed.

Old Sam was driving the lorry, a rattle-trap Bob had purchased from army surplus. The canvas hood had been replaced by a crude slat-sided cage. The trip would take an hour or longer. The lorry invariably ran short of breath on the hill that climbed up to the Cleavers's ranch. Her Shelties would be in a high old state of nervous agitation before they were shooed out into the field to join Bob's collection of equine odds and ends.

She hated to see her ponies going off to spend the rest of their lives hauling laden tubs along airless tunnels deep underground. She wondered if they would remember Picton's green pastures as clearly as she remembered her childhood in Blairgowrie where her father had been a carrier until the flax mills had closed and trade had

72

dwindled. He had died of a sudden apoplexy when she was ten, long before she'd heard of Picton or tasted beer or met up with Andy McCall.

'I'll come inside with you,' the doctor said.

'No need for that,' she told him. 'Wait by the fence, please, and keep out of the herders' way.'

He tipped his hat like a salute. 'Yes, ma'am.'

She wouldn't let him into her house for all the tea in China. The hut was a mess. Greasy dishes were piled in the tub, underwear strewn about, the bed was unmade and the floor ankle-deep in beer bottles. She was no more a housewife than she was a gardener but she had enough pride left not to flaunt her slatternly habits before a gentleman who was plainly used to better things.

Old Sam steered the lorry across the yard to the paddock gate. He climbed from the cabin, opened the cage and lowered the ramp. The rest of the crew were already in the paddock cutting out the Shetlands while the Highlands, half curious and half alarmed, trotted round in circles tossing their handsome heads. Beatty watched for a moment before she went indoors. She found her boots and, seated on the bed, hauled off the ill-fitting wellingtons. She didn't change out of Marion Kelso's cast-offs but paused only long enough to check that her cash box really was missing—which it was—before she went out to join Dr Kelso at the fence.

'This is quite exciting,' he said. 'I had no idea such things still went on. They look wonderfully untamed, your ponies. What happens to them now?'

'They're taken to a ranch on the outskirts of Glasgow. Bob Cleavers—he's the dealer—sells

73

them on to colliery managers to be broken in.'

'I see. They're pit ponies,' the doctor said. 'I assume the very small ones are required to haul tubs from narrow rooms near the face.'

'I didn't know you were a miner.'

'I'm not, thank God. How much did you make on the sale?'

'Eighty pounds.'

'Is it all gone?'

'I've lost about seventy.'

'Can't you sell more ponies to cover your bills?'

'The next lot won't be ready for market until September.'

'How will you manage in the meantime?'

'I'll manage,' said Beatty grimly.

'Haw!' old Sam said. 'That's a fine new woolly jumper, Beatty. Never saw you in pink afore. Did your fancyman buy it for you?'

'He's not my fancyman,' Beatty said. 'He's the new animal welfare officer for Ottershaw district.'

Old Sam glowered suspiciously at the tall, well-dressed man who had wandered over to the lorry. 'Zat a fact?'

'That is, indeed, a fact,' Alan answered, straight-faced.

'You'll find nothin' out o' order wi' our animals, sir.'

'Oh, I don't know. I might—if I look hard enough.'

The old man swallowed and called out, 'Hurry it along, lads. We havenae got a' day.' Then, after closing the gate of the cage on the Shetlands, he clambered into the cabin, closed the door and fired the engine.

'Why is he afraid of the animal welfare officer?'

Alan whispered.

'We all have our bogeymen, don't we?' Beatty answered.

The lorry lurched on to the open road, the terrified ponies braying and kicking in the cage. Minutes later the Highlands trotted across the mud, veered on to the road and clattered away out of sight.

Beatty stared across the empty paddock to the pasture where mares and young stallions hid among the gorse bushes. It was quiet now, too quiet. She had provided the robbers with easy pickings and whether they were locals or Glasgow hooligans, she was afraid they might come back. She'd fix the bolt on the door, make sure the rusty iron bar was dropped every night and that she was never again so drunk she couldn't defend herself.

And next time she'd any cash to spare, she'd buy herself a gun.

Alan put a hand on her shoulder. 'Are you all right?'

'If you don't mind, Dr Kelso, I think I'll go for a lie down.'

'Best thing for it,' he said. 'Tomorrow, off to see Tom Currie.'

'Yes,' she said. 'Yes, of course.'

And with a nod in lieu of a handshake, she let him go.

*   *   *

Alan knew perfectly well that Mrs McCall had no intention of presenting herself to the GP. The mere matter of having to pay Currie's fee would deter her. He did not doubt that she had lost her money or that what she had told him was essentially the truth. She was a countrywoman, of course, stubborn, proud and independent, and fathoming the motives of country folk was beyond him. He had already pricked his housekeeper's Presbyterian sensibilities by asking a few innocent questions about the occupants of Preaching Friar and didn't dare ask Mrs Mackintosh about the pony woman without revealing that she'd spent Saturday night on his couch.

He polished off a second boiled egg, stuffed a last piece of cold toast into his mouth and washed it down with tea.

Rising, he went into the parlour, took the blanket from the couch, shook it, folded it, carried it upstairs and stowed it away in the cupboard in Marion's room. He went next to the bathroom and removed from the bowl of the washbasin three fair hairs that he placed on a piece of toilet paper and flushed down the pan.

Dear God, he thought wryly, I'm behaving like a criminal.

He hurried downstairs to the kitchen, washed the teacup and glass from which the widow had drunk—no lipstick, he noticed—and checked the kitchen, hall and parlour for bloodstains. When he found himself outside inspecting the doorstep and gravel drive for incriminating evidence, however, he let out a self-mocking howl, 'Enough, Kelso. Enough.'

And took himself off to bed.

*   *   *

She had not expected to see him at church but had

76

hoped she might bump into him on the ridge road in the course of the afternoon. She had enjoyed his company, his conversation and had been flattered by his interest in her.

'Are you going out again?' her mother said. 'What's wrong with you?'

'Bruce needs the exercise.'

'Bruce is worn out. Look at him, he's half asleep.'

'He's eaten too much, as usual.'

'Let him sleep it off,' her mother said.

'It's not like you to take Bruce's side,' Christine said.

She had already been out for an hour after lunch, pushing into the blustery March wind as far as the crossroad. It was bracing weather, she told herself, and with nothing much doing in the old homestead—the Brigadier snoozing, her mother sewing, the radiogram switched off—she had surrendered to an urge to go out once more in the hope that Dr Kelso might come looking for her.

'Look at it'—her mother nodded towards the window—'it's as black as the earl's waistcoat out there.'

'I shan't go far.'

'You're hoping you'll run into that Kelso chap, aren't you?'

'No, no. I just fancy another breath of air before tea, that's all.'

'I hope you're not getting ideas?'

'Ideas? I don't know what you mean.'

'You know fine what I mean.'

The Brigadier opened one eye. 'Let her go, Maude, if she wants to.'

'If she catches her death of cold . . .'

'Blame me,' said the Brigadier gallantly.

* * *

Rain battering against the bedroom window wakened him. The room was filled with bleak afternoon light. He lay motionless on his back contemplating the shadows on the ceiling for half a minute then sat up and groped for his watch. Twenty-three minutes past four. He had slept for the best part of nine hours.

The day was gone, his plans shot.

He rolled from the bed, crossed to the window and peered out into the gloom.

His chance of meeting up with the dog-walker had vanished. Surely she would have better things to do than hang about in the rain in the hope that he might show up again. And there were no trains to wave to on Sunday. He watched the tops of the trees toss in the wind and rain sheeting against the glass. He wondered if the pony woman, Beatty McCall, was still asleep, wrapped in blankets like a chrysalis in her snug wooden hut and how much cosier it would be there than here in Moss House. There was something to be said for the simple life, though he doubted if Mrs McCall, in her penniless state, would agree with him.

Then, shedding his pyjamas, he headed for the bathroom to relieve himself.

* * *

Christine stood in the hallway, dripping wet. Bruce, drenched too, padded off into the kitchen to scrape his muddy paws on the clean linoleum

78

and, by way of protest at her cruel treatment of a poor, dumb animal, spray rainwater in all directions.

She had no reason to be disappointed, let alone hurt. There had been no 'arrangement', no hint of one. For all she knew the doctor had put her out of mind as soon as he had turned for home yesterday afternoon.

'Christine, is that you?' Maude called from the kitchen.

'Yes, Mother.'

'Are you soaked?'

'A bit.'

'Well, as soon as you've dried off please come and get this blessed dog out from under my feet. He smells to high heaven.'

'Yes, Mother.' Christine sighed.

She took off her coat and hat. Her stockings clung to her calves, her skirt to her thighs and trickles of water down her neck made her shiver. Coat over her arm and hat in hand, she was on the point of going upstairs to change when, to her surprise, the Brigadier appeared from the sitting-room and the strains of the 'Paradise Waltz' floated into the hall.

He had played the record four or five times last evening. The waltz was just as wistful and sad as most of the songs in his collection and Sylvia Froos's warm wavering voice and the saxophone and strings of the Manhattan Orchestra had already fixed the melody in Christine's head.

'He didn't show up, did he?' the Brigadier asked.

She could not bring herself to lie to the frail old man who seemed to understand her better than

79

anyone.

'No,' she answered. 'He didn't show up.'

'Never mind, my dear. One day he will,' the Brigadier assured her.

Then he slipped back into the sitting-room and closed the door.

*   *   *

Monday morning was a carbon copy of Friday evening, though a little more smudged. He could barely see the train as it chugged around the bend and crossed the bridge below which nestled Mrs Beatty McCall's little pony farm.

Eighteen minutes past seven on the dot. Alan shook out his umbrella, furled it carefully and stepped up into the carriage where, as always, the gentleman from nowhere was already immersed in his newspaper. Nods were exchanged. Alan dumped brolly and briefcase on the rack and sat down. He took a cigarette from his case, lit it with a match and drew in the sharp taste of tobacco.

The carriage jerked and rolled away from the platform, gathering speed.

He tried not to lean forward and incline his head as the train pulled on to the line that bordered the ridge road. He was, of course, looking out for the girl, who, sense told him, would be dressing or eating breakfast or possibly still be in bed.

Naturally there was no sign of her on the road; nothing, not even a tractor.

The train trundled on. He sat back.

'Quiet weekend?'

'What?' Alan looked up. 'Yes, very quiet. You?'

80

'Much the same,' said the gentleman from nowhere and went back to reading his newspaper.

PART TWO

The Teasing Board

CHAPTER EIGHT

Christine had never been in love, at least she didn't think she had. How could she possibly be in love with a man she had only just met? It wasn't love or even the possibility of love that troubled her but some vague notion that love had drifted by while she'd been looking the other way and that when she was very old and very alone she would glance back at her windy encounter with the handsome doctor on the ridge road and make far too much of it.

It was all the Brigadier's fault, the Brigadier and his obsession with sweet-voiced singers and sad, sad songs that, like it or not, ran round in your head like mice in a wheel. For the next few days Chris found herself humming the silly tunes while she hurried through the rain to school, washed dishes, polished the Brigadier's shoes or walked the dog. Every evening she watched the carriages clattering past, windows blurred by drifting rain, but she no longer waved just in case the doctor happened to be on board and thought her forward.

Suffering, she decided, was really quite fun.

All she had to do to bring her 'suffering' to an end was wander down to the railway halt one evening and, batting her eyelashes, say, 'Why, Dr Kelso, what a surprise.' Or turn right at the top of the drive from Preaching Friar and head for Moss House to see, metaphorically speaking, if the lights were on. Or she could simply wait for another Saturday, a blue-sky day, and camp on the ridge road until he appeared; then she would know for sure what he really thought of her and what she really thought of him.

And there, of course, fell the shadow.

What if he didn't recognise her? What if he simply tipped his hat and walked on? What if she discovered he was not the gentleman she supposed him to be but a middle-aged lecher who winked at everything in skirts and, as Charley had once done, tried to take liberties.

What, she thought, if she hated him?

That evening, Wednesday, the BBC Dance Orchestra signed off with a jolly rendition of 'Yes Sir, That's My Baby', full of whistles and cowbells.

The following morning, Thursday, Chris wakened not with a head full of love songs but with a bizarre image of Dr Kelso tap dancing over the brow of the hill like lanky Hal LeRoy. She realised then that it was time to talk to someone who might, just possibly, know a little something about falling in love.

*   *   *

'Me?' Freddy McKay said. 'What makes you think I know the least little thing about falling in love?'

'You've been to Paris, haven't you?'

'Whatever you may have heard to the contrary, sweetheart, Paris during the war was not a cradle of romance. What went on there had less to do with love and more do with—well, never mind all that.'

'I thought you met your wife in Paris.'

'I met my wife in Northolt.'

'Oh, I thought she was French,' said Christine.

'Only on her mother's side.'

86

'Love at first sight, was it?'

Freddy laughed callously and wiped a trail of mustard pickle from his moustache with the back of his hand.

'First sight? Hardly! Lucille was the belle of the ball or, should I say, the training station. Everyone fancied her: staff officers, parachute instructors, pilots, observers, right down to the chaps who swept the barracks. She was a civilian secretary to our liaison officer, Captain D'Offay, who, in spite of his name, couldn't speak a word of French.'

'Did he fancy her too?'

They were seated in the cupboard that passed for a staffroom and in which they ate lunch while those children who did not trek home for a midday meal huddled outside on the so-called veranda making do with bread and jam.

Freddy wiped his moustache again, a little more delicately this time.

'What is all this, Christine? Why the sudden interest in my love life?'

'I read in a magazine that men don't believe in love at first sight,' said Christine, unconvincingly. 'I just wondered if you had an opinion.'

'It's one thing to spin the kiddies tales of my derring-do with the Royal Flying Corps, quite another to . . . Damn it! D'Offay was sleeping with her, if you must know. He was her man, her one and only.'

'Why didn't he marry her?'

'He was already married.'

'I see.'

'I doubt if you do,' said Freddy. 'However, to answer your question—yes, I do believe in love at first sight. God knows, I fell for Lucille the

87

moment I clapped eyes on her. I knew she was D'Offay's girl but it made not a blind bit of difference. I wanted her.'

'Wanted her?'

He reached for the mug of tea that was cooling on the ledge by the hot-plate.

'There you are, sweetheart,' he said. 'That's one man's definition of love at first sight. I just plain wanted her.'

Christine cleared her throat. 'Physically, you mean?'

'Oh, I don't know. Yes, I suppose—physically, yes.'

'Did she want you?'

'Look at me,' Freddy said. 'Five feet six in my stocking soles with a face like a turnip and an unfortunate habit of spraying saliva in all directions when I talk. Lucille Medway didn't want me. She didn't even know I existed. She was D'Offay's little chickadee and had eyes for no one else.'

'What happened to change her mind?'

'Our dear Captain D'Offay fell out of a balloon.' Freddy snorted. 'I know what you're thinking but, no, I wasn't in the basket with him at the time.'

'Where did this happen? In Northolt?'

'Soissons. We were spotting for the guns. D'Offay had a couple of Frogs up there with him, showing off, and not a parachute among the lot of them when the German plane came zooming in.'

'Where were you?'

'Hanging upside down twenty-odd miles away observing the passing scene from the wing of a Sopwith Camel.'

'Oh, Freddy, you're such a liar.'

88

'No, it's the truth for once.'

'Uh-huh,' said Christine. 'As true as that story you tell about throwing an apple core at Baron von Richthofen.'

'And hitting him on the back of the head? Yes, well, the kiddies like it.'

'They don't know any better.'

'Do you, sweetheart?' said Freddy. 'If you did I doubt if you'd be asking me daft questions about love at first sight. I'm telling you the truth—but not the whole truth, not the unvarnished truth. The unvarnished truth is, to mix a metaphor, unpalatable. I prefer my version. I feel safer with my version.'

'So,' Christine said, 'you carried the bad news back to Lucille, comforted her and she fell in love and married you?'

'Not quite.' Freddy fumbled in his jacket pocket, brought out his cigarettes and lit one. 'Lucille—my wife—was pregnant when D'Offay bit the dust. She tried to do herself in by drinking Lysol. Failed, lost the child, went on the bottle. I bumped into her again a couple of years later in a bar in Piccadilly. She didn't really remember me, of course, but she'd got it into her head that I'd been D'Offay's friend, his special pal. All she wanted to do was talk about D'Offay. She'd broken off with her folks, with everyone. She had no one—well, no one except the men she slept with and they didn't give a toss about her. I brought her back to Scotland with me. She was too far gone by then to care where she went or who she went with. An undersize Scottish school teacher with malfunctioning salivary glands was better than nothing. I didn't touch her, didn't even kiss her for nigh on six months before I asked her to marry me. And she said yes. I mean, what choice did she have, poor woman?'

'But she loves you, doesn't she?'

'I suppose she does,' the headmaster said. 'Yes, I suppose she does.' He ground his cigarette into a tin ashtray. 'Now you know the whole squalid story of how Freddy found a wife. Not frightfully romantic, is it?'

'Not frightfully,' Chris agreed. 'May I ask you one more question?'

'In for a penny, I suppose. Fire away.'

'How long have you been married?'

'Twelve years. Thirteen come April.'

'Do you still want her? Physically, I mean?'

'God, the cheek of it! What are young women coming to these days?'

'Do you?'

'Of course I bloody do,' said Freddy and, handing Chris his tea mug, escaped into the classroom to ring the electrical bell.

*   *   *

Todd Thomas had been behaving strangely all week. Perhaps, Beatty thought, I'm being oversensitive and the boy is just going through one of his spells. His sister was easier to deal with. Maggie chattered merrily in response to Beatty's questions as to what she and her brother had been up to at the weekend and where, in particular, Todd had spent Saturday evening.

Todd, it seemed, had been ensconced, quite illegally, in the bar parlour of Kennart's Harvester Inn when Maggie had left for the Young Farmers' dance. He had remained there until closing time when he'd been accompanied home by his cousin Rab Campbell and his Uncle Jimmy, all three barely sober enough to stand up. Todd had had his ears boxed for his stupidity in squandering his wages buying drink for the Campbells.

Maggie's account had the ring of truth to it. The Campbells were notorious scroungers who would think nothing of parting a young boy of diminished responsibility from his wages.

Beatty ticked the boy off her list of suspects, and to apologise for doubting his honesty slipped him two of her last three cigarettes.

Being low on tobacco and out of bottled beer was the least of her worries. She had two pounds, fourteen shillings hidden away in a jar under her bed—emergency money—and not another penny to her name. The vet's bill was overdue and the kids' wages would have to be paid on Friday night. There was precious little fodder left in the bin for the ponies and even less to keep her nourished, a few eggs, two tins of soup and one of garden peas being about the best of it. She was close to flat broke and, with nothing to sell or pawn, was left with no choice but to swallow her pride and go in search of a loan to tide her over.

'A loan?' Charley said. 'I thought you were rollin' in it?'

'I'm not. I'm skint.'

'What happened to the dough you got from Cleavers?' Charley asked. 'Hasn't the old bugger paid you yet?'

'He paid me,' Beatty answered. 'I lost it.'

'Lost it? How in God's name did you lose it?'

'I did. I just did.' Even to her ears 'I just did'

91

sounded lame.

'That's an awful lot o' beer, Beatty. What pub did you blow it in?'

'It wasn't the ale, Charley. It was something else.'

'You're not gonna tell me, are you?'

'I—I can't.'

Charley remained seated on the skinny metal seat of the tractor, looking down on her. 'How much do you need?'

'How much can you spare?'

He pursed his lips. 'Thirty bob?'

'How soon can you let me have it?'

'Are things that bad?'

'Aye, they are,' Beatty admitted.

'If you can wait until Friday night I can up it to a couple o' quid.'

Sunlight raced over the field and picked out the shell of McCall's farmhouse far away across the glen. Charley followed the line of her gaze. 'You should've kept in with old McCall, Beatty. I'm told he got a packet from Vosper for the ground.'

'He got nothing for the ground,' Beatty said. 'All his acres were leased from Vosper in the first place. The only thing he owned was the farmhouse and Vosper didn't pay much for it, which is why his lordship's let it run to rack and ruin.'

'Nobody wants farmhouses these days,' said Charley. 'Any roads, Andy saw you right, didn't he? I mean, he had the Picton patch wrote into his will in your name just in case he didn't come back. And you've the widow's pension.'

'It's a pittance,' Beatty said. 'Better than nothing, I suppose.'

'I'm glad I missed the war,' Charley said. 'Fancy

92

a wine gum?'

'I fancy a ciggie, actually.'

She watched him vault down from the tractor. For someone as square-shaped as him he was almost graceful. She had no recollection of what he'd been like with his clothes off—young then, of course—or how he'd performed. At the time she'd convinced herself she was being charitable by introducing him to the joys of love but it had been nothing but pure selfishness on her part and she'd made sure it had never happened again.

Charley tapped two Woodbine from the pack, balanced both cigarettes on his nether lip and, with a gesture a little too continental to sit well with dungarees and an old cloth cap, lit them from one match.

Beatty took the cigarette, pinched between finger and thumb, drew in a lungful of smoke, coughed, and nodded her thanks.

'What happened to your leg?'

She had put on her old cotton skirt to hide the bandage around her thigh. She hadn't dared remove the dressing, though it was horribly frayed and grubby.

'What's wrong with my leg?'

'You're limping.'

'Age, Charley,' she said. 'Age and decay.'

'Get off,' he said, frowning. 'You're in trouble, Beats, aren't you?'

'I'm only in trouble 'cause I'm broke,' she said, then, inspired, 'My mother's sick and I sent most of Cleavers's cash to my sister to help pay the doctor's bills.'

'Oh!' Charley was almost persuaded. 'I'm sorry to hear it.'

'It's left me strapped, really strapped, but my sister's man's out of work and the dole won't stretch to—'

'Aye, right,' Charley interrupted. 'I've got the picture.'

'Thirty bob would help a lot. Two quid would be even better. The only thing is, I don't know when I'll be able to pay you back.'

'When you can,' said Charley, 'just when you can.'

'You're a decent chap,' Beatty said, 'and a good friend.'

'Never mind the smarm, Beatty. You'd do the same for me, wouldn't you?'

'Actually,' Beatty said, 'I'm not sure I would.'

She wasn't at all surprised when Charley, laughing, told her to bugger off.

*   *   *

Matrimonial ambitions were rife among the nursing staff and flirting, though frowned upon, was a universal pastime that no amount of finger-wagging or the posting of rules of behaviour had managed to stifle. Unattached junior doctors were regarded as fair game but even some wise old owls, bachelors born and bred, had fallen victim to the wiles of twentieth-century womanhood and had wound up, a little dazed perhaps, on the steps of the altar.

So far Alan had escaped the attentions of the predatory younger set who no doubt regarded him as far too dry a stick to bother with even if he hadn't already had a wife. He had never cultivated much of a personality and had no obvious eccentricities, unlike visiting consultants, many of whom led colourful lives, professional and private. It hadn't crossed Alan's mind that becoming a widower had changed the situation or that, quite unwittingly, he somehow conveyed the impression that he was no longer impervious to the attractions of the opposite sex.

The little patient, barely eight weeks old, had failed to respond to treatment for hypertrophy of the pylorus. Lavage and rectal feeding had not effected an improvement and it was agreed that surgery would be necessary to open up the pyloric lumen before the infant became too debilitated to survive the trauma. The procedure—Ramstedt's operation—was simple enough but the mortality rate was high, a fact of which all the members of the theatre staff were well aware.

Alan spent Wednesday night at the Caledonian Club. He arrived by cab at the hospital at a quarter past six with nothing in his stomach but a cup of coffee and a single piece of toast. He visited the ward to examine the poor, wizened wee creature, who looked more like an old man than a baby. The mother had been given a cot in the visitors' room. Bewildered and frightened, she too was a sad sight. The little boy's father had not been able to find work in Scotland, had gone off to England in search of a job and had not been heard of for months.

At least, Alan thought, the woman had enough sense to bring the baby to us. Far too many women in Glasgow chose to send for a priest in preference to a doctor and the priests, some of them, were too inclined to wring their hands and accept congenital malfunctions as God's will.

He spoke to the woman for three or four minutes, striving to make her understand that he was no miracle worker and there was a possibility that her son would not pull through: the usual juggling act, reassuring and warning at one and the same time. He left her, weeping and fiddling with her rosary, in the care of the ward sister and headed, via the back stairs, for the surgical wing.

'Ah, here you are at last.' Josie Carmichael, the senior anaesthetist, was already scrubbed and gowned. 'I thought you'd been carried off by some harpy.'

'Chance would be a fine thing,' Alan said. 'I was talking to the mother.'

'How's she taking it?'

'How do you think she's taking it?'

'I mean, does she care?'

'I'm not sure she understands but, yes, she cares.'

'Some don't. Is she suffering from guilt?'

'Guilt?' Alan said. 'Why would she feel guilty?'

'Women do. Any misfortune they don't understand they blame on their own inadequacies. Surely you knew that, a man of your experience?'

'I'm a surgeon, Josie, not a . . .'

'Philanderer?'

'Psychologist.'

She lifted her hands and very carefully adjusted her cap. Every strand of dark brown hair had been tucked away. The sweep from her neck to the edge of the cap showed the marks of the razor. She always wore her hair short though not bobbed, which, she'd once declared in Alan's hearing, was a style best reserved for horses. If anyone knew about horses it was Josie Carmichael. She spent her weekends galloping about the countryside in point-to-points or following the hounds across the fields of Lanarkshire. She was always weather-brown, her figure trim, apart from her bottom which had begun to spread a bit.

Alan cleared his throat. 'I met a woman at the weekend who breeds ponies.'

'Ponies,' Josie snorted, 'are for little girls.'

'These ponies aren't. They're destined for the pits.'

'God!' she said. 'That's a frightful trade, that is.'

'But necessary.'

'Yes, I concede—necessary. Who is this woman? Is she a friend?'

'Hardly,' Alan said. 'She's a local—what— farmer, I suppose.'

'Married?'

'Josie!'

'Oh, Mr Kelso, do I detect a little blush upon the marble cheek? Surely you know whether or not your friend has a husband.'

'No husband.'

'Well, well, well!'

On top of her academic achievements and her standing in the medical community, Miss Carmichael had a bawdy sense of humour. She was neither callous nor careless in her work—far from it—but she was prone to making remarks during simple surgery that Alan considered immodest. At staff dances and formal dinners, however, Josie fairly turned on the style and in a sheer black cocktail dress or chiffon dinner gown was the acme of sophistication.

'If I invite you to supper,' Josie said, 'will you tell me all?'

'There's nothing to tell.'

'I'll bet there is. And if there's not there soon might be.'

'Josie—'

The wheels of the trolley-cot squeaked in the corridor.

Josie Carmichael tightened the belt of her gown and murmured, 'Oh, yes, Mr Kelso, we'll have you in the saddle yet,' then, all business, followed the tiny patient into the operating room.

CHAPTER NINE

Charley had been sulking all week. On Monday when the potato planters had descended on the field behind the school he had stationed himself on the tractor on the crest of the hill like a knight on his charger and, much to the dismay of his juvenile fans, had pointedly refrained from coming within three hundred yards of the fence. He had repeated his aloof performance again on Tuesday and on Wednesday had appeared only to pay off the hands.

'What's wrong with Charley, miss?'

'Nothing,' Christine snapped. 'He's busy, that's all.'

'But, miss—'

'You're not here to chatter, Doris. You're here to learn.' Christine tapped the culprit's desk with the long ruler. 'Now get on with it.'

Much as she resented Charley Noonan's attentions, Christine did not take kindly to being cold-shouldered. Enquiries in the Ottershaw Co-operative store had brought forth the information that Charley had been spotted on the bus to Glasgow on Saturday afternoon. Precisely what had lured him into the city even Co-op gossips had been unable to determine, though Christine knew Charley well enough to guess what he'd been up to.

Football was not one of Charley's passions nor was he much enamoured by the 'entertainment' offered in Glasgow pubs which all too often involved fisticuffs. When spared from farm work he took himself off to one of Glasgow's numerous cinemas and now that words and music had been added to the flickering images Charley, like nine-tenths of the population, was in total thrall to the movies.

Christine liked moving pictures too, but queues, crowds, the darkness and anonymity of city cinemas frightened her. She knew by reading and rumour that many a young woman had come to grief in the back row of the stalls and that agreeing to go to the pictures in town with a man—even Charley—was roughly the equivalent of agreeing to be kissed, fondled and probably having to fight to hang on to one's virtue.

For three nights a month, however, the upper room of the Vosper Halls in Ottershaw was transformed into a picture palace where Christine felt perfectly safe; a noisy, friendly, community jamboree where the lights were never quite dimmed and the screen—dropped from rollers near the ceiling—was so bright that any young man with hanky-panky on his mind would be hard pressed to pursue his nefarious ends without being spotted by his auntie, his mammy or his victim's dad. Not being entirely a prig, Christine had let

99

Charley take her to the pictures in Ottershaw now and then, though she'd refused to let him walk her home.

When posters appeared in the Co-op announcing that *Morocco* would be shown in the Vosper Halls for three days after Easter there was considerable excitement among local buffs. After its opening in Glasgow a year ago the film had been denounced as filthy, lewd and depraved, which was recommendation enough for the good folk of Ottershaw and district.

Naturally, Charley had seen it and had told Christine all about it, laying emphasis on the kissing rather than the fighting. But with Charley sulking and the Brigadier too fragile to be left alone, it looked as if the legionnaire and the cabaret singer would have to conduct their steamy affair without her.

'Now there's a picture I wouldn't mind seeing again.' Mr Woodcock rested his bum on the bonnet of the new red mail van in the forecourt of the school yard. 'I saw it in the Gem in Lime Street with my girlfriend. Wasn't the Palais, exactly, but it wasn't no fleapit neither.' He grinned. 'Got quite carried away, Angie did. Couldn't keep her hands off me.'

'What happened to—ah—Angie?' Christine asked.

The postman shrugged. 'Got lost in the crowd, I expect. We was young at the time, her an' me—well, younger.'

'Aren't you young now?'

'Just reachin' me prime, love.'

'What? Twenty-one?'

'Thirty-three, I'll have you know.' He paused to

tip his cap to Freddy McKay who, wheeling into the forecourt on his bicycle, scowled by way of a greeting. 'I thought of joining the Foreign Legion, like, but my mum wouldn't wear it.'

'I'm not surprised,' said Christine.

'You an' me would make a nice couple.'

'A nice couple of what?'

'Tell you what, why don't you an' me go to *Morocco*?'

'It's a little too far for a weekend.'

'The picture, love, the picture.'

'Mr Woodcock, are you asking me out?'

' 'Course I am. You daft or something?'

'Daft I may be,' said Christine, 'but not that daft.'

She was well aware that she was being observed, not just by her pupils, who would stare uninhibitedly at anything and anyone, but also by her boss. Having taken off his bicycle clips and propped the machine against the wall, Mr McKay glowered and with an urgent little tick-tack motion of the head instructed her to break off her all-too-public tryst and come indoors.

'Gotta go,' said Mr Woodcock, ' 'fore I get you in trouble.'

'You won't get me in trouble,' Christine said. 'Never fear.'

'Be nice to try, though, dontcha think?' He rolled off the bonnet, opened the van door and leaned on it. 'Saturday week—*Morocco*?'

'The letters, Mr Woodcock?'

'The what?'

'The mail.'

'Oh—yeah.'

He reached into the van, brought out the bundle

101

of letters and brochures that made up the morning's delivery to the school and gave it to Christine.

'Think about it, love, will you?'

'No need to think about it,' Christine said.

'I'll betcha will, though,' the postman told her. 'That's the thing about girls: they just can't help thinking about it.' Slithering into the driver's seat, he closed the door, tooted the horn, and drove off.

Freddy waited in the entrance hall. 'Who the devil's that?'

'New postie. He's from Liverpool.'

'Didn't take the beggar long to get his lamps on you, did it?'

'Don't be ridiculous,' Christine said. 'He's a boy.'

'He doesn't look like a boy to me,' said Freddy. 'What's his name?'

'Woodcock.'

'Dear God!' Freddy muttered and, shaking his head, carried the mail off into the sanctuary of the classroom.

*   *   *

Alan was seated in an armchair in the residents' lounge drinking coffee and eating a sandwich when Josie Carmichael came for him. She had changed out of her surgical gown and had combed her hair. He waited for her to pick up a cup from the buffet trolley and steeled himself for more of her teasing. Then he caught sight of the expression on her face and, setting down his plate and cup, rose to greet her.

'What is it? What's wrong?'

'The boy,' she told him quietly, 'died.'

'When?'

'A few minutes ago. We need you for the certificate.'

'Is he still in the ward?'

'Yes, the sister and a nurse are with him.'

'And the mother?'

'She's with him too. She wants us to fetch a priest.'

'Then fetch one,' Alan said. 'The chaplain will have a number.' They were already heading for the stairs that led up to the ward. 'The surgery—there were no obvious complications. The stomach was perfectly empty and the pylorus came through cleanly. Everything seemed fine to me.'

'Everything was fine,' Josie told him. 'He was awake and taking liquid.'

'Breast milk?'

'Yes.'

'Did he choke?'

'No, no choking or vomiting.'

Alan moved on to the staircase, Josie behind him. 'And there was no fault in the regulation of his temperature?'

'Are you suggesting that I—'

'I'm not suggesting anything, Josie.'

'It appears he simply closed his eyes and stopped breathing.'

'Heart,' said Alan. 'Blood clot probably.'

'You'll ask for a post-mortem, of course.'

'Of course.'

'The mother may object.'

'Or the priest,' said Alan. 'I'm signing nothing until we have an answer.'

'What if there is no answer?' Josie Carmichael

103

said. 'Surely, you're not going to drag in the Fiscal.'

'Not unless the governors insist. They'll have to be informed.'

'Under the circumstances,' Josie said, 'they'll leave it to you. They trust your judgement.'

'My judgement?' said Alan bleakly. 'Did the child have a name?'

'Iain.'

'Iain,' Alan said. 'Right!' And, pushing through the door into the ward, he headed for the screens that surrounded the cot.

*   *   *

Seated at the table in the hut, Beatty tore the end-paper from one of the detective novels she'd picked up for a penny at the pedlars' market in Stirling and, tongue between her teeth, scribbled down figures.

Two pounds and fourteen shillings plus Charley's two quid wouldn't go far. Come September there'd only be three Shetlands old enough to sell plus two or three Highlands and, God knows, that small lot wouldn't fetch much.

She nibbled the pencil stump and thought of her brother-in-law up in Peterhead, far to the north-east. She'd told Charley a lie. Her mother wasn't sick and her brother-in-law was well in work. Jackie was a trawler-hand and the fishing trade continued to thrive even in these miserable times. No help would come from that quarter, however. Jackie had tried it on with her when she was fourteen. She'd kicked him in a sore place and he'd never forgiven her. Andy's folks, the McCalls, had cut her off right after the war when they'd sold up in Ottershaw and moved away. The only thing she had of any worth was Picton's meagre acres and if she sold those she'd be homeless.

She threw down the pencil, tossed the paper into the fireplace, opened the door and stepped out into the darkness. The clouds had skittered away, the sky was clear. Ewes bleated across the hill and the bark of a dog fox came from the edge of the pine wood. She sensed, rather than saw, her ponies stirring in the pasture and was seized by a terrible panic at the thought that she might lose them.

She returned to the hut, closed the door and crossed to the bed where she'd laid out Marion Kelso's clothes. She lifted the pink cashmere jumper and held it against her cheek. It was still soft, still redolent of the woman who'd lived in the big house and whose belongings meant so much— or was it so little?—to her husband that he'd preserved them just as the woman had left them, stuffed away in drawers and wardrobes. Gosh, Beatty thought, what wouldn't I do to get my hands on the rest of those clothes to sell at the Stirling market?

What wouldn't I do, I wonder?

*　　　*　　　*

Another restless night in the Caledonian and another early rise had washed Alan out. He slouched through ward rounds before hurrying down to the pathology laboratory where Dr Munro had gathered the results of the post-mortem examination which were, to say the least of it, inconclusive. He followed Munro to the boardroom where they were joined by Josie Carmichael, a senior theatre nurse and, traipsing in one by one, four of the fifteen governors, including Robert Foster, a distinguished Glasgow stockbroker and the board's current chairman.

Questions were asked and answered: when pressed, Munro reluctantly admitted that the weight of the child's heart had been less than one would normally expect to find in a male of that age and that while he had discovered no defects in the tiny pump or evidence of clotting in the arteries, the delicate and unformed nature of the arterial system did not rule out a fatal embolism.

After some discussion the Board members declared themselves satisfied that the child had died of post-operative heart failure which, as far as Alan was concerned, was more excuse than solution. The sad fact was that very young children died for no obvious reason and even among doctors there was grudging acceptance that some things must be put down to the will of God.

'You don't believe that nonsense, do you?' Josie Carmichael said.

'Not really.'

'Do you still think it was your fault?'

'No,' Alan told her. 'I did nothing wrong.'

After a moment, Josie said, 'Do you know what day it is?'

'Friday.'

'Good Friday.'

'Am I supposed to find some significance in that fact?'

'My mother used to tell me that when little babies died on Good Friday they went straight to heaven and became cherubs,' Josie said.

'And you believed her?'

'I believed her then,' said Josie. 'God knows, I wish I believed her now.'

*   *   *

Easter was not a trades holiday but the banks were closed and city types took full advantage of it. On Friday afternoon the station was crowded with lawyers and stockbrokers heading home for the long weekend. Alan's friend with the pipe and the *Scotsman* was not on board the train. Alan was obliged to share the first class compartment with three young men who, full of high spirits, were heading off for a spot of fishing. Josie Carmichael had offered to cook him dinner and put him up for the night but he suspected there was more to her invitation than professional sympathy, and had politely declined.

When he stepped from the carriage at Ottershaw Halt, however, an odd sort of despair came over him and he regretted his decision. He looked around in hope that someone he knew— the girl with the dog, or even the pony woman— might be there to greet him. But there was no one, no one at all.

Moss House was in darkness. Mrs Mackintosh had left a note to inform him that as she hadn't seen him all week she'd taken it upon herself to go home early.

He dumped his coat, hat and briefcase in the hall and checked the contents of the larder: frying steak on the cold shelf, a packet of salted bacon, eggs, a pair of kippers, a loaf, butter and a brown paper bag containing vegetables. He was too tired to cook. He wanted someone to talk to. He went into the library, poured a Scotch and for no other reason than to escape the horrible emptiness of the house carried the glass out into the garden.

Late afternoon shadows strode across the lawn. He could just make out a corner of the ridge road half hidden by hedges. He debated if it would be worth while going for a walk. If he did meet the girl with the dog, though, what would he say to her? He had never discussed hospital affairs with Marion and to open up to a complete stranger was unthinkable.

He returned to the house, put a match to the fire in the parlour, then, bone weary, kicked off his shoes and stretched out on the couch. He found himself thinking not of Josie Carmichael or the slim, knock-kneed girl on the back road, but of the baby, Iain, who had died without reason in a cot in his ward. The infant's mother had defied the priest and given the doctors the nod to have her child cut up in search of an answer that might assuage her guilt and blunt her grief.

If only, Alan thought, it was that easy.

Then, in spite of his resolve not to, he fell asleep.

CHAPTER TEN

She wore a crêpe-de-chine middy jumper and a loose skirt in streaky mauve that might have been the height of chic a decade ago but that had definitely seen better days. 'It's me,' she said. 'I hope I'm not disturbing you?'

'You are, rather,' Alan said. 'What can I do for you, Mrs McCall?'

'You remember my name.'

He did not rise to the bait, if bait it was. 'What can I do for you?'

'I brought your clothes—your wife's clothes—back.' She had a parcel under her arm, a very neat parcel tied with twine. 'Washed and ironed.'

'You shouldn't have bothered.'

'Least I could do. I'll return the wellingtons another time.'

He took the parcel and waited for her to leave.

'Is there something else, Mrs McCall?'

'I didn't go to see Dr Currie.'

'Why not?'

'Since I was coming here anyway I thought you might change the dressing.'

'All right, I suppose you'd better come in.' He stood back and let her enter the hall. 'I'm not a charitable institution, Mrs McCall. Dr Currie won't be too pleased at me robbing him of a fee.'

She accepted the reprimand meekly. 'I won't do it again. Promise.'

He laid the parcel on the hall table and ushered her into the kitchen.

She glanced at the bare table. 'Haven't you had your supper?'

'Not yet, no.'

'Your stove needs stoking.'

'Mrs McCall . . .'

'I'm sorry. Old habits. Where shall I sit?'

'Anywhere.' Alan drew out a kitchen chair. 'Here.'

She took off her hat, placed it on the floor, shook out her hair, smoothed her skirt and sat down. 'I see you've an electric hot-plate,' she said. 'Very handy. I'd love one but, like the song says, we ain't got no 'tricity down on the farm.'

'The leg, how's the leg?'

'It's fine.' She toyed almost playfully with the hem of her skirt. 'You'll want to take a look, I suppose?'

He had heard lots of stories about amorous female patients seducing doctors but he had never been invited to do anything that wasn't strictly ethical, except during his service in Egypt where language difficulties had thrown up some hilarious misinterpretations.

He nodded warily.

She parted her knees, furled up her skirts and, reaching between her legs, did something with the garter. She peeled the stocking from her thigh and left it curled about her kneecap like a dancer in a sleazy nightclub.

Changing a dressing doesn't call for any great medical skill, Alan told himself, so at least I'm not liable to kill this patient like I did the last one.

He went off to fetch the first-aid box.

When he returned, the woman kicked off her shoe, propped her leg on a chair and showed him rather a lot of white thigh. He poured lukewarm water from the kettle into a clean baking bowl, added a drop or two of iodine, then washed his hands at the sink in the corner.

'Isn't that what you do before you operate?' Beatty McCall asked.

'It is.'

'Are you going to operate on me?'

'One can't be too careful with a knife wound.'

He knelt at her feet and rolled the stocking over

her calf.

The bandage was grey and frayed. There was no staining on the outer layer, however, and no evidence of leakage. He put a hand beneath her calf. Her skin was smooth, almost silky. Did she shave with a razor or apply wax, he wondered, or was there some lotion on the market now that removed all trace of hair? Marion had been modest to a fault. Any amendments to nature had been carried out in privacy. In bed at night he had navigated by touch alone, tracing her thighs to the patch of hair between her legs which he'd stroked until the rhythm of her breathing told him she was prepared to accept him.

He slipped the point of the scissors under the bandage, inserted his little finger into the gap and cut away the binding.

The pony woman let out a little, 'Ow!'

He glanced up. 'Sorry. I didn't mean to hurt you.'

'You didn't hurt me,' the pony woman said. 'It tickles, that's all.'

*   *   *

He had long fingers and muscular forearms scrolled with dark hair. He looked grave, brow wrinkled, eyes piercing.

'Something wrong?' Beatty asked anxiously.

'No, no, you're healing beautifully.' He ran a finger up and down the spongy line of the scar. 'I'll bathe it with mild antiseptic and apply a light bandage. That should do the trick. No trouble walking?'

'Not now—thanks to you.'

111

The finger stopped moving and withdrew. He lifted the baking bowl from the table and placed it on the floor, dipped a pad of lint into the bowl, wrung it out and began to wash her leg.

She shivered.

'Cold?' he asked.

'No,' she answered.

She lifted her skirt a little higher and let her knee fall outward to give him access to the upper part of her thigh. She peeped down at the crown of his head. His hair was almost as thick as hers, with hardly a sign of grey. He dabbed her leg with a towel, cut an oblong strip from the lint and slid it carefully along the length of the scar. Holding it with a forefinger, he rolled out a piece of bandage to keep the dressing in place.

Beatty sucked in a deep breath. 'Couldn't lend me a fiver, could you?' she blurted out. 'I know I've a cheek asking after all you've done for me, but . . .'

'You do have a cheek,' he said, 'a damned cheek. How broke are you?'

'Stony. If I wasn't I wouldn't be here.'

'Well, I'm not giving you something for nothing,' he said. 'Can you cook?'

'Cook?' Beatty said. 'Cook what?'

'Whatever you find in the larder.'

'Are you offering to pay me to make your supper?'

'Exactly,' he said. 'Enough for both of us—if you're hungry, that is.'

'Oh, I'm hungry,' Beatty said eagerly. 'I'm always hungry.'

*   *   *

She fried steak and eggs and warmed up a tin of beans. They ate at the kitchen table and when they'd finished he suggested they adjourn to the parlour where they'd be more comfortable. Beatty had read enough cheap fiction to know what that meant and when he drew the curtains, lighted a lamp and threw a big log on the fire, she was sure they were settling in for the night.

He poured a whisky and soda and delivered it to her with a little bow. She took the glass and held it against her breast.

He fished a worn case from his pocket and flicked it open. 'Cigarette?'

'Why, thank you.'

She held the glass steady, made to pluck a cigarette from under the band and then, pausing, looked up at him; a ten pound banknote, folded into a strip, lay pinned by the band.

'Take it,' he said. 'Go on.'

'I'm not sure I should,' she said, still looking up at him.

'Do you want it or don't you?'

She nodded, tucked the banknote into the pocket of her skirt and extracted a cigarette from the case. She put the cigarette to her lips and touched his wrist lightly to guide the match flame.

'Thank you,' she said. 'I mean—well, thank you.'

She waited for him to snuggle down beside her, put an arm around her and get what he'd paid for. When he crossed to an armchair on the far side of the room and slumped into it she experienced a wave of disappointment, almost of annoyance.

He said, 'No sign of the thieves, I suppose?'

'No, they're long gone.'

'I still think you should have informed the police. What do you have to hide?'

'I don't keep proper books,' she told him.

'Half the farmers in the country don't keep proper books.'

'Aye, but they're men.'

'How long have you lived this way?' he asked.

She bristled. 'What way?'

'Hand to mouth?'

'I do all right.'

'You cherish your independence, don't you?'

'What's wrong with being independent?'

'Not a thing.'

'Are you making fun of me, Dr Kelso?'

'No, I'm not making fun of you. I'm the last person qualified to criticise you for hanging on to your liberty. But things happen, yes, things do happen, unexpected things that render us more dependent than we'd like to be.'

'Like your wife dying?'

'That,' he said, 'yes, that too.'

'Do you miss her?'

'Oh yes,' he said. 'I miss her. Don't you miss your husband?'

'I can barely remember my husband.'

He emptied his glass then said, out of the blue, 'I lost a patient yesterday, a little boy; a baby, eight weeks old.'

Beatty had been treated to sob stories before but she was sure this was no pitch to lure her into bed. Besides, he'd paid her and while she'd never taken money from a man before—a few free drinks didn't count—she'd taken money now.

'Did it happen when you were cutting him up?' she asked.

'Afterwards.'

'So it wasn't your fault?'

'That's what everyone keeps telling me. Why did you come here tonight?'

'To return your wife's clothes.'

'And to borrow money?'

'Yes.'

He sat forward in the armchair. 'Ten pounds means nothing to me.'

'That sounds like boasting.'

'I suppose it does,' Alan said. 'My point is, something that means nothing to me means a great deal to you.'

'I'm not sure where this is heading,' Beatty said. 'Perhaps I should go.'

'No.' He beat a little rhythm with his palms on his thighs. 'Stay. Have another Scotch.'

'You're not trying to get me drunk, are you?'

'Actually,' the doctor said, 'I'm trying to find a polite way of asking you to come upstairs with me.'

Oh, Beatty thought, is that all.

'Upstairs, Dr Kelso? Why do you want to take me upstairs?'

'To sort out my wife's clothes. It strikes me you might get more benefit from them than the Salvation Army. Anything that fits you may keep for yourself. I've no objection to that.'

'What about your housekeeper?'

'What about her?'

'She won't approve.'

'What I do with Marion's stuff is my business. Isn't there a ready market for second-hand clothes?'

'There certainly is,' Beatty told him.

'Then sell them,' he said firmly. 'Sell them and

keep the cash.'

'Why are you doing this?'

He got up and came towards her. She rid herself of the cigarette and the glass and waited for him to take her in his arms.

'Oh,' he said, looking down at her, 'I'm sick of pretending that everything's fine. Everything's not fine. Why am I coming home to an empty house or, rather, to a house that isn't empty enough? I'm not an old man, you know. It's just habit, really.'

'That little kiddie dying yesterday knocked you for six, didn't it?'

'Eight weeks, eight weeks of stomach pains and sickness and then—gone. It's so random, isn't it? So blessed random as to be almost pointless.'

'Not for me, it's not,' Beatty said. 'But then I'm not religious.'

'What are you, Beatty?'

'Bit of a pagan, I suppose.' She patted the back of his hand. 'Come on, Dr Kelso, take me upstairs. That's what you want to do, isn't it?'

'Yes, that's what I want to do,' he said.

*   *   *

He seemed like a novice at first, like Charley all those years ago. Some doctor, she thought, when he can't remember enough about anatomy to find the right place to put it. Then it dawned on her that he was afraid of offending her, of failing to please, which made a pleasant change from the rough treatment she usually received from men.

He was long in the bed, awkward, all knees and hip bones. Long in that other part, too. It had been an age since she'd made love to a man in a proper bed, a broad, soft, elegant bed. She was tempted to reach for him with her hand or push him down and mount him but something told her he wouldn't take kindly to that sort of thing. She lay motionless while he stroked her, but even with his hand cupping her belly, it seemed he couldn't quite bring himself to kiss her. She tangled her fingers in his hair and, lifting her shoulders from the pillow, opened her legs as wide as they would go and kissed him hard while his finger worked in and out and the pulse in her belly quickened and, arching her back, she boxed him between her thighs and swallowed him up.

*   *   *

'I'm sorry,' he said.
　'Sorry for what?'
　'That fiasco, that mess.'
　'You'll do better next time.'
　Throwing back the sheets, he thumped his feet to the floor, stumbled across the bedroom and switched on the corridor light. He came back a moment later and handed her a spotless white towel.
　'Here,' he said; then again, 'I'm sorry.'
　He seated himself on the side of the bed and stared into space.
　She hoisted herself up against the pillows and worked the towel across her stomach in the hope that the fall of light from the corridor would add a certain mystique to her nakedness.
　On cue, he said, 'You're very beautiful.'
　'No, I'm not,' she said. 'But do feel free to continue.'

117

He smiled faintly. 'Mrs McCall, you are very beautiful.'

'For a middle-aged widow, you mean?'

'You're not middle-aged,' he told her. 'You're in the bloom of youth.'

'How much whisky have you had?'

'Not enough, apparently—or too damned much. Are you cold?'

'I'd be a lot warmer if you gave me a cuddle.'

'Would you settle for a cigarette?'

If she'd been seventeen, a shivering kid riddled with self-doubt, she'd have leapt to the conclusion that her body repelled him, but being thirty-eight years old did have advantages when it came to riding over the rough spots.

'Sure. I'd love a cigarette.'

He crossed to the chair, fumbled in his trouser pockets and found his cigarettes and matches. He cupped the match in his palms, trapping them in a halo of light. He blew out the match, dropped the blackened end behind him and kissed her breasts. In a moment she was wet again, wetter than she'd been before.

'Here,' he said, 'give it here.'

She transferred the cigarette from her fingers to his. He held it as if it were a pencil or a fountain pen and let her pull on it. Smoke trickled away like milk in the shaft of light from the door and when he rose to find an ashtray, she saw that he had shed his uncertainty and wanted her once more.

And that, for the time being, was enough.

*   *   *

'Someone's been here,' Mrs Mackintosh said. 'My

pots are all over the place.'

'I had a friend in to supper last night.'

'They might have had the decency to wash up.'

'It was late,' Alan said. 'So late, in fact, she stayed over.'

'Stayed over?' his housekeeper said. 'Who stayed over? Was it that girl from Preaching Friar?'

'No,' Alan answered. 'It was not that girl from Preaching Friar.'

'Who was it then?'

'It may come as a surprise, Mrs Mackintosh, but I'm under no obligation to explain myself to you.' He tugged his dressing-gown about him and helped himself to coffee. 'A friend from Glasgow, if you must know.'

'Where is she? Is she still upstairs?'

'She's gone.' That at least was the truth. 'She left early.'

'There's no early train from Ottershaw on Saturday.'

'She has a motorcar.'

'Does she now?' Mention of a motorcar seemed to placate Mrs Mack as if somehow possession of a vehicle conferred rectitude on its owner. 'Are you for marrying again, Dr Kelso?'

'Good lord, no!'

'Is she just—just your sweetheart then?'

'She's a friend,' said Alan. 'Nothing more.'

He sipped coffee and watched his housekeeper's hunger for gossip wax before his eyes. 'I'll—I'll need to be making the beds,' she said at length. 'Two sets o' sheets I'll be needing if she's just a friend.'

He studied the dumpy country woman over the rim of the cup and wondered what sort of

119

vocabulary she and her husband used when sexual matters came up for discussion—if they ever did.

'One bed, Mrs Mackintosh,' he said. 'The double.'

'Oh!'

'While we're at it,' he went on, 'would you be good enough to unearth some cardboard boxes.'

'Cardboard boxes?' Mrs Mack said shrilly, as if she suspected some terrible perversion was in the offing. 'For what, may I ask?'

'To pack up Mrs Kelso's clothes.'

'You're—you're clearing out?'

'Yes.'

'Mrs Kelso's clothes, all her lovely clothes?'

'They're serving no purpose hanging in closets. I'll pack them this afternoon and have them collected some time next week.'

'Collected by who?'

'Charity,' Alan said curtly. 'Now, did I see kippers in the larder?'

Coffee cup in hand, he sauntered out into the hallway to pick up the morning's mail: two bills, a heavy brown envelope containing the latest issue of the *Lancet* and a small square envelope with his name and address written in copperplate in bright green ink.

He slit open the letter with his thumbnail. The paper was expensive but had a yellowish tinge around the edges as if it had been stored too long. It bore at centre top a regimental crest that had been crossed out by two slashing strokes of the pen.

Dear Dr Kelso,
If you are not otherwise engaged on Sunday

afternoon, it would give me great pleasure to provide you with lunch. We have been neighbours for some years, I believe, and it strikes me that it is high time we met. Unless I hear to the contrary I will look forward to greeting you at Preaching Friar after church service at, shall we say, one o'clock.

It was signed, without flourish, *Alexander Crockett (Brig. Ret.).*

He felt a flicker of excitement and then, in the same heartbeat, remembered Beatty and the long night of love-making.

'Damn!' he murmured. 'Damn, damn, damn!' and tucking the letter into the pocket of his dressing-gown, went back to the kitchen to eat his kippers and brood on the fickleness of fate.

CHAPTER ELEVEN

Beatty was in no fit state to greet visitors. She groped for the alarm clock hidden beneath the cot but was so bleary-eyed she could barely focus. She'd slipped from the doctor's bed at a quarter past five, dressed without waking him and had crawled home to Picton around six. It was now ten past ten. She let the clock fall and lay belly down while the thumping on the door continued.

'What?' she shouted, at length. 'Who is it?'

'It's Charley. Who do you think it is?'

'Go away.'

'I've brought your money,' Charley yelled. 'But if you don't want it ...'

121

She heaved herself from bed, found a coat to cover her modesty and unbarred the door.

Charley peeped timidly into the hut. 'You alone?'

' 'Course I'm alone,' Beatty croaked.

'Since when did you start locking the door?'

'Since tinks like you kept barging in on me.'

'God, you look terrible. You been at the beer?'

'Now where would I get the money to be at the beer?'

Charley grunted and, hunkering, opened the door of the barrel stove. 'You're down to ashes, Beats. Want me to light it?'

'Please.'

She watched him shake the grid, drop ash into the pan and lay out a few sticks of kindling from the basket by the hearth. On the shelf above the fireplace was the banknote Alan Kelso had given her. Coat flapping, she reached the shelf before Charley got up to search for matches. She dropped the matchbox into his hands and, turning away, stuffed the note into her pocket.

Charley glanced up. 'Is that a garter?'

'No, it's not a garter,' Beatty answered.

'It's a bandage, isn't it?'

'What if it is?'

Flushing a little, he looked away. 'Woman's trouble?'

'Yes,' Beatty told him. 'Woman's trouble.'

'Is that why you're so grouchy?'

'I'm grouchy,' Beatty said, 'because I need a pee, a cup of tea and a cigarette; not necessarily in that order.'

Stretched out on the floor like an Indian scout, Charley struck a match and placed it very precisely under the pyramid of twigs.

'For God's sake, go and pee, Beats,' he told her. 'I'll see to the rest.'

'You're a good lad, Charley. You'll make somebody a good wife some day.'

'Hah bloody hah!' said Charley.

*   *   *

When Maude marched into the sitting-room, the Brigadier knew he was in for it. He had freed himself from the confines of the armchair and had no intention of letting his housekeeper bully him back into it.

'I want a word with you, sir,' she said.

He steeled himself. 'Where's Christine?'

'Gone out.'

'With Bruce?'

'Yes—that's what I want to talk to you about, sir.'

'Oh, stop "sir-ing" me, Maude. You're not my sergeant-major.'

'Very well,' Maude said. 'What about this lunch?'

'What about it?'

'Sunday lunch for four in the dining-room?'

'We're entertaining a guest. At least I hope we are.'

'I saw the letter you gave Woodcock to post for you.'

'All right, so I sneaked a letter to that Post Office feller. Am I not entitled to a modicum of privacy?'

'It won't be so private when Dr Kelso turns up at the door.'

123

'You *read* my letter?'

'Certainly not,' said Maude Summers indignantly. 'I put two and two together.'

The Brigadier braced his elbows on the radiogram. 'What's wrong with giving Christine an Easter surprise? She was obviously impressed by this Kelso fellow and enjoyed his company.'

'You're match-making, aren't you?'

'Nothing of the sort.'

'Why the sudden interest in Christine's affairs?'

'I'd like to see Chris settled before I slough off this mortal coil.'

'Christine will manage fine without you fussing about her future,' Maude said. 'You've done enough for her already. She has her teaching, and she has me.'

'Quite!' the Brigadier said. 'However, that's not the same thing as having a man to look after her. By which I mean a husband.'

'You old devil,' said Maude. 'You *are* match-making.'

'Nudging,' the Brigadier said. 'Just nudging.'

'Dr Kelso's not her type. He's far too old.'

'He's not much older than your husband was when he married you.'

'Bertie was ten years older than I am. This Kelso chap's a good twenty years older than Christine.'

'No, he's not. He's only forty-six,' the Brigadier put in.

'How do you know?'

'Looked him up in *Who's Who*.'

Maude was impressed. 'He's listed in *Who's Who,* is he?'

'He's a senior paediatric surgeon with a bit of military history—Egypt—so of course he's listed in

124

Who's Who.'

'Then he's not going to be interested in our Christine.'

'Why not?'

Maude Summers hesitated. 'She won't be posh enough for him.'

'Posh!' The Brigadier exploded. 'Good God, woman, Christine's a well-educated, personable young woman, not some wittering dolt. Would you have her marry Charley Noonan and be a farmer's wife? Let's see what this Kelso fellow's made of before we throw him in the bucket. Now, please, go away. I'm busy.'

'Busy? Huh! Doing what?'

'Sorting out my gramophone records.'

'Gramophone records!' Maude shook her head. 'What do you think this doctor chap would like to eat?'

'Pot roast,' the Brigadier answered. 'Pot roast and treacle tart.'

*   *   *

For once she didn't flinch when Charley put an arm about her. He'd just given her two quid of his hard-earned, had lighted her stove and coaxed the kettle to boil. The least she owed him was a cuddle, though, having just given herself to a doctor, she felt she'd rather priced herself out of Charley's bracket.

'Feeling better?' he asked.

'Much,' Beatty said. 'Thanks, Charley. You're a pal.'

He had boiled a couple of eggs, frightened a slice of stale bread into believing it was toast, had dumped the food on the table and more or less ordered her to eat. She was just beginning to feel the way a girl should after a night in the hay with a handsome man when Charley said, 'Okay, tell me who you were with last night.'

'I wasn't with anyone, Charley. I was here—alone.'

'Liar! I know you weren't here, 'cause I came down about ten to give you your dough and the place was in darkness. You've a feller, Beats, admit it.'

'I do not have a feller,' she informed him.

'Well, you sure could do with one.'

'Are you volunteering?'

'Maybe,' he said.

'What about the school teacher?'

He shrugged. 'The snooty bitch can hardly bring herself to give me the time o' day. I don't know who she's saving herself for but it certainly isn't me.'

'Okay, Mr Noonan. You've been a pal to me so let me return the favour.'

'What do you mean by return the favour?'

'You'll see,' said Beatty darkly.

*   *   *

Alan experienced a flutter of guilt as he climbed the steps to the church to be greeted, not all that warmly, by an elder who handed him a hymn book. Gloom had dogged him in the wake of his indiscretion with the pony woman. McEwan, that inveterate womaniser, would have suffered no such doubts but, unlike McEwan, he had no yardstick by which to measure Beatty McCall's response. He

126

had been intimate with only one woman in his life—Marion.

'Why, Dr Kelso, what a pleasant surprise.'

Her linen tweed suit seemed too gay for a Presbyterian service and she looked, Alan thought, disconcertingly youthful. 'Miss Summers, how nice to see you again. Have you been sent to collect me?'

'Collect you?'

'Accompany me to lunch.'

'Lunch?'

'Oh!' Alan said. 'I've spoiled the surprise.'

'Are you alone?'

'Yes.'

'In that case perhaps you'd care to sit with me . . .'

'I would very much care to sit with you.'

'. . . and explain yourself.'

He shuffled after her, hat in hand. He was too tall to lose himself in the crowd and his appearance at Christine Summers's side would no doubt cause much idle speculation among Marion's friends. As he followed the young woman down the aisle he almost expected the organ to break into the Wedding March.

The girl slid into a vacant seat in a crowded pew and drew him after her; a tight squeeze. The elders, moving briskly among the flock, were packing every pew.

Alan tucked in his elbows and made himself as small as possible.

'What's all this about lunch?' the girl whispered.

'I've been invited to lunch at Preaching Friar. Didn't you know?'

'No, I did not know. Who invited you?'

127

'Brigadier Crockett.' Barely an inch separated Alan's freshly shaven chin and her lightly powdered cheek. 'Would you care to see my invitation?'

'That,' Christine said, rather tartly, 'will not be necessary.'

'Probably just as well,' Alan said. 'If I so much as wiggle a finger four old ladies will fall off the far end of the bench.'

The girl stared at him, all brown eyes, then nudged him in the ribs.

'Oh, you fool. You great fool,' she said and under cover of the Bible ledge allowed her knee to brush against his.

*   *   *

Sherry was taken in the sitting-room before the Brigadier led them into lunch. The saying of grace was followed by the consuming of soup, pot roast and treacle tart, her mother and she bobbing up and down to serve and clear while the conversation flowed as naturally as if Alan and the Brigadier had known each other for years.

Alan told amusing stories of his time with the Medical Corps in Ras el-Tin and less amusing stories of the casualties that had poured through the General Hospital in Alexandria. The Brigadier countered with tales of the Afghan campaigns and the bitter fighting in the salient of the Somme, tales that Christine had heard many times before but that the Brigadier recounted now without exaggeration.

Lunch over, they moved back to the sitting-room for coffee. The Brigadier instructed

Christine to put on one of his gramophone records and urged Alan to ask her to dance. She placed her hand in Dr Kelso's and put an arm about him.

'I haven't done this in years,' he said, 'absolute years.'

Christine said, 'I've never done it at all.'

'What, never danced?'

'Not to a waltz, not this waltz.'

'You have, my dear,' said the Brigadier. 'Of course you have.'

'With you, yes, but you don't count.'

'Oh, thank you,' the Brigadier said and, not in the least inhibited by the presence of a guest, crooned along with Sylvia Froos while Alan waltzed round and round the sitting-room with Christine in his arms.

CHAPTER TWELVE

The Shetland mares had been wormed some weeks before and were ready to be covered by Beatty's most reliable stallion, Nelson, who romped about in the paddock with not a care in the world.

Beatty kept a close eye on the big boy, though. He was a lot more sensitive than she was to signs that the mares were coming into season and stallions, even Shetlands, could become uncommonly aggressive with maiden mares. For this reason, she stalled the females beforehand and introduced them to the stallion as if they were strangers, preferably when Maggie and Todd were not around. The blacksmith's kids were well used to animals, of course, but Beatty was wary of letting the youngsters watch Nelson in action, for he could be raw and rough and dauntingly large when roused.

Early on Sunday she led the bridled mares to the teasing board, which was nothing more elaborate than a chest-high gate at the far end of the paddock. When the mares showed no alarm, Beatty let them loose and, just as church bells began to ring, seated herself on the doorstep to wait for Nelson to do his stuff.

She was still sitting there when, without warning, a total stranger appeared round the end of the barn. Beatty scrambled into the hut, snatched up an iron rod and gripping it in both hands like a cricket bat, shouted, 'One more step, mister, and I'll beat your brains out.'

'Whoa, whoa! Keep your hair on. I'm looking for Mr McCall.'

'What do you want with Mr McCall?'

'I heard he might have a place to rent. Seems like I was misinformed.'

'Seems like you were,' said Beatty.

'I mean, is this it?'

'Is this what?' said Beatty.

'McCall's farm.'

'McCall's farm's across the glen on the back side of the hill. But if somebody told you McCall has rooms to let they're having you on.'

The man had a knapsack on his back but he didn't look like a rambler. He didn't look like a thief either.

Beatty said, 'Where are you from?'

'Liverpool.'

'Ah!' Beatty said. 'So that's where you got that funny accent.'

'Oy!' the stranger said. 'Have a care. Three million people speak this way back in God's own country.'

'God's own country?' Beatty relented a little. 'This is God's own country.'

'Well, if it is, God should've provided a few more places to rent.'

His fair hair fluttered in the breeze and his blue eyes twinkled. If it hadn't been for the daft wee moustache on his upper lip, Beatty thought, he'd be quite a tasty proposition.

'I take it,' she said, 'you haven't walked all the way from Liverpool.'

'Kennart. I'm the new postman. I drive the red van. I'm lodged with Mrs Lorimer right now. She don't much care for me and I don't much care for her so I thought I'd scout for a better billet. This, if you'll pardon my candour, ain't it.'

'Who told you about McCall's farm?'

'Bert Lowden.'

'He's pulling your leg,' said Beatty. 'McCall's been gone for years.'

'Who owns the farm now?'

'Sir Maurice Vosper. It's more or less a ruin.'

'Ruin or not, I think I might toddle over and take a gander.'

'No skin off my nose,' said Biddy. 'By the way what's your name?'

'Woodcock. Call me Les, if you like. Now which way to . . .' He turned, stared, and glanced back at Beatty. 'Is that horse doing what I think it's doing?'

'It isn't a horse. It's a pony,' Beatty said. 'And, yes, he is doing what you think he's doing.'

'Gawd!' Mr Woodcock exclaimed. 'Never seen nothin' like that before.'

131

'What a sheltered life you lead in Liverpool,' Beatty told him. 'Stick around here long enough and you'll see a whole lot worse than that.'

'Gawd!' Mr Woodcock said again, then, turning his back on the mating pair, cleared his throat. 'So where's this farmhouse then?'

'Come on,' Beatty said. 'Shoulder your little pack and I'll show you.'

*　　　*　　　*

It had been years since Beatty had last visited the house where, in another lifetime, it seemed, she'd arrived as a bashful bride. In those days Andy's father had leased the grazing from the Vosper Estate and the fields had been peppered with sheep and cattle. Only a handful of hill sheep were scattered across the pastures now and a few hairy-looking bullocks nosing for winter bite since Vosper or, rather, his manager had let the grazings run to seed.

'Looks okay from here,' Mr Woodcock said. 'Four walls and a roof, that's a good start. You coming?'

An hour, Beatty thought, I can spare an hour. She was curious to see how much damage weather had wrought on the farmhouse and if the room in which she'd lost her virginity was, so to speak, intact.

'Lay on, Macduff,' she said and trailed the postman into the glen.

*　　　*　　　*

'No gas?' the postman said.

'Gas way out here? Don't be so daft.'

'No electricity neither?'

'Four walls and a roof,' said Beatty. 'What more do you want?'

'Where's the toilet?'

'Out in the back.'

'Do I need a spade and a parasol, like?'

'Chemical. In a shed.'

'Lovely!' Les Woodcock said.

For a moment Beatty assumed he was waxing sarcastic but then, dropping his knapsack, he gleefully announced, 'I can do something with a place like this. Handy, you know, I'm very handy.'

'I can well believe it,' said Beatty.

'The rent won't be all that much, will it?'

'No idea,' said Beatty. 'Are you serious?'

'Dead serious. It would be my place, my very own place.'

'Miles from anywhere.'

'Twenty minutes by bike to the sorting office and fifteen to the pub.'

'Have you seen what passes for a road?' Beatty said.

'Rough riding won't put me off. It's fun.'

'Dear God!' said Beatty. 'You *are* serious.'

'Be one in the eye for Bert Lowden if I settled down here, wouldn't it? How come the door ain't locked?'

'We're a trusting lot round here,' said Beatty. 'But before you get too carried away, I think you'd better look upstairs.'

'What's special about upstairs?'

'Nothing,' Beatty said quickly. 'Except it's probably riddled with woodworm and dry rot.'

'I can fix all that,' Les told her. 'Upstairs?'

133

Same steep wooden stairs, same low-roofed corridor, same ill-hung wooden doors; Beatty pushed open the door of the small bedroom. The bed she'd briefly shared with her husband was still here, the mattress rotted and smelly. She closed the door and followed the passage between the bedrooms, like a ghost from her past.

When the postman called out, 'Oy! Where are you?' she almost jumped out of her skin.

'Where are *you*, for God's sake?'

'In here,' Les told her.

The big bedroom had been occupied by Andy's parents. It was lit by one window and a skylight and contained no furniture save two rickety old chairs. Les Woodcock was precariously balanced on one of them. He'd pushed open the rusty hinge of the skylight and heaved half his long body through the opening.

'Hey,' he said, 'you should see the view.'

'I've seen the view,' said Beatty.

'A few tiles missing here and there,' he informed her. 'Crack in the chimney head, but look at those outbuildings. Perfect!' He closed the skylight carefully and climbed down. 'How do I find this Vosper guy to see what he'll soak me in rent?'

'Sir Maurice Vosper's far too grand to deal with riff-raff like you,' Beatty answered. 'The factor's name's Tait. He has an office in the lodge house at the gates of the Balnesmoor Estate.'

'I know it. I deliver there.'

'Tait's your man. He'll give you all the information you need. I should warn you, though, Tait might be persuaded to rent you a few lousy buildings but he'll never sell one acre of land. Vosper won't let him.'

'I don't want to buy ground, just rent the place.'

'Don't tell me you're taking up farming?'

Les Woodcock chuckled. 'What I know about cows you could put on the back of a postage stamp. No, Miss . . .'

'Beatty.'

'No, Miss Beatty, it ain't cows I'm hoping to stock here.'

'What is it then?'

'Motorbikes,' the postman said and, grasping a pair of invisible handlebars, uttered the immortal words, '*Vooom, vooom.*'

*   *   *

It had not escaped Christine's notice that Dr Kelso took his leave at precisely five o'clock. To linger much longer would have hinted that he expected to be invited to dinner which, she knew, would have been a breach of good manners. Dr Kelso was nothing if not polite; too blessed polite. He even apologised for taking her in his arms and dancing to the strains of the 'Paradise Waltz' which the Brigadier had played over and over again.

'He did keep insisting,' Alan said. 'It seemed to give him pleasure to see us dancing together. Did he teach you the steps?'

'In fact,' Chris conceded, 'he did. Who taught you how to dance?'

'A very large Australian lady, Miss Elsie Norris, RRC with Bar. She was deputy matron-in-chief for Egypt.'

'Were you in love with Miss Norris?'

Alan laughed. 'Heavens, no! There was very little time for dancing or anything else in

Alexandria, what with wounded coming in from the beaches and hospital trains ferrying them out to Cairo. I was sent down to Alex to patch up the worst cases and get them fit enough to travel. Elsie was so delighted to have an inexperienced young man to dance with she took it upon herself to give me lessons every spare minute we had, which were, I assure you, precious few.'

Halfway along the road between Preaching Friar and Moss House on a tranquil Easter Sunday evening; Christine had never felt so close to anyone before.

'In the midst of all that carnage, all that chaos,' Alan went on, 'dear old Elsie still found time to teach a boy—I wasn't much more than a boy—to dance. She had a portable, hand-cranked gramophone—the first I'd ever seen—that she lugged about with her and eight or ten records, very warped and scratchy, and a little purse, a reticule, in which she kept the needles. She'd play those records over and over until, I suppose, they eventually wore out.'

'What tunes did she play?' Christine asked.

'Strauss, American ragtime, one bitter-sweet French thing that always made me sad. I received my lessons in the corridor between the wards, sand and slops everywhere, Elsie very proper and correct, guiding me round while the orderlies, somewhat embarrassed, I imagine, ducked around us and pretended to look the other way. She tried to teach me the Turkey Trot and the Grizzly Bear but I was no Vernon Castle and she soon gave up on those.'

'She taught you how to waltz well enough.'

'I suppose she did, really. Did you like my

136

"hesitation"?' It used to be considered rather a novelty. Old hat now, I expect.'

'Were you happy then?' said Christine.

'What? Yes I was, I think, given that we were trapped in the middle of a bloody war and people were dying all around us.'

'You've more in common with the Brigadier than you might imagine.'

'I was never a military man, never a fighter.'

'That's not what I meant,' Chris said. 'What happened to Elsie Norris?'

'Haven't a clue. Probably went back to Australia after the war. I like to think she's teaching the foxtrot in some comfortable suburb of Melbourne, but'—he spread his hands—'who knows?'

He had given her something valuable, an almost-forgotten memory. She felt an urge to give him something in return.

'I remember my father very clearly,' she said. 'He was a teacher in Hamilton Crescent.'

'In Partick? I know the school. It's still there.'

'Of course it is,' said Christine. 'They didn't knock it down just because my daddy didn't come back from France.'

'Have you no sisters or brothers?'

'Only me,' she said with a little grimace. 'The apple of my father's eye.'

'I take it the Brigadier was a friend of your father's.'

'He didn't know Daddy from Adam.'

'Weren't they in the same regiment?'

'Gordon Highlanders, yes,' Chris said. 'But Daddy was an infantryman, a private. According to the Brigadier they never met. When the Brigadier was forced to retire and needed a housekeeper, he obtained a list of war widows and picked my mother's name from the list simply because Daddy had fought at Neuve Chapelle; died at Neuve Chapelle, actually.'

'I'm sorry.'

'Oh, really, Dr Kelso!' Christine said. 'You're not to blame for the war. Besides, the Brigadier looks after us very well. I miss my daddy, though. Even now I'm grown up, I still miss him.'

'And always will,' said Alan.

*   *   *

'Well, Maude, that went rather swimmingly, don't you think?'

'She's been gone long enough,' Maude said. 'She could have walked him to Glasgow by this time.'

'Oh, stop moaning,' the Brigadier said. 'Admit it: you liked him?'

'He's very polite, I'll say that for him.'

'Chris obviously likes him even if you don't.'

'She likes everyone. She's too trusting for her own good.'

'Come now, Maude. Kelso's no wolf in sheep's clothing.'

'I don't know what he is,' Maude said. 'And neither do you.'

'I've always considered myself rather a good judge of character, actually.'

'You might be a good judge of men but you know nothing about women.'

'True,' the Brigadier conceded. 'True. I mean, look at the dreadful mistake I made when I picked you out of the hat.'

'It's not too late to change your mind.'

'It is, alas. It's far too late. Besides, I don't know what I'd do without you.'

'I know what I'd do without you,' Maude said.

Look at her, the Brigadier thought, standing at the window wringing her hands because her daughter's walking out with a gentleman. What's wrong with the woman? Has she forgotten what it's like to be young, or is she afraid of being left high and dry if Christine takes a husband? Dear lord, he thought, suddenly, perhaps she's jealous.

'Maude,' he said cagily.

She glanced round. 'Do you want the wireless on?'

'It's nothing but hymns at this hour.' He hesitated. 'Tell me, if you were Christine's age wouldn't you regard Dr Kelso as a good catch?'

'I had a good catch and I lost him. What if there's another war?'

'Oh, what a pessimist you are, Maude Summers. Would you have Christine stay single on the off chance that Britain will go to war again?'

'There are other ways to get hurt,' Maude said.

'By a man, you mean?'

'Other ways,' Maude murmured.

And turned to face the window again.

CHAPTER THIRTEEN

By Monday Beatty had recovered her equilibrium. She had high hopes that Alan Kelso would keep his promise and donate her some of his wife's clothes to sell. There was also the question of what the doctor would expect in return. The borrowed tenner made it awkward. She wasn't a tart and had no intention of following that particular road to hell.

The sun shone over Picton. Children shrieked in the distance, three or four paper kites quivered in the wind above the pines and members of the Kennart Cycling Club whirred along the road past the stable.

Schools were closed, banks and big city institutions too, but farmers were hard at it and the Liverpudlian postie was out and about delivering mail.

He whizzed past the road-end in his red van twice in the course of the morning and tooted cheerily on both occasions, once while Beatty was lugging water from the tap and once as she emerged from the privy. The mares had been returned to the pasture but Nelson remained in the paddock for he still had work to do. Beatty had given the Thomas kids a couple of days off and intended to spend the afternoon rounding up more Shetlands for servicing.

She'd slapped two pieces of cold bacon on a slice of bread, brewed a pot of tea and was seated on the doorstep when the Wallis growled into the yard. 'Hello, Charley,' she said. 'I thought you'd be out on the hill with the lambing ewes.'

'I was.' Charley clambered down from the tractor and sat beside her. 'You told me a lie, Beats, didn't you?'

'A lie, Charley? What sort of a lie?'

'You didn't send Cleavers's dough to your poor sick old mother.'

' 'Course I did.'

'Well, that's fine. It couldn't have been you he

140

was talkin' about.'

'Who?'

'Rab Campbell.'

'Todd's cousin?'

'That's the one,' said Charley. 'He an' his uncle were in the Harvester on Saturday evening scattering money about like confetti. I'd popped in for a quick pint but the Campbells didn't notice me. They were with the usual rough crowd and looked as if they'd been boozin' for quite a while.'

'What did they say, Charley?'

'Rab Campbell was bragging about how Jimmy and he had found a pot o' gold under a woman's bed an' how she'd chased them with a hatchet. They'd borrowed Flem Aitken's truck to drive out to Picton an' escaped before the woman could catch up with them.' Charley paused before he went on, 'Look, Beatty, I didn't mean to eavesdrop. I couldn't help it. I'd a notion it might be you even before they mentioned your name.'

'You're right, Charley. They broke in while I was asleep and stole every penny I got from Cleavers. Todd probably told them I had cash.'

'Why didn't you send for the coppers?'

'No point,' said Beatty.

'Well, there's point now,' said Charley. 'I'll tell the coppers what I heard.'

Beatty grabbed him by the arm. 'No, Charley. If you point the finger at the Campbells you'll be looking over your shoulder for years to come, waiting for them to poison your ewes or wreck your tractor.'

'We can't let those bastards get away with it. They work for Vosper, don't they? You could have a word with Mr Tait.'

141

'And tell him what? It'd be your word against theirs.'

'How are you going to manage without money?'

'I'll get by somehow.'

Charley got to his feet and, digging his hands into his pockets, looked down at her. 'Does anyone else know about this?'

'No.' Beatty hated herself for lying again. 'Just you, Charley, just you.'

*   *   *

Christine dug out his panama hat but sensibly left the linen jacket in the wardrobe and put him in a warm old vicuña overcoat instead. Cardigan, scarf, gloves and a pair of fur-lined boots completed the ensemble that Maude deemed necessary to keep the Brigadier comfortable out of doors on a warm and sunny afternoon.

Seated in the basket chair that Chris had carried from the outhouse, he leaned into his stick and watched everything that was going on—which wasn't very much—on the drying lawn.

'Why,' he called, 'aren't you out rolling your Easter egg?'

'Easter Day was yesterday. Besides, I'm too old to roll eggs,' Christine told him. 'I'm not a wee girl any more.'

'Really!' the Brigadier said. 'I must have blinked.'

There was something medieval about Preaching Friar's cauldrons, wringers and scrubbing boards but, wreathed in steam and drenched in perspiration, Maude was in her element in the washhouse. The Brigadier was used to his housekeeper's bursts of activity but he felt sorry for Chris on laundry day when the poor girl staggered under loads that would have buckled the knees of a stevedore. 'Why don't you take Bruce for a walk?'

Tired out by chasing stray ends of clothes rope, Bruce was curled up at his master's feet, fast asleep.

'Bruce doesn't need another walk.'

'How long will this kerfuffle go on?'

'Until it's done,' said Christine. 'Then we'll start spring cleaning.'

'Oh, God!' said the Brigadier. 'Spring cleaning! You should be out having fun, my dear. Why don't you fetch your bicycle and go for a run?'

'Can't. Chain's broken.'

'Have it fixed then.' He sat forward, fists cupped on the crook of his stick. 'I'll bet that doctor chappie—'

'You *can* use his name, you know.'

'I'll bet Alan Kelso would fix it if you asked him nicely.'

Christine pinned her mother's voluminous flannel nightgown to the rope and emerged from behind it.

'Stop pushing, Sandy,' she said.

'I thought you liked him?'

'I do. But it's not up to me.'

'What's not up to you?'

'The next move.'

'Ah-hah!' the Brigadier exclaimed. 'The rules of amorous engagement haven't changed much, I see. Just don't wait too long, dearest.'

'Why—in case he stays away?'

'He's a fool if he does,' said Sandy Crockett.

'And a rogue if he doesn't?' said Chris and glided off across the grass with the clothes basket balanced on her hip.

*   *   *

Soon after he arrived at the hospital on Tuesday morning Alan was summoned by Professor Roy Stillwater, a visiting physician. The patient was a girl of five. In attendance were a nurse, a matron and Stillwater himself, a wiry wee chap in a morning coat and striped trousers.

'Now, Jenny,' Stillwater said. 'I'm going to lift you up a wee bit while this gentleman tickles your tummy. He'll try not to hurt you but if he does, you tell me and I'll—I'll punch his nose.'

'Aye.' The child's reply was barely audible. 'Punch his nose.'

'Well,' said Alan, 'I don't want my nose punched so I'll be as careful as careful can be. Are you ready, Jenny?'

'Aye.'

Seated on the side of the bed, Stillwater elevated the girl into a half-sitting position, a gentle movement, Alan noted, that caused her pain. She began to cry. So far neither Stillwater nor the matron had told him what was wrong with the child, just that she had been brought in at half past three in the morning by a gang of male relatives piled on the back of a horse-drawn cart.

Alan slid his right hand under the sheet.

'Abdomen?'

Stillwater nodded.

He pressed his palm carefully on to the child's stomach.

The professor and his little patient both flinched.

'How long has she been like this?' Alan asked.

'According to her father, twelve or fourteen hours,' the matron answered.

Rigidity and a degree of distension were already evident. The girl wriggled in Stillwater's arms and continued to weep fractiously.

'How high is her temperature?'

'One hundred and three,' said the matron.

'No symptoms of appendicitis?'

Stillwater answered, 'None.'

'Diarrhoea?'

'Present but not excessive.'

'If it's simple pleuro-pneumonia,' Alan said, 'you wouldn't have sent for me. Pneumococcal peritonitis would be my best guess. Is she toxaemic?'

'The results haven't come forward from the lab,' said Stillwater, 'but there's every indication that she is.'

Riding into Glasgow on the morning train Alan had thought of nothing but Beatty and Christine, Christine and Beatty. He was relieved to be given a difficult case to restore his professional focus. He withdrew his hand from beneath the sheet and got to his feet.

'That's your diagnosis, Roy, isn't it? Pneumococcal peritonitis?'

'In the sub-acute phase with localised abscess formation, yes. What do you have on the slate, Alan?'

'Tonsillectomies, two of the blessed things. Ungar can cover those. I assume you want me to drain the child's peritoneal cavity as soon as

145

possible?'

'If you're up for it,' Stillwater said.

'Why wouldn't I be up for it?' Alan said. 'The fact that you sent for me indicates that you trust me or, perhaps, that you trust me to trust you.'

'Exactly,' Stillwater said.

The child had stopped whimpering and seemed to be falling asleep. Her colour was bad, her breathing shallow. Stillwater held her as lightly as if she were a soap bubble.

'Have her moved to the surgical ward—my ward—and prepped,' Alan said. 'If the labs come through in the next hour I need to be informed. Failing which, I'll open her and hope for the best.'

'Who do you want to assist?' said Stillwater.

'Hargreaves and Josie Carmichael, if they're available.'

'May I—ah—stand in, please?' Professor Stillwater asked.

'Of course,' Alan answered. 'But only on one condition.'

'What's that?'

'No twittering, sir, no twittering under any circumstances.'

'You have my word on it, Mr Kelso,' the learned professor said and, being well aware of his reputation as a worry wart, crossed his heart with his thumb.

*   *   *

It was close to four o'clock before Alan sat down to lunch. The staff dining-room was almost deserted. He had taken no more than a couple of mouthfuls when Josie appeared. She had changed into street clothes and snaked between the empty tables as if she were dancing a tango. She placed her hands on her hips, leaned over the chequered tablecloth and squinted at Alan's plate.

'What the devil is that?' she asked.

'Macaroni pudding.'

'Oh, dear God! Kiddy food! What happened to the steak and kidney?'

'Gone.'

'And the chops?'

'All gone.'

'So it's mush or bust, is it?'

'Seems so,' said Alan.

She remained hanging over him, displaying the valley between her breasts. A week ago he would have discreetly averted his gaze but Josie had raised the bar or, more accurately, lowered the neckline.

'Is the girl all right?' she asked. 'Will she pull through?'

'Stillwater seems to think so. He was right to insist on surgery.'

'Why didn't you let Hargreaves close for you? He's an excellent stitcher.'

Alan shrugged. 'I was in a mood for stitching, I suppose.'

'You ripped through those two tonsillectomies too.'

'Nothing complicated.'

'Well,' Josie said, 'if you're finished for the day, how about taking me out for a cocktail? It's close enough to the witching hour, isn't it?'

'Love to,' Alan said gallantly, 'but I can't. I'm going home this evening.'

'Really!' She raised her brows. 'Why?'

'If you like,' Alan said, 'you may join me in a macaroni pudding.'

'If I do, will you answer my question?'

'I might'—Alan batted his eyelashes—'if you ask me nicely.'

'Oh, for God's sake!' Josie said and strode off to the serving hatch to forage for something to eat.

*   *   *

'Hello, hello, hello! And who might you be?' Mr Woodcock enquired.

'I might be Maggie Thomas,' Maggie Thomas answered. 'An' I might bash you wi' this bucket if you don't tell me who *you* are.'

'Call me Les, sweetheart.'

'You're the new postie, aren't you?'

'Famous at last,' said Les.

'Do you read other folk's letters?'

'Certainly not. Wouldn't mind taking a gander at your letters, though.'

'My letters?' said Maggie. 'Nobody ever writes to me.'

'What? No boyfriends? You must have a lover tucked away somewhere.'

'Watch it, mister!' Maggie warned. 'Just watch it!'

'I've been watching it since you stepped out of the cowshed.'

'It's a barn, daftie; a barn not a cowshed.'

'I knew that,' said Les.

'Bet you didn't.'

'Bet I did.'

'What's that then?' said Maggie, pointing.

'Easy. That's a horse.'

148

'Yah! It's no' a horse. It's a pony.'

'A "pownie?" Ain't never heard of a "pownie" before.'

'Are you makin' fun o' me?'

'I never make fun of beautiful young girls,' Mr Woodcock told her with just sufficient sincerity to bring a blush to her cheek. 'But,' he added, 'I might make an exception in your case. Who's that over there?'

'My brother, Todd.'

'He's a big lad, ain't he? How old is he?'

'Fifteen.'

'Geeze!' the postman said. 'How old're you?'

'None o' your business,' Maggie said.

'Lemme guess. Twenty-two, twenty-three?'

'Sixteen,' said Maggie proudly.

'Never!' Les feigned surprise. 'You look much too mature for sixteen.'

'Now I know you're at it,' said Maggie. 'Anyway, have you got mail for us?'

'Nope, no mail today.'

'Why have you stopped then? What do you want?'

'He wants me, I think.' Beatty had been observing the flirtation from the hut doorway. 'So, Mr Woodcock, what's the word?'

'I got it.'

'Got what?' said Maggie.

'I'm gonna be your neighbour,' Les told her.

'What's he talkin' about?' said Maggie.

'McCall's farm,' Beatty told her. 'When did you see Tait?'

'Yesterday evening. Caught him at home. Went in uniform.'

'That would impress him, I'm sure. Didn't he

ask for references?'

'Said he'd talk to his boss but saw no difficulty, etcetera. Dropped in this morning with the Balnesmoor post. Mr Tait was in the office and gave me the nod. Ten bob a week for the buildings. Not bad, eh?'

'Can you afford that much?' Beatty asked.

'No problem,' Les Woodcock answered airily. 'Mr Tait says he'll fix the tiles and the chimney and put in a new toilet, but the rest's up to me.'

'How long's the lease?' said Beatty.

'Three years. I'll sign the paper as soon as Mr Tait writes it up.'

'McCall's farm?' Maggie put in. 'What do you want wi' that dump?'

'I'm gonna live there, like,' Les said. 'I've always wanted a place where I can do what I like.'

'An' what,' Maggie asked injudiciously, 'would that be?'

'Ride your "pownie" over the hill some evening and I'll show you.'

'Careful, Mr Woodcock,' Beatty told him. 'She might take you up on it.'

'Not me,' said Maggie. 'I'm not that daft.'

'How about you, Miss Beatty?' the postman said. 'Are you that daft?'

'Do I look that daft?' said Beatty.

'Actually,' Les Woodcock said, 'you look like you'd eat me for supper.' He gave Maggie a formal bow. 'Duty calls, sweetheart. Gotta rush. See you soon.'

'Not if I see you first,' Maggie retorted.

But the shock-haired postman had gone.

*   *   *

Josie Carmichael was a good deal more adept at injecting atropine than she was at coaxing ketchup from a bottle. Alan was not in the least surprised when a great dollop of tomato sauce plopped all over her macaroni pudding. She scowled at the mess for a moment then, lifting her fork, delicately punctured the cheesy crust and let sauce seep into the wounds.

'Well,' she said, 'is it the horse farmer?'

'I don't know what you mean,' said Alan.

'Come off it, Kelso, I'm not entirely stupid. You're behaving like the cat that ate the canary. I've never heard you humming while you planted sutures before.'

'Humming? I wasn't humming. Was I?'

'You most certainly were, chum, humming away good style while you plied your little needle. Lord knows what Stillwater made of it.' Josie shovelled a forkful of pasta into her mouth. 'You're having a fling, aren't you?'

'No, I am not having a fling.'

'Is it this pony farmer you told me about?'

'It is not the pony farmer I told you about,'

'Who is it then? It's someone. I know it's someone.'

'Josie . . .'

'What?'

'You're dripping.'

She peered into the depths of her cleavage and removed a crumb of pasta from the crown of her breast.

She said, 'What I really want to know is why it isn't me?'

'Isn't you—what?'

151

'Do not be obtuse.'

'I'm only a man, Josie, obtuse by nature.' He mopped cheese from the corner of the dish with a pinch of bread and pushed the dish away. 'However, yes, I have struck up a friendship with a young lady.'

'Some freckly child out of the wild wood, no doubt.'

'In point of fact, she's in her late twenties.'

'Then why call her a young lady? How many girls do you have at your beck and call out there in the wilderness?'

'Umpteen,' said Alan. 'I'm beating them off with a stick. Now you've raised the subject, perhaps you'd be good enough to share a little of your experience on the subject of—ah—dating.'

'Dating? What do I know about dating? Good God, I can't even persuade you to buy me a cocktail.'

'What would a girl—a young woman—expect? What would please her?'

'Dinner for two at the Rogano.'

'She isn't that kind of a girl.'

'What kind of a girl is she?' Josie enquired slyly.

'Educated, articulate, not awfully sophisticated.'

'Why isn't she married? Or is she?'

'No, she isn't married,' Alan said. 'What do you take me for?'

'I'm not sure what I take you for. You've changed.'

'So you keep telling me,' Alan said. 'Come on, Josie, how *do* I make a good impression on my friend?'

'Drive up to her hovel in a Rolls-Royce and sweep her off her feet.'

152

'Off where?'

Josie spread her hands. 'The theatre.'

'In Ottershaw?'

'The pictures then,' Josie said. 'I refuse to believe there isn't a cinema in Ottershaw. But'—she waved her fork—'do not, repeat not, have the usherette show you to the back row unless you want to scare the drawers off your tender young flower—which may be precisely your intention, of course.'

'There are times,' Alan said, 'when your vulgarity astounds me.'

Josie fixed him with her sad, dark eyes. 'Whatever fairytales your mother may have told you, Mr Kelso, whatever myths were drummed into you at school, women are sexual creatures. The moment you invite this wench to accompany you anywhere, the first thing that'll pop into her head is just how soon you'll kiss her and, when that's been taken care of, just how soon you'll—'

'Josie, please!'

'You're a well-to-do widower, Alan, reasonably well preserved. While you may have romance in mind your unsophisticated little miss will be dreaming of sex or, should I say, of sex preceded by marriage. Now if you won't carry me off and get me plastered, the least you can do is buy me dessert.'

'Of course,' Alan said. 'What would you like?'

'What's left?'

'Prunes and custard.'

'Thank you,' Josie said. 'I'd rather die.'

'You don't know what you're missing,' Alan said.

'Neither do you,' said Josie gravely, and pushing back her chair, left him at the table to stew in his

153

own stubborn juice.

CHAPTER FOURTEEN

Hiring a motorcar was easier than Alan had anticipated. After early ward rounds on Friday afternoon he rode a cab out west to Anniesland where a certain Mr McNair gave him a tour of a recently opened showroom of high-class vehicles. He was tempted by an enormous Rolls-Royce Phantom—which would certainly have impressed Josie—but given that the last car he'd driven had been a rattle-trap ambulance conversion, he settled for a 1929 Alvis instead.

Fortunately Mr McNair did not ask to see his driving licence which was one of the old-style 'county' things and as tattered as a pirate's map. Mr McNair did, however, accompany him on a test run through quiet suburban streets to explain what all the knobs and switches were for, how to rein in the power of the engine and, most importantly, how to operate the clutch without sending them both flying through the windscreen.

Terms were arranged, insurance settled, the petrol tank filled and, around five thirty, Alan set off in a north-westerly direction heading, he hoped, for Ottershaw. He arrived at Moss House, tense and shaken, forty minutes later, just as Mrs Mackintosh was leaving.

'What's this?' she grizzled. 'What have you been doing now?'

'It's a car, Mrs Mack, a motorcar, that's all.'

'You've bought a motoring car, Doctor, have

154

you?'

'Hired.'

'Hired, is it? And for what, might I ask?'

By his housekeeper's reckoning a Saturday evening jaunt to the picture show would be unlikely to justify the expense of motorcar hire. 'To see if I like it?'

'Surely you're not thinking of buying a thing like that?'

'I don't see why not,' said Alan. 'I'd be home every evening in forty minutes and would have a good half-hour—more—extra in bed of a morning.'

'Who'll look after it?'

'Me, of course,' said Alan confidently and, uncoupling his hands from his armpits, headed indoors for a drink.

*   *   *

Christine had been ready for well over half an hour. She had smoked two cigarettes to soothe her nerves and on the off chance, however remote, that Dr Kelso might attempt to kiss her at some point in the evening had chased away the odour with a peppermint imperial.

'You look lovely, my dear,' the Brigadier told her.

'Except for the shoes,' her mother added.

'I can't walk to Ottershaw in heels,' Chris said.

'In any case,' said the Brigadier, 'I doubt if your doctor friend will spend much time admiring your feet, even if he is a paediatrician.'

Christine was too tense to respond to the feeble joke.

155

She glanced furtively at her wristwatch.

'He's late,' her mother said.

'No, he's not,' Christine corrected. 'It's not half past six yet.'

'Perhaps he's not coming,' Maude suggested.

'Of course he's coming,' said the Brigadier. 'He's probably hanging about outside the gate so that he doesn't appear too keen.'

'Is that what you'd do?' said Maude.

'What I did many a time,' the old man answered.

Silence in the sitting-room, a silence so profound that the ticking of the grandfather clock in the hall sounded ominous. Then Bruce, locked up in the kitchen, started barking and a throaty roar from the driveway shook the glass in the long windows.

The Brigadier hoisted himself from his armchair and hobbled towards the window. 'By God, he's got transport. What is it, Christine? What's he driving?' But Christine had already dashed out into the hall and, pausing only to tuck away an errant lock of hair, threw open the door.

'Alan,' she said, 'you're early.'

*   *   *

'This isn't what I expected, Charley,' Beatty said. 'This isn't my idea of a date.'

'It isn't a date,' Charley told her. 'If it had been a date we'd be hoofing it. What's wrong with you, woman? Sit still. You're perfectly safe.'

'Don't feel safe,' Beatty admitted, 'not with your—with you digging into me.'

'Sorry.' Taking one hand from the iron wheel, he wrapped an arm about her waist and shifted her

156

position on his lap. 'Better?'

'Not much.' The tractor leapt over another pothole. 'What happened to chocolates and flowers?'

'There are wine gums in my pocket if you fancy one.'

'Later,' Beatty said. 'I don't want you to spoil me.'

The tractor bounced again. Beatty let out a shriek. She was seated, side-saddle, across Charley's lap, the wheel and big gear lever pushing into her.

'You smell o' soap, Beatty.'

'Would you rather I smelled of ponies?'

'All the perfumes o' Arabia,' Charley threw at her.

'Good God, you've been at the Shakespeare.'

'Looked it up in a poetry book. I *can* read, you know.'

'I thought Edgar Wallace was more your style.'

'Not spicy enough for me,' said Charley. 'Not like Shakespeare.'

'Listen,' Beatty said, 'how do you know she's going to be here tonight?'

'Christine, you mean? I don't. But I'm hopeful.'

'Perhaps she went on Thursday or Friday?'

'Thursday, it's usually kids. Friday's for mammies and daddies. On Saturday, mostly, it's the likes o' us. Anyhow, even if Christine doesn't show up, it's a night at the pictures, so relax and enjoy yourself.'

'Relax?' Beatty said, as Ottershaw church hove into view. 'Oh, sure!' And draping an arm about the young farmer's shoulders, she hung on for dear life.

*　　*　　*

However reluctant Sir Maurice Vosper might be to consort with his tenants—no one had clapped eyes on him in months—he had certainly done them proud when it came to providing a community hall. On the ground floor a maze of stairs and corridors linked meeting rooms, cloakrooms and toilets. The basement housed a billiard room—two tables— and a polished wooden rink where 'summer ice' was played with pucks instead of curling stones. At the top of the building Sir Maurice had really gone to town. He had equipped the upper floor not only with a curtained stage but also a projection booth, a drop-down screen and the latest in broadcasting equipment. The hall was mainly used for public meetings, dances, concerts and educational lectures but once a month a professional projectionist arrived from Glasgow with a programme of feature films and shorts, and movie fans, young and not so young, traipsed into the Vosper to shoot it out with Tom Mix or swoon into the arms of the Vagabond King.

The bus that toured the outposts was packed by the time it reached the village and the queue outside the hall's narrow doorway soon became a mob.

Alan parked the Alvis in a side street close to the Black Bull. He had only just applied the handbrake when a big tank-like tractor nosed around the corner and rumbled to a halt behind him.

'Hey, Christine,' Charley Noonan shouted. 'Travellin' in style, I see.'

158

He shovelled Beatty from his lap, jumped down from the tractor and confronted his true love who, he was just beginning to realise, might not be his true love after all.

'Who's this guy then?' he said.

'Dr Kelso, Charley Noonan,' Christine said. 'I'm sorry I don't know your name, Miss . . .'

'Call me Beatty. That'll do.'

'We've met before, Mrs McCall,' Alan said. 'Haven't we?'

'You patched up my knee one time.'

'Did he?' Charley rounded on her. 'You never told me that.'

'How is your knee now?' the doctor asked politely.

'In sound working order, thank you.'

To Alan's relief, two couples converged on the awkward little gathering. The postman had an arm draped over Maggie Thomas's shoulder as if they had just completed a three-legged race.

'Fancy meeting you here, Miss Beatty,' he said. 'Never took you for a film fan.' He glanced over the top of Maggie's head at Christine. 'Nor you neither, sweetheart.'

Before Christine could answer, a familiar voice said, 'Hey, Christine. Enjoying your holiday?'

She had an impression that Freddy and his wife might have emerged from the Black Bull but she could not be sure. Freddy's mouth was moist at the corners, but Freddy's mouth was often moist at the corners. The woman clung to his arm in a manner that was either tipsy or possessive; possibly both. Christine had met Lucille McKay half a dozen times at school concerts and prize-givings and had always found her standoffish.

159

With her head against her husband's shoulder, Lucille gave Alan the once-over. 'A doctor,' she purred, with just the trace of an accent. 'You are a doctor who takes care of women, no?'

'No,' Alan said. 'Not women. Children, small children.'

'So you cannot take care of—'

'Lucille,' Freddy put in, with a sigh. 'Leave the poor chap alone. Come on, we don't want to miss out on the decent seats, do we?' He dragged his wife off along the pavement while Lucille, head angled just so, gave Alan a last, long, lingering glance from her sultry dark eyes.

*   *   *

First up was a cartoon about a fat king and his courtiers that had the audience in stitches. It was followed by a short Movietone musical in which a plump Irishman sang two mournful songs and a bottle-nosed comic in a top hat pretended to be drunk which, Alan whispered, probably didn't require much rehearsal.

The ceiling lights went on then off again. The grey-blue shaft of light from the projection booth cut a swathe through the haze of tobacco smoke.

Christine was aware of Charley and the woman from Picton three rows in front of her. The woman huddled close to Charley and Charley seemed to be holding her hand. There was no sign of Les and Maggie who had fought their way up the steep stairs to grab chairs at the back of the hall. Immediately in front of Alan, Freddy and his wife appeared to be spooning like love-birds but were, Christine soon realised, actually sharing a hip

160

flask.

Music suggestive of the Arabian Nights swelled from the loudspeakers.

The Paramount banner filled the screen and the audience settled down.

Soon after that the commotion began.

'Izata donkey?'

'Aye, it's a donkey.'

'Izat the Boys' Brigade?'

'No, they're French soldiers.'

'Are they gaun tae shoot somebody?'

'Wait an' we'll find out.'

Several older children were tucked away in the crowd. Four or five from Freddy's class squatted, engrossed, directly beneath the screen.

The voice that pierced the background music was unmistakable.

Christine winced.

It was unfortunate that young John Thomas had been abandoned by his sister, Maggie, and, by dint of much wheedling, had been escorted to the Saturday showing by his Granny Campbell whose only control over her inquisitive grandson rested in a bag of toffee balls that was already half empty.

'Izata boat?'

'Aye, it's a boat.'

'Whaza boat doin' in the desert?'

'Sshh! We'll see in a minute.'

A bribe in the form of a toffee ball changed hands.

For several minutes the drama proceeded uninterrupted.

Then, loudly: 'Izata wumman?'

'It's the same woman we saw on the boat.'

'Naw, it canny be a wumman. She's wearin'

161

breeks.'

A sharp word from Mr McKay might have done the trick but Mr McKay seemed more amused than annoyed by young Johnny's remarks. A few seconds later—vindication: 'Look, look, Granny. I telt ye it wasnae a wumman. A wumman wouldnae be kissin' yon other wumman, would she?'

'Johnny,' Christine called out crisply. 'Be quiet.'

A tousled head bobbed up and obliterated the lower half of the screen.

'Whozat, whozat?' Johnny Thomas yelled. 'Izat you, Miss Summers?'

'Yes. Now sit down and shut up or it'll be the belt for you on Monday.'

It probably hadn't dawned on Johnny Thomas that the spheres of his existence were inextricably linked and that how he behaved on Saturday night might have a bearing on what would happen on Monday morning. He was sufficiently shaken by the revelation to sit down and hide behind his grandmother. Cheers and whistles endorsed the fact that the audience was not on his side and not a peep was heard from the blacksmith's son for the rest of the performance.

Christine slumped in her chair, shaking her head.

She glanced at Alan and told him she was sorry for making a fuss.

He assured her there was no need to apologise.

Then he knitted his fingers with hers and continued to hold her hand until whispering desert winds and swirling sands brought the movie to an end, and the screen went suddenly blank.

CHAPTER FIFTEEN

Granny Campbell's relationship to the louts who commandeered the corner of Main Street and Greenhill Road was tenuous at best. Maggie, Todd and Johnny might claim Rab as a full cousin and Jimmy as their uncle but the bonds of kinship were stretched too thin to be sure of any such thing.

By the time Granny Campbell steered the small, sulking boy out into the street at the end of the picture show the bulk of the audience had given the ruffians a wide berth and were gathered at the bus stop.

The five men who loitered on the corner had forsaken the Harvester in Kennart for the Bull in Ottershaw in the hope of stirring up trouble. They had carried their pint pots into the street and lounged against the wall of the Vosper Halls, sniggering and passing remarks in loud voices. If luck ran their way they might even rile some snot-nosed softie from one of the farms into showing off to his girlfriend by challenging them. There was nothing the Campbell crew enjoyed more than slapping a gormless lad around while his girlfriend wet her knickers and shrieked for help; help that was rarely forthcoming.

'There's Rab,' said Johnny, brightening. 'Todd's no' here, though.'

'Todd's at home; just as well for him.' Granny Campbell reached for her grandson's hand but the boy was off, darting through the crowd to throw himself against the trouser leg of his hero, Rab.

Rab Campbell started back, almost spilling his

beer. He might have clipped his little relative's ear if Uncle Jimmy hadn't stayed him. He pulled Johnny against him and ruffled his hair with a beer-soaked hand and when Granny came up to him smoothly passed young Johnny round behind his back.

'Haw, auld woman, an' what do you want?'

'She's lookin' fur a man,' Flem Aitken jeered.

'She's too old fur a man,' said another hanger-on.

'Give him here, Rab,' said Granny Campbell evenly. 'It's past his bedtime.'

'Past your bedtime an' all, ye nosy auld bitch.'

'Give him here,' said Granny again, and stretched out her hand.

*   *   *

Beatty grabbed Charley's arm. 'Isn't that Rab Campbell over there?'

'Come on, Beatty. No point in lookin' for trouble.'

'That's the swine who stole my cash.' Beatty's voice rose. 'What's he doing with Johnny Thomas?'

'They're cousins. Leave it alone, Beats, please.'

Greenhill Road was no more than thirty yards wide. The lamp that guarded the corner had not been converted to electricity and the worn gas mantle flared in the breeze that flirted up Main Street.

Granny Campbell stretched out her hand.

Rab batted it away.

'Leave her alone, you pig,' Beatty yelled.

Then, before Charley could stop her, she

164

charged across the road and swiped the beer glass from Rab Campbell's fist.

*   *   *

'Here,' said Mr Woodcock, 'I don't like the look of that.'

'It's only my cousin, Rab, havin' a bit o' fun.'

'Don't look like fun to me.'

'I thought you were gonna walk me home?' said Maggie.

'I am,' said Les, 'in a minute.'

'If you don't like it, don't look,' Maggie told him.

'I'll look if I like,' the postman said. 'If he doesn't give over pawing Miss Beatty, I'll do more than look. Hoy, you, keep your bleedin' hands to yourself.'

Flem Aitken roped his arms round Beatty's waist and hoisted her, flailing and cursing, two or three inches above the pavement. Frightened by the commotion, Johnny Thomas ran to his grandmother who grabbed his hand and trotted him around the corner out of harm's way.

'You should've took her when you had the chance, Rab,' Jimmy Campbell said. 'By Geeze, she's beggin' for it now.'

The crowd at the bus stop looked then looked away and only one enterprising citizen, a lad of seventeen, sprinted off into Main Street in search of Constable Birkett who, naturally, was nowhere to be found.

Alan opened the passenger door of the Alvis and pushed Christine inside.

'Stay put,' he said.

165

Les reached the corner a step ahead of Charley and two steps ahead of the doctor. Flem Aitken didn't know what hit him. An arm snaked about his throat and yanked him away from the protection of his peers. He dragged Beatty with him a step or two then shoved her away. Alan caught her before she fell and swept her round into Charley's arms while Les, without a qualm, kicked out at Flem Aitken who lay, cowering, on the ground. Les was quite calm about it. He didn't aim for the head or chest but delivered a short stabbing blow close enough to Flem's delicate parts to cause a maximum of pain with a minimum of damage.

'Want more, like?' the postman said. 'If not, push off.'

Flem Aitken took off like a whippet, followed by two other louts who scattered the crowd at the bus stop as they raced by.

'Now, now then, feller.' Jimmy Campbell squared up to Alan. 'What's your grouse? We're just standin' here peaceful like when that woman—'

Alan ignored the olive branch. He scowled down at Rab. 'Is it true?'

'Is what true?'

'Did you steal her money?'

'Who the hell're you?'

'Is it true?'

'What if it is?' Rab shrugged. 'You'll never bloody prove it.'

'I don't have to prove it,' Alan said. 'Return the sum you stole from Mrs McCall and we'll say no more about it.'

Rab rocked on the balls of his feet. 'Think I'm scared o' a toff like you?'

'Probably not,' Alan said, 'but only because you're too stupid to realise the trouble you're in.'

'I'm in no trouble.' Rab Campbell spoke with less conviction. 'You're the one in trouble, mister. Anyhow, I canny gi'e her back her dough. It's spent.'

'That's too bad,' said Alan. 'Too bad for you, I mean.'

'Bugger you!' Rab Campbell aimed a round-house right at Alan's head.

From the corner of his eye he saw the youngster grab Jimmy in a bear hug and at the same split second felt his fist slam into the tall guy's forearm just before a hand closed round his neck and a thumb pressed into his Adam's apple.

'Seventy pounds, Campbell,' Alan said softly. 'Seventy pounds in cash to Mrs McCall by the end of the week. And if you're thinking of getting your own back, I wouldn't bother. My friend here knows more ways to torch a barn than you ever dreamed of and I'—the thumb pinched Rab's windpipe—'let's just say I have my own area of expertise. Do you understand?'

'Aye,' Jimmy Campbell said, 'he understands.'

'Then get him out of here,' said Alan.

*   *   *

'Is she all right?' Christine asked.

'Yeah,' Charley answered. 'She's fine. Where did you find *him*?'

'He's a doctor.'

'I know who he is. I just didn't know you two

167

were acquainted.' Charley stepped back as a bus rounded the corner from Main Street and sucked up the crowd. 'Looks like you've got a bit of competition, though.'

Beatty nuzzled Alan's arm. 'Maybe it's not as bad as it looks.'

'As what looks?' said Christine.

Alan peeled back his sleeve and undid his cufflink. He turned his arm this way and that, grimacing. 'I think that barbarian might have broken my wrist.'

'Hospital?' said Beatty.

'No,' he said. 'No hospital. Take me home, please.'

'You can't drive a car with a broken wrist,' said Charley.

'I can drive,' said Mr Woodcock. 'I'll take you home.'

'Beatty,' Charley said, 'what about you?'

'I'll go with Alan—with Dr Kelso. He'll need help.'

'Will he?' said Charley. 'Can't she help him?'

'I don't need anyone's help,' Alan said. 'Can you really drive that thing?'

'Drive anythin' with wheels,' Les Woodcock said. 'You insured?'

'Probably,' Alan said. 'Yes, the car's insured.'

'Okay, pile in,' said Mr Woodcock coolly. 'Where's the kid I came with?'

'She caught the bus,' said Charley. 'I'll follow you on the tractor.'

'No,' said Beatty, quickly. 'Just go home, Charley.'

'What about you? How'll you get back to Picton?'

'For God's sake, Charley,' Beatty said testily. 'Do as you're told. Go home.'

Les helped Alan into the passenger seat and slithered behind the steering wheel. He switched on the ignition and ran his fingertips lightly over the dash.

'Are you sure you can drive this thing?' Alan asked.

'Oh, yeah,' Les answered and, to prove his point, revved the engine, released the handbrake and shot the car off down Main Street like a bullet from a gun.

*   *   *

'I don't think we've been properly introduced,' Christine said. 'I'm Christine Summers.'

'I know who you are,' said Beatty. 'Charley told me all about you.'

'Is Charley a friend of yours?'

'I've known him since he was a boy.'

'How long have you known Dr Kelso?'

'Long enough,' Beatty answered.

Crushed into the back seat, shoulder to shoulder, knee to knee, every twist in the road threw them together.

'He's obviously a close friend,' Christine said.

'What makes you think that?'

'He knew you'd been robbed.'

'Gossip.' Beatty shrugged. 'Can't avoid it in this village, can you?'

'Where are we going?' Christine said.

'We're taking you home.'

'Alan—what about Alan?'

'I'll take care of Alan,' said Beatty.

169

*   *   *

'Where did you learn to drive?' Alan asked.

'My dad taught me. He drove lorries in the war.'

'He taught you well. Does he still drive lorries?'

'Nah, the Spanish flu got him: March, after the Armistice. He coughed it real quick. Nearly got me, too, but I struggled through.'

'I'm glad you did,' said Alan.

He held his left arm across his chest, hand tucked into his overcoat. He would bathe the wrist, strap it and get through Sunday as best he could. On Monday he'd have it X-rayed to find out precisely how much damage had been done.

'Is it painful?' Les Woodcock asked.

'Yes, it's painful.'

'You won't be able to doctor properly for a while, will you?'

'Probably not.'

'Tough!' the postman said. 'Who were those guys?'

'I really don't know,' said Alan. 'They stole money from Mrs McCall.'

'*Mrs* McCall? I didn't know she was married.'

'She's a widow.'

'She's a good-lookin' widow,' Les whispered.

'Yes,' Alan agreed. 'She is.'

*   *   *

Dressed in pyjamas and a dressing-gown, the Brigadier was seated in his armchair, a glass of brandy and warm milk in his hand and the Scottie on his knee. The wireless was playing dance music, a foxtrot. Perhaps it was the music or the sight of the frail old man by the fireside or just her relief at being safe home again but, without quite knowing why, Christine began to cry.

'Oh, my!' The Brigadier pushed Bruce from his lap. 'What's all this, my dear? Tears?' He placed the brandy glass on the mantelshelf and opened his arms. 'Come on, old thing. Tell me all about it.'

'See,' said Maude from the doorway, 'I told you he wasn't right for her.'

'We don't know that yet, do we?' the Brigadier said and, bracing his back against the chair, let Christine weep into his shoulder like a child.

*   *   *

Sunlight found a crack in the curtain and rippled on the ceiling. He was on his back in the centre of the bed and someone was lying across him, knee cocked over his thigh, her belly pressing into his hip, her breasts soft and warm against his stomach. He knew at once that it wasn't Marion. Marion was slim and small-breasted and slept, always, with her back to him. He glanced to his left and saw the woman's face flushed with sleep and framed by a tangle of thick fair hair.

Cautiously he lifted his left arm straight up in the air. The heavy bandage remained intact, neatly laced over his thumb, over the heel of his hand and round his wrist almost as far as the ulna. Aspirin had taken the edge off the pain but it hadn't dulled his senses or lessened his desire. There had been several comical moments when Beatty had supported him while he'd slipped and slithered in the lower depths before he'd found her.

171

He waved his arm about in the air above the bed, admiring his handiwork.

Beatty opened her eyes and yawned. 'Sore?'

'No, it's not bad.'

She trickled her fingers down the length of his thigh.

'See,' she whispered, 'you didn't need a splint after all. What time is it?'

'Early.'

'Too early?'

'No,' Alan answered. 'Not too early, not too early at all.'

PART THREE

Nobody's Sweetheart

CHAPTER SIXTEEN

It was a relief to be back in school again. Over the next few weeks she would help Freddy conduct a series of tests he had purchased to assess the progress of the Junior class and enable him to compile a report for the Board of Rural Education.

Christine couldn't imagine what value such a report would have for gentlemen and ladies whose main concern was balancing a budget and doubted if Mr Warrender, HM Inspector of Rural Schools, would be thrilled to learn that Freddy was experimenting with advanced teaching methods that he, Mr Warrender, regarded as anarchistic.

Freddy had other things on his mind than charts and graphs, however. As soon as Christine and he were settled in the closet with their lunchtime tea and sandwiches, he began his inquisition.

'I hear that Lucille and I missed all the fun on Saturday night.'

'Fun?' said Christine. 'I'd hardly call it fun.'

'Ticking off our Johnny in public is one thing— you were quite right, by the way—but squaring up to his uncles and, I hear, getting the better of them quite another.'

'Who told you?'

'It's the talk of the town,' said Freddy. 'Your name or, more particularly that of your gentleman companion, is on everyone's lips. He's the hero of the hour; no mean feat for a mere physician.'

'He's a surgeon, actually.'

'And a widower, I believe?'

Christine nodded grudgingly.

'Well, whatever he is,' said Freddy, 'he certainly made an impression on my dear wife. Probably just as well she didn't catch the showdown. Any truth in the rumour that he knocked one of the Campbells out cold?'

'No truth at all.'

'Blows were exchanged, though?'

'Not really.'

'And yet,' Freddy persisted, 'your feller has a broken arm?'

'He's not my feller and to the best of my knowledge he does not have a broken arm,' Christine said. 'According to the postman it's only a sprained wrist.'

'Ah!' said Freddy. 'So you're not about to kick off your shoes like the lovely Miss Dietrich and follow him into the desert.'

Chris snorted. 'I'm not that much of a fool.'

'I don't suppose you are,' said Freddy, 'which may, in fact, be your undoing. According to my dear Lucille, who's expert in such matters, Dr Kelso is definitely a man worth pursuing.'

'It's none of your business, Mr McKay—or your wife's.'

'Touchy, touchy,' said Freddy. 'Next thing, I suppose you'll deny there's any connection between your interest in my theories on love at first sight and your appearance on the hand of a tall, dark, handsome and somewhat mysterious stranger.'

'Alan's not mysterious. He's lived in Ottershaw for years.'

'No one ever saw him until you lured him into the light.'

'I did not lure him anywhere.'

176

'Love at first sight,' said Freddy, rolling his eyes. 'Ah, the joys, the joys.'

'I've had enough of this.' Christine pushed back her chair. 'If you've nothing sensible to say I'm going back to my classroom.'

'Hang on,' he said. 'I do have something sensible to say.'

'What?' Christine snapped.

'How's my favourite film critic this morning? I mean young Johnny.'

'Chastened,' Christine said. 'But it won't last.'

'No,' said Freddy. 'Unfortunately it never does.'

*　　　*　　　*

Beatty was not surprised when Maggie and Todd Thomas didn't show up for work. Blood, after all, was thicker than water. Some sort of pow-wow had probably taken place with Rab and Jimmy laying down the law to the blacksmith and Maggie and Todd caught in the middle.

At least Les Woodcock was enjoying himself scooting about in Alan's motorcar. He'd turned up at Moss House on Sunday morning in time to catch them having breakfast together. He'd shown no surprise at finding her in one of Marion Kelso's dressing-gowns. While she'd bathed and dressed, Alan and Les had gone out to admire the motorcar and, as men will, poke about under the bonnet. Later, Alan had despatched Les to the petrol pump at Harlwood to fill the Alvis's tank while he'd steered her upstairs to pick out a selection of Marion's clothes.

Four cardboard boxes stood in the middle of the hut; four boxes filled with a dead woman's possessions; four boxes smelling of lavender and mothballs; four boxes whose contents would keep her ticking over until she could decide what to do about Alan. Or he could decide what to do about her.

*   *   *

When Alan arrived in the ward, the child, Jenny, was sitting up in a railed cot sucking lime-green jelly from a spoon. She did not remember him and, with no Stillwater to mediate, kicked up a fine old fuss while he examined her. Liveliness in a young patient was a good sign. The little girl wasn't terrified, just cross that her breakfast had been interrupted.

He conducted the examination with his left hand tucked behind his back, a senatorial pose that would have drawn sarcastic comments from outspoken interns had there been any about to witness it.

Teddy Hargreaves—five feet five inches tall and as strong as a bull—was the only house surgeon that Alan trusted to be both thorough and discreet. Sealed in an examination-room in the bowels of the hospital, Teddy, tongue in cheek, asked what the problem was and when Alan stuck out his bandaged wrist, stroked his chin and said, 'That's a hand, isn't it?'

'Oh, stop fooling about, Teddy. If it's fractured I'll be sidelined for weeks.'

'Yes, of course. Sorry.' Teddy unwrapped the binding. 'How'd it happen?'

'Not a word to anyone.'

'Cut my throat,' said Teddy.

178

'I got into a fight.'

'Really? Who won?'

'I did.'

'Shake my hand.' The young surgeon applied traction to test the limit of flexion and extension. 'I assume you've done all this?'

'As best I could.'

'The nature of the trauma, please.'

'I blocked a punch with my forearm—hence the bruising—and jarred the area of the wrist in the process.'

'One punch?'

'Just one.'

'This will probably hurt.' Teddy rotated the inferior radial-ulnar joint.

Alan, through his teeth, hissed, 'It certainly does.'

'I think,' Teddy said, 'it might be as well to wheel you through to radiography for a quick X-ray.'

'Can't you do it?'

'Only if I can lay hands on the new mobile unit.'

'Have you used it before, Teddy?'

'Once or twice. Haven't you?'

'No,' Alan admitted.

'Be a tad less dangerous if a radiographer—'

'Trot off and see if you can find the mobile.'

'Sir,' said Teddy and, laying Alan's arm gently on the padded examination table, slipped away to scour the corridors for the most modern piece of equipment that the hospital possessed.

*   *   *

It was a brisk sort of day with streaky cloud over

179

the mountains and blinks of sunlight dappling the moor. Beatty felt quite light-hearted as she climbed to the crest of the hill. Unlike stallions, mares were seldom truculent. They emerged from the bushes and nuzzled her in friendly fashion. She petted them casually while looking for early signs that the servicing had taken and, less casually, stroked the round bellies of the mares who were due to foal in May. She was tempted to linger on the hill but she was hungry. With nothing in the larder but mouse-droppings, she would have to hoof up to the Co-op to buy something to eat.

When she reached the paddock she found Maggie Thomas, all alone, leaning on a fence post. The girl said, 'Todd's not comin' back.'

'Can't say I'm surprised,' Beatty said. 'What's his excuse?

'No excuse,' said surly Maggie. 'He's got a proper job now.'

'A proper job?' said Beatty. 'What sort of a job is that?'

'Estate worker. Balnesmoor.'

'I see,' said Beatty. 'You mean he's digging ditches, like your cousin?'

'Will you be keepin' me on?'

'Of course. Why wouldn't I?'

'After what happened, I wasn't sure.'

'All right,' Beatty said. 'Out with it. I assume Rab wanted you to leave my employment and your old man was forced to settle on a compromise.'

'Some compromise!' Maggie dug into her pocket and produced a wad of crumpled banknotes. 'Sixty-two quid; that's all you're gonna get.'

'Good God!' Beatty said. 'I never dreamed I'd

180

see a penny of my money again. How did your old man do it?'

'It wasn't my daddy. It was that guy in the motorcar. They're scared o' him. They think he's a pal o' Sir Maurice Vosper. My daddy told Rab one word from your friend an' Mr Tait would sack him an' Jimmy both.'

'Good for your daddy,' said Beatty.

She held out her hand and the girl counted out the banknotes which, to judge by their grubby state, had been riding around in someone's pocket for the past couple of weeks or, more likely, had been forth and back across the counter in the Harvester or the Bull.

'That doctor feller?' Maggie said. 'Is he your man?'

'He might be,' said Beatty cagily. 'What would you say if he was?'

'I'd say you were bloody lucky,' Maggie told her and, tittering, covered her mouth with her hand.

*   *   *

Josie said, 'So it's true, is it? You have been in the wars? Let's have a look.'

He had hoped to make good his escape before morning surgery was over. No such luck. He almost ran into the anaesthetist as she emerged from the ladies' cloakroom in the passage between the units. She prodded the still moist plaster that coated his arm from hand to elbow.

'Nice job,' she said. 'Hargreaves?'

Alan nodded.

'Useful little devil to have at your beck and call, isn't he?' said Josie. 'How long?'

181

'Couple of weeks at least.'

'God! How miserable. You'll need to be more careful with railway carriage doors in future, old chum,' Josie said. 'Could have cost you fingers, then where would you be?'

'Carriage doors? Oh yes, of course. Teddy told you, I suppose.'

'One of the technicians, actually. I think he overheard you talking to Teddy in the plaster-room.'

Alan was not unduly surprised that the lie Teddy had cooked up to cover the unpalatable fact that a senior surgeon had been involved in a brawl had leaked as far as the operating-room.

'I can still take ward rounds,' Alan said. 'Lecture. That sort of thing.'

'How long since you had time off? Marion's funeral, wasn't it?'

'Yes, I suppose it was.'

'You're due a holiday. Take one,' Josie said. 'Is there someone at home to look after you?'

'I can look after myself perfectly well.'

'If you're really stuck,' Josie said, 'I'll look after you.'

'I appreciate the offer, but . . .'

'Look'—she glanced towards the swing doors that shielded the theatres—'I'll have to go. Catch up with you at lunch—if you're still here.'

'Where else would I be?' said Alan.

She walked away, waving over her shoulder.

'Go home, Kelso,' she called out. 'For once be sensible and go home.'

At half past twelve o'clock, feeling decidedly seedy, he did.

She was halfway down the road from the Co-op when she spotted Charley or, rather, his collie in the field in which old Mr Noonan kept his lambing ewes.

The dog was working the flock in a series of crouching manoeuvres that nudged the sheep, three and four at a time, past the tractor so that Charley could give them the once-over. Screened by the hedge, Beatty slipped the bulging canvas shopping sack from her shoulder and put it down on the verge. She had shopped heavily, extravagantly. The sack was stuffed with tins, packets and bottles, bread, vegetables, eggs and meat, topped off with a juicy orange.

When the sheep were quietly cropping the thin spring grass once more, the collie trotted to the tractor, swarmed on to the hay bale wedged behind the driver's seat and lay down, panting.

Charley shouted, 'All right, Beatty, I know you're there.'

She clambered up the steep bank and peered over the hedge. 'Spare me a minute, Charley, please.'

He climbed from the tractor and cut across the corner of the field. 'Only a minute, Beats,' he said. 'I've a lot to do today.'

'Here.' She passed two banknotes across the hedge. 'Now we're square.'

Charley held the notes up to the sunlight. 'What's this?'

'Two quid,' Beatty told him. 'Unless you're charging interest.'

'Huh!' Charley exclaimed. 'You're doin' well out

183

o' that doctor, aren't you?'

'I got my cash back from the Campbells,' said Beatty, 'most of it.'

'Good God!' said Charley. 'I've never known the Campbells back down before. Kelso, I suppose, him and his fancy motorcar, put the wind up them. Have you been nursin' him, Beatty?'

'I made his supper, that's all.'

'What about breakfast?'

'Why must you think the worst of me, Charley?'

He reached behind his ear, removed the stub of a cigarette, lit it and blew out the match. 'I can't compete with Kelso, not for her and not for you,' he said, then, flipping away the rags of the cigarette, returned to the tractor and left Beatty to meander home alone.

CHAPTER SEVENTEEN

Alan arrived home in mid-afternoon, much to the surprise of Mrs Mackintosh who immediately demanded an explanation. He exhibited his plastered arm and, playing it up a little, appealed to her better nature to put aside her recriminations until he'd been fed and watered.

Mrs Mack had already been treated to several lurid accounts of the Saturday night incident and was not well pleased that her employer had taken to consorting with louts or, for that matter, to flitting about the countryside in a motorcar filled with fast young women. She was even less pleased to learn that Mrs Kelso's beautiful clothes had been given away but, smothering her annoyance, she dismembered his mutton chop and mashed the potatoes so that he could cope with lunch one-handed.

She lit the fire in the parlour, plumped up the cushions on the couch and brought him coffee on a tray while Alan lay back and pressed his hand to his brow in a pose he hoped might defuse the woman's resentment.

The ruse might have succeeded if Mr Woodcock hadn't screeched up to the front door to enquire what the 'Doc' wanted done with his motorcar.

Only minutes later Christine arrived to ask after his health.

And as if that wasn't enough Beatty turned up too and following a brief altercation on the doorstep, was ushered into the parlour. Mrs Mackintosh, her face like fizz, pulled on her coat and stalked out without a word.

Alan thought, I don't need this. In my condition, I definitely do not need this.

'Coffee,' he said gallantly. 'Help yourselves to coffee. It's still warm.'

'We'll need cups,' Beatty said.

'In the kitchen,' Alan told her.

'I know where they are,' said Beatty.

Seated on a pouffe at Alan's feet, Christine struggled to remember what the Brigadier had told her. 'Backbone,' he'd said. 'Show a bit of backbone, Chris. If you think this woman's infiltrated your lines don't dive into a foxhole and wave the white flag. Get out there and fight.'

Rattled by Freddy's suggestion that she wasn't bold enough to hold a lover and spurred on by the Brigadier's pep talk, she had combed her hair, slipped into her prettiest dress and hurried uphill to Moss House.

Only to discover that the blowsy pony breeder'd had the same idea.

Beatty McCall returned with cups. She put one down on the carpet at Christine's feet.

'Coffee?'

'No, thank you.'

She watched the woman fill Mr Woodcock's cup, then, sashaying to the couch, shift Alan's legs and sit down beside him.

'Have you moved in yet, Les?' Beatty asked.

'Nope, not yet. I'll lug some groceries up there next weekend.'

'Watch out for the mice.'

'Mice?' said Alan. 'What's all this about mice?'

'Les has rented the old McCall place,' Beatty answered. 'He's going into the motorcycle business.'

'What? Giving up the Post Office?' said Alan.

'No fear. Not yet. Sideline, that's all,' Les said. 'How are you gonna get the Alvis back to the garage, Doc? You'll never manage the gear shift with that arm. Believe me, it's like pumping wet sand.'

'I'm not taking the Alvis back to the garage,' Alan said. 'I've decided to buy it. It seems a manageable sort of vehicle for an old boy like me.'

Beatty McCall nudged him lightly. 'You're not an old boy, far from it.'

'Yeah,' said the postman, 'a car would sure be useful for fast getaways.'

Everyone, except Christine, laughed.

Oh, Beatty thought, she really is in love with him.

For a moment she felt sorry for the school

teacher who, for all her education, seemed lacking in experience not just of men but of the world at large. Here they were, assembled in the parlour like characters in one of those modern plays by Noël Coward or Bernard Shaw and, Beatty realised, she was being thrust into a role she hadn't asked for and didn't know how to perform.

Alan said, 'You didn't bring the dog?'

Christine looked up. 'No. He's been in the garden all day.'

'Will you walk him tomorrow?'

'I expect so.'

'I might join you, if you don't mind.'

She glanced at Beatty and her smile was far from innocent. 'Oh, no, Alan,' she said. 'I don't mind at all.'

Beatty hoisted herself to her feet, dug in the pocket of her skirt and dropped the notes into Alan's lap. 'The Campbells shelled out this morning,' she said. 'So here's the ten quid I owe you. I'd hate to see you starve now you're out of work.'

'I'm not out of work, Beatty. I'm on holiday.'

He got to his feet too and, as Beatty had hoped, Les and the school teacher followed suit. 'What you need, Dr Kelso, is a good night's sleep,' she told him and dabbed her forefinger to his nose in a gesture of calculated familiarity. 'Do you hear me, lad? A good night's sleep for once.'

'I hear you, Beatty,' he said.

'If that motorcar of yours is sitting outside doing nothing perhaps Les would be good enough to drive us home,' Beatty said and, buttoning her overcoat, led the little troupe of well-wishers out of the parlour before anyone could protest.

'You really are a wicked woman,' Les told her, 'dumping that poor girl off with never a kind word.'

'I have no idea what you're talking about.'

'She's mad about him, ain't she?' said Les. 'Okay, I'm just a feller an' I'm not supposed to notice these things but, you ask me, she's a cooked goose as far as the Doc's concerned. What was all that stuff about money?'

'Alan—he made me a loan.'

'Sure it was a loan?'

'What else would it be?' said Beatty.

Les didn't answer. He looked quite at ease behind the wheel and in his Post Office uniform with his cap tipped back there was a certain dash to him that Beatty hadn't remarked before.

She said, 'You'd make a good chauffeur, you know.'

'Yes, sir, no, sir, three bags full, sir? Nah, not for me,' Les said. 'I wanna be my own man. What's your ambition—to get spliced to Dr Kelso?'

'And give up my independence? Not likely.'

'Probably just as well since you've got a rival in Miss Summers.'

'If I did decide to set my cap at Alan Kelso I'd soon see her off.'

'Wouldn't be so sure, if I were you,' Les said. 'She's kinda cute.'

'Cute?' Beatty shook her head. 'Is that what you'd look for in a wife?'

'Not me,' Les said. 'I know my limitations.'

'Are you implying I don't?'

'Not implying nothing.'

'You're a cheeky beggar, aren't you?'

The railway bridge loomed over them. Les eased the Alvis to a halt and applied the handbrake. Beatty looked past him into the field. On the breast of the hill she could make out eight or ten of her ponies, small as toys, nibbling the spring grass. High above the herd a fragment of new moon looked down on Ottershaw and, though the sun hadn't set yet, a few stars shone bright as steel studs.

'Have you had your dinner?' she asked.

'Is that an invitation?'

'One time only.'

'What's on the menu?'

'Steak pie,' said Beatty. 'Fray Bentos.'

'Fray where?'

'Tinned, you idiot.'

'Just the way I like it,' the postman said.

* * *

The evening wireless programmes had begun. The Brigadier, hidden under a copy of the *Radio Times*, was rapt in the BBC Dance Orchestra's rendering of 'After You've Gone'. He slouched in his armchair, legs stretched out, one foot gently tapping. Bruce snoozed by the side of the chair.

'So, Chris,' the Brigadier said, 'did Kelso welcome you with open arms?'

'He had visitors.'

The Brigadier sat up and stripped the paper from his face. 'Really? Who?'

'The postman—and that woman from Picton.'

'What an incongruous lot. Still, if our postman's

189

looking after his car for him perhaps it's not surprising. How's Kelso's arm?'

'Wrist,' said Christine. 'Torn ligaments. It's set in plaster.'

'I was plastered once—no, not drunk, though that's another story, or several other stories—plastered from hip to ankle. Fell off a camel, would you believe. Was he pleased to see you?'

'I do believe he was,' Christine said.

'Oh, come now, surely you know.'

'Yes. Yes, he was pleased to see me.'

'Didn't he ask you to stay?'

'He was tired, very tired. We left him to rest.'

'I see,' said the Brigadier. 'What's that they're playing now?'

'"Where the Blue of the Night", I think.'

'Of course it is. Will you see him again soon?'

'Oh, yes,' said Christine brightly. 'Tomorrow—if it doesn't rain.'

*   *   *

Stretched out on the couch, Alan slept for over an hour. When he wakened it was almost dark and the house had seldom felt so empty. The plaster had tightened and his arm ached all the way up to his shoulder. Tendons, he thought, it would have to be tendons; a clean break would have been easier to deal with. Hargreaves had been adamant that insertion of primary sutures would only lead to prolonged synovitis, an opinion with which he reluctantly agreed. He was not entirely crippled, however. He could swing the arm about, use the tips of his fingers for pinning things down and by careful positioning of the cast would probably be

190

able to bathe, shave and dress himself.

In spite of the late lunch he was hungry. He would boil a couple of eggs and chop them up with butter in a cup, like his mother used to do when he was sick. He must visit his mother soon. She was comfortable in the nursing home by the sea, but too vague to tote up the weeks since he'd last shown his face there.

Rolling from the couch, he switched on the lamp, poured himself a whisky and knelt in front of the radiogram that had been Marion's pride and joy.

Knobs and dials, strange little lights within the casing reminded him of the mobile X-ray machine that Hargreaves had trundled into the examination-room that morning. He had no idea where music might be found and toyed with a silly sort of notion that Marion's voice might emerge, helpfully, from the cloth-covered speaker if only he could find the right wavelength.

It had shaken him to have both women together in the room.

He had flirted with the little school teacher and had spent two exhausting nights in bed with Beatty. His mother, if she'd been at all *compos mentis*, would have told him in no uncertain terms that he was a cad—which, he supposed, was true.

He experienced a sudden explosion of self-disgust at what he had become and anger at Marion for abandoning him. He gave up on the radiogram, polished off the whisky, and headed for the shelves where he stored his old medical textbooks and, mixed among them, the dry and dusty novels that Marion had read to while away the hours.

CHAPTER EIGHTEEN

It was, thank heaven, a pretty morning, cloud high, the sun fixed in blue. In eight hours' time she'd be walking the ridge road with Alan and he would hold her hand and might even take her in his arms and kiss her, and . . .

'What are you doing out here?'

'Mr McKay told us to wait outside, miss.'

'All of you?'

'Aye, Miss Summers.'

'Does anyone know why?'

'He's got a mannie wi' him, miss.'

'A mannie? What sort of—I mean, where are they?'

'Our class,' one of the Juniors informed her. 'There's his car.'

'It's just an old sheep-shearer,' sneered one of the boys from Balnesmoor.

Christine peered at the vehicle parked in a corner of the playground. 'A what?'

'A Wolseley, miss, only eight horsepower. I can run faster.'

Three or four late-comers trotted through the gate and joined the crowd in the playground. 'Can we go home, Miss Summers?'

'Certainly not,' Chris said. 'Form up in lines. I'll be back in a minute.'

She went into the building, crossed the foyer to Freddy's classroom and was on the point of opening the door when the shouting match began.

'Damn it, I don't care if you're empowered by the Lord God Almighty, as far as I'm concerned you're just another pipsqueak inspector sticking his nose where it has no business to be.'

'There you're wrong, Mr McKay. Your business, as you call it, is very much my business. Do you suppose the Board would send me out here if we weren't concerned?'

'Concerned about what? Me?'

'The pupils.'

'The pupils are fine. Thriving, in fact.'

'They are not being taught according to the curriculum.'

'Oh!' Freddy cried. 'It's the nature study issue, is it? Well, let me tell you, those kids know more about tits than I do.'

'I beg your pardon?'

'I've no intention of wasting valuable time explaining the mating habits of marsh warblers to young people who already know all about them.'

'I'm sure they don't.'

'Well, if they don't, what matter?' Freddy cried. 'You're here to make sure I toe the party line, aren't you? Discipline and development at all costs. Development for what? To be ditch diggers or thrifty wee housewives or—the thought makes me shudder—breeding machines for another bloody war.'

'There's no need to swear, Mr McKay. The children will hear you.'

'They've heard me often enough,' said Freddy. 'Come clean, Harrison, your cohorts are scared of the deficiencies in the system that my tests will expose.'

'It's not up to me to interpret Board policy.'

'Just to close the bloody door on my report without allowing me my say.'

'You're having your say now, Mr McKay, are you not?'

'So I can push ahead with the testing, can I?'

'Actually,' the inspector said, 'no.'

At which point Christine thought it politic to intervene.

*   *   *

'I hope you're not going to be lying in bed every morning, Dr Kelso. Ten o'clock is far too late for me to be making beds,' Mrs Mackintosh said. 'I suppose you'll be wanting a lunch.'

'Probably,' Alan said. 'In fact, yes, I will be wanting a lunch.'

'Will your friend be joining you?'

'No, I doubt it.'

'Will she be here for her dinner?'

Alan had no idea whether or not Beatty would call this evening. He had doped himself on aspirin last night and with only one cup of coffee inside him, his head was not as clear as it might be.

'I have to shop, you know,' his housekeeper said. 'I'll need to buy extra.'

Alan refilled his cup from the pot. 'I'll be out all day tomorrow. I've business in Glasgow. On Thursday I'll probably go down the coast to visit my mother.'

Mrs Mackintosh sniffed. 'Are you bringing her back with you?'

The possibility hadn't even crossed his mind. 'My mother is being well taken care of where she is,' he said. 'For your information, Mrs Mackintosh, she suffers from a serious medical condition.'

'She should be here with you.'

'If you're not happy with the arrangements, Mrs Mackintosh, I'm prepared to accept your resignation.'

'Resignation?' Her voice rose. 'Are you giving me the sack, Dr Kelso?'

'No, a simple choice,' he said. 'If you wish to continue to work for me you will take care of my house and keep your opinions to yourself. Is that clear?'

She pursed her lips. Her red cheeks grew even redder.

'Well, Mrs Mackintosh, is it?'

'Aye, Dr Kelso,' she said, at length. 'That's clear.'

*   *   *

'Christine,' the inspector said. 'How lovely to see you again.'

'Don't tell me you actually know this guy?' Freddy said.

'We were at training college together,' the inspector explained.

'At the same time,' Christine corrected him.

'I knew you were teaching at Greenhill and hoped I might bump into you.'

'Be hard to avoid bumping into her,' Freddy pointed out, 'given that Greenhill's a two-teacher school. He's taking old Warrender's place.'

'Not exactly,' Ross Harrison said. 'I'm not here to make an inspection.'

'What are you here for?' Christine asked.

'To haul me over the coals,' said Freddy, 'for daring to challenge the Board.'

195

Ross Harrison gazed at Christine with such mournful longing that it was all she could do not to hide behind the headmaster. 'You've hardly changed,' he told her. 'You're just as lovely as you were ten years ago.'

'He's obviously confusing you with someone else,' said Freddy.

'Oh, Christine, don't you remember the wonderful times we had together in Trencher's class?' Mr Harrison went on.

Christine remembered Ross Harrison well enough but any memory of wonderful times had been completely erased.

In training college Ross had been a suave, charming, handsome narcissist who believed—not without reason—that a snap of the fingers would bring any girl leaping into his arms. Grappling for Ross's attention had been a universal sport among the more impressionable young ladies, occupying as much of their time as the study of educational method. In the months during which they'd shared lectures and classrooms, however, the great Ross Harrison had exchanged not one word with Christine and had never snapped his fingers in her direction.

'I missed you, Chris,' he crooned, 'terribly.'

'Oh, for God's sake!' Freddy exclaimed.

And being a man to whom sentiment was anathema, he reached over his desk and pressed the buzzer to bring the bantam army charging to Christine's aid.

*   *   *

Christine stuck her nose around the staffroom

door. 'Has he gone?'

Freddy capped his hip flask and dropped it into his sandwich box. 'Yes, he's gone,' he said. 'But I greatly fear the bugger will be back.'

Christine came into the room and pulled out a chair. She glanced at the cupboard where materials were kept as if she expected Mr Harrison to leap out in a shower of compliments.

'What did he want, Freddy?'

'Apart from ravishing you on my desk, you mean?' Freddy wiped his mouth with the back of his hand. 'He's the newly appointed deputy convenor of the Board of Rural Education and his first task as a big gun is to shoot me down. Were you and he really star-crossed lovers?'

'Of course not. He never looked the road I was on.'

'Are you sure there wasn't a romantic interlude you've forgotten about?'

'Absolutely positive. I don't know what's come over him.'

'A fit of the great what-might-have-beens would be my guess.'

'He's not much older than I am. And he had his pick of the girls.'

'Tall, blond, smooth as a well-pressed trouser leg.' Freddy dug a gammon sandwich from his lunch box and bit into it. 'I can see why Harrison romped up the career ladder. If you have the looks you don't need intelligence, just enough savvy to smile and say "Yes," to all the questions put to you.'

'Is that how you climbed the ladder of success?'

'Very funny, I don't think,' said Freddy. 'Dealing with old Warrender is bad enough, but this guy has considerably more clout.'

'Why are the Board reluctant to let you test our pupils by a new method?'

'Achievement testing's too radical for them. The education board in Fife tried it and found it invaluable. Fife, of course, is notoriously progressive. Even has a child psychiatrist on its books. Can you imagine that happening here?' Freddy drew his chair closer and lowered his voice. 'Between you and me, Chris, I intend to carry out the tests whether the Board likes it or not. I need solid proof that half the stuff on our rural curriculum is out of date.'

'Isn't the mainstay of rural education to encourage a spirit of investigation?'

'That's the theory,' Freddy said. 'We're supposed to foster a scientific turn of mind through disciplined opinion. But since when has "disciplined opinion" been anything other than a means of telling kids *what* to think, not *how* to think? Do you suppose any boy with half a brain would have galloped off to the recruiting station in 1914 if he'd been taught to think for himself?'

'That's a very dangerous premise.'

'I know, I know,' the headmaster said. 'But I don't intend to take a leaf out of the book of rules for advancement and smile and nod like an idiot. After all, I'm only a primary school teacher in a backwater community. What difference can I make to the fate of nations? What harm can I do?'

'You taught Peter McFee to play "MacCrimmon's Lament" on the comb and paper, Freddy. No mean achievement, that.'

He stared at her bleakly for a moment then snorted. 'It's a start, I suppose, one end of the golden string.'

'And where's the other end?' Christine asked.

'God knows!' Freddy answered. 'Just so long as it isn't a line of trenches soaked in blood in a foreign field somewhere.' He reached into his sandwich box and fished out his hip flask. 'Fancy a snifter?'

Christine shook her head. 'The tests—I'll help if you want me to.'

He sipped from the flask and studied her cautiously.

'Good girl,' he said. 'Now I've one more favour to ask of you.'

'Which is?'

'If Ross Harrison shows up here on parents' night,' Freddy said, 'just keep him away from my wife.'

*   *   *

To Christine's dismay the Wolseley was parked across the road from the gate. The deputy convener for the Board of Rural Education was leaning on the wheel arch, smoking a pipe. When he caught sight of her he raised an arm, then, pausing only to knock out his pipe on the heel of his shoe, loped across the road and, before she could escape, trapped her against the railings.

'Christine,' he said in a deep, tobacco-enriched baritone, 'is it really you?'

'I—I thought you'd gone.'

'I had to come back to make sure you were real, not just a spectre of happy times from my long-lost youth.'

'Ten years is hardly long, Ross, or lost.'

199

'It seems that way to me.'

One of his hands rested on the pillar of the gate, the other grasped the railings as if they were prison bars.

'Cheerio, miss,' a little girl called out in passing.

Christine responded automatically. 'Cheerio, Joyce.'

'You know them all by name, I see,' Ross Harrison said.

'Of course I do.'

It was already four o'clock. It would take her all her time to rush home and change into something fetching before Bruce and she set off for her rendezvous on the ridge road. She had a horrid feeling that if she was just one minute late Alan would assume that she had changed her mind and head back to Moss House where the pony woman from Picton would be lying in wait.

'Ross, I really must go.'

'But I've so much to tell you.'

'What can you possibly have to tell me?'

'That I've missed you'—he paused—added again, 'terribly.'

'How can you have missed me when you barely knew me?'

'Oh, my dear, I knew you. I knew you in my heart.'

For a moment Christine thought he might be making fun of her but his voice quivered with sincerity. She realised then that for some inexplicable reason she had become Ross Harrison's last resort.

She said, 'Whatever happened to Janice?'

'She married someone else.'

'And Muriel?'

'Our engagement ended.'

'Hold on,' she heard herself say, 'just how many times have you been jilted?'

'Janice, Muriel, Alice, Hazel—they were not for me, not really for me.'

'For heaven's sake, Ross, you must have met other girls since you left training college.'

'None like you.'

'Me? Why me? You don't even know me.'

'But I do,' Ross Harrison assured her. 'I know you liked me. Have you forgotten how much you liked me?'

'Oh, this is ridiculous!' Christine exclaimed. 'Everyone in college liked you. Well, almost everyone. All the girls.'

'I was special, though, special to you, Christine, wasn't I?'

Deputy convener of the Board of Rural Education or not, the man was clearly a candidate for a rubber room.

'No, Ross,' she said emphatically. 'You were nothing special to me then and you're nothing special now. Goodbye.'

'We'll see, Christine,' he said. 'We'll see.'

Slipping the pipe from his top pocket, he blew into it as if it were an Indian flute and, tapping the stem against his teeth, watched her hurry off along the Greenhill road.

*   *   *

When Christine came into view Alan waved and ambled down the hill to meet her. The Scottie barked a warning then went back to foraging in the ditch.

201

'I'm late,' Christine said. 'I'm sorry.'

'You're not late,' Alan said. 'But you do look flustered.'

Christine told him about Ross Harrison's unexpected appearance.

'I take it you didn't have a romance with this chap?' Alan said.

'Ross may have nodded once or twice, but that was all. Plenty of other girls were hanging on his coat-tails, girls prettier than I am by a long chalk.'

'Did you resent being ignored?'

'I don't know. Perhaps I did.'

'From what you've told me convener of a rural education board wouldn't have been high on this chap's list of aspirations after he left training college.'

'He has plenty of time to improve himself.'

'It's different for women,' Alan said. 'There's marriage for one thing.'

'I see. If a woman's not married by thirty, she's finished, is that it?'

'I didn't say that.'

'Like your Mrs McCall?'

'She isn't my Mrs McCall,' Alan said. 'And it wasn't her fault her husband was killed in the war.'

'I wonder if Ross knows I'm single.'

'He probably looked up your employment card,' Alan said. 'There's nothing a man in love won't stoop to. Aren't you even a tiny bit flattered?'

'No, I'm not.'

'Or a tiny bit curious?'

'Curious? Why would I be curious?'

'If someone I hadn't seen in years turned up out of the blue and told me I was the light of their life, I'd be curious.'

'You think he must be desperate, don't you?'

'I wish you wouldn't put words in my mouth, Christine. What's wrong with you? By the way you're going on,' Alan said, 'I can only conclude that you were in love with this Harrison chap at one time.'

'Oh, is that what you conclude, Dr Kelso? You think I'm just a silly wee girl, don't you? Well, perhaps I am. Silly enough to believe you cared for me.'

She darted behind him and clambered over the gate into the sheep field.

'Bruce,' she called. 'Bruce, come here.' The dog wriggled under the gate and, a moment later, dog and mistress disappeared behind the hedge.

Alan watched her dash up the hill, scattering the flock, the Scottie panting behind her. 'Chris,' he shouted. 'Christine,' then, knowing he would never catch up with her, set off, angrily, for home.

CHAPTER NINETEEN

She was propped up in a worn tapestry chair, dwarfed by its huge curved back. Her hands lay in her lap, palms uppermost, as if waiting to receive a blessing.

'Mother, it's me. Alan. How are you? Are they treating you well?'

There was no wind to speak of and the islands across the firth were laced with slender ribbons of cloud, tinted pink and baby blue. Below the big picture window of the visitors' lounge, just yards from the railway line, the sea lapped gently on a brown sand beach.

Crouched by the side of the chair, Alan reached out and took her hand. Her fingers were icy cold. He gave them a little squeeze but there was no response, neither acknowledgement nor reflex. When he shifted position to insert his face between her gaze and the window he felt like a rude little boy.

'Mama?' he said. 'Mama, don't you know me?'

'Herbert,' she murmured. His father's name had been Andrew. Her brothers were William and George. He had no idea who Herbert was, or had been, and knew better than to ask. 'We're going to the toy fair in Daddy's cart tomorrow.'

'Yes.' Alan patted her hand lightly. 'Yes, you are.'

She had shared that memory with him long ago; the toy fair in Pickford's Emporium, her father, a merchant, taking the family in one of his drays, all tricked out in flags and bunting as if it were a holiday or a birthday treat.

He knelt at his mother's feet. She wore shoes not slippers but they were not her shoes. Her ankles bulged against the leather and her stockings were wrinkled. He tugged down the hem of her skirt to cover them.

He was well versed in the difficulty of nursing patients who were unaware of their condition. She was clean, neat and the long-skirted frock was her own, one that his late Aunt Lizzie had coveted when it had been brand new, a little victory over her fat sister-in-law that had given his mother great satisfaction at the time. No point in reminding her of it now.

Soon after Marion's funeral she had drifted

away. Her days came and went, shuffling off into darkness. The wind blew and the waves broke and the islands appeared and disappeared and none of it meant anything to her.

In September he had brought her down in a chauffeured car. His Uncle George, ancient and frail, had accompanied them just to make sure everything was done by the book. George had cried all the way back to Glasgow in the hired motorcar, embarrassing the driver.

All too often during medical training Alan had watched relatives, a husband or wife, a son, a daughter, bent over the bed of a patient who was close to death. He had listened to their desperate chatter. He had thought then—being young—how selfish it was of them to unload their petty achievements on someone so far gone, as if they hoped to wring one last approving word to assure them that they would never come to this, become, in turn, the lonely figure in the hospital bed.

Standing just behind his mother, he laid his good hand upon her shoulder. He stared out across the calm, rose-tinted waters of the firth and longed to share with her—what? His woes, his plans, his future?

He stayed for ten minutes, hand on her shoulder, but she didn't look up and didn't speak again.

'Mama,' he said, at length, 'I'm going now.'

He leaned down and kissed her cheek.

She did not so much as blink.

*   *   *

'Look, Beatty,' Les Woodcock said, 'if you're

planning to lug this stuff all the way to the brass balls in Stirling by bus you're nuts.'

'I'm not taking it to a pawnshop,' Beatty said. 'I'll get a far better price at the pedlars' market.'

'I've still got Doc's motorcar. Why don't we load the clothes into the boot and do the whole trip in one go? Saturday, I finish early. We could be on the road by half past two.'

'I'm not rolling up in a fancy motorcar. The hawkers'll think I'm well off.'

'Wrong, sweetheart, wrong,' Les said. 'If you roll up in an Alvis they'll be too intimidated to offer you owt but top dollar.'

'God, but you're a persuasive wee devil when you're roused.'

Les winked. 'Baby,' he said, 'you ain't seen nothin' yet.'

Soon after Les left, Beatty set about sorting out Marion Kelso's clothes: a jacket in white wool stockinette, a suit in two shades of green, a coat frock in russet wool—beautiful clothes, not much worn. Underwear too; Beatty held a corset against her body and realised it would never fit her no matter how she stretched it. She had no image of Marion Kelso beyond a glum black and white portrait that Alan kept on his desk, but lounging pyjamas and a pair of French knickers hinted at a naughty streak in the woman's character. She pressed the French knickers against her tummy and wondered what the dealers in Stirling would make of them.

'Very fetching, Beatty. May I come in?'

He was already halfway over the threshold.

'Alan, what a surprise.'

'You don't mind, do you?'

206

'Of course not, but I wish you'd given me warning. Look at the place. It's a midden.' She tossed the knickers on to the cot and covered her confusion by kissing him. 'I'm not the world's best housewife. What are you doing here?'

'I didn't feel much like being on my own tonight.'

'No Miss Summers, then?'

'No Miss Summers,' Alan said. 'Would you happen to have a drink handy?'

'What's wrong, Alan? Is your arm painful?'

He placed his forearm on the table as if it were an anatomical specimen. The plaster had already begun to turn grey and shiny and the padding that protruded from between his fingers was stained.

'Bloody arm,' he said. 'Bloody nuisance.'

Beatty dug out the whisky bottle, poured two shots and put them on the table. She filled a milk jug with fresh water and placed it before him. He pulled her down on to his knee and kissed her.

'What's that for?' she asked.

'Absolutely nothing.'

'It didn't feel like absolutely nothing,' Beatty said.

He kissed her again. She put her tongue in his mouth.

Opening the buttons on her shirt, he pushed his fingers under her vest. She had been working with the mares that afternoon and for comfort's sake had removed her brassiere. Her skin was sticky but his eagerness, his desperation, annulled her embarrassment. Out of nowhere she was suddenly wet.

'Do you want me to stop?' he asked.

'No,' she answered.

She slid from his knee, went to the bed and began to remove the dresses that covered it. She heard the door close, the bolt snap. Then he was behind her, coat and jacket thrown aside. He thrust a hand between her legs and threw her on to the cot, Marion Kelso's fine expensive clothes crushed beneath her. He drew her legs down until she lay diagonally across the bed. He lifted her skirt, pulled off her drawers, pushed her knees apart and punched into her.

She knew she should stop him, tell him to wait, withdraw, be careful, but all sense of responsibility had gone out of her.

The only sounds that escaped her lips were, 'Yes, dearest, yes.'

By which time it was too late.

*   *   *

Charley Noonan was waiting by the gate of the sheep field, plus dog but minus tractor. Bruce yapped and made several unconvincing advances towards the collie who, crouched behind the gate, glowered with such mute malevolence that the little Scottie backed away, whining, and hid behind Christine's legs.

Christine tugged the lead from her pocket and clipped it to Bruce's collar.

'Come to scare my sheep again?' Charley said. 'If you saw dead lambs all over the field, you wouldn't be so careless. Not that you give tuppence about Charley and a bunch of silly sheep.'

'Oh, Charley, I'm sorry.'

'What got into you, Christine? You know better than to worry pregnant ewes near their time. My old man would have shot your dog without thinkin' twice.'

'It wasn't Bruce's fault. I had him on the lead.'

'From what I hear, the dog isn't the only thing you have on a lead. First me, now this doctor chap,' Charley said. 'While we're on the subject, who was the joker who kissed you outside the school?'

'Kissed me? No one kissed me.' Christine paused. 'Mr Harrison is the deputy convener of the Board of Rural Education. He was visiting Greenhill on official business. We were at college together. We were reminiscing, that's all.'

'I suppose you were reminiscing with the postman too?' Charley said. 'You've been seen with him in the doctor's car.'

'What a place this is,' Christine cried. 'It's like living in a goldfish bowl.'

'Your "nobody's sweetheart" act doesn't wash with me, Christine. Perhaps you weren't ready to settle for a man with mud on his boots—I can just about understand that—but be careful you don't miss your chance. And please keep away from my lambing ewes in future.' He leaned over the gate and spat, something she had never seen him do before. 'At least my sheep repay the attention I give them.'

'I'm not going to be lectured by you, Charley Noonan.'

'Then go,' he said. 'I'm not stoppin' you. But if you're lookin' for lover boy, you won't find him here. He's down at Picton with Beatty McCall.'

'How do you know?'

''Cause I saw him from the hill,' Charley answered.

'You're mistaken.'

'Am I? Well, maybe I am,' Charley said and stalked off around the edge of the sheep field with the collie slinking behind him.

*　　　*　　　*

Alan had never given much thought to money. His salary was paid directly into the bank and Marion had taken care of all the domestic expenses. Shortly before Christmas his Uncle George had advised him to obtain court permission to sell his mother's flat and manage on her behalf the income from shares that his father had accumulated. Until that sunny morning in the manager's office in the Royal Bank in St Vincent Street, however, Alan had no idea that he was, by any reasonable standard, quite wealthy.

'Have you prepared a will, Mr Kelso?' the manager asked.

'Yes,' he answered. 'Of course.' A will that, stupidly, he had neglected to revise since Marion's death.

'Children?'

'No, no children.'

No children, no heirs to benefit from his hard work and his father's acumen. Thousands of pounds at his disposal in the midst of a national depression and he could think of nothing better to do with it than buy a second-hand motorcar.

He withdrew one hundred pounds and caught a cab to Anniesland.

Mr McNair was only too pleased to negotiate a cash-down deal for purchase of the Alvis and tactful enough not to enquire where the motorcar was or how the doctor had damaged his wrist.

210

It was not much past noon when Alan stumbled out of the showroom.

He dithered by the side of the road while tramcars hurtled past, buses whizzed out to half-built suburbs and horse-drawn carts clattered among the tenements. He felt peculiarly vulnerable all of a sudden. What would become of all that cash if fate hurled him under a bus or tram or if he was felled by a blood clot in the brain? Who would bury him? Uncle George? Who would inherit? Uncle George? And if he survived a few more years, who would kneel at his feet in a seaside nursing home and try to make sense of his memories?

He walked to Anniesland Cross and picked up a taxi to carry him to the hospital where, with luck, he might find a sympathetic ear.

*   *   *

'Many things I can and would do for you, Alan,' Josie Carmichael said, 'but bearing children isn't one of them.'

'Why ever not?' Alan said. 'I thought you were my friend.'

'It may come as news to you, chum, but I'm past it,' Josie said. 'It might be fun to tease dear old mother nature by engaging in a little *ooo-la-la* with you, Mr Kelso, but in terms of providing you with heirs, alas, mother nature would have the last laugh.'

'Just how old are you?'

'Older than you might imagine.'

They were seated on the hospital roof above the almoner's office, Josie slouched in a deckchair that

211

one of the juniors had graciously vacated, Alan on a wooden bench that the nurses used when they came up for air. He watched Josie exhale a lungful of smoke.

'I was under the impression that you were in the market for a female companion,' she said. 'It never occurred to me that you might be nurturing dynastic tendencies.'

'Never occurred to me either,' Alan admitted, 'until this morning.'

'Perhaps the urge will pass as swiftly as it came.'

'Possibly,' Alan conceded. 'But now it's on my mind—well, you know how obsessive I can be.'

Josie blew more smoke, quite a cloud of it. 'So it's not just a wife you want but children, which does rather put me out of the running. Won't your horse farmer fill the bill? How old is she?'

'Thirty-seven or -eight, I think.'

'Before you summon the gypsy violins, Alan, I'd advise you to have a dekko at her birth certificate.' Another cloudy pause. 'Are you compatible?'

'What do you mean by compatible.'

'Have you slept with her?'

'In that sense, yes, if you must know, we are compatible.' Alan hesitated. 'However, there's someone else.'

'Oh, God!' Josie cried despairingly. 'What's got into you, Kelso? Is this the one you told me about? I trust she's still capable of performing the rites of spring?'

'She's quite young and inexperienced.'

'Where have I heard that before?' Josie dropped her cigarette to the concrete and rubbed it out with her shoe. 'What does *she* do?'

'Teacher.'

'That's a little more like it. At least she's educated.'

'Just because a woman breeds ponies doesn't mean she's not educated,' Alan said. 'In fact, she reads Shakespeare.'

'Anyone with a library card can read Shakespeare. Do you?'

'Do I what?'

'Read Shakespeare.'

'Actually, no.'

'What on earth do you find to talk about if you don't read Shakespeare?' said Josie sarcastically. 'Never mind the horse farmer, tell me more about your teacher. Is she dazzled by your gravitas?'

'I've taken to reading Chekhov,' Alan said evasively.

'For God's sake, why?'

'Marion liked the Russians.'

'Nothing happens in Chekhov, nothing much anyway,' said Josie. 'What does this have to do with your teacher? She's not a Bolshevik, is she?'

'No, but she does have a little dog,' said Alan.

'You're kidding me? Not a bloody Pomeranian?'

'A Scottie.'

Josie looked over the rooftops to the cranes and half-empty slipways that ribbed the river. 'Do you really want to embrace fatherhood at your age, Alan, or are you just bored?'

'I've never been less bored in my life.'

Josie clambered out of the deckchair. She did something with the front of her dress, drawing it away from her to peer down into her bosom and, finding everything in place, settled the dress again and smoothed it over her hips.

'I've missed the boat, haven't I?' she said.

213

'I'm not sure there was ever a boat to miss,' Alan said.

'But there is now, isn't there?'

'Yes,' Alan told her. 'There is now.'

'Then good luck, old boy,' she said. 'Jolly good luck.'

'Josie, where are you going?'

'Blockage of the bowel,' she said, 'at four o'clock.'

And went off and left him, alone, on the sunlit roof.

CHAPTER TWENTY

The tea-room that looked out on the tower of the Wallace Monument hadn't been there last time Beatty had visited the pedlars' market. It was one of several jerry-built constructions that had sprung up to provide the impecunious folk of Stirling with a glorious view and a cheap bite to eat.

However greasy and crowded, the Monument tea-room certainly tickled Mr Woodcock's fancy. Mr Woodcock, in turn, tickled the fancy of the miners' wives and daughters who'd dropped in for a Saturday afternoon treat in the form of a poached egg or slab of fried sausage meat. It wasn't the postman's good looks that caught the girls' attention, of course, but the shiny motorcar from which he emerged in the company of a woman too young to be his mother and just a little too old to be his wife. The motorcar driver and the good-looking blonde ordered haddock and chips from the top of the menu and followed it with cakes.

'God, that's better.' Les dabbed crumbs from his moustache. 'I was starving, in case you hadn't noticed. I hope you haven't blown all the profits.'

'Even you couldn't eat your way through seventeen pounds, nine shillings and sixpence worth of cast-off clothing.'

'Been a pig, have I?'

'Not at all,' said Beatty. 'I like a man with a hearty appetite.'

'Does he have a hearty appetite? The Doc, I mean.'

'Now, now, Leslie, no fishing.'

'Nobody calls me Leslie, not even my mum. You gonna marry him?'

'He hasn't asked me. I doubt if he will.'

'If you can't make him happy, Beatty, nobody can.'

'I'm not in it for what he can give me, you know.'

'Never thought you were,' Les said. 'Still, he's done all right by you so far. Not many guys would lend their motorcar to an 'umble postman either. By the by, he's bought the car. He'll be banging up an' down to Picton once his wrist heals, unless you're planning on moving in with him.'

Beatty hesitated. 'I'm not sure I'm classy enough for a man like Mr Kelso.'

'You're sure classy enough for me,' Les said. 'If you ever get tired of the Doc or he gets tired of you, Beatty, I'll be waiting to catch you.'

Beatty cleared her throat and reached for the check.

'Are you ready for the road, young man?'

'As ready as I'll ever be,' said Les. 'Don't forget what I said.'

'No,' Beatty promised, 'I won't forget.'

*   *   *

The tests arrived by first post on Monday in a heavy parcel sealed with tape. Mr Woodcock hefted it from the back of the van and carried it to the school steps where he deposited it, like a trophy, at Christine's feet.

'Looks interesting,' he said. 'What's your boss buying now?'

'Exam papers,' Christine answered. 'Not a word to anyone, please.'

'What's so secret about exam papers?'

'It's a form of testing of which our education board does not approve.'

'What's that then?' Les said. 'A sex test, like?'

'Les, really!'

'Some queer things being done in schools these days, I hear,' the postman said.

'In Greenhill Primary?'

'Yeah, well, maybe not.'

A ring of nosy onlookers had assembled round the steps. Discussion as to the contents of the mysterious parcel was already under way.

Christine accompanied the postman to the gate.

'Have you seen anything of Dr Kelso over the weekend?' she asked.

'Sure,' Les answered. 'Saw him Friday night and again on Saturday.'

'Where did you run into him?' Christine enquired casually. 'Picton?'

'His place.' Les gave her a quick, darting glance. 'He's been busy, Christine, very busy. Drop in. He'll be pleased to see you.'

216

'I'm not so sure he will.'

'Sure he will,' Les said. 'He likes you.'

'Does he? Did he tell you that?'

'Doesn't have to,' Les said. 'I can tell by the way he looks at you.'

'How does he look at me?'

'Who do you think I am, bleedin' cupid?' Les said, grinning, and climbed back into his van and drove off.

*　　　*　　　*

Two strong-armed ten-year-olds lugged the parcel into Mr McKay's classroom and hung about the half-open door in the hope that they would be first to carry word of impending doom to the multitude milling in the playground.

'Scram,' Freddy told them, and shut the door with his foot.

He pulled a penknife from his pocket and deftly slit the tape, folded back the wrapping paper and exposed the box in which the test papers nestled.

'Now I'll show the beggars what progress is all about,' he said. 'The way they've resisted it, you'd think there was something subversive in a simple— well, not so simple—series of tests for third and fourth graders. Heck, these tests are used all over Canada and North America.'

'And Fife,' Christine reminded him.

'Yep, and Fife,' Freddy said. 'Approved, you know, by the Council for Educational Research.'

'Then why are we doing it on the sly?'

'Because of idiots like your Mr Harrison.'

'Nonsense!' said Christine. 'You're doing it for your own satisfaction.'

217

'No,' Freddy said. 'Not entirely. I want to find out why Greenhill Primary promotes so few pupils into higher education.'

'Because no more is expected of them?' Christine suggested.

'Give that lady a coconut.' Freddy dug into the box and brought out a fat paper-bound book. 'Here. Read all about it. It'll take your mind off your love life.'

'My love life?' said Christine. 'What love life?'

*   *   *

Long ago, in her training days, Chris had learned to walk and read without bumping into lampposts or tripping over kerbstones. Nose buried in the manual that Freddy had given her, she turned into the gate at Preaching Friar so absorbed in grading ratios and growth curves that she almost side-stepped the Wolseley in the drive before she realised quite what it was.

She hurried into the house to find Ross Harrison taking tea with the Brigadier. Her mother, all simpering smiles, danced attendance.

'Here she is now,' Maude said. 'Mr Harrison's been waiting for you.'

'Has he?' Christine put down her satchel. 'Where's Bruce?'

'Locked up,' Maude said. 'Mr Harrison doesn't care for dogs.'

'Does he not?' said Christine. 'Perhaps dogs don't care for Mr Harrison.'

'Christine, dear,' Maude admonished, 'do not be rude. I'm sure she doesn't mean it, Mr Harrison. Mr Harrison's come all the way from Harlwood,'

Maude said, as if Harlwood were somewhere in the Arctic Circle. 'He's been telling us all the things you two got up to at college.'

'All what things?' said Christine. 'We didn't get up to anything at college.'

'Come now, Chris,' Ross Harrison said. 'Why should we be embarrassed by the follies of our youth?'

'Flappers,' the Brigadier said. 'Ah! Those were the days.'

'What do you know about flappers?' Maude said. 'You were locked up in Preaching Friar by 1920.'

'More's the pity,' said the Brigadier.

'You looked so beautiful in tassels, Chris,' Mr Harrison said.

'Tassels! I never wore tassels in my life.'

'I'll never forget how you appeared on the night of the spring ball, gliding down the steps to join me in the Hoochy Koochy.'

'That wasn't me. That was Alice Dinwiddie.'

'The Hoochy Koochy!' said the Brigadier. 'I saw that performed in Egypt, oh, umpteen years ago. Did you really do the Hoochy Koochy, my dear? That must have been a sight to behold.'

'This,' Christine said, 'has gone far enough.' She paced across the sitting-room and confronted Ross Harrison. 'What *are* you doing here, Ross? What do you want with me?'

'It's a fair question, Mr Harrison,' said the Brigadier from the depths of his armchair. 'What *do* you want with her?'

'To marry her, sir. To marry her.' The deputy convenor of the Board of Rural Education smiled blandly and smoothed a large hand over his blond

219

curls. 'I do not expect your answer here and now.'

'Well, thank God for that,' said the Brigadier.

Mr Harrison rose to his feet. 'Sir,' he said, 'I have declared myself prematurely. For that you have my apology. It's now up to me to persuade Miss Summers that my intentions are honourable and sincere.'

'You can be as honourable and sincere as you like, Ross, I wouldn't marry you if you were the last man on the planet.'

'Now, now, my dear,' the Brigadier said. 'Let's not be hasty.'

'Hasty?' Christine said. 'I'm not the one being hasty. How many other girls have you tried to sweep off their feet, Ross? Am I the last in a long miserable line? What do you have to offer apart from honourable intentions?'

'Love,' said the deputy convenor. 'I offer you love.'

'What else?' said the Brigadier. 'Something a little more concrete, perhaps.'

'Tell us something about yourself, Mr Harrison,' Maude suggested.

'I'm a teacher serving on the Board of Rural Education. My prospects are—I say it without false modesty—excellent. I've a house in Harlwood, a fair size of a house, where I live with my stepfather. My mother succumbed some time ago.'

'Succumbed to what?' said Christine. 'Boredom?'

For the first time since entering the sitting-room Ross Harrison's composure wavered. He bared his teeth in a grimace that swiftly—but not swiftly enough—transformed itself into a withering smile.

'Consumption. We miss her terribly.'

'Of course you do,' said Maude. 'How awful for you.'

'I've a few pounds in the bank and my position is secure,' Ross Harrison continued. 'Christine would want for nothing.'

'She wants for nothing now, Mr Harrison,' the Brigadier pointed out.

'Except a husband,' Ross said.

To Christine's dismay she saw her mother nod.

The Brigadier said, 'Perhaps she doesn't want a husband.'

'Every young woman of a certain age wants a husband,' Ross said, which Christine thought sounded suspiciously like a line from a Jane Austen novel.

He reached for Christine's hand but she would have none of it.

'Well, I certainly don't want a husband,' she said. 'Or, to put it bluntly, I certainly don't want *you* for a husband.'

Ross smiled his gilded smile and stroked his hair again. 'Then I must find a way to change your mind, dearest. It's unfortunate that circumstances have forced me to put the cart before the horse but at least I've made my intentions plain.'

'All too plain,' said the Brigadier.

'And I cannot be accused of deception.'

'Certainly not, Mr Harrison,' Maude agreed, with far too much unction for Christine's liking. 'You've been very honest with us. I'm sure we all appreciate it.'

'Speak for yourself, Mother.'

'I think it best if I take my leave,' Ross Harrison said, 'to allow you time to mull over my proposal and weigh up the advantages.'

'Well, that won't take long,' said Christine.

'Show Mr Harrison to the door,' her mother said.

'He found his own way in,' Chris said, 'he can find his own way out.'

'What a charming young man,' Maude said, as soon as she returned to the sitting-room. 'So handsome—and just the right age for you, Christine.'

'I thought you didn't want me to get married.'

'Nonsense! I just don't want you throwing yourself away.'

Chris turned to the Brigadier. 'Sandy, tell me—what does he really want?'

'He's after your money,' the Brigadier informed her.

'But I don't have any money.'

'No, but I do,' said the Brigadier.

*　　　*　　　*

With the annual village fete coming up the Boys' Brigade had been invited to help prepare the field in front of the church. Charley was scheduled to meet with big-wigs from other organisations that evening to lay out plans. He was tired, though, and his bum ached as the Wallis rumbled down the lane to the low pasture.

He cocked his head to listen for the tell-tale bleat of a new arrival or the disgruntled *baaah* that some ewes uttered when their contractions began but, to his relief, heard nothing. He laid his foot to the pedal, increased the tractor's speed and, jouncing about on the rutted road, almost ran head-on into the Alvis as it tore around the corner.

222

Charley swerved, felt the nearside wheel plunge over the edge of the ditch and, frantically jerking the gear lever, just managed to prevent the Wallis from tipping over.

'You bloody maniac,' he shouted, waving his fist. 'Don't you know a blind corner when you see one? You could've killed us both.'

Mr Woodcock reversed, braked and wound down the window.

'Yeah, sorry about that. Hadn't realised the hedges had growed so thick.'

'They're in leaf,' Charley told him. 'It happens every spring.'

'Next year, I'll remember,' Les promised. 'Anyhow, it's you I want to see.'

'Me?' Charley anchored the tractor. 'What d'you want with me?'

'You got a trailer for that machine?'

Charley scowled suspiciously. 'What if I have?'

'Supposin' I want to hire your tractor an' trailer.'

'Not on your bloody life,' said Charley.

'And you with them, of course,' said Les, 'what would it set me back, like?'

'What do you need a trailer for?'

'Hauling.'

'Haulin' what?'

'A motorbike.'

'A motorbike?' Charley was intrigued. 'How come you can't just drive it wherever you want to go?'

'Not driveable,' Les answered. 'Not—ah—roadworthy.'

'I get it. It's lyin' in pieces in somebody's shed?'

'Not exactly in a shed. You know the pond out behind McCall's old place?'

'You don't mean the Dhu Loch?'

'I think I do, yeah,' the postman said. 'Well, it's there, stuck in the mud in the reeds. It don't belong to nobody far as I can tell.'

'Aye, an' do you know why it don't belong to nobody?' Charlie said. ' 'Cause it's been stuck there for years an' none of us could ever get it out.'

'I'll bet we could get it out.'

'We?' said Charley.

'You, me and the tractor.'

'I dare say we could,' said Charley warily. 'What do you want it for? It'll be nothin' but a heap of rust by now.'

'It's a Triumph Model H, probably military, like despatch riders used,' Les told him. 'If the frame ain't fractured and the cylinder's sound I can put the rest together from parts. Any idea how it got there?'

'Haven't a clue,' said Charley. 'Ask Beatty. She lived up there for a while.'

'Well, I live there now,' said Les, 'and I want that bike. So, what do you say, Mr Noonan? How much for an hour's work with tractor, trailer and rope?'

Charley shrugged. 'Five bob?'

'I can manage that,' said Les. 'We got a deal?'

'Can't do anythin' right now. We're into lambing. But if you're prepared to wait a week or two, aye, okay.'

'O-*kay*!' Les said and, climbing out of the motorcar, reached up and shook the farmer's hand.

CHAPTER TWENTY-ONE

They were propped up side by side in bed, sipping tea, when Beatty said, 'Alan, I'm foaling.'

He stiffened. 'You're *what?*'

'Not me, you clown. My mares.'

'Well, that's a relief.'

'Would it be so awful if it was me? Wouldn't you like to have children?'

'I'm probably too old now.'

'Rubbish!'

She felt the mattress tilt as he changed position. She considered letting him off the hook but the opportunity had come her way without conniving on her part.

She said, 'If I *was* foaling would you do the right thing?'

'Marry you?'

She nodded.

He answered, 'Of course.'

'Then you'd be stuck with me for ever?'

'I wouldn't mind being stuck with you.' He was clearly trying to appease her. 'I can't think of anyone I'd rather be stuck with.'

'You,' she said, 'are such a hypocrite sometimes. Just Beatty and me and baby makes three, eh?'

'I don't understand.'

'It's a song, Alan: "My Blue Heaven". Duncan McLean sings it every time there's a concert in the village. I don't think either of us is ready to believe in a cosy little nest for two, though, not as things stand.'

'How do things stand?'

'I was on the point of asking you the same question,' Beatty said.

He lay back against the bolster, hands behind his head and stared at the pool of lamplight on the ceiling. At length, he said, 'I wish I had an answer for you, Beatty. The truth is I don't know where I stand in relation to anything these days.' He turned on his side and brushed her hair with his knuckle. 'It's all so new to me.'

'What is?'

'All this.'

'Sex, you mean?'

He frowned, as any dour Presbyterian would, at the mention of the word, which, Beatty thought, was ironic given what they'd been up to half an hour ago.

'Not only sex,' he said. 'I've been cut off from the world for so long I've forgotten how to engage with it. Does that sound overly dramatic?'

'Well, it isn't Shakespeare, but I think I know what you mean.'

'I'm not used to examining my feelings.'

'That's a different kettle of fish from not having any feelings,' Beatty said. 'Didn't you love your wife?'

'Of course, but that was a long time ago. Besides'—he hesitated—'there was an element of convenience in our marriage.'

'Convenience?'

'We were suited to each other,' Alan said, 'socially.'

'I see.'

'I'm not sure you do,' he said. 'Whatever it was that drove me, whatever held me together—it's gone.'

'And you miss it, do you?'

'It's infuriating to have one's inbuilt habits suddenly stripped away.'

'By me?'

'By you, by this,' he held up the plastered arm, 'by not being at the hospital every day, by discovering there's a different sort of order out here in Ottershaw.'

'Pony breeders and postmen?' Beatty said. 'And village school teachers? She's very sweet, isn't she?'

'Mrs Mackintosh doesn't think so. She thinks she's poison.'

Beatty snorted. 'She thinks I'm poison too.'

'Take no notice of Mrs Mack. She resents change of any sort.'

'Inbuilt habits,' Beatty said. 'We know all about those, don't we? Anyhow'—she peeled back the covers—'I'd best be on my way.'

'Can't you stay the night?'

'I told you: I'm foaling.'

'When? Tomorrow?'

'Soon,' Beatty said. 'Like a good little Boy Scout I must be prepared.'

'Some Boy Scout!' said Alan. 'Give me five minutes and I'll walk you as far as the road-end.'

'Five minutes? What do you need five minutes for?'

'This,' he said and, reaching across the bed, pulled her beneath him again.

*   *   *

'What the devil's that?' said Freddy.

'Flowers.' Christine held the paper-wrapped

227

bunch at arm's length. 'Roses.'

'Bit early for roses, isn't it?'

'Hothouse blooms, I imagine.'

'Expensive?

'Probably.'

'So who's been sending you roses then?' said Freddy.

'I'd rather not say. In fact, I'd rather not think about it.'

'It's a beautiful bucket, though. How was it delivered?'

'Left on the front steps. The cleaner found it.'

'Old Jeanie? How did she know the flowers weren't for her?'

'There's a card.'

'Uh-huh!' Freddy held out his hand. 'Let's have a squint.'

'Certainly not,' Christine said. 'I thought there was a vase in this cupboard.'

'Top shelf, behind the hymn books.'

Christine placed the bouquet on the table and, on tiptoe, groped for the vase and brought it down.

Freddy lifted the bouquet to his nose and sniffed. 'Not much scent,' he said.

'Never is with forced blooms.'

'Lovely gesture on someone's part, though.'

Christine filled the vase with water from the tap at the washbasin. She didn't think it was a lovely gesture. She thought it was an act of impertinence. The flowers, fresh-cut, had been placed on the school steps some time before half past six o'clock that morning which was when the cleaner usually arrived. Half past six, Christine thought, meant that Ross Harrison had left home before dawn to drive all the way to Greenhill to deposit them.

'Is it the doctor?' Freddy said.

Chris rammed the roses into the vase. 'I suspect this may be the start of a protracted campaign, so I may as well tell you.'

'Do,' said Freddy eagerly. 'Please do.'

'The deputy convenor of the Board of Rural Education wants to marry me.'

'Harrison? Surely not Harrison?'

'The same.'

'Far be it from me to condemn any man for falling arse over—I mean head over heels for a pretty young thing like you, but isn't it all a bit sudden?'

'Sudden? It's ludicrous!'

'How do you know he wants to marry you?'

'He came right out and said so in front of witnesses.'

'Witnesses?'

'My mother and the Brigadier.'

'He's a bold lad is our Mr Harrison.'

'I know what you're thinking,' Christine said. 'You're thinking I must have encouraged him but, honestly, I haven't.'

'I believe you, sweetheart,' the headmaster said. 'Just because you've a pretty face doesn't mean to say you're simple-minded.'

'I do not have a pretty face. I'm as plain as rice pudding,' said Christine. 'It's not my looks he's attracted to. It's my prospects. He seems to have got hold of the notion that when the Brigadier passes away I'll inherit a fortune.'

'Oh, so you're a wealthy young heiress now. Harrison's been reading too many trashy novels, if you ask me. Is the Brigadier ailing?'

'No, but he is knocking on.'

'How did Harrison find out about your situation? I'll bet he ran across your employment card. My, my! He's more enterprising than I gave him credit for. If it's your money he's after, Chris, you can be sure he'll make a thorough nuisance of himself. Are you taking the flowers into the classroom?'

'The children may as well have the benefit of them.'

'Why not?' Freddy said. 'But next time Harrison decides to leave you a gift, ask him to make it chocolates.'

* * *

In her early days as a pony breeder Beatty had let the mares foal in the open. But after she'd lost a foal to torrential rain and another to late snow she'd taken to bringing them into the stable where, with dry wheat straw for bedding, she set up a clean and airy foaling bay. In theory mares dropped eleven months after impregnation but the gestation period was exceedingly elastic. Barley, the smaller of the mares, had 'that look' about her though and her teats were tipped with the waxy substance that indicated her time was near.

Maggie was more excited than Beatty at the prospect of watching a foal dive into the world. Even Mr Woodcock was interested enough to toddle over the hill from his farmhouse in the hope that he'd be lucky enough to observe a birth. Neither Barley nor Primrose seemed disposed to oblige, however, and a week floated by with no activity at all.

And no sign of Alan Kelso.

Tense from lack of sleep and with her period overdue, Beatty finally tackled the postman. 'Where is he?' she said. 'Dr Kelso, I mean?'

'Search me.' Les shrugged. 'I ain't seen him since he took the car back.'

'Oh, he took the car back, did he?'

'Well, it is his car. Haven't *you* seen him?'

'No, I have not.'

'Got other things on his mind, I expect.'

'Other things like that school teacher?'

'Christine? Nah. I think she's found another guy.'

'What other guy?' Beatty said. 'You don't mean Charley?'

'Not Charley, no. Big tall handsome beggar. He's with her every afternoon. I see them when I take the van back to the sorting office. He's got a motorcar. He parks outside the school. Christine comes over and talks to him.'

'Does she get in the car?' Beatty asked.

'I only saw her do it once.'

'When?'

'Last Friday.'

'Was she going off with him, do you think?' said Beatty.

'For God's sake, Beatty, I don't know,' Les said. 'If you're so concerned about the Doc why don't you go and talk to him?'

'I can't,' Beatty said. 'I'm stuck here until the foals arrive.'

'At this rate it could be bleedin' Christmas,' Les said. 'What's wrong with them ponies? Didn't you get your arithmetic right?'

'My arithmetic—' Beatty began just as Maggie rushed from the door of the stable, crying, 'Come

231

quick. I think she's started.'

*　　　*　　　*

'This,' Christine said, 'will have to stop.'

'If that's the case,' Ross Harrison said, 'why are you here with me now?'

'To tell you it will have to stop. What do I have to do to convince you?'

'Convince yourself first of all.'

He looped an arm around the back of the seat and pressed his handsome face close to hers. She knew he was about to kiss her. Ten days of determined courtship had almost worn down her resistance; almost, but not quite.

'Ross,' she said, 'please don't.'

He sighed and sat back. 'Very well, Christine. If that's how you feel, I'll abide by your wishes. I'm not the rotter you take me for. Your mother likes me. Why don't you?'

'My mother doesn't know you as well as I do.'

It had been a mistake to step into his motorcar in the first place but last Friday it had all become too much for her: the flowers, the boxes of Paynes' Poppets—why Paynes' Poppets?—a copy of the poems of Christina Rossetti and, bedded in cotton wool, a small heart-shaped metal brooch. Some of the gifts were delivered to the school in the early hours of the morning, others left on the doorstep at Preaching Friar, as if the deputy convenor of Rural Education was a sprite who didn't take on fleshly form until late afternoon.

'Dear God, Christine,' Freddy complained, 'can't you at least lure him away from the gate? It's becoming manifestly embarrassing, not to say

232

annoying, having to interrupt my lessons to explain just who the fellow is and why he's out there.'

So, stupidly, she had capitulated.

Every day thereafter Ross had swept her into the Wolseley before she could think to refuse. Three days boxed up in the stuffy little motorcar while Ross showered her with promises and compliments; three days of romantic twaddle that highlighted the fact that his wooing had been rehearsed in the course of many courtships— Janice, Muriel, Alice, Hazel—that had somehow gone askew.

Now, parked on a cart track just off the ridge road, it was time to put a stop to it once and for all.

'You're after my money, Ross, aren't you? If you are after my money why don't you admit it?' He opened his mouth but Christine gave him no opportunity to interrupt. 'Didn't it cross your mind that I might be perfectly willing to marry a fine upstanding gentleman who would probably make a perfectly good husband even although his motives for marrying me were less romantic than mercenary? Of course, the fact that I have no money—not a red cent—and my benefactor, Brigadier Crockett, has already indicated that he intends to leave most of his vast wealth to the regimental welfare fund—'

'Not true,' Ross Harrison blurted out.

'Oh, really? How do *you* know it's not true?'

A bead of perspiration trickled from his brow and landed like a teardrop on the bridge of his nose. 'He—he's not going to leave you penniless?'

'I don't know what he's going to do,' Christine said. 'Strange as it may seem, Ross, I've given it no thought.'

'Haven't you had sight of his will?'

'No,' Christine said. 'Have you?'

'How could I possibly have sight of his will?'

'Why are you pursuing plain wee Christine Summers when you might marry the daughter of a shipping magnate or—Muriel, wasn't it?—the heiress to a fortune in steel castings? Did their daddies see through you? If you'd exercised a degree of patience, Ross, you might have won me round, though, to be frank, I doubt it.'

'What are you saying?'

'Isn't it obvious? I'm saying I've not the slightest intention of marrying you and you'll save yourself a great deal of time and trouble if you find another victim.'

At last, a flicker of pride: 'I think you've made your position clear, Christine. I'm more in love with you than you give me credit for, however, and I will not give up easily because I know, even if you do not, that one day you'll regret it.'

'Regret what?'

'Turning me down.'

She reached for the door handle. 'I'm not rich and I'm not pretty but, by God, Mr Harrison, I'm not crazy.' She threw open the door. 'I've no idea why you picked on me, apart from some mad notion that I'm in line to inherit a fortune. Who told you about the Brigadier? Why are you in such a furious hurry to make me your wife?' She groped for her satchel, dragged it across her knee and threw it out on to the ground. 'You're either very cunning or very stupid, Ross. In either event I've no wish to see you again.'

'What a bitch you are, Christine,' he said. 'What an absolute bitch.'

'I think that says it all, don't you?' she told him
and, scrambling from the car and snatching up her
satchel, set off up the incline to the ridge road with
the Wolseley's engine snarling behind her.

She stepped on to the macadam road just as the
Alvis drew up beside her.

Alan opened the passenger door.

'Get in,' he said.

Which, quite sensibly, she did.

*   *   *

She slumped in the passenger seat with her satchel
on her lap and, in the side mirror, watched the
Wolseley weave along the ridge road behind them
and eventually shear off at the crossroads.

Alan stopped the car and rested his forearm on
the steering wheel.

'You do have some very odd friends, Christine.'

'He's not a friend,' Christine said. 'How did you
know where to find me?'

'The Brigadier told me. He seemed to think you
might need rescuing.'

'Oh, is that what it was—a rescue?' Christine
said.

'Are you still angry with me?'

She pursed her lips, unsure whether she wanted
to cry or laugh. 'He called me a bitch.'

'Not terribly courteous of him, was it?' Alan
released the handbrake. 'Why don't I deliver you
back to the Brigadier and we'll say no more about
it. Will you take Bruce for his walk later?'

'Yes, I expect I will.'

'Oh, good!' Alan said. 'You never know who you
might bump into.'

'As long as it isn't Ross Harrison, I can put up with anyone.'

'Even me?'

'Yes,' Christine assured him. 'Even you.'

PART FOUR

The Paradise Waltz

CHAPTER TWENTY-TWO

Palmy Days with Eddie Cantor had come and gone, Nancy Carroll in *The Devil's Holiday*, too. Charley had missed both films. In any other season he would have been able to slip away for an hour or two but with lambs dropping thick and fast he was kept hard at it from dawn until after dusk.

It was during his last round-up of the day, a very long day, when the ewe took off with half the lamb still inside her, its greasy head bobbing, bug-eyed, under her tail. With no dog to help him, Charley chased the beast downhill in the hope that the burn would give her pause and allow him to pull the lamb, clearly alive, out on to the grass. He was too intent on catching the sheep to notice the couple sprawled on the grass in the lee of a gorse bush.

The ewe didn't spot them either until she was almost upon them. Braying, she swerved and the lamb, its bag torn, slipped out another inch or two and waggled a foreleg like a cry for help.

'Jump her, Leslie,' Beatty cried. 'She won't bite you.'

Les leapt like a cat and pinned the sheep to the ground. Beatty supported the lamb's head in her cupped hands while the ewe, rather ungratefully, broke wind, made water and bleated as loudly as a bugle call.

'Can you hold her, Liverpool?' Charley shouted.

'Yup.'

'Beatty, lift her up.'

Hitching her skirt, Beatty threw a leg over the

ewe's back, plunged both hands into the smelly fleece and elevated the ewe's hind end. Charley fished a tin of soft soap from his pocket, anointed his hands, slipped them under the lamb and fished about in the fluid tissue.

Glancing up at Beatty, he winked. 'Fancy meetin' you here.'

'Yes, fancy.' Beatty grinned. 'Is she knuckled?'

'Aye, that's all. Elbow caught on the pelvic bone. Here we go.'

He drew the lamb out, swung it gently by its forelegs and stretched it on the ground. He wiped its nose and mouth with a pluck of grass while the ewe grunted and puffed and shook her head.

'Are you sure she's empty?' Beatty said.

'Aye, there's just one, thank God.'

Charley continued cleaning until the lamb prodded out a tiny pink tongue and released a blethering *meeeh* that made the ewe struggle even more frantically.

'Can I get up now?' Les asked.

'I don't see why not,' said Charley.

The ewe, released, rounded on Les, butted him by way of thanks, then fell to licking her one and only.

'Another life saved, Charley?' Beatty said.

'Another fiver earned.' He wiped his swollen hands on his trouser leg. 'What the heck are you doin' here, anyway?'

'Out for a stroll,' said Beatty.

'Is that what they call it these days?'

'What a grubby mind you have, Charley Noonan,' Beatty told him.

'Have you got those foals on grass yet?' Charley asked.

'I'll run them out next week. You?'

'Near done,' said Charley.

Ewe and lamb moved quietly away, the lamb's tail wriggling as it nosed around its mother searching for the teat.

'Well,' Charley said, 'thanks for your help. I'd best push on. I've a couple o' stragglers to track down before I turn in. Are you two off up the pub?'

The postman exchanged a swift glance with Beatty.

'Not tonight,' Beatty answered. 'No, Charley, no pub tonight.'

'Where are you goin' then?'

'Back to my place,' said Les.

*   *   *

The kitchen was furnished with two chairs, an old table, a wooden rocker by the fire, a patch of rug, two kerosene lamps, and four shelves above the sink that hadn't been there in her day. The range had been black-leaded, the arch of the chimney brushed free of soot. Even the treacly stains that had so plagued Beatty's mother-in-law had been scraped away.

'You've been busy.'

'My place,' Les said, 'my responsibility.'

'Where do you sleep?'

He nodded to the nook beneath the stairs. 'In there. It's not much for space but it's warm. I'll do up a bedroom when I have some money. My kid sister, Pearl, sent me ten bob for furniture, which was nice of her.'

'What does she do?'

241

'Secretary to some big-wig on Liverpool Council. Good job. She was lucky to get it. Well, maybe not lucky.'

'What do you mean?'

'When Pearl bats her baby blues she can get most anything she wants.'

'It runs in the family, does it?' Beatty said.

'Does what?'

'Charm.'

'Guess so. If you wanna get ahead, you gotta use what God gave you.'

'What did God give you, Les?'

'That's for me to know, Beatty,' he said, 'and for you to find out.'

She followed him across the kitchen and stood behind him at the range while he removed the lid from a pan and stirred the contents.

'What's cooking?'

'Irish stew—Liverpool style. You hungry?'

Beatty wrapped an arm about his waist. 'I see you've mastered that blasted range. I never got on top of it when I lived here.'

'Wouldn't get on top of it now, love,' Les said. 'It's roaring hot.'

'It's not the only thing that's roaring hot,' Beatty said.

He lifted his head and pulled away from her.

'What's wrong?' Beatty said.

He dropped the lid back on the pan. 'This is my place, Beatty.'

'What's that got to do with it?'

'I'm responsible for what goes on here.'

'I'm sorry. I thought you liked what we were doing out on the hill.'

'I did,' Les said. 'But out on the hill I knew when

to stop.'

'What if I didn't want you to stop?' Beatty said.

'It isn't up to you.'

She pulled out a chair and propped an elbow on the brand-new oilcloth that covered the table. Les had his back to her, staring into the maw of the chimney where the flue from the back of the range disgorged thin trickles of smoke.

'Bet you wouldn't be saying that if Maggie was sitting here,' Beatty said.

'Maggie's just a kid.'

'And what are you?'

'Old enough to know better.' He came to the table and planted both hands on the oilcloth. 'Okay, Beatty, what's the game? What're you up to?'

The muscles of her stomach clenched and a wave of nausea pumped acid into her throat. 'I thought you said you were ready to catch me.'

'Oh, yeah, I am,' Les told her, 'but what about the Doc?'

She studied the pattern of rosebuds sprinkled on the cheap green oilcloth. She knew it was wrong to throw herself at Les Woodcock but if her late period meant she was pregnant she had no time to lose.

'I haven't seen Alan in weeks.'

'I like you, Beatty—I even fancy you—but there's something else going on, something I don't think is right.'

'You think I'm cheating, don't you?'

'Yeah, frankly, I do.'

The cramping had subsided into a familiar throbbing ache.

She knew what was coming next.

243

'You're right,' she said. 'I am cheating.'

'Who are you cheating? You, me or the Doc?'

'All three of us,' Beatty said. 'Awful, isn't it?'

'Awful, just awful,' Les said. 'Don't do it again.'

'No,' Beatty said contritely. 'I won't.'

She watched him shake his fingers as if to discharge the last of his animosity, then, shrugging, he said, 'You staying?'

'I'm staying,' Beatty said. 'Do you have enough in the pot for two?'

'More than enough,' Les Woodcock said.

He turned again to the stove while Beatty, excusing herself, went out into the fading sunlight to find the chemical toilet and do what she had to do.

*　　　*　　　*

There had been an outbreak of respiratory fever in the Clydeside tenements north of the river and the almoner's staff and dispensary sisters were run off their feet. Hallways and corridors were bustling with activity and no one noticed when Mr Kelso sailed up in a sleek new motorcar.

Four small patients and two babies occupied the surgical ward. Hargreaves was completing a post-operative examination on a boy whose hare lip had been repaired. Alan elected not to interfere and made his way down to the theatre wing to see what was going on there.

'Oh, it's himself, is it?' Josie Carmichael said. 'How's the wrist?'

Alan waved his fingers in a spider crawl. 'Nearly better.'

'You're not on the slate, you know.'

244

'I didn't expect to be. I'm here, however, and raring to go.'

'You don't look as if you're raring to go,' the anaesthetist told him. 'You look half asleep to me.' She stepped closer and peered into his face. 'My God, you've got yourself a sun tan and I think you've put on weight. What have you been up to while my back's been turned?'

'I haven't been entirely absent, you know.'

'I heard you'd been in for a lecture or two. Somehow I missed you.'

'Did you?' Alan said. 'Did you really, Josie?'

'Don't push it, chum.'

'I'll report to Cairns and have myself put on standby for emergencies,' Alan said. 'Who's operating today? Anyone I know?'

'Professor Bryce,' Josie told him. 'It's heavy stuff. He's trephining a severe case of oxycephaly. You don't see that done very often.'

'Really! How old's the child?'

'Six. Bryce brought his own team with him. It's rumoured he intends to scrape and widen the orbits to relieve the child's headaches. He's just about to start. I'm sure he wouldn't mind if you observed.'

Alan hesitated. 'No,' he said, at length. 'I think I'll pass.'

'Personally,' Josie said, 'I wouldn't miss it for the world.'

'By the by,' Alan said, 'I've bought myself a motorcar.'

'Later,' Josie told him and scuttled off upstairs.

*   *   *

245

'Is this test for marks, sir?'

'Of course, it's for marks,' said Freddy. 'Now get your head down, laddie, and concentrate. You've thirty minutes'—he peered at the wall clock—'starting now.'

Papers rustled, thirteen heads dropped; he could almost hear their busy little brains beginning to hum. Someone—Gordon Blaine—applied himself to sharpening his pencil for the third or fourth time and Eileen West, a timid girl, let out a gasp as she scanned the list of questions. Little Maisie Moscrop, pretty as a picture and tough as a farmer's boot, raised her hand.

'Yes, Maisie,' Freddy said, patiently enough.

Most of the class stopped studying the test paper to listen to her question and his answer, hoping perhaps for a key that would guarantee gold stars all round. Only Drew Walker, smart as well as industrious, kept on writing, his new HB pencil flying down the page.

'It's ticks, Mr McKay,' Maisie said.

'Yes, Maisie, ticks it is.'

Master Blaine blew a heap of wood shavings to the floor, inspected the point on the stump of his pencil and said smugly, 'There's no space for answers, but.'

'The ticks *are* the answers.'

'How can ticks be answers?'

'Oh, for God—for goodness sake! Weren't *any* of you listening when I explained the rules?' Freddy closed his eyes, counted to three. 'It's what's called "multiple-choice testing". Drew, do you mind stopping for a bit, please.' Reluctantly Master Walker stopped writing but, Freddy noted, did not stop reading or, for that matter, thinking.

'For the last time, the purpose of the test is to examine the breadth of your knowledge on a lot of different subjects and to save you having to strain yourselves writing out long answers. Look, a question—three boxes. One box has the right answer. Two boxes have the wrong answer.'

'How do we know what box has the right answer?'

'Gordon,' the headmaster said, with a sigh, 'do you want to die young?'

'Naw, Mr McKay.'

'Then shut up and let me finish.'

He snatched a piece of chalk from the ledge, turned to the blackboard and with speed born of much practice, drew three large boxes, printed *London*, *Paris*, *Copenhagen*, one city to each box. He swung round to face the class.

'If the question says, "Which city is the capital of France—"'

'Paris,' Maisie piped up.

'Right. Paris. Which box do you tick?'

'Paris.'

'Right again. *Now* do you understand?'

Light bulbs flickered over earnest heads: 'Aye, Mr McKay.'

'Good. Now the object of the test is to see how many questions you can answer—tick—correctly in exactly thirty minutes. So I'm going to start again.' He studied the second hand, waiting, arm raised like a race official. 'Go.'

Every head in the classroom dipped; every head bar one.

'What's wrong now, Gordon?'

'It's not there.'

'What's not there?'

247

'Paris: it's not in any o' ma boxes.'

'Forget Paris,' Freddy hissed.

'But you said—'

'Forget bloody Paris, Gordon.' Freddy leaned over the boy and hammered the chalk on the desk top like a pianist playing ragtime. 'There! That's the first question. It has nothing to do with capital cities. What I wrote on the blackboard was an example. Put a tick, just put a tick in one of the boxes.'

'Which one, but?' said Gordon.

Freddy closed his eyes, counted to five this time. He straightened, smiled and, with the hand that was free of chalk, lightly brushed the boy's hair.

'Any one at all, Gordie. Any one that takes your fancy.'

'This one?'

'Fine,' said Freddy. 'Fine.'

Then with the class, including Gordon, finally engaged, he ambled out into the hallway and, leaving the door wide open, treated himself to a cigarette and a long pull from his whisky flask.

CHAPTER TWENTY-THREE

'Miss Summers, a word, if you please.'

'I'm in the middle of a lesson, Mr Harrison.'

'Give them something to get on with and step outside.'

'I'll do no such—'

'It's a matter of urgency, Miss Summers,' Ross Harrison insisted.

Christine was well aware that Freddy was

deliberately flouting the Board's authority and administering a test that morning.

The class had gone quiet, very quiet. 'Put away your readers,' Christine said, as calmly as possible. 'Gillian and Peter, distribute the crayons and one sheet of drawing paper to each desk. The cupboard isn't locked. I'll be no further away than the hall and if I hear any noise, any noise at all, it'll be the worse for all of you. Is that clear?'

'Yes, Miss Summers.'

Ross Harrison ushered her out into the hall and closed the classroom door. There was no distinct sound from Freddy's class only sibilant whispering pierced now and then by some dumb cluck shouting, 'Sshh, sshh, sshh!'

There had been no gifts, no notes or other communication from Ross Harrison since the incident on the ridge road. He rocked on the balls of his feet and, head thrown back, peered down at her then shot out his hand so abruptly that Chris thought he was about to slap her.

'I take it,' he said, 'you know about this?'

The test paper had a name pencilled in the slot at the upper left corner and, as far as Christine could make out, five or six carefully applied ticks in the boxes.

Playing for time, she said, 'What is it?'

'A multiple-choice testing paper.'

'Yes, I know about it.'

'Did you also know that the Board expressly forbade this method of testing as detrimental to curricular procedure?'

'Curricular procedure? Really?'

'Do not play innocent with me, Miss Summers.'

'I wouldn't dream of it.'

'You will be brought to book, you know.'

From within her classroom came the crash of a crayon box hitting the floor and, like an echo stretching across the hall, someone cried out, 'Sshh, sshh.'

'I've already sent McKay home,' Ross Harrison said.

'You can't do that.'

'Indeed, I can.'

'For administering a test approved by the Council of Education?'

'For being in charge of a class while under the influence of drink.' From his pocket he produced Freddy's silver flask. 'I caught him red-handed in the foyer not ten minutes ago and confiscated this receptacle which, as you see, is inscribed with his initials. Do you doubt that it contains alcohol?'

Christine said, 'I know what it contains.'

'Whisky?'

'Probably.'

'I'll take over McKay's class for the rest of the day. I'll report to the Board and in due course a temporary headmaster will be appointed to replace McKay who will, I assure you, never be employed in education again.'

'Freddy wasn't drunk.'

'I didn't say he was.'

'He—he wasn't feeling well.'

'Your lies won't save him, Christine.'

His superior attitude so infuriated her that she poked a finger into his chest. 'Save him from what? Save him from you, Ross? This has nothing to do with Freddy having a snifter to keep him going. It's not even about multiple testing. It's sheer bloody-minded malice.'

'That,' Ross Harrison said, 'is nonsense.'

'Everything about you is nonsense, Ross. Why are you intent on ruining Freddy McKay's career when he has nothing to do with what's between us?'

'Nothing's between us, Miss Summers. You made that perfectly clear.'

'Do you have your eye on the headmastership of Greenhill Primary, by any chance? Is that what this is about?'

'I can have my pick of schools, Christine. If I was inclined to return to blackboard teaching it would not be here.'

'Not even to be close to me?'

'You flatter yourself.'

'If that thought *is* lurking in that muddled head of yours, I may as well tell you that I won't be teaching here much longer. I'm resigning.'

'Resigning in support of a drunken little nobody?'

'My reasons for resigning will be set out in my letters to the Board of Rural Education *and* the Educational Institute. You may have the local committee in your pocket, Ross, but I doubt if the Institute will brush my complaint aside.'

'Complaint? What do you have to complain about?'

'Molestation,' Christine said. 'Specifically sexual molestation.'

The noise from both classrooms had grown almost deafening. Christine darted across the hall, threw open the door of Freddy's room and yelled, 'Be quiet.' Crossing the hall, she repeated the instruction to her Infants.

The din died away and for a moment or two

251

silence reigned.

She returned to her stance in the foyer.

'Well?' she said.

'You won't get away with it.'

'Try me.'

'My reputation will protect me against your slanders.'

'Your reputation, Ross? What sort of reputation is that, I wonder?' She took a pace towards him. 'Just how would "your reputation" stand up to a board of enquiry, particularly as I have witnesses to back my story?'

'Witnesses?'

'Two classrooms full of witnesses.'

'Children! No one takes their word on anything.'

'Children can be very observant, I assure you. The Institute would almost certainly send an expert to question them. As any mere blackboard teacher knows, once you get the little blighters started there's no stopping them.'

'I never laid a hand on you, Christine.'

'Prove it.'

'I don't have to prove anything.'

'Ah, but you do, Ross. The reason for my resignation will be taken seriously. If you do manage to wriggle out of it your reputation will be tarnished—believe me, it will—and your progress up the monkey-puzzle tree come to a grinding halt.'

'I was right. You are a bitch.'

'And,' Christine went on, 'if the evidence of juveniles isn't enough to sink you, the testimony given by my headmaster, to whom I frequently complained of your unwanted attentions, and by my fiancé—'

'Your fiancé?'

'Dr Kelso. He rescued me from your clutches, if you recall. He'll confirm that I was considerably upset by your disgusting behaviour; quite hysterical, in fact.'

'Jesus Christ!'

'Blaspheme all you like, Ross, it won't alter my story. I couldn't possibly be expected to remain here with you as headmaster, not after what you did to me.'

'I asked you to marry me. Otherwise, I behaved like a perfect gentleman.'

'Who'll believe that a perfect gentleman would propose marriage to a woman he hardly knew? No, Mr Harrison, that isn't the way perfect gentlemen behave; that's the way of the seducer.'

Ross took a pipe from his pocket and tapped his teeth with the stem.

'What do you want from me, Christine?'

'Freddy's whisky flask, for a start.' She held out her hand and, to her relief, saw him drop the flask into it. 'And the test paper.'

'What do you want with the test paper?'

'I intend to return it to the pupil and let her, or him, complete it.'

'You're not going ahead with this stupid test, are you?'

'Absolutely,' Christine assured him. 'It's Freddy's baby and he has every right to see it through. What's more, Mr Harrison, I'll expect you to give it your full support when Freddy's report comes up before the Board.'

'I do not approve of the American method of—'

'The test paper, if you please.'

He glanced down at it then handed it over too.

'Is that all?'

'By no means. Freddy will take the rest of the day off to recover from his indisposition. I'll manage both classes as best I can. Freddy will be here tomorrow, in full charge, as if nothing had happened. There will be no adverse report from you and no repercussions.'

'If I don't agree?'

'My letters of resignation will be in the post first thing tomorrow.'

'I've half a mind to defy you,' Ross Harrison said.

'And risk your career? You've more to lose than I have.'

'Are you really engaged to this doctor fellow?'

'On the brink,' Christine lied. 'Right on the brink.'

'Does he know what a bitch you are?'

'I do wish you'd stop calling me that, Ross, or I might not be so forgiving.'

'Forgiving?' he shouted. '*You* are forgiving *me*?'

'I'm letting you off lightly, very lightly,' Christine said. 'When you pause to think about it, you'll realise what a narrow escape you've had. Now, I've one more question to ask before I dismiss you. Who told you about the Brigadier's will?'

Colour drained from his face. He glanced towards the door as if he had half a mind to make a dash for it.

'Well, Ross? Who was it?'

'No one. I—I heard a rumour . . .'

'I don't believe you.'

'It wasn't his fault. He knows nothing about it. Please, Christine, promise me you won't tell him.'

'Tell who?' said Christine.

254

'My stepfather,' Ross Harrison said.

*   *   *

Freddy was seated at the table in the living-room, fork in one hand, knife in the other. He was clad in an under-vest and a pair of stained flannel trousers, his braces hanging loose about his waist. He looked, Christine thought, more like a tramp than the headmaster of a respectable village school. The glass of beer was almost empty but the plate of watery mince and mashed potato had hardly been touched.

'Frederick,' said Lucille McKay, 'you have a visitor.'

In contrast to her husband, Lucille McKay was a model of fashion. Her hair was pinned up, her make-up—rather a lot of make-up—perfectly applied, as if she were about to lunch in town, not serve mince and tatties to a husband in his gallowses in a seedy little bungalow on the outskirts of Kennart.

'I'm done, Chris,' Freddy said. 'I'm finished. I finally buggered up.'

'No, you didn't.'

He sighed heavily and wiped his mouth with his hand. 'I'm forgetting my manners. Pull up a pew. Have some mince?'

'No, thank you all the same.' Christine remained penned between the sideboard and the dining-table. She braced her satchel on the edge of the table, opened it, flopped out the pile of test papers and put it before him, just shy of the beer glass.

Freddy frowned. 'What's this?'

'What does it look like?' Christine said. 'Given

255

the unusual conditions under which the test was conducted I can't guarantee accurate results. But while you're recuperating from the intestinal upset that overtook you this morning, you might care to get on with marking. I'll expect them on my desk—on your desk—first thing tomorrow morning. I've also warned the Juniors that a second series of tests will be coming their way tomorrow afternoon and that they'd better smarten up their ideas before they bring shame on the school.'

'What about Harrison?'

'Mr Harrison will not be putting in a report about anything. Mr Harrison will not be bothering either of us again. As far as Greenhill Primary is concerned the *status quo* will be maintained under the present system of management—except for one thing.' She fished the monogrammed silver flask from the satchel and handed it to Lucille. 'It might be as well if you left this at home in future. Now, I must get back to school before the rebels realise I've gone.'

'Wait a second,' Freddy said.

He put down his knife and fork, thumbed his braces over his shoulders, slid out from behind the table and, before Christine could step away, wrapped his arms about her and kissed her, French style, on both cheeks.

'Frederick!' said Madam McKay, not quite menacingly.

'How did you do it, Chris?' Freddy was close to tears. 'I mean, how in God's name did you get that snotty bastard to change his mind?' He pulled back and peered at her. 'Hey, you didn't promise to marry him, did you?'

'Not even for you, Freddy,' Christine said. 'It

turns out Mr Harrison has a few skeletons of his own in the closet. A bit of bluff on my part did the rest.'

'Oh, you darlin', you darlin'.' Freddy hugged her again.

'*Frederick!*'

'Yes, my dear. Sorry.'

Lucille McKay put an arm about Christine. 'Today you have saved a life,' she whispered. 'In your debt we will be for ever,' then led her to the door while Freddy, beaming, celebrated by filling up his glass.

*   *   *

Both Barley and Primrose were thick with milk and the foals had already begun to lose the spindly appearance of newborns. She'd introduced them to the paddock early that day and had watched them trip about, amazed at the width of the world in which they found themselves.

In late afternoon, after Maggie had left, she walked up the hill to check on the Highlands. She'd a notion she might encounter Les who would be on his way home from the sorting office riding on a wobbly old push-bike he'd picked up for a song from Bert Lowden. It amused her to watch the postman pedalling along the bumpy track, his long legs pumping furiously, and to receive a cheery wave in which there was no hint of recrimination for the way she'd behaved towards him.

There was no sign of Les that evening, though, no sound of hammering drifting across the glen from the farmhouse, no smoke hanging at the chimney head.

She was halfway down the hill on her way back to the hut when the unmistakable whine of the Alvis cut through the evening air.

Beatty forced herself to walk calmly downhill.

Alan Kelso was leaning on the ledge of the teasing board.

'Hello, stranger,' Beatty said. 'Long time no see.'

'My fault,' Alan said. 'Entirely my fault. I apologise.'

'Well, I've been too busy to notice, really,' Beatty told him.

He glanced at the foals who'd come across to inspect him. 'Yes, I can see that,' he said. 'Lovely, aren't they?'

'Lovely if you don't have to feed their mothers every ten minutes.'

'Are they healthy? They look healthy.'

'Yes, they're fine.'

'More to come?'

'Three Highlands.'

'Earmarked for Mr Cleavers?'

'Eventually,' Beatty said.

'You do have to look to the future in this business, don't you?'

It hadn't occurred to Beatty that, in spite of all that had happened, all the changes that had occurred recently, she *was* still looking to the future.

'No bad thing,' she said.

'I'm sorry I haven't been in touch,' he said.

'I know. You've been busy too. Are you back doing your surgery?'

'Started this morning.'

'Do you want to come in?' Beatty asked.

'No,' he said. 'Thanks all the same.'

'Is she waiting for you?'

'Christine? Not tonight.'

Something fell away within her. She had lost him, and she didn't know why.

He said, 'Are you going to the fete on Saturday week?'

'Are you inviting me?'

'It's awkward, Beatty. I can't. I'm sorry.'

'For God's sake, Alan, stop apologising. I've no claim on you.'

'Ah, but you have.'

'Because we went to bed together?' Beatty said. 'That's not my idea of a binding contract. It suited me just as well as it suited you.'

'Don't be so offhand. I care for you.'

'I don't need cared for.'

'I think you do, and just don't know it.'

'You patronising bugger,' she said. 'Just because you gave me a few quid when I needed it doesn't mean you own me.'

'I doubt if anyone will ever own you, Beatty.'

He had slept with her, made love to her, had, by his lights, used her. He was struggling now with his conscience, a real old-fashioned conscience. There were all sorts of reasons why falling love with Alan Kelso had been a mistake. Style, good manners, education were all things she lacked, but the sad fact was that she didn't need him, didn't need anyone. A baby would have changed all that but, fortunately, the baby had been a false alarm.

'Listen,' she said, 'if you've made promises to the teacher, go ahead and keep them. If this is your version of "Goodbye and Don't Cry", Alan, please

259

get on with it. I've better things to do than hang around while you dump me.'

'Trouble is,' Alan said, 'I don't want to dump you.'

'Oh, I see,' Beatty said. 'You want to keep me as your bit on the side, do you? Well, that's not on, Dr Kelso.' Oh, God, she thought, please don't let me cry. 'You're going to marry her, aren't you?'

'That's by no means certain.'

'For God's sake, Alan, I'm not some kid you finagled into bed.' She let out a nasty little 'hah' which was better than dissolving into tears. 'Don't tell me you want us to be friends?'

'I do,' he said. 'Is that insulting?'

'Pretty much,' Beatty told him.

She closed her eyes for half a second and opened them again. There was no breath of breeze across the paddock but on the shoulder of the hill the pines swayed in the warm wind that strayed up from the glen.

The doctor hadn't gone away. He was still there.

She knew that he would always be there.

'Yes,' she said. 'Friends,' then headed for the hut before he could see her tears.

CHAPTER TWENTY-FOUR

Maude had brought him a glass of sherry which he sipped while looking out of the window at magpies squabbling on the lawn. The evening radio programmes had started but, for once, the Brigadier had more to interest him than dance music.

Maude said, 'I hope you don't think I had anything to do with it.'

'No, Maude.' The Brigadier addressed himself to the window pane. 'Christine was right to bring the matter to my attention. Heavens, woman, you'd have had her married to the upstart if you'd had your way.' He finished the sherry, placed the glass on the window ledge, then, picking up his stick, inched round to face them. 'Let's exercise the old brain-box and see if we can deduce who the upstart's stepfather might be and why he has access to information that, by rights, should be confidential. Christine, what do you know of Harrison's history?'

'Not much,' Christine said.

The Brigadier rested his shoulders against the window glass.

Ten years ago he'd have been pacing the room like a Victorian detective, Christine thought, the bit between his teeth.

'He told us where he lives, did he not?'

'Harlwood,' Christine said.

'How on earth he hoped to sustain his deception as far as the altar is beyond me. But who am I to question the intelligence, let alone the morals, of the rising generation.'

'You know who he is, don't you?' said Maude.

'I do,' the Brigadier admitted. 'I think Harrison's stepfather is my lawyer, Geddes Johnston.'

'I didn't even know you had a lawyer,' Maude said.

'Of course I have a lawyer,' the Brigadier retorted. 'Everyone has a lawyer.'

'Where does your lawyer live?' Maude said.

'Harlwood,' said the Brigadier.

'Why haven't we met him?'

'He's my lawyer, Maude, not my bosom pal. In fact, he has been here, rather a long time ago when I employed him to tackle the thorny problem of my estate.'

'I don't think your estate is any of our business,' Maude said. 'What would you like for dinner?'

'Maude, Maude,' the Brigadier said, 'like it or not, it is your business.' He pushed himself from the window and leaned into his stick. 'Christine, dearest, I wonder if you'd be good enough to give me a helping hand. Been on my feet too long and the old pins are beginning to object.'

She offered him her arm which he gripped a little more tightly than usual. He hobbled to the armchair and allowed Christine to ease him down into it. He grunted and, using his free hand, swung his left leg into position as if the limb had lost all power.

'Are you all right?' Maude asked.

'I'm perfectly fine,' the Brigadier answered. 'I'd have preferred not to upset you—or myself, for that matter—by discussing my demise, but it seems it's been forced upon us. I knew Geddes Johnston had a son but I'd always assumed he was blood kin. Mr Johnston is a man of few words, however. Our conversations over the years have been confined to the state of the weather and the rotation of crops. Now, suppose we concoct a wee history of our own for Mr Harrison. Let's say his father dies in or before the war. Widow Harrison remarries. Ross finds himself with a new stepfather who expects him to make something of himself.'

'Which the boy does not,' said Christine. 'He

262

becomes a teacher.'

'Hardly the lowest of the low,' said the Brigadier, 'but nevertheless lacking the stature of a member of the legal profession. Now if I were young Harrison—he of handsome visage and noble mien—I'd be very keen to prove myself.'

'He sets out to marry money,' Christine suggested, 'and fails at that too.'

'Precisely,' said the Brigadier. 'Then, one day, Ross discovers that his college chum lives not far from Harlwood and, conveniently, she's not only a spinster but the ward of a rich old buzzard—his stepfather's client—who will obligingly die one day and leave her all his ill-gotten gains. Plausible?'

'Highly plausible,' Christine said.

'However, there is one fly in young Mr Harrison's ointment.'

'The spinster, being no fool, wants nothing to do with him,' Christine said.

'Yes,' said the Brigadier, 'but there's an even more important detail that somehow escaped Ross Harrison's attention as he rummaged through his stepfather's files.'

'Which is?' said Christine.

'Unfortunately, my dear, you won't inherit much of my so-called fortune.'

'Why ever not?' Maude enquired indignantly.

'Because,' the Brigadier answered, 'I also have a wife.'

*   *   *

The wooden-wheeled, horse-drawn cart that had been used to carry turnips, hay and manure for as long as anyone could remember did not fit behind the Wallis and, four years back, Charley had saved enough from his wages to buy a trailer to replace it. The trailer was beautifully balanced on two stout rubber tyres. It rolled smoothly along the roads even when fully loaded and did not bog down in the fields unless the ground was exceptionally wet.

The track that led from the Kennart road along the glen to the farmhouse had been bedded with stones by old man McCall and in the dry month of May was firm enough to tempt Charley to bump tractor, trailer and all at top speed to the Dhu Loch, which was little more than a stretch of black, brackish water not much larger than a pond.

Les had replaced his Post Office uniform with patched overalls rolled up to expose bare feet and skinny legs. He looked, Charley thought, like some odd bird vaguely related to the heron family as he stalked about in the reeds.

Charley eased the tractor close to the water's edge and cut the engine.

Black smoke puffed from the exhaust stack and the stench of kerosene chased away the cloud of insects that hovered over the shallows.

'Howdy, partner,' Charley said, leaning on the steering wheel.

'Howdy yourself,' said Les. 'I thought you were still lambing.'

'Finished last night. Dad's doing the evenin' round-up.'

'Did you bring a rope?' said Les.

'I brought a rope,' said Charley. 'Is the bike still there?'

'Yep. What's more, I've dug out the forks an' tank.'

'I still think you're daft.' Charley hopped down from the Wallis. 'But what the heck, we'll give it a go an' see what comes up.'

He was almost as keen as Les to retrieve the motorcycle for, as a boy, he and his pals had tried to dislodge the machine from the mud, if only to solve the mystery of how it got there and to whom, if anyone, it belonged. He pulled a stout rope from the trailer, tied one end to the tractor bar and threw the coil to Les.

After two or three minutes' splashing and fumbling, Les looked up, his face, hands and forearms streaked with mud. 'I've secured the front forks and chain housing. Take it steady now, Charley. I don't want her breaking up.'

Charley clambered on to the tractor and started the engine.

'All set?'

'All set.'

The rope tightened and the trailer lifted a little behind him. He worked the gear lever and inched the tractor back in a straight line. The rope sprang taut, flicking water drops in all directions then, with a horrible gobbling sound, the body of the motorcycle emerged from the mud.

'Easy, easy, easy,' Les cried as the machine freed itself, skated like a huge fish through the reeds and before either of the young men could stop it, bumped up on dry ground. 'Whoa!'

The motorcycle lay wet and glistening on the grass like something that had just been born. Charley climbed down and clawed mud from the frame.

'Geeze!' he said. 'Look at that. It's hardly rusted at all.'

'Amazing.' Les hunkered. 'Absolutely amazing. I can't understand why the acids in the water haven't done more damage.'

Charley snatched back his hand. 'What's that?'

The men craned forward, peering at the frond-like thing that snaked about the handlebars.

'Is it alive?' Les asked.

'Naw,' Charley answered. 'Pull it off.'

'You pull it off. You're the farmer.'

'What's that got to do with it?'

'Okay, okay.' Les caught a fistful of the material and tugged it loose. 'It's ribbon, I think. Red ribbon, by the look of it.'

Puzzled, he sat back on his heels. 'Rum,' he said.

'Very rum,' Charley agreed and, with hands that were not quite shaking, reached into his pocket for his cigarettes.

*   *   *

Alan was late returning from Picton. Mrs Mack had gone. He had no appetite to speak of and had mooched about the garden, brooding, with a glass of whisky in his hand for a good half-hour before going indoors to make supper.

He was in process of putting a pie in the oven when Christine showed up. She did not have the dog with her and was so out of breath that he almost had to help her into the kitchen.

'I'm sorry for calling so late but I have to talk to someone.'

'Well, here I am,' Alan said. 'All ears.'

'It's the Brigadier.'

'Is he ill?'

'No, not ill—married.'

266

'Good God! How did he manage that at his age?'

Christine tugged off her headscarf. 'Not now. Years ago.'

'All right, take a deep breath, calm down and tell me all about it.'

Alan filled the kettle and put it on the stove while Christine told him how the Brigadier had revealed his secret.

'I know precious little about the workings of the Scottish legal system,' Alan said when she had finished, 'but I'm fairly sure a man can dispose of his chattels any way he wishes—with certain provisos, of course.'

'Provisos like a wife he hasn't clapped eyes on for fifteen years,' Christine said. 'He's tried to change the terms of his will, apparently, but the woman—her name's Irene—refuses to divorce him. He even sent his lawyer to negotiate with her but it came to nothing.'

'When did he marry her?'

'In 1911. He was almost sixty. She was twenty-two. He met her at a regimental ball and fell head over heels in love. I still don't understand why he kept it from us.'

'Well,' said Alan, 'it does rather smack of folly.'

'I don't think he ever got over her.'

'How long did they live together?'

'About three years, I think, or even less.'

'Where's the woman now?'

'Eastbourne.'

'Eastbourne?'

'She's English, you see.'

'That's no excuse for living in Eastbourne,' Alan said. 'What is she—forty-two, forty-three? Not old by today's standards. Why hasn't she married again?'

'She knows the Brigadier will die eventually and provided she can prove the marriage is still valid she'll inherit most of his worldly goods.'

'What worldly goods?' said Alan.

'I've no idea,' said Christine. 'Preaching Friar for one thing, I suppose.'

'I'm surprised Crockett's lawyer hasn't managed to sever the knot. There must be lots of precedents. Predatory women marrying old soldiers was commonplace before and during the war. I take it no children came of the union?'

'Sandy said nothing about children.'

'Has he been paying her a pension?'

'It's possible. He's generous by nature.'

The kettle hissed on the hot-plate. Alan ignored it.

'Did the Brigadier marry in England or did he bring the girl to Scotland to be married here? That's something you'll have to find out. Domicile is important.'

'I don't really care about his money,' Christine said. 'I care more about him. I can't help feeling he's let us—I mean, my mother—down.'

'He loves you, you know,' Alan said. 'You're all he has to hang on to.'

'Ah, but it turns out I'm not.'

'How can you possibly be jealous of a woman you never heard of before tonight, a woman who drifted out of the Brigadier's life long before you knew him? You're not his daughter, are you?'

'My mother never set eyes on Sandy Crockett until we arrived in Ottershaw.'

'Are you sure?'

268

'Of course I'm sure. I'm not Sandy Crockett's daughter, so don't go supposing I am. However, he has taken care of my mother and me for all these years and I—I don't want to be without him.' She looked up. 'He's really all I have.'

'Not quite true.'

'Who else is there?'

Alan was suddenly on his guard. 'Well,' he said, 'there's always Mr Harrison.'

'That isn't even funny.'

'The next move must come from the Brigadier,' Alan said. 'It's up to him to sue for divorce and make it stick.'

'How could he do that?'

'Pay the woman off.'

'Can he do that—legally, I mean?'

'I don't see why not,' Alan said. 'On the other hand, she may have no claim on him at all or— think of it this way—she may die before he does. Stranger things have happened.'

Christine rose and put on her headscarf.

'Thank you,' she said. 'You've been very helpful.'

'I'm glad,' he said. 'Now, how about some tea?'

'Tea?' she said. 'No, no tea. I've troubled you enough as it is.'

'You haven't troubled me at all,' he said. 'Won't you stay a little longer?'

'I think not,' she said.

'In that case,' Alan said, 'I'll drive you home.'

'I'm perfectly capable of—'

'I know you are,' he said, 'and I'm perfectly capable of driving you home—which is precisely what I intend to do, whether you like it or not.'

＊　　　＊　　　＊

There was firelight in the long window of the sitting-room. The strains of a radio orchestra floated in the air like the smell of honeysuckle. The Alvis smelled of leather and cigarette smoke. The seat creaked when he leaned across to open the passenger door. When his arm brushed her breast he drew back and kissed her. She let out a gasp. He kissed her again, as surprised as she was to find his mouth on hers.

'Saturday?' he said.

'Yes, Saturday.'

'Goodnight, Chris.'

'Goodnight, Alan,' she said and went off into the house.

＊　　　＊　　　＊

Bruce was curled up in his basket in the kitchen. Maude had helped the Brigadier to bed and had gone to bed too. Christine, though, was still wide awake. All that had happened that day, and Alan's unexpected kiss, had left her restless.

It was close to midnight when a muffled thump brought her upright in bed.

Scraping, shuffling, a door opening and closing; she threw on her dressing-gown and hurried downstairs just in time to catch a glimpse of Bruce pattering across the hall. Her first instinct was to cry for help but the dog appeared more playful than anxious. She followed him around the corner to what had been—indeed, still was—the Brigadier's study.

The narrow little room was hardly ever used.

Her mother gave the roll-top desk and bow-fronted bookcase a whisk with a feather duster now and then and chased spiders from the shelves where the Brigadier's mementoes, more sporting than military, were ranked. Christine watched the Scottie dab at the door and, tail wagging, open it just enough to slip into the room. Light from a desk lamp seeped across the hall and, to her relief, she heard the Brigadier's gruff whisper: 'Sit now, sit like a good lad. No barking or you'll be out on your ear.' When she heard the click of a lock and the rattle of the desk top, inquisitiveness got the better of her. She pushed open the study door. Bruce whined but, as if he were party to his master's game, did not greet her with his usual noisy fervour.

The Brigadier was clad in his oldest dressing-gown, a frayed ankle-length garment of patterned silk that Maude said made him look like Aladdin's wicked uncle. He spun round from the desk so quickly that the robe billowed open and exposed his white shanks and bony ankles.

He staggered, gripped the edge of the desk and groped for his stick.

'Damn it to hell, Christine!' he snapped. 'Can't a man have a bit of privacy in his own house even in the middle of the night?'

'I thought you might be ill.'

'If you keep sneaking up on me like that, I will be ill.'

She gave him her arm and helped him to the swivel chair. The Brigadier sank gratefully on to the pocked and faded leather and for ten or fifteen seconds concentrated on regaining his breath.

'Caught,' he said, at length. 'Caught red-handed.

271

Can't get off with anything in this house, can I? It's worse than being a prisoner of the Boers.'

'Nonsense, Sandy. You were never a prisoner of the Boers.'

'Might have been, though, might well have been. Did I ever tell you about my tour in the Transvaal?'

'I'd much rather you told me why you're wandering about in the dark.'

'Couldn't sleep.'

'Do your legs hurt?'

'It's my heart,' he said. 'Well, not so much my heart as my head.'

'Were you thinking of her?'

'Can't help but think of her with all that stuff coming out and Maude blathering on and on about it. Don't suppose you've any notion what it means to an old man to have his memory shaken up like salts in a bottle.'

'I don't suppose I have,' Christine said. 'But that doesn't explain what you're doing in the study.'

'Look in the little drawer at the top right-hand side of the desk,' he said, 'and you'll find a key.'

Christine opened the drawer and brought out a small, not-quite-rusty key. She held it up between finger and thumb, like a minnow.

'That's it,' the Brigadier said. 'It fits the lock of the drawer below the three pigeon holes on the left. Open the drawer, slide it out and bring it to me.'

The key fitted easily into the tiny lock but the drawer was difficult to dislodge. It took Christine half a minute to free it.

She placed it on the Brigadier's lap.

'Haven't looked in here for some time,' he said.

272

'Haven't felt the need.'

Bruce placed a paw on the arm of his master's chair, peeped into the drawer and sneezed. The Brigadier pushed the Scottie away and extracted from the drawer a postcard-size photograph which he passed on to Christine.

'That's her,' he said. 'That's my Irene.'

'She's beautiful.'

'She is,' the Brigadier said. 'Or, should I say, she was. I shudder to think what the years might have done to her. I mean, look what they've done to me.'

'When was this taken?'

'In 1911, March 10th, a Friday. Drayton's Studios in Regent Street. We were married by special licence and held a wedding breakfast—Irene's idea—in the Café Royal. Ten or a dozen of my chums were there, together with Irene's sister, Gladys, and several of her friends.'

'What about her—Irene's parents?'

'They weren't invited.'

'Why ever not?'

The Brigadier shrugged. 'Her father was a miner from a village I'd never heard of somewhere in Derbyshire. Irene assured me that neither he nor her mother would be interested in attending. I had the distinct feeling that the girls were ashamed of their parents—or perhaps it was the other way around. I never did meet them. We saw a fair bit of Gladys, though. She took up with one of my friends, Major Leonard—Iain—whom she later married.'

'What happened to Major Leonard?'

'He went down on the Messines Ridge. June, 1917.'

'And Gladys?'

'I have absolutely no idea,' the Brigadier said. 'Irene and I parted company before mobilisation. I was involved in planning the landing of the Expeditionary Force in France and was here, there and everywhere on battalion business. Irene didn't care for barracks life. She stayed in a rented flat in Marylebone High Street which, as she kept reminding me, wasn't exactly Mayfair.'

'Sandy,' said Christine quietly, 'were there other men?'

'Several.'

'Why didn't you divorce her at that time?'

'I had a war to fight, two battalions and a division of tanks to command,' the Brigadier said. 'Besides, I still . . .'

'Loved her?'

'Had hope.'

'And after the war?'

'The last I saw of Irene was just before I retired to Preaching Friar. We lunched at Simpson's. I wasn't in great shape. I think she was rather disappointed I hadn't copped it in France. Silly girl should have realised that brigade commanders rarely venture anywhere near the fighting. I wanted her back but she was having none of it. I offered to divorce her but she wouldn't wear that either. The lunch straggled on into the evening. I didn't want to let her go, you see. I thought, foolishly, that she was the best thing that had ever happened to me, that ever would happen to me. I agreed to pay her a monthly sum in lieu of a settlement in the hope that she'd be grateful.'

'Which she wasn't, of course.'

'Actually, after her fashion, she was.'

He fished in the drawer again and brought out a bundle of cards fastened with a wrinkled rubber band. He picked off the band, shuffled the cards and displayed them. 'Irene had the decency—the guile, perhaps you'll say—to keep in touch. Christmas, always Christmas, my birthday, an occasional seaside postcard enclosed in an envelope. "Darling Sandy", always "Darling Sandy", always signed, "Your Loving Wife".'

'In other words she wasn't going to let you forget her.'

'As if I could.'

'Did you correspond with her?'

'Cards, just cards; a word here and there.'

'And gifts?'

'No, no gifts.'

'Did she ever ask for money?'

'Never did.' The Brigadier boxed the cards and returned them to the drawer. He glanced up at Chris and smiled, sheepishly. 'Irene was a girl in a million as far as I was concerned, the only girl in the world until you came along. Have no fear, Christine. I'm an old fool, but not that much of an old fool. When I went in search of a housekeeper and unearthed your mother, I was convinced I wanted someone to look after me. It didn't take me long to realise that what I really wanted was someone to look after. Which is why we're in the pickle we're in right now.' He passed her the drawer to put away. 'I suppose I should thank that rogue Harrison for giving me a shake. I've let things drift for far too long. I must do something about Irene. I owe her nothing, nothing at all compared to what I owe you.'

'I wish you wouldn't talk like that.'

'Would you believe,' he said, 'that I used to hold the fate of five thousand men in my hand? Now look at me. Dear Lord, I'm so feeble in mind and body that I can't even take care of you properly.'

'You've always taken care of me,' Christine said. 'I'll always be grateful for it, more grateful than you can possibly imagine.'

'Grateful enough to get that dog out from under my feet and help me back to bed?' the Brigadier said. 'I'll write to Geddes Johnston on Monday and put my cards on the table. It's time he knew what his stepson's up to, and high time he found a legal way to cut Irene out of a share of my estate.'

'I'm sure that won't be too difficult,' Christine said.

'Oh, but it will,' the Brigadier said. 'You don't know Irene.'

Then, taking Christine's arm, he let her guide him through the darkened hallway with the Scottie pattering at his heels.

CHAPTER TWENTY-FIVE

Parish minister and parish priest were the best of friends and often shared a tipple in the manse. There were few Roman Catholics in Ottershaw, not many more in Kennart and none at all in Greenhill where, in a tiny chapel near the school, Father Donovan conducted mass for his scant congregation.

When the clergymen met at the gate of the glebe that May morning, however, it was weather not religion that concerned them.

276

The glebe was a broad skirt of grazing land owned by the Church. Until last century it had provided the minister with a portion of his livings. The ground was still let for sheep but the present incumbent, Reverend Willie Williams, received a salary in lieu of mutton and no share of the ground rent. On Friday evening the sheep had been driven off to temporary pasture, while gangs of men and boys erected tents and open-sided stalls and dragged tables and chairs and all sorts of weird paraphernalia from the village hall to be put in place first thing on Saturday.

When the morning of the fete dawned bright and clear priest and pastor, together with most parishioners, regarded it as more of a miracle than a meteorological anomaly.

'We prayed for good weather, of course,' Mr Williams announced.

'And so did we,' said Father Donovan.

'There are more of us,' Mr Williams pointed out.

'Ah, but we lit candles.'

'I didn't know you could light candles for fine weather.'

'Can light candles for just about anything. Look round you, man.' Father Donovan waved an arm. 'It worked, didn't it?'

'Aye,' said Mr Williams. 'God heard our prayers all right. But tell me, Sean, if there's a sudden deluge before teatime, will you take the blame for it?'

'Not I,' said Father Donovan. 'Floods are all your fault.'

'Because Noah was allegedly an Ulsterman?'

'Precisely.'

Members of Ottershaw's Boys' Brigade company might hold their minister in awe and be suspicious of the priest but no such respect was accorded to Charley Noonan who, when out of BB uniform, was really just one of the lads. Surrounded by boys, small and large, he was kneeling on the grass with a mallet in his hand giving the pegs of the big marquee a last tap or two when the Post Office van zoomed up to the field gate and squealed to a halt.

Mr Woodcock loped across the grass and, vaulting guy ropes and sundry other obstacles, approached his farmer friend.

'What,' he said, 'are we gonna do about Beatty?'

Charley sat back on his heels. 'What's wrong with Beatty?'

'Says she ain't coming this afternoon.'

'What?' said Charley. 'For why?'

'Don't know for why. Do you?'

'Not me. She isn't mad at me.'

'She isn't mad at me either,' said Les.

A group of boys gathered round Charley like bodyguards and when he got to his feet clamoured to relieve him of his mallet, which Charley handed off without a second thought.

'Beats always shows up for the fete,' he said. 'One time she loaned us a couple of ponies but that didn't work out too well, though no one blamed her for what happened.'

'What did happen?' said Les.

'One stallion; one mare. Big mistake. 'Nuff said?'

' 'Nuff said.'

'Is she sulkin', do you think?' Charley asked.

'You know her better than I do,' Les answered.

'But if you ask me, I'd say she was pining.'

A yell rose from the skirts of the tent. Charley looked over his shoulder at a lanky boy who was sucking his fingers and hopping about on one leg with the mallet lying at his feet.

'Careful, guys,' Charley growled, then, to Les, repeated the word, 'Pining?'

'What it looks like to me,' Les said. 'My sister, Pearl, gets that way when she's love-sick.'

'Beatty's not love-sick, is she? I mean,' said Charley, 'she's a grown woman.'

'Grown women get it too,' Les said. 'I figure it's the Doc.'

'Kelso?' said Charley, scowling. 'Geeze, do you think he's got her in the family way? If he has an' he's left her in the lurch, I'll beat the bugger's brains out.'

'Take it easy,' Les said. 'I don't think it's that at all. She's just sitting on her porch moping, like, and positive she ain't coming out to play.'

'Are the ponies okay?'

'Far as I know,' Les said. 'Maggie says they're fine.'

'Was Maggie there?'

'Yep.'

'Are you bringin' Maggie to the fete?'

'I'm not interested in Maggie,' Les said. 'Are you?'

'God, no!' said Charley. 'Anybody takes on Maggie Thomas gets the whole blasted family thrown in. No, no, no.' He hesitated. 'If the Doc's bowed out, though, I might be interested in another party.'

'You mean Beatty?'

'I do mean Beatty.'

279

'Funny that,' Les said.

'What's funny about it?'

'I'm interested in that party too.'

'Uh-huh!' said Charley quietly. 'So it's every man for himself, is it?'

'Or maybe, just for today, a little bit of teamwork might be in order.'

'What do you mean—teamwork?' said Charley.

*   *   *

The setting up of a beer tent at the Ottershaw and District fete was a contentious issue but after several rowdy meetings of the Community Fellowship, it had been agreed, though by no means unanimously, that it was better to serve light alcoholic refreshment—no spirits—on the ground than have men and boys slipping off to the pub across the road or slyly slugging whisky behind the chemical toilets.

Beatty couldn't help but dwell on how pleasant it would be on a warm afternoon to sit on the grass with a glass in her hand listening to bagpipers vying for attention or watching wee boys and girls ride the rocking boat or, with mum or dad close at hand, tiptoeing across the fairy bridge to collect a handful of sweets. Even more pleasurable was the display of muscular young farmers tossing the hay bale or, balanced like ballet dancers, attempting to walk the length of a stripped pine pole slathered with axle grease without damaging their family jewels.

She'd always had fun at the Ottershaw fete—the year of the ponies excepted.

She preferred to go with a man, though, even if

it was only Charley. Too many temptations otherwise, too many drunken louts, too many married men who saw her as an easy target just because she lived alone in a hut under the railway bridge and was known to enjoy a pint.

All that had gone, though, all the innocent possibilities that never came to anything but ran through the afternoon like a tingle in the blood. That, Dr Kelso, she thought morosely, is what you've taken from me. Worst of all, I don't even have the heart to blame you for it. However bold I am, though, however self-reliant, I will not turn up at the fete to see you fawn over your school teacher.

She was still sitting on the doorstep at twenty minutes to two o'clock, still stubbornly brooding, when Mr Charles Noonan and Mr Leslie Woodcock rode into Picton on the Wallis tractor and drew up in front of the hut.

'What do you think, Charley?' Les Woodcock said. 'Will she do?'

'Dunno,' said Charley. 'She don't look like she'd be much fun.'

'Might be better when she's dolled up, like.'

'Look at the face on her, though. Could curdle milk, a face like that.'

'I've heard a rumour she smiles now and then.'

'Aye, third Monday in every month an' one extra in leap year.'

'No good then?' Les said.

'Nah, no good,' said Charley.

'All right, all right.' Beatty slapped her hands to her thighs and projected herself to her feet. 'Give me five minutes to change and you can do what you like with me.'

'Now there's a tempting offer,' Les said.

'Best we've had all day,' said Charley.

'Sod off, the both of you,' Beatty told them and vanished into the hut to unearth her summer frock.

* * *

Lunch was served early to allow Christine time to dress and do her hair. She came down looking lovely, so the Brigadier declared. With ten or fifteen minutes to spare before Alan was due to collect her, she fiddled with the radiogram in the hope of finding dance music or some other programme that might entertain the old man while she was gone.

Reception on Saturday afternoon was not of the best. Fragments of jazz were interspersed with urgent voices announcing sporting events and at one point a sudden burst of classical music that the Brigadier dismissed, scathingly, as 'blasted Bach'. Eventually Chris put on one of his favourite gramophone records—the High Hatters tearing through 'Sing You Sinners'—that set the Brigadier's feet tapping and Christine spinning gaily around the room.

She knew he was watching her, admiring her and she wondered if he was comparing her to Irene in some other time, some other tempo, when he had been as happy as she was now.

'Your mother can't stand that song. Thinks it's immoral.'

'I suppose it is, in a way,' Christine said, still whirling. 'But what the hell!'

The Brigadier chuckled. 'Salty talk like that will shock the socks off your Mr Kelso, you know.'

'I doubt if he's quite as sensitive as all that.'

'You're happy with this chap, aren't you?'

'I am,' said Christine. 'Very.'

'Don't let it slip away.'

'I've no intention of letting it slip away.'

'Bring him back for dinner.'

'He may have other plans,' Christine said.

'Oh, really!' said the Brigadier. 'Like what?'

'Who knows?' Christine said. 'Who cares?'

She started the record at the beginning once more then as the Alvis drew into the drive, flirted over to the armchair and kissed the old man on the brow.

'Do you know, my dear,' the Brigadier said, 'if I had my life to live over again I think I'd learn to play the saxophone.'

'What on earth brought that on?'

'Dreaming,' he said, 'just dreaming,' and sent her off to enjoy herself with a smile and a wave of the hand.

*   *   *

Tea tent and beer tent had been going great guns all afternoon. Mr Williams and Father Donovan, in ecumenical harmony, divided their time between one and the other, smiling and chatting to parishioners.

Only down in the bear pit, as Charley called it, where the shies were situated was there conflict or, rather, a little too much competition while he and Mr Woodcock—no mean hand with a horseshoe or an air pistol—dragged poor Beatty round the stalls, showing off to her like mad.

Charley had the advantage in that an honour

283

guard from the Boys' Brigade accompanied him and cheered every time his horseshoe hooked the stake or a pellet from his air rifle clipped the paper target. Then Mr Woodcock, waggling his fingers and measuring his shot, would mutter, 'So that's the way of it,' in his strange, vowel-flattened accent and, with a shimmy of his lean hips, draw a bead and smugly top his rival's score.

'Damn it, man, you've been practising,' said Charley.

'Pure natural talent,' said Les.

'How far can you toss a hay bale?' said Charley.

'Further than you can, I'll bet,' said Les.

That was the last straw for Beatty. Firmly, she led the men away from the sawdust rinks and, arms linked, steered them, not unwillingly, up the slope to the beer tent which, like its tea-stained neighbour, was pretty much a bedlam.

Charley and Les argued about who would buy the first round and might have been arguing still if Beatty hadn't given them a shove and told them, in plain speech, that she was dying of thirst and could probably handle two half-pint glasses if it wouldn't break the bank. She watched the men, still gabbing, wade into the crowd. Moving away from the mouth of the tent, she rested her shoulders against the sagging canvas and surveyed the sunlit field in search of Alan.

Then, as if she'd conjured him up by wishing, he appeared before her.

'Where did you spring from?' she asked.

'The tea tent. We've been queuing for what seems like hours.'

'We?'

'Christine—Miss Summers and me.'

284

'Where is she?'

'Gone to powder her nose.'

'Powder her nose?' said Beatty. 'Hasn't she learned how to pee yet?'

'Beatty,' he said, 'don't be cruel.' He looked at her and then away. 'I've never been to one of these things before. Marion loved them. I can see why. Great fun, isn't it?'

'Yes,' Beatty said. 'Great fun.'

'Can I fetch you something; a glass of beer, perhaps?'

'I'm being taken care of, thank you.'

'Beatty,' he said, 'I'm truly sorry at the way things worked out.'

She shrugged. 'Or didn't.'

'Yes, or didn't.'

'You're better off with her,' Beatty said. 'She's young enough to keep you on your toes. Any roads, I'd never desert my ponies for a mere doctor.'

'Is that all I am, Beatty? A mere doctor?'

'Yeah,' she said. 'Nothing special.'

'Well, you were—you are rather special, Mrs McCall.'

'I'm almost tempted to believe you,' Beatty said. 'Perhaps you'd better cut along before Miss Summers catches us together and has another fit of the vapours.'

'She isn't too sure of herself, I'll admit.'

'She isn't too sure of you, you mean.'

'I'm not even sure of myself these days.'

'I wouldn't tell her that, if I were you,' Beatty said. 'You're supposed to be a paragon of all the virtues, remember. Don't disillusion the poor kid just yet.'

'What's this? Advice from the lovelorn?'

'Lovelorn? Don't flatter yourself, Dr Kelso.'

'To the lovelorn, that's what I meant to say.'

'However you say it . . .' Beatty began and then, nudging him with her elbow, nodded down the slope to the coppice of birch trees in whose shadow the toilets had been erected. 'Isn't that your little teacher, nose all freshly powdered, heading this way? I think you'd better go now, Alan.'

The doctor stood his ground.

*　　　　*　　　　*

The ladies' toilet had a double flap at the entrance and a sagging canvas roof to keep out flies. The gentlemen's convenience, thirty yards to the right, was much less sophisticated, being nothing but a long trench hidden behind a shoulder-high wall of hay bales and tarpaulins.

Fastidious females trotted off to the cloakroom in the Vosper Halls three hundred yards down the road but Christine was reluctant to leave Alan alone for long and, swallowing her pride, joined the unruly queue of mothers and girl children at the flap.

There was a certain amount of giggling from the girls of Greenhill Infants at the sight of their teacher lining up to relieve herself and, behind Christine's back, a few guffaws from the boys, Johnny Thomas among them, who, for some unfathomable reason, chose to hang about the lavatories rather than the beer tent.

'Dirty devils,' said a voice behind her. 'It is a beating they are in need of.'

Summer's day or not, Lucille McKay was

wrapped in a peacock shawl and a long red flannel skirt that, together with her bangles and beads, gave her the appearance of a gypsy fortune-teller.

'Freddy has been looking to find you.'

'Has he?' Christine said. 'Why?'

'Today, this post this morning, he received a letter from that man.'

'Mr Harrison, do you mean?'

'Him, yes, the controller deputy.'

'Surely Freddy hasn't been sacked after all?'

'No, nothing like that,' Lucille McKay said. 'It is a sorry letter in which the man offers apology to Frederick and his congratulations on the work he is doing for advancement in Greenhill School.'

'Good Lord!' said Christine. 'Freddy must be pleased.'

'Full of delight.'

'Where is Freddy now?'

'In the tent with the beer.'

'Of course,' Christine said. 'I'll go and have a word with him.'

'I see you have the doctor secured,' Lucille said.

Christine raised an eyebrow. 'Secured?'

'He is your man now, no?'

'I wouldn't go that far.'

'Oh, but you *will* go far with him,' Lucille said. 'He is the right man for you.'

'Well, thank you for saying so.'

'So handsome, so handsome,' Lucille McKay said and pushed Christine forward into the odorous enclosure to powder her nose.

*   *   *

For a split second Christine thought she might

faint. There was something so protective in the way Alan leaned over the pony woman that they might have been husband and wife. Her knees buckled as she climbed the slope towards the couple. She was unaware of the children who flew about her or the crowd that flooded from the big marquee clutching cups, saucers and plates laden with sandwiches and home-baked scones. She stepped over the litter and around the boys that Charley had delegated to retrieve the crockery and return it to the wash tubs. She moved blindly into the throng at the mouth of the small marquee, into the stench of spilled beer and tobacco smoke, into a froth of doubt that Alan did nothing to dispel. And then she was rescued from misery by Charley Noonan and Les, the postman, who, juggling glasses, elbowed out of the crowd and, with barely a nod to dear Dr Kelso, scooped up the pony woman and carried her away.

Grinning, Alan took Christine's arm.

'What a bunch they are,' he said. 'They'll all be plastered by nightfall.'

'I doubt it.' Christine pulled him close. 'Charley's far too sensible to make a fool of himself in public. I don't know about her, though. Will she be all right?'

'The lads will look after her,' Alan said. 'She's not my problem.'

'Isn't she?' Christine said.

'You're my problem,' Alan said, 'just you and no one else.'

She felt a great rush of affection, of love, well up in her.

'I think I like being your problem, Alan,' she said.

The canvas smelled hot behind her and the din from the tents melted into a strange, soothing hum. She had a vague notion that she should go in search of Freddy, had made a promise of sorts to Freddy's wife, but she had lost all volition, all sense of obligation to anyone or anything.

Charley Noonan grabbed her arm. 'Chris,' he said, 'isn't that your mam?'

She followed the line of Charley's finger and saw beyond the low stone wall that bordered the glebe her mother with her arms raised up above her head and heard, faintly, the screeching that came from her mother's throat.

Heads turned one after another: minister, priest, pony woman and postman. Boys rose from the grass like dragon's teeth. Alan's housekeeper, Mrs Mackintosh, upset her teacup, and Freddy and his wife, glasses in hand, emerged from the beer tent to see what the fuss was all about.

By then Chris was running wildly towards the gate.

'Mama,' she cried. 'Mama, what's wrong?'

CHAPTER TWENTY-SIX

Peacetime reorganisation had thinned the ranks of the Gordon Highlanders but soon after the obituary notices appeared in the *Scotsman* and *The Times* letters of condolence trickled in from officers and men who had served with the Brigadier and remembered him for his courage and good humour.

Maude read every card and letter and Christine

acknowledged them.

Because Sandy Crockett's death had been unexpected, Dr Tom Currie was obliged to report the circumstances to Fiscal authorities and, to be on the safe side, had arranged for the body to be taken away late on Saturday evening. Poor Sandy had lain under a sheet in the mortuary in Stirling for thirty-six hours until the Procurator's office had sensibly agreed that heart failure was the cause of death and that chopping up the corpse of an eighty-year-old veteran would serve no purpose at all. Sandy's body, still intact, was delivered to a funeral home in Stirling to await the issuing of a death certificate and the instructions of Sandy's next of kin as to the form the funeral would take.

The Brigadier's parents and sister were buried in the graveyard in Kennart, a lovely green place below the big hill, but the Brigadier had been adamant that he had no wish to be laid to rest so far from Preaching Friar and that a plot in Ottershaw's new cemetery would suit him perfectly well.

On Monday at lunchtime Freddy called to inform Chris that a temporary replacement—no, not Mr Harrison—had been brought in to cover her absence but that he would be darned glad to have her back as soon as she felt up to it.

'If I'm still here, Freddy.'

'What do you mean—if you're still here?'

'The house doesn't belong to us.'

'Oh, yes, of course,' Freddy said, and tactfully changed the subject.

On Monday evening Alan drove from the hospital to Preaching Friar to share an early supper with Christine and her mother. They ate in the kitchen and stayed in the kitchen, for Maude could not bring herself to enter the sitting-room where she had found the Brigadier's body. Christine too was upset by the sight of the armchair in which the Brigadier had passed away with Bruce snoozing at his feet and the radio playing.

'I thought he was sleeping. I thought he was sleeping. I honestly thought he was sleeping.' Maude went on and on, remorselessly, until Christine told her to stop.

As soon as supper was over Alan and Chris left to walk the dog.

Bruce was subdued, his bewilderment palpable. He scratched and whined at the closed door of the sitting-room, snuffled and sniffed around the garden and hugged Christine's heels, head down, as if he feared that she too might vanish if he went rooting in the ditch.

'He doesn't know what to do with himself,' Christine said. 'He's lost.'

'Aren't you?' Alan said.

'Of course I am. I've no idea what will become of us. I'm doing the best I can but I feel as if—oh, I don't know.' She burst into tears and buried her face in Alan's shoulder. 'I—I don't know who I'm crying for—Sandy or myself.'

'Little bit of both, I think.'

Alan gave her a handkerchief. She wiped her eyes and blew her nose.

Bruce squatted by her ankles, staring up at her, head cocked.

'What are you looking at, daftie?' she said then, mouth crumpling once more, added, 'Oh, I'm so silly, so silly, aren't I?' and wept again.

291

When they arrived back at Preaching Friar they found Ross Harrison's Wolseley parked outside the house. Ross was seated behind the wheel smoking a pipe and reading a newspaper. As soon as Alan and Christine appeared, he put the pipe on the dashboard, tossed the paper into the back seat and climbed out of the car.

Bruce growled and might have thrown himself on the intruder if Chris hadn't grabbed his collar. Holding the wriggling Scottie in check, she said, 'What do you want here, Ross? Go away.'

'First,' Ross Harrison said, 'may I say how sorry I am—'

'Yes, yes. Now please go away.'

'My stepfather's inside,' Ross said. 'He'd have been here sooner but he was visiting friends at the weekend and I had the devil's own job tracking him down. He was as shocked as I was to hear what happened. If there's anything I can do to lighten your burden—'

'Nothing, thank you.'

'My stepfather's here officially, you know. It may come as a surprise but—'

'I know who he is and why he's here,' Christine said.

'You won't tell him about us, will you?'

'I made you a promise and I'll keep it.'

'May I come in?'

'No,' Christine said, 'you may not.'

*　　　*　　　*

292

When Alan stepped into the dining-room he drew up with start at the sight of the gentleman from nowhere, grey spats and all, standing by the window with a teacup and saucer in his hand.

'Good God!' Alan said. 'It's you!'

'Indeed, it is.'

'Why didn't you tell me you were Crockett's lawyer?'

'The subject never came up.'

'Well,' said Alan, 'given that we are about to do business—'

'Are we?' Geddes Johnston said. 'Without wishing to give offence, may I ask if you are related to the deceased?'

'No, I'm not—as you know perfectly well.'

'To Maude Summers?'

'No. Where is Mrs Summers, by the way?'

'Infusing more tea, I believe,' the lawyer said. 'She was somewhat overwhelmed by my appearance. I suspect the infusing of tea is an excuse to make herself scarce. You—Dr Kelso, isn't it?' Alan nodded. 'You, I take it, have struck up an acquaintance with Miss Summers with whom, as I recall, you were quite enamoured when you first spotted her from the train.'

'I'd hardly say enamoured.'

'But you are enamoured now, are you not?'

'I'm a friend—a friend of the family.'

'You didn't waste much time, Dr Kelso, did you?' Geddes Johnston put cup and saucer on the dining-table, dug a stubby briar and a box of matches from his pocket and lit his pipe. 'Are you no longer travelling by train?' he asked.

'I've bought a motorcar. An Alvis.'

'I find the railway more convenient,' Geddes

293

Johnston said. 'Miss Summers doesn't much care for my stepson, does she?'

'I don't believe she does, no.'

'Has he given her reason to dislike him?'

'You must ask her that yourself,' Alan said.

Christine, he guessed, was upstairs in the bathroom attempting to repair the damage wrought by her tearful outburst.

Alan lit a cigarette and tried to compose himself.

He was uncomfortable in the presence of the gentleman who, in his loneliness, he had stupidly supposed was more friend than acquaintance. He experienced a prickle of resentment at the realisation that he had been duped. He assumed that the lawyer's blunt questions were intended to keep him off balance. It also occurred to him that stepfather and stepson might be in cahoots and that Johnston, lawyer or not, was not to be trusted.

'Are you Brigadier Crockett's sole executor?' he asked.

'I am, so nominated.'

'I take it you're here about the will?'

'I'm here to offer my sympathy.'

'But that's not all, is it?' Alan said.

'No, that's not all—which is why I would prefer you to leave.'

'And why I would prefer Dr Kelso to stay,' said Christine from the doorway.

She had washed her face and applied a little make-up to restore colour to her cheeks but her eyes were still red.

The lawyer delivered a nod by way of greeting. 'Miss Summers.'

'Mr Johnston.'

'I see that you know who I am?'

'The Brigadier told me all about you.'

'Did he?' No surprise showed on the lawyer's face, no emotion at all. 'Did he also tell you that he has a wife?'

The blow was low, Alan thought, deliberately intended to unsettle Chris and put her in her place. He moved around the dining-table and stood by her side, not touching, not quite.

'He did,' Chris said. 'I take it, Mr Johnston, you've informed Mrs Crockett that she is now a widow.'

'I have.'

'By telegram or telephone?'

'I don't quite see the point of your question.'

'The point of my question,' Christine informed him, 'is to discover just how much communication you've had with Irene Crockett and what the nature of that communication might be.'

'I know where she is, if that's what you mean.'

'Telegram or telephone?' Christine persisted.

'Telephone.'

'You talked with her?'

'I did.'

'So,' Christine said, 'when may we expect her?'

'That,' Geddes Johnston said, 'depends.'

'On what?'

'On the funeral arrangements?'

'Surely it's up to you and Mrs Crockett to make the arrangements.'

'Have you done nothing?'

'I've done what had to be done,' Christine said.

'And what, if I may ask, is that?'

'In accordance with the Brigadier's wishes,' said Christine, 'he will be buried in Ottershaw new

295

cemetery. I've been in touch with the funeral directors this afternoon by telephone from the public box. They've received the death certificate from the Fiscal's office, the death has been duly registered and they are free to proceed. They require us—someone—to call at the funeral home to deliver a suit for the Brigadier and to choose a coffin.'

'Will he not be laid out here?'

'Not unless Mrs Crockett wishes it.'

'Mrs Crockett does not wish it. What else?'

'The Brigadier was emphatic: no service in church. The coffin will be brought from Stirling on the morning of the funeral. Mr Williams has agreed to hold a short service for friends and—and family here in Preaching Friar, after which we will follow the cortège to the cemetery for the interment.'

'A trifle unusual, is it not?'

'Modest,' said Christine, 'which is how the Brigadier liked things. Of course, Mr Johnston, if Mrs Crockett prefers something more flamboyant, it's not too late to order a gun-carriage and plumed horses.'

'No horses, Miss Summers, thank you,' Geddes Johnston said. 'I've no quibble with what you've done so far. When do you propose that the committal takes place?'

'Friday morning at eleven,' Christine said. 'Service here at ten fifteen. Someone will have to visit the funeral office tomorrow to make a decision about the coffin, the flowers and motorcars.'

'You may do that.'

'Won't Mrs Crockett wish to be consulted?'

'That won't be necessary.'

'When will Mrs Crockett arrive?'

'Friday.'

'In time for the funeral?'

'No,' the lawyer answered. 'In time for the reading of the will.'

*   *   *

Two Highland mares gave birth in the high pasture in the small hours of Sunday morning. Beatty left them to get on with it. It was noon before she trailed up the hill lugging a sack of feed. As soon as the foals found their feet, she would lure them down to the paddock where she could keep a weather eye on them. The breed was hardy and the mares made good mothers but she was extra cautious now that Alan had gone from her—and Alan *had* gone from her—and she was once more obliged to take stock and look to the future.

The weekend had been blighted by news of the Brigadier's death. Beatty had never met the man, though she'd seen him now and then, in his younger days, fishing on the banks of the Kennart or out with one of his dogs.

'Saw him last week,' Les told her as they'd walked back to the tractor. 'Shouted at me through the window when I dropped off a parcel of gramophone records. He didn't have much time to enjoy them, poor guy.'

'Well,' Charley said, 'someone will.'

'What do you mean?'

'It's an ill wind, that's all I'm sayin'.'

'Hey,' Les said, 'do you think Christine will inherit?'

'Damn sure she will,' said Charley.

He had dropped Les and Beatty at Picton and had hastened back to the glebe to assemble his boys to clean up the field and dismantle the shies and stalls. The two marquees would be left in place, empty and sad, until Monday when the hirers would send a gang and a lorry to collect them.

After Charley had gone, Beatty had fried eggs, bread and bacon and Les and she had eaten supper seated on the step. The evening was as fine as the day had been, though there was a melancholy edge to it now as if Ottershaw had gone into mourning for a man no one had really known.

After Les had trailed away Beatty had gone indoors, had taken off her summer dress and had lain on the cot in the half dark, thinking what it would mean to die—not old, like Brigadier Crockett, but to die now, suddenly. Who would mourn for her, she wondered, who would inherit the debris of her ramshackle life and who would take care of her ponies?

Perhaps, she thought, I'd better make a will. I wonder what it costs to hire a lawyer? Then she thought of the girl, Christine, and how strange it must be for her to be alone in the big house without the old chap to look after and to look after her; or, she thought, not alone for Alan would be with her and Alan would no more let Christine Summers down than Charley would let her down.

Yes, she thought, just before she fell asleep, she has him now.

If she wants him, she has him now.

*   *   *

298

'Hello, stranger.' Les Woodcock looked up. 'What an unexpected pleasure.'

'You don't mind me dropping in, do you?' Beatty said.

'By heck, no. We're neighbours.'

'Have you heard any news about the old man? Maggie tells me nothing.'

'Delivered lots of letters and cards this morning. Curtains were drawn, though, and the place looked—well, dead.'

'Did you see her?'

'Christine? Nope, no one.'

'I wonder what's happening.'

'Notice in the *Scotsman* yesterday. You see it?'

'I haven't been out since Saturday.'

'The funeral's on Friday at eleven.'

'Friends and family only, I suppose.'

'Is there a family?' Les said.

'Just her, I think, and her mother.'

'Charley's right. She will be in for a bit of a windfall,' Les said. 'She'll have that big house for one thing and probably enough cash to hang on to it.'

They were in the yard behind the farmhouse. The yard, Beatty noted, had been cleared of rubbish, hosed and swept. The concrete her father-in-law had laid to give the cattle footing had cracked in places but still provided a sure, well-drained foundation. In a pair of faded overalls and not much else, Les was seated cross-legged on a canvas sack with a tarpaulin spread before him like a prayer mat. Several mechanical parts were laid out on the tarp. Les was polishing one small part with emery cloth, his long fingers nimbly buffing

299

the metal.

Leaning over his shoulder, Beatty said, 'What is that?'

'Cylinder head.'

'What are you doing with it?'

'Cleaning it. Wish I had a vice, like. Need to wait for a vice till I've saved some more cash. Can't really do spit on spindles and valve stems without a vice.'

'Is that all you've got?' said Beatty. 'Parts?'

'Nah, got the frame too.'

'What frame?'

'Didn't Charley tell you? We found a bike. Well, it wasn't lost, like. Nobody thought to dig it out of the mud. Can't quite figure why it ain't more wasted but'—he shrugged—'never look a gift horse, so they say. There's more than enough of it in solid shape to get me off on a rebuild.'

'Leslie, I've no idea what you're talking about.'

He laughed, placed the cylinder head on the tarp and stuffed the emery cloth into his pocket. A lift of the shoulders and a twist of the hips brought him to his feet.

'Step this way.'

He gestured to Beatty to follow him into an outbuilding.

The outbuilding, an old cowshed, had also been thoroughly cleaned, though it still niffed a bit. She was pleased that Les hadn't knocked down the swallows' nests that were tucked under the rafters. A paraffin lamp hung from a hook on the wall. Another old lantern stood on the dirt floor like an offering to the sheet-shrouded object that occupied most of the space.

Les lit the paraffin lamp and held it high.

'There you are,' he said. '*Tah-rah!*' and plucked off the sheet. 'Me bike.'

It didn't look like much to Beatty. The forks were balanced on an apple box, the front mudguard was bent out of shape and it had no tyres.

'Ain't she a beau?' the postman said.

'What's that stuff hanging from the handlebars?'

'Yeah,' said Les. 'It's ribbon. Red ribbon. Don't know what it's doing there.'

Beatty reeled back from the skeletal frame, hands to her mouth.

'Oh, God!' she whispered. 'Oh, God!'

'Beatty, what's wrong with you?'

'The bike—it's my husband's. It's Andy's. No, it's not Andy's. He never saw it. His dad bought it to surprise him when he came home from the war. But he never came home from the war. And after the telegram—I remember that telegram, that khaki paper—Mr McCall took the bike away. I thought he'd sold it.'

Les lowered the lamp to the floor and put an arm about her.

'He didn't sell it, Beatty. He threw it into the loch.'

'So nobody would find it, so nobody would ever ride it—yes, of course.'

'Beatty, love, I'm sorry,' Les said. 'I'll toss it back first thing tomorrow and you'll never see it again. I mean, if I'd known . . .'

She leaned against him and stared, dry-eyed, at the wreck.

'Ah, Andy,' she said, 'Andy McCall, if only you'd known what was waiting for you back here in Ottershaw. If only you'd known what you'd be

301

missing.' Swinging round, she touched the postman's chest with the flat of her hand. 'Keep it, Les. Repair it, if you can. Ride it round the village and down the lanes. Make a lot of noise with it, a joyful noise. That's what my Andy would have done.'

'Beatty, are you sure?'

'Oh, yes,' Beatty told him. 'I'm sure.'

CHAPTER TWENTY-SEVEN

On Tuesday Alan had surgery and could not drive Christine to Stirling. She went alone, by bus, to the funeral office, lugging a suitcase. Her mother and she had argued about what was suitable for a retired high-ranking officer to wear to his funeral but just as the discussion grew heated it dawned on them that it hardly mattered. The coffin would be closed and no one, apart from the undertakers, would ever know how they had dressed Sandy for his final journey.

It was not an easy trip for Christine. The bus meandered across half of west Stirlingshire, dotting from village to village, before it reached town. She had too much time to ponder her uncertain future and, on the run home, with the suitcase full of the garments the Brigadier had been wearing when he'd died, she had been unable to hold back her tears.

The sight of her dear friend and counsellor laid out on a shelf had affected her more than she had supposed it would. There was nothing gruesome about the body. It was just the Brigadier, just

Sandy, pale-skinned and motionless, eyes closed as if he were asleep. But it had not been Sandy. Something had gone, the spark—the soul, perhaps—and had left only a shell behind. She had chosen a coffin, selected a wreath and a spray of lilies to adorn it. She had ordered two motorcars to accompany the hearse in case any of the mourners were too infirm to walk the short distance to the graveyard.

She couldn't imagine who the mourners might be or calculate how many old comrades would turn up to bid the Brigadier farewell. Would they expect a piper to play a lament while the coffin was lowered into the ground? If so, they would be disappointed. Sandy Crockett, though Scottish, had no great love for the music of the bagpipe and, Christine guessed, would have preferred to be lowered into the ground to the strains of 'Sing You Sinners', or perhaps the 'Paradise Waltz'.

She got home late in the afternoon to find that her mother had tackled the sitting-room. The tea things and plate of stale teacakes had vanished. The lid of the radiogram, which had lain open for four days, had been closed. Maude hadn't thought to switch the radiogram off at the plug, though, and it hummed drowsily in the spotless room.

Housework had revived Maude. Without the Brigadier to hinder her, she had swept, dusted and polished every surface in the sitting-room and hall, and had stripped the Brigadier's bed. The clothes lines on the drying lawn were weighed down with wet sheets and pillowcases. To Christine's surprise her mother had opened the curtains and, flouting convention, had flung open all the ground-floor windows as if to let in the scents from the garden and the smells of the countryside or, Christine thought, to allow the old man's spirit to escape.

'Sausage hotpot,' Maude said. 'Do you think he'll like that?'

'Do I think who'll like that?'

'Alan.'

'I'm sure he will,' Christine said.

'What time do you expect him?'

'I really have no idea.'

Maude was clad in a cotton skirt, a floral blouse and a stained canvas apron. Her sleeves were rolled up and her arms, flushed from the wash tub, looked as muscular as a man's. 'Have I time to make him a chocolate pudding?'

'Mother, I doubt if Alan expects anything grand.'

'We must take care of him, you know.' Maude tugged open the larder door and fished for a slab of cooking chocolate. 'After all, dear, he's all we have now.' She emerged from the larder with the chocolate block and a packet of gelatine, darted a little smile at Christine and, tossing the items on the table, bent to the cupboard to dig out a saucepan. 'Did it go well in Stirling?'

'Well enough. Everything's under control.'

'Did Sandy look nice in his navy blue suit?'

'Yes, Mama,' Christine said. 'He looked very nice.'

'I knew he would. He was always such a handsome man.' Maude straightened. 'Is that Bruce barking?'

'Where is Bruce?'

'I put him the back garden on a lead. Yes, that's Bruce. And, unless I'm mistaken, that's Alan arriving in his motorcar.'

304

'There's not much point in speculating,' Alan said. 'Might be ten, might be twenty. I suggest, Maude, that you set out a sandwich buffet in the dining-room and let everyone help themselves. The butcher in Kennart will do you a boiled ham and two or three roast chickens at a reasonable price.'

'How do you know what the butcher in Kennart will do?' Christine asked.

'It was Mrs Mackintosh's idea—when my wife died. Tasty piece of boiled ham, too, if I recall.'

'I'm surprised you recall anything about that day, especially the boiled ham.'

'It's the inconsequential details that stick somehow,' Alan said. 'Is there enough drink? I mean, did the Brigadier keep a stock of spirits?'

'Only a few bottles in the cupboard in his study, I think, plus what's in the cabinet in the sitting-room.' Christine said. 'What should I order?'

'Whisky, gin and brandy, a bottle or two of sherry—and soda water,' Alan told her. 'You'll also need glasses. The manager of the Black Bull will deliver everything you need, including glassware. If you can, Chris, do try to arrange it so that you only pay for what you use. Oh, and ask him to present you with a thirty-day invoice. All funeral expenses will be met from funds controlled by Johnston. It's not your affair, not financially.'

'I have money put by,' Christine said, 'a little.'

'Sandy took nothing from us,' Maude put in. 'Wouldn't hear of it even after Christine was drawing a wage. I didn't think he'd leave us high and dry, though.'

'We don't know that yet, Mama,' Christine said.

'One thing's for sure,' Alan said. 'It's all going to take time. No matter how efficient he is, Geddes Johnston will be tangled in red tape. Inventories to be compiled, valuations made, tax to be calculated before the issue can be put to the Sheriff Clerk for confirmation, and before anyone will see a penny.'

'She'll have it all, if she can,' Maude said.

'I doubt it,' Alan said.

'She'll have Preaching Friar,' Maude Summers said. 'It's Preaching Friar she's after, I'm sure.'

'We've no idea what she wants or what she's entitled to, Mama. The woman's an unknown quantity. She may turn out to be perfectly reasonable and accommodating.'

'Do you believe that, dear? Do you really believe that?'

'Actually,' Christine said, 'I don't.'

*   *   *

'Here,' Charley said, 'she's beginnin' to look like a bike again. I'll say this for you, Liverpool, you really do know what you're doin'.'

'Every man to his trade, Charley,' Les Woodcock told him. 'She's a long way from being fit for the road. I'll need to hop into Glasgow and start scouring the scrapyards for parts. Cheap parts at that.'

'Money's tight, I suppose?'

' 'Course, money's tight.'

'When she's all bolted together and runnin' sweet, will you sell her?'

The Triumph had been carried from the outbuilding and propped up on a crude wooden frame in the yard. The front mudguard had been beaten out and every functional part of the machine oiled. The tubular frame was spotted with tiny pimples of rust but the handlebars were whistle clean.

Charley ran his hand lightly, longingly over the bars.

'What's your offer?' Les said. 'Three sheep and a sack of spuds?'

'Funny! I am interested, though. Always fancied a bike.'

'Not this one, Charley,' Les said. 'This one belongs to Beatty.'

'That's daft. Beatty's not the sentimental type.'

'Wouldn't be too sure of that, Charley.'

'Hey! Are you chancin' your arm, Liverpool?'

'Yeah,' Les said. 'I think I probably am.'

'She'll never wear it. She thinks you're just a boy.'

'No, Charley. She thinks *you're* just a boy 'cause she's known you so long. Okay, so she's five, six years older than me. What does that matter?'

'Kids, if you want kids . . .'

'We'll have to be quick.'

'You fancy her, is that it?'

'Yep, I fancy her.'

'Well,' said Charley, before he could stop himself, 'I've had her.'

'Have you now?' the postman said thinly. 'How was it?'

'Great!'

'I thought you were after the teacher?'

'Old hat,' said Charley. 'Anyhow, Christine's latched on to the doctor an' even if she doesn't collect a fortune from the Brigadier, she'll want

307

nothin' more to do with me.' He glanced up and watched two swallows, a breeding pair, loop and plunge, beautifully, into the old cowshed. 'All right, Liverpool, all right. Christine never wanted anythin' to do with me. I was just too pig-headed to see it.'

'She wouldn't have made much of a wife for a farmer.'

'I'm not lookin' for a day labourer,' Charley said. 'Farming's not like it was in my dad's time, unless you're running a dairy herd, which we're not.'

'What sort of a woman are you looking for, Charley? There's plenty round here for you to choose from, plenty would jump at the chance.'

'I don't know what I'm lookin' for.' Charley sighed again. 'I thought it was Christine, somebody with just that—that wee bit o' whatever it was I never had the chance to acquire.'

'Glamour?' Les Woodcock suggested.

'Yeah, maybe.'

Les raised his brows. 'Like Beatty?'

'I had her once, just once, ten years back. We were both drunk. It was my first time an'—aw, hell, I can't remember a bloody thing about it.'

'Ten years is a long time to wait for seconds,' Les said.

'I've known Beats for so long I don't even fancy her any more.'

'What are you telling me, Charley? That I've a clear field?'

'Aye, that's about it.'

Les glided around the motorcycle, aimed a punch at Charley Noonan's chin, a punch that didn't connect, of course.

'Thanks, Charley,' he said. 'Thanks for coming clean.'

Charley shrugged. 'Guess I'll just have to keep lookin', eh?'

'Guess you will,' Les said. 'You going to this funeral, Friday?'

'Aye, I'd better show my face.'

'Out of respect for the old man, like?'

'For Christine,' Charley said. 'For the sake o' auld lang syne.'

'Whatever *that* means,' said Les.

*   *   *

If Christine's replacement had been more man than mouse, Freddy might have left the guy in charge on Friday morning while he attended the Crockett funeral. The Board of Rural Education, however, had seen fit to saddle Freddy with a teacher—Mr Tippet—who was on service training; a timid wee laddie who, in Freddy's opinion, lacked sufficient bottle to control a ladies' tea-party let alone a class of Juniors whose wiles had been honed by three years' practice in the subtle arts of recalcitrance. The idea of handing Greenhill's Juniors over to a trainee—or the trainee over to Greenhill's Juniors—made Freddy shudder. An act of Machiavellian cunning was called for if disaster was to be avoided.

Five minutes after the buzzer summoned the herd back to class on Wednesday afternoon, a strange figure dismounted from Freddy's old boneshaker and strode into the hallway. She threw back her shawl, paused to listen to the avian chatter from the Infants' class, flung open the door and stepped into the room.

The peacock shawl and black hat were unmistakable. Everyone, except Mr Tippet, recognised her immediately. She raised an arm. Bangles rattled down her wrist. She shook them as if she were casting runes.

'I know you,' she said. 'I know you all,' and then went out again.

'Wh—who was that?' Mr Tippet asked.

'Mrs McKay,' whispered the cowering Infants. 'It's Mrs McKay.'

'My wife,' Freddy informed the Juniors across the hall, 'the honourable lady McKay will be looking after you on Friday while I'm away. Woe betide anyone who gives her any lip. Understood?'

No response from the multitude.

'*Understood*?' Lucille shouted, shaking her bangles.

'Yes, Mrs McKay.'

'I didn't hear that,' said Freddy.

'*Yes, yes, Mrs McKay.*'

'Good,' Freddy purred.

And with the fear of God well struck and Friday taken care of, he escorted his beloved out to the playground and helped her back on her bike.

CHAPTER TWENTY-EIGHT

The anxiety that had plagued Christine and Maude Summers throughout the week was eased by the arrival of the mourners. They came by train from Glasgow, by bus from Stirling and by motorcar from heaven knows where: ten, then twenty, then thirty of them, not quite a battalion but enough to add gravity to the modest affair.

They were sober and respectful, of course, for they were or had been soldiers and death was meat and drink to them. It had not occurred to Chris that the reclusive old man she had loved and looked after had been famous in his day and that half the tall tales he had told her over the years had been at least half true. When she watched his comrades gather in the garden in braid and cock-feathers, in tartan and khaki, with medals and ribbons blazing on the pockets of their dark suits, she felt as if she had not known Sandy at all.

A colonel and a major had driven down from Aberdeen bearing an official wreath: a huge horseshoe of shiny laurel with the regimental crest wired into the centre and, to Christine's surprise, a ragged cloth cap that the Brigadier, in defiance of regulations, had worn in India when the colonel and he had served there in their youth. Wreath and cap would adorn the coffin for all to see when the hearse led the march uphill and would lie on the grave until wind and weather rotted them and they vanished into the earth.

The folk who had come from Ottershaw—precious few, in fact—were awed by the turnout and stood apart, not so much pushed aside as outnumbered. Freddy and Charley were somewhere at the back, Tom Currie and Alan too. Geddes Johnston, without his stepson, was penned in by a couple of old poachers who had fished the Kennart with the Brigadier in days gone by.

Four chairs were placed on the lawn. Maude was dragged from her hiding place in the kitchen and, veiled and gloved, seated by Christine's side. The

311

colonel and the major occupied the other two chairs while the rest of the men—all men— gathered in a half circle around the minister.

Mr Williams offered a blessing for the life of Alexander Crockett and spoke briefly of his fondness for country life. He then ceded his place to the colonel who, in turn, praised Sandy Crockett's dedication to the regiment and read from a list of honours and campaigns. Finally he delivered a prayer in a loud, strong voice, as if the lawn at Preaching Friar was close to a battlefield and all that was missing was the drumhead and the sound of guns.

The service ended with a rousing hymn.

The men moved off, subdued and orderly. Ignoring the hired motorcars and frock-coated drivers, they formed up in column of route behind the hearse. The colonel, major and minister were in the vanguard, followed by officers and serving men and, last of all, civilians.

'Alan,' Chris called out. 'Wait.'

She hurried into the house and came back with Bruce fastened to a lead.

She handed the lead to Alan who, saying nothing, brought the Scottie to heel.

Maude vanished into the kitchen to cut sandwiches.

The hearse rolled quietly away from Preaching Friar.

Christine remained at the gate until the procession was swallowed up by hedges and all she could see was Bruce's stumpy little tail wagging before he too rounded the corner and passed out of sight.

*   *   *

The colonel and the major stayed only long enough to toast the departed and murmur a few words of condolence to Christine and Maude in lieu of family before they left for the long drive north. Once the high brass had gone the atmosphere relaxed. Men spilled from the dining-room on to the lawn carrying plates and glasses and the wake took on the air of a garden party.

Laughter, no longer subdued, rose over the shrubs. Traffic to and from the dining-room, heavy at first, dwindled as every scrap of food was devoured and, mysteriously, bottles, decanters and soda siphons found their way out of doors. Uniforms were unbuttoned, ties loosened, caps and hats discarded and in the pale afternoon sunlight men sprawled in convivial groups upon the grass.

Bruce was in his element. He raced about, begging titbits and generally being fussed over until, overcome by heat and exhuastion, he settled with his head in the lap of a young corporal who stroked his ears and tickled his ruff until he, and the corporal, fell asleep in the shade of the magnolia tree.

Christine had no need to play host, to shake hands. She was not the Brigadier's daughter, his sister or his wife. After a while, she grew tired of trying to explain herself to grizzled veterans who claimed to have known the Brigadier well, but not well enough apparently. She knew no one, and no one knew her. Freddy had swallowed a sandwich, downed a glass of whisky and had hastened back to Greenhill to save his pupils from his wife. Charley, her unrequited lover, had slipped off straight after the committal. Geddes Johnston had also disappeared, but Christine knew that he would be back when the time of reckoning arrived.

It was almost two o'clock before Alan found her in the hall with a tray of dishes in her hands. 'Take off your apron and come outside, Chris. The Brigadier would have loved all this. For his sake, come outside.'

She balanced the tray carefully on the hall table and, untying her apron, dropped it there too. She let him lead her out into the garden. He put an arm about her, and pointed. 'The big fellow with the side whiskers. He was in Egypt. I don't remember him but he remembers me in a vague sort of way. We both remember Egypt, though, and had a long chat about it.'

'I see,' Christine said.

She was hot and sticky and wanted them gone, to take the war away with them. She could not relate to any of them. She was annoyed at Alan for bringing her out to face them. She would have pulled back and gone to hide in the kitchen with her mother if Alan hadn't tightened his hold.

She looked around for Freddy but he, of course, had left.

She looked for Charley, who had never been there at all.

'The little chap over by the rhododendrons, the one standing up,' Alan said, 'he was the Brigadier's clerk when Sandy was stuck in garrison HQ organising draft-finding units. Sandy hated it. He raged against the posting but he did a wonderful job.'

'It's all so long ago. I really have no interest in

314

what happened.'

'Ah, but you do,' Alan said.

Taking her by the arm, he led her across the lawn to the shady corner where the young corporal lay against the roots of the magnolia tree. His eyes were closed and his legs stretched out. He looked so peaceful, Christine thought, that he might as well be dead. Bruce was sprawled across his stomach. The corporal held him lightly with one hand and dog and man breathed in unison.

'Corporal Kenny,' Alan said quietly. 'I found her.'

The soldier sat up, blinking. He peered up at Chris for a moment then tipped Bruce on to the grass and scrambled to his feet.

'Miss Summers, is it?'

'Yes,' Christine said. 'It is.'

He lifted his hand then put it down again. He fumbled with the buttons of his uniform, adjusted his collar, picked up and put on his cap.

Still half asleep, Bruce wandered off into the bushes.

Christine waited impatiently for the young man to compose himself.

'I think,' Alan said, 'he'd quite like to shake your hand.'

'Aye,' the corporal said. 'I would, if that's all right.'

He wiped his hand against his trouser leg and held it out.

Christine took it, shook it and, for some reason, did not let it go.

'My father said I was to look for you,' the corporal said. 'He thought you'd be here, see. He heard you was with the Brigadier. My father knew

315

your father, see. He was with him when he died.'

Christine said. 'Was he there at Neuve Chapelle?'

'Aye, miss. On the Aubers Ridge. They were good pals.'

'Shall I fetch your mother?' Alan said. 'Will I get Maude?'

'No,' Christine said, then, sharply. 'No.'

She was still holding the corporal's hand, his fingers laced in hers. She drew him away from the veterans sprawled on the grass, from the house and the kitchen, from Alan. She walked with him as if they were sweethearts on the path that bordered the garden.

'Did the Brigadier tell you what happened that day, Miss Summers?'

'He never spoke of it. He told me a lot about the war, but not that.'

'It was a bungle, a mistake. The second battalion had gone in on the left of a fruit orchard. They was moving through the orchard when the jerry machine-guns caught them out.'

'Is that where it happened? Is it?'

'Near enough,' the corporal said. 'Headquarters thought the twenty-first Brigade was on the flank and would draw cross-fire. But the twenty-first wasn't there at all. By the time HQ found out, it was too late. Brigadier Crockett came chargin' out in a staff car, just him an' a driver, to sort things out but by then the lads had been chopped to bits. My father thinks it was a mortar shell upended the Brigadier's car, but he was wounded and can't really be sure.'

'He—he didn't . . . ?'

'Die? Nah, nah. Not him. He lived to fight

316

another day.'

'And my father?'

'Shot in the head; the head an' chest. They was together, inches apart, your pappy an' mine. They fell one on top o' the other an' stayed there till dusk when the battalion dug in an' the stretcher-bearers found them.' He turned to her and, freeing his hand from hers, pulled back his shoulders. 'He was killed outright, miss. There was nothin' nobody could do to save him. I've been told to make sure to tell you he didn't suffer. He was dead, poor man, before he struck the ground.'

'Thank you,' Christine said. 'Thank you for telling me.'

'Pappy said he thought you'd want to know.'

'Yes,' Christine said, 'thank you again. What happened to your father?'

'Lost a kneecap, near lost the leg.'

'So he didn't fight another day?'

'Not in the war, miss, no,' the corporal told her. 'He was a regular, a soldier before. He had a pension but it was still quite a struggle afterwards.'

'What does he do now?'

'Gateman at the steel works in Coatbridge.'

'And you,' Christine said. 'You became a soldier?'

'I did that, Miss Summers. Do you know where he's buried, your pappy?'

'Yes, in the cemetery at Neuve Chapelle.'

'Mogg's Hole it was called then but they've changed the name,' the corporal said. 'Only a handful were put down there, my pappy says, an' they're all English. Imagine a Gordon Highlander lying among Englishmen. Not that it matters, I suppose. One Gordon's good enough.'

317

'Have you visited the grave, Corporal Kenny?'

'Not yet,' the young man answered. 'One day, miss, one day we'll get there.'

'Yes,' Christine said, 'one day we will.'

*　　*　　*

Alan waited until the corporal left before he came to her. There was a time, and that time was now, when she needed him to say, 'I love you more than life itself. I will give anything to be with you.' The feeling flickered before her and was gone, like a last glance backward. He said nothing at first, just touched her, very lightly.

'How did you find him, Alan?'

'I didn't find him; he found me. He asked if he might speak with you. He was too shy to approach you himself. Are you all right?'

'Did he tell you what he told me?'

'Some of it,' Alan said. 'Enough. I take it you didn't know?'

'No, we didn't know.'

'Is it—is it comforting?'

'Yes, I suppose it is.'

'An ending?'

'Of sorts,' Christine said. 'An ending of sorts, yes.'

She looked across the lawn towards the house. Afternoon sunlight gleamed in the windows and from the sitting-room she thought she heard the strains of a dance band playing the 'Paradise Waltz'. It was nothing but her imagination, of course, a little bit of wishing for what might have been, what had been and wouldn't be again.

One Scottish soldier buried among the English

318

in Mogg's Hole; an error of judgement, a fault in communications, the troubled conscience of an honourable man. She knew now not only how her father had died but why the Brigadier had picked her out and brought her here to Preaching Friar.

There had been nothing random about it.

He had chosen her to help him make amends.

CHAPTER TWENTY-NINE

The years had not been kind to Irene Crockett, Christine thought. She wondered what the Brigadier would make of her now. She still looked a little like the girl in the photograph that Sandy had preserved but her high cheekbones and pointed chin had been swallowed up by fat and the nipped-in waist of her linen skirt and short mannish jacket could not disguise the fact that when she walked, she wobbled. She was not, Christine noted, in mourning.

It was after eight o'clock before the Wolseley prowled into the drive. Bruce, in his basket in the kitchen, heard it first and set up such a racket that Christine had to rush him out to the washhouse.

The dining-room had been cleared, the table set and fresh flowers arranged in a crystal vase on the sideboard. The glasses that had been hired from the Black Bull had been washed and, together with empty bottles and soda siphons, placed on a board in the study for collection on Saturday morning. Maude had swept the hall and would have waxed the wooden floor too if Christine had not insisted that her mother go upstairs and wash her face before the lawyer and his guest arrived.

Seven o'clock came and went, however, and at half past the hour Alan lost patience and demanded that someone poach him an egg before he died of starvation.

They were, all three, seated at supper when Bruce began barking.

Maude and Christine went out into the hall.

Shaking and simpering, Maude opened the front door.

Mrs Irene Crockett stalked into the house, followed by Geddes Johnston.

Drawing herself up to her full five feet, she looked straight through Maude and Christine and, turning her head this way and that, surveyed the walls and staircase, corridor and ceiling. 'So,' she said, in a nasal English twang, 'this is where Sandy lived, is it? This is the famous Preaching Friar. Well, it'll just have to do, I suppose.' She snapped her fingers. 'Have the boy bring in the luggage, and you'—she flicked a glance at Maude—'show him where to put it in my room.'

'Your room?' Christine said. 'Are you staying here tonight?'

'Of course I'm staying here,' Irene Crockett said. 'It's my house, isn't it?'

*   *   *

Friday night was parade night, when members of the Boys' Brigade met in the old church hall to learn how to form fours, dress ranks, march and salute and, later in the evening, in skimpy shorts and sandshoes, how to participate in team games without actually maiming each other.

It was still daylight when the boys came tearing out of the hall and, energy undiminished, scattered in various directions, racing, chasing, shouting and beating each other about the head with their pill-box caps. A staff sergeant and a young officer paused to light cigarettes and, strutting a bit, tipped their cheese-cutters in Beatty's direction and wished her goodnight before heading off down Main Street.

Charley came out at last. He locked the door of the hall with a key the size of a bread knife, put the key carefully into his pocket, immediately lit a cigarette and, with a sigh and a slump of his broad shoulders, crossed the church grounds to the pavement where, seated on the low stone wall, Beatty was waiting for him.

'Ah, it's yourself, Beats,' he said, cheering up a little. 'Been at the pub?'

'Not ladylike.'

'When did that ever bother you?'

'I've reformed,' Beatty said.

'Aye, that'll be the day,' said Charley. 'Pigs might fly.'

She was tempted to take his arm but the forage cap and anchor badges in the lapels of his suit put her off. He was in uniform and, she supposed, still duty-bound to set a chaste example to any impressionable young males who happened to be hanging around. He took a draw on his cigarette and passed it to her.

'Where're you going?' she asked.

'Down to Mrs Walkinshaw's house.'

'Who's she?'

'Church hall caretaker. More than my life's worth not to return the key.'

'Can I walk with you?'

'Sure,' Charley said, then, 'What's up?'

'Itchy nose,' said Beatty.

'Uh, you mean the funeral? Not much to tell, really.'

'Big turnout?'

'Big enough. Soldiers an' ex-soldiers. Quite a surprise. I thought they'd have forgotten him by now.'

'What is it they say about old soldiers? They never die, they only . . .'

'Fade away,' said Charley. 'Aye, well, Ottershaw's very own Brigadier sure faded away in style. Couple o' big cheeses from the regiment drove from Aberdeen with a wreath the size of a tractor tyre an' one o' them—a colonel, no less— gave a whajacallit—an oration. Pretty impressive, really. There were no women except for Christine an' her mum an' they didn't go to the burial. Tradition still rules the roost round here. They were left behind to comfort each other.'

'And make the sandwiches?'

'That's about it. They were—'

'Bereft?'

'Whatever that means,' said Charley, 'they weren't. Not a tear was shed, not that I saw. I didn't go back afterwards, though.'

'Why not?'

'It was all pretty much soldiers, in an' out o' uniform.'

'And Alan Kelso, of course,' said Beatty.

'Aye, and Alan Kelso.'

Six or eight boys had accumulated under the streetlamp at the corner of the Vosper Halls, not mischief-making just letting off steam.

322

'Hoy,' Charley called out to them. 'Time you lot went home.'

They glanced across the street, then, one by one, sprang to attention and saluted, with just a hint of mockery. When Beatty and Charley had passed, though, a catcall and a wolf whistle followed them and Charley, not in the least put out, raised an arm and, without looking back, bade his little Christian soldiers goodnight with a gesture that bordered on obscene.

'They like you, Charley, don't they?'

'Nah, they're terrified o' me,' Charley said. 'Can't you tell?'

He stopped at a door in the row of old weavers' cottages at the end of the village and pushed the long key through the letterbox.

'All right, Mrs Walkinshaw?' he called out.

'All right, Charley,' came a voice from within.

They turned and headed back up the main street.

The boys had gone from the corner and the street was quiet.

The only noise came from the direction of the Black Bull where Ottershaw's inveterate drinkers were downing pints and supping whisky as if the call for 'last orders' meant an end of boozing for ever. There was no sign of the Campbells who hadn't shown their noses in Ottershaw for weeks and, it was rumoured, had taken to drinking in Toddy Martin's tiny dump of a pub in the hamlet of Balnesmoor where they still had the respect of their peers.

'Seen anythin' of our Leslie lately?' Charley asked.

'Our Leslie?' said Beatty. 'When did he become

"our" Leslie?'

'He's a good lad—for an Englishman.'

'I didn't say he wasn't,' Beatty said, waiting.

'You're not goin' to get off with the doctor, you know.'

'I know that, Charley. I'm not entirely daft.'

They walked on, their footsteps echoing in the empty street.

The church looked very grand in the spill of light from the streetlamps, its sandstone walls mottled with shadows from the blossom trees in the garden. Behind the church, sheltered by it, the vale of Kennart stretched away in a boundless twilight pricked by the lights of farmsteads and hamlets and the headlamps of a solitary motorcar moving along the high road under the shoulder of the hill.

'Do you think he'll marry her for her money?' Charley said.

'He doesn't have to,' Beatty said. 'He's well off as it is.'

'My guess,' Charley said, 'is he'll either marry her, or leave.'

'Leave?' said Beatty. 'Leave Moss House, you mean?'

'I wouldn't stay in that gloomy hole on my own if I had a choice.'

'It's not so bad,' Beatty said. 'Maybe he likes it.'

They had stopped at the crossroad beyond the church. Eight large houses, hidden behind hedges, were laid out along the road to Kennart and four new bungalows on the slope that led down to the railway halt and the low road to Picton.

'I'd walk home with you, Beatty,' Charley said, 'but it's been a long day, one way or another, an'

I'm knackered.'

'Beddy-byes for you then,' said Beatty.

'Will you be okay on your own?'

'Yes, I'll be fine. I've walked home in the dark hundreds of times. At least I'm sober tonight.' On impulse she kissed him on the cheek then turned away to head downhill into the half dark.

'Beatty.'

She glanced back at him.

'Les Woodcock really isn't so bad, you know,' he said.

'You're not so bad yourself, Charley,' Beatty told him and, with a douce little smile, steered a steady course for home.

*   *   *

The reading of Brigadier Crockett's last will and testament took place in the dining-room within ten minutes of Irene Crockett's arrival. She had already eaten and, it seemed, was anxious to get down to business. She was not well pleased when Christine Summers's friend, the doctor, attempted to impose himself and, supported by Mr Johnston, refused to allow the proceedings to go forward while the fellow remained in the room.

Unsure of his standing, Alan reluctantly retired to the kitchen where 'the boy', as Mrs Crockett called Ross Harrison, was helping himself to tea.

Alan pulled out a chair, lit a cigarette and sipped from the cup he had abandoned when Bruce had started barking. Bruce was quiet now. He had probably fretted himself to sleep on the washhouse floor. If the meeting in the dining-room went on for any length of time, Alan told himself,

325

I'll make sure the Scottie has food and water and a blanket to lie on. If the worst comes to the worst I'll take the dog home with me and Christine can pick him up tomorrow after Irene Crockett leaves—if, that is, the widow from Eastbourne intends to leave at all.

Ross Harrison held out the teapot. 'Top-up?'

Alan shook his head and studied the man who had caused Christine so much trouble and who, he supposed, had every right to be jealous of him. Ross Harrison was anything but jealous, though. He exuded a strange, almost squirming obsequiousness and, Alan realised, was probably so eager to be liked that he might be vulnerable to a kind word and a little understanding.

'She's quite a lady, isn't she?' he said.

'Hmm?' Ross Harrison said. 'Christine?'

'Christine too, of course; a lovely young lady, I think we're both agreed. However, I meant Mrs Crockett. Rather—rather sharp, though, don't you think?'

'She is, rather,' Ross Harrison said.

'Do sit down,' said Alan affably. 'I suspect we might be here for some time while your father—sorry, stepfather—explains the nuances of the law to the benefactors. Are you hungry?'

'What? No, we—I dined—earlier.'

'I assume you picked Mrs Crockett up at the station in Glasgow.'

Ross Harrison struggled with an innate desire to please and a need for discretion. At length, he said, 'We did.'

'Was the train on time?'

'Spot on.'

'Long journey from Eastbourne, though.'

'Yes, I suppose it is.'

'Lovely part of the world,' Alan said, treading carefully. 'Beautiful beaches.'

'Beautiful.'

'You've been there, have you?'

Ross Harrison nodded.

'As a boy, I suppose,' Alan said, 'before the pier was built.'

'Oh no, the pier's been there for . . .' Ross frowned and to cover his gaffe fished for his pipe, stuck it in his mouth and fumbled in his pocket for matches.

Alan pushed a box towards him. 'Where did you eat tonight? The Rogano?'

'The Corn Exchange.'

'Handy for the railway station,' Alan said. 'Just a pity Mrs Crockett couldn't make it in time for the funeral.'

'Pity, yes.'

'On the other hand,' Alan said, 'she might have felt out of place.'

The flame teetered on the bowl of the pipe. 'Out of place?'

'Among all those old soldiers.'

'Possibly, possibly.'

'Old friends among them, perhaps.'

'What are you driving at, Mr Kelso?'

'Nothing in particular. Just making conversation,' Alan said. 'Did your father—your real father—die in the war?'

'Before it: 1913. TB.'

'Insidious disease,' said Alan. 'Not much we surgeons can do about it.'

'I was twelve.'

'You and Christine have much in common.'

'Oh, do you think so?'

'Both left without a father at a young age. Both trained as teachers,' Alan said. 'When did your mother remarry?'

'Three years after—what would that be?'

'Middle of the war,' Alan said. 'That's close enough. He did well by you, your stepfather? Brought you up properly?'

'Yes.'

'Was he strict? I mean, did he like things done his way?'

'Well, he didn't let me off with much.'

'I guessed as much,' Alan said.

'Did you? How?'

'We often travel together on the train, as you probably know; not by arrangement, just as it happens. I've come to know Geddes quite well. He strikes me as a quiet man, but firm in his convictions.'

'He's that all right,' Ross Harrison agreed.

'If Christine had been more—I mean, if she hadn't already been with me and had decided to marry you . . .' Alan paused. 'I've really no right to ask you all these questions.'

'No. Do go on.'

'Would your stepfather, would Geddes have been pleased?'

'Delighted. He's very keen for me to marry.'

'But not just anyone?' Alan said.

'No, not just anyone.'

'Someone with—position, shall we say? With a bit of substance?'

Ross Harrison was watching him now, alert for pitfalls but not apparently smart enough to avoid them. He nodded warily.

'Yes,' Alan said, 'Christine would have been ideal.'

'No,' Ross Harrison said, 'not ideal.'

'Oh, why not?'

'I don't know. Something to do with the Brigadier.'

Alan leaned on the table and stared at the handsome young buccaneer. 'Tell me, Mr Harrison, just when did your stepfather point you in Christine's direction?'

'He had nothing to do with it.'

'Did you know she lived in Ottershaw and taught at Greenhill School before your stepfather brought it to your attention?'

'I'm the deputy convener of the Board of Rural Education, for heaven's sake.'

'That doesn't mean a thing,' Alan said. 'Did you, or did you not know that Christine, your old college chum, lived here in Ottershaw before your stepfather pointed it out?'

'I'd have bumped into her eventually, I imagine.'

'Would you have recognised her?'

'What a thing to say. We were friends, such friends, back in—'

'In training college, yes, where you barely acknowledged her existence,' Alan said. 'He told you, didn't he? He told you who she was and where to find her. If you'd been a wee bit less eager to impress your stepfather and a wee bit more adept at courtship, it might all have worked out for the best—the best for you and Mr Johnston, that is, not for Christine.'

Ross leapt suddenly to his feet. 'Are you going to marry her? Well, are you?'

'I might,' Alan said. 'If she'll have me.'

'She isn't rich, you know, and she's not going to be rich. Oh, she'll have a share, at least her mother will. I mean, he's not leaving them penniless after all they did for him. But it's not what you think it's going to be.'

'And what do I think it's going to be?' said Alan.

'The lot, the lot, the whole caboodle.'

'What does that amount to in, say, sterling?'

'Fifty thousand—upwards of fifty thousand pounds.'

'I see,' Alan said. 'Definitely a sum worth getting one's hands on.'

'Christine's not going to get that much, not a half, not a quarter,' Ross Harrison said, showing off now.

'How much is she going to get?'

'After taxes, fees and processing—she'll be lucky if it's five.'

'Still, in this day and age,' Alan said, 'it's not to be sneezed at.'

'No, no, of course not, but compared with what's on offer . . .'

'On offer?' Alan said.

'I mean—I mean . . .'

'You mean compared with what Irene Crockett's going to inherit,' Alan said, 'with the aid of a good lawyer. Tell me one thing more, Ross.'

'I think I've said too much as it is.'

'I think you have, too,' Alan said, 'but, to satisfy my curiosity, answer me just one more question.'

'What's that?'

'How the devil do you know what the Brigadier put in his will?'

* * *

If Maude had understood half the legal gobbledegook that Geddes Johnston spouted Christine reckoned she would have burst into tears much sooner than she did.

The lawyer was seated at the head of the table, Irene Crockett on his left. Her mother and she were relegated to the end of the long table. The curtains had been closed, the electrical chandelier switched on but there was no fire in the grate and now that the sun had gone down the room was chilly.

Now and then the lawyer would detach a page from the document and hold it up to the light as if he could not quite decipher the typewritten print or make out a marginal amendment. He was meticulously correct in all that he did, however, and after reading a particularly obscure paragraph would pause to explain what it meant. As the reading went on an icy lump formed in Christine's chest.

'Is that clear to you, Miss Summers?'

It took her all her time to answer, 'Yes.'

'What's he saying, dear?' Maude whispered.

Christine patted her mother's hand and promised to explain later.

The Brigadier's widow sat back in her chair, smoking a cork-tipped cigarette and smiling fatuously, her gaze fixed on Geddes Johnston. Not once did she glance at the table's end to catch Maude or Christine's eye.

'I direct that unless otherwise specified any legacies granted herein shall be paid as soon as my executor considers it practical after my death, free of government duties in respect of my death and of delivery expenses but without interest. Thereinafter I direct my executor, Mr Randolph Geddes Johnston, to make over the residue of my estate to my wife, the said Irene Hobbs Crockett, if she survives for thirty days after my death. If my said wife does not survive for thirty days or does survive but disclaims in whole or part the bequest of residue in such an event only I direct my executor to make over the residue, or such part as may have been disclaimed, to my housekeeper Maude Summers.'

'Is that me, Christine?'

'Yes, Mama, it is.'

'I knew he wouldn't forget us.'

A frosty pause: 'Do you wish me to explain, Miss Summers?'

'No, that will not be necessary.'

'In recognition of her faithful service I hereby direct my executor to grant to Maude Summers a sum not to exceed ten percentage of the worth of my net estate, all bills, fees and taxes paid, or in the event that said Maude Summers predeceases me, the percentage to be granted to her daughter, Christine Grace Summers, on her reaching the age of responsibility, which is twenty-one years.'

Christine cleared her throat and, like a child, raised her hand.

'Yes, Miss Summers?'

'Are there no amendments to that clause?'

'None.'

Her mother had been the Brigadier's housekeeper for six years at the time the will had been drafted. Had Irene Crockett still been so vivid in Sandy's memory that he could not bear to admit that he had lost her for ever?

'May I go on?' Geddes Johnson enquired.

All Christine could do was nod.

The lawyer rattled through the rest of it.

'Executor shall have full power either to pay or apply the whole or any part of the income or capital . . . full power of retention, realisation, investment, appropriation, transfer of property and management of my estate.'

Dated, signed and witnessed.

Mr Johnston placed the last page of the document on the table, sat back, and reached for his pipe. He filled and lit it expertly, then slid a sidelong glance at Irene Crockett who stabbed her cigarette into an ashtray and ground it to pulp.

She picked a fleck of tobacco from her teeth. 'Well,' she said, 'I think that's all perfectly clear, Geddes. Thank you,' and made as if to rise.

Christine said, 'It's not perfectly clear, not all of it.'

'In which case you haven't been listening,' Irene Crockett said.

Two puffs on the pipe, smoke drifting: 'What isn't clear, Miss Summers?'

'What about the house?' Maude blurted out. 'What about Preaching Friar?'

'The house is part of the estate,' said Mr Johnston patiently. 'The contents will be incorporated into the general inventory and the property assessed by an independent evaluator who will calculate its worth.'

'Who appoints the independent evaluator?' Christine enquired.

'I do,' Mr Johnson replied. 'That is the prerogative of the executor.' He took another pull on the pipe then put it in the ashtray. 'If you are

333

dissatisfied with anything contained in the will you are at liberty to appoint a lawyer of your own to inspect it. Challenging the legality of a will, however, is an expensive business.'

'They don't have a leg to stand on,' the widow said. 'It's all down there in black and white, just the way the Brigadier wrote it.'

'In 1921,' Christine reminded her.

'He had his chance to change it—and he didn't,' Irene Crockett said. 'If you ask me ten per cent is more than you deserve since you sponged off the poor old sod for all these years.'

'Sponged?' Maude said. 'I worked for every penny.'

'What did he pay you?' said Irene Crockett.

Maude glanced at Christine. 'I don't know.'

'Weren't you indentured?'

'I—I don't know what that means,' said Maude plaintively.

'Under contract. Surely you signed a contract?'

'No, we—we just shook hands.'

Christine jumped in. 'My mother received a personal allowance of thirty pounds a year, paid annually by cheque. The Brigadier met all our other expenses.'

'You soaked him, didn't you?'

'We did nothing of the sort.'

'Well, you won't soak me, you can be sure of that.'

Christine bit her lip. 'I gather, Mr Johnston, it will take some time for the will to be processed—is that the correct term?'

'It is.'

'How long?'

'Impossible to say—a year perhaps, perhaps

longer.'

'What, if I may ask,' said Christine, 'do we live on in the meantime?'

'I'll tell you what you don't live on,' Irene Crockett put in. 'You don't live off me. I'll give you five pounds in lieu of wages—that's generous—and ask you to vacate the premises by noon tomorrow.'

'Vacate the premises,' Christine said. 'What do you mean?'

'I mean leave my house.'

'But this is our home,' Maude cried.

'No,' the woman said, 'it's not your home, never was your home. I'm Alexander's widow so I'm entitled to reside here until the valuation's completed.'

'What do you want with Preaching Friar? You live in Eastbourne.'

'None of your business what I want with it.' Irene Crockett got to her feet, tightened the belt of her linen skirt and tugged down her jacket. 'You've been pampered by my old man for so long you've forgotten what you really are—servants, both of you, just servants. Tell them, Geddes.'

'Mrs Crockett is correct, I'm afraid. You've no claim upon the property and, as minor beneficiaries, no right to remain here. If Mrs Crockett desires it . . .'

'Which I do.'

'. . . then, Miss Summers, you must leave.'

'And don't go thinking you can filch any of the stuff.' Irene Crockett advanced upon them. 'If you lay a finger on any of the old—my husband's stuff I'll have the law on you. You can keep what he gave you, clothes anyway, but I'll expect you to show me what's in your suitcases before you put a

335

foot out of that door.'

'Where will we go? What will we do?' Maude cried.

'Rot, for all I care,' Irene Crockett said. 'Now, show me to the kitchen. I'm dying for a nice cup of tea.'

CHAPTER THIRTY

'Every man's dream,' Josie Carmichael said, 'and every man's nightmare. On the one hand you've a gorgeous young creature, skint, homeless and absolutely at your mercy, taking shelter under your roof. On the other hand you're saddled with her mother. Honestly, Kelso, I'm at a loss to understand how you get yourself into these situations. You breeze off on Thursday afternoon relatively footloose and fancy-free and arrive back Monday shackled to two women.'

'What else could I do?' Alan said. 'I couldn't leave them stranded.'

'Oh, come on now; they're not totally helpless. She's a teacher, isn't she?' Josie said. 'All right, I admit it must have been a fearful shock losing her protector.'

'He was more than that to Christine.'

'Whatever he was,' Josie went on, 'losing him one day and the next you're being kicked out of the only home you've known for the past twenty years.'

'Seventeen years.'

'How old is Mama?'

'Now don't start on that tack, Josie, please.'

'This lawyer feller, I gather he's not being

helpful.'

'He gave me sight of the will when I asked for it,' Alan said. 'She wasn't very pleased about that.'

'She being the wife nobody knew about?'

'Unfortunately,' Alan said, 'the Brigadier and she kept in touch.'

'Well, that takes estrangement out of the picture, I suppose,' Josie said.

'She's a complete and utter cow, if you must know.'

'Fighting talk, Mr Kelso. Did you lose your temper?'

'Not quite,' Alan said.

'Were they both in tears, mother and daughter?'

'Yes, though Christine was more angry than anything.'

'You didn't stand a chance, old chum, not a chance.'

'I couldn't hang fire and watch Christine being humiliated. I told them to pack their bags and took them off there and then.'

'Back to your lair in the forest.'

'Josie, this isn't funny.'

'You do realise,' the anaesthetist went on, 'it can take years for estates to be wound up. You've read *Bleak House*, haven't you? If the lawyer decides to tread water you could be stuck with them until your hair falls out—unless, of course, that's part of your dastardly plan.'

It was early for lunch, barely half past eleven. Alan had no appetite.

There had been a general purposes meeting that morning to discuss the possible purchase of a second mobile X-ray unit and other bits and pieces of equipment; a full afternoon of surgery was

337

slated to start at twelve thirty. The lounge was crowded with theatre staff stoking up for a long shift and it had taken Alan all his time to find a quiet corner where he could unburden himself to the only friend whose judgement he trusted.

'I have no plan, Josie, dastardly or otherwise.'

'Well, in spite of your ingenuous denials, Alan, you might just have bought yourself a darned good deal.' She leaned over the plates and sauce bottles. 'Hasn't it occurred to you that you've acquired a housekeeper and a lover in, shall we say, one fell swoop?'

'That,' Alan said, 'is ridiculous. Besides, I already have a housekeeper.'

'Old Grumpy? How long do you think she'll last if she's sharing her kitchen with a woman she can't stand, while you're sharing your bed with—'

'No,' Alan said sharply, 'that won't happen.'

'Why? In case you have to commit yourself?'

'Commitment has nothing to do with it. It just wouldn't be right.'

'La, la, la!' Josie said. 'Integrity and intimacy make odd bedfellows.'

'Is sex all you ever think about?'

'More or less,' Josie said. 'Sex, horses and where my next gin and tonic's coming from. Talking of horses, what's your friend the pony farmer going to say when she finds out you're providing room and board for a sweet young thing?'

'There was never anything between Beatty and me,' Alan lied. 'Even if there had been, I'm sure she'd understand.'

'I'm damned sure she wouldn't.'

'Country folk aren't like you and me, Josie.'

'I know all about country folk, Mr Kelso, at least

338

the horsy sort. Believe me, they're not that much different from normal human beings when it comes to playing the mating game.'

'I'm not playing the mating game.'

'No? What about all that stuff you were giving me not so long ago? Don't tell me your dynastic urges were nothing but a whim? Whether you know it or not, Alan, you *are* playing the mating game; you're just not playing it very well.'

'I'm a victim of circumstance, that's all.'

Josie frowned, unsure whether he was making a joke or merely being pretentious. Until recently he'd been confident and self-contained, a little too self-contained perhaps. Now he was all at sixes and sevens, scared of the situation in which he found himself.

She felt sorry for him—almost.

'Listen,' she said, 'it doesn't matter if your house guest has a glass eye, a gammy leg and looks like an old boot, if she's living cheek by jowl with you, you're in trouble, chum, deep, deep trouble. Breakfast on the terrace, candlelit suppers, surprise encounters in dead of night as you scamper to the toilet; to say nothing of summer frocks, bare arms, scanties hanging on the washing line. Have you forgotten what it was like?'

'It was never like that,' Alan said.

'Poor you,' Josie said. 'Poor Marion.'

'What are you driving at?'

'Sooner or later you'll surrender,' the anaesthetist told him. 'You'll make her your mistress then you'll make her your wife. Hark to my words of wisdom: if you don't want to change your life, if you really don't want a wife, then get rid of her, and her dear old mater, now—*now*, do

339

you hear me?—before it's too late.'

'I don't think I can—get rid of them, I mean.'

'Of course you can. Tell them you're moving back into the city. Make them a loan against this modest fortune they're about to inherit. Find them a cottage, a lodge, a tent, for God's sake, just get them out of your house before you become responsible for them.'

'I'll think about it.'

'Don't think about it. Do it, do it tonight.'

'Not tonight,' Alan said. 'Definitely not tonight.'

'Why not tonight?'

'It's too soon.'

'Too soon for what, Mr Kelso?'

'I told them I'd look after them.'

'Then you're sunk, sunk without trace.'

'Do you really think so, Josie?'

'I don't think so; I know so,' Josie said. 'Now, are you going to eat that slice of Grosvenor pie?'

'No.'

'Then give it here,' said Josie.

*   *   *

It seemed odd to be walking to school by an unfamiliar route. The building itself looked different, as if the events of the past week had spun everything around to face the other way. It reminded her of that day, seventeen years ago, when she had first been brought to Ottershaw and how different Greenhill School had seemed from her school in Glasgow, a massive, drab building hemmed in by tenements, and how out of place she had felt until Charley Noonan had taken her under his wing.

340

Alan had left early in the Alvis. When, ten minutes later, his housekeeper, Mrs Mackintosh, had turned up, there had been a nasty confrontation in the kitchen that had ended with the woman scuttling out, muttering, 'We'll see about this, we'll see about this.'

The fracas had delayed her. She was several minutes late arriving at school. The ritual chant of morning prayers came from Freddy's room and the babble that accompanied the taking of the register from her own. She knocked on Freddy's door and heard him call out, 'Amen. Enter,' as if it were all one word.

She opened the door and put her head around it.

'Miss Summers, as I live and breathe,' Freddy bawled, then, stepping out into the hall, said, *sotto voce*, 'Thank God you're back, Christine. How is it? Are you okay? Are you sure you don't need more time to—what—recover?'

'No, I'm fine. I have something to tell you but it can wait. What do you want me to do?'

'Do?' said Freddy. 'For heaven's sake, woman, I want you to get in there and show that young man what teaching's all about. Tippet's his name, by the way. He's wetter behind the ears than the average haddock. We'll let him finish the day then pack him off from whence he came. Are you really okay?'

'Not really.'

'Oh!' said Freddy, frowning. 'Fit to face the firing squad, though?'

'Yes'—Christine smiled—'fit to face the firing squad.'

*   *   *

Gossip, not love, brought Les Woodcock post haste to Picton. Beatty was leaning on the gate of the paddock when the red mail van swerved into the yard, much to the alarm of the foals who trotted gaily about in the bright morning sunshine.

The postman cranked down the window. Beatty leaned a forearm on the roof of the van and bent down.

'She's gone,' Les said.

'Who's gone?'

'Christine. She's moved in with the Doc, her an' her mother both.'

'What!' Beatty exploded. 'Are you sure?'

'Certain.'

'Dear God, that was fast.'

'Nah, Beatty, it's not like that. I think she was given her marching orders,' Les said. 'There's another woman in the old boy's house. And here's the cruncher: she's his wife—well, his widow, like.'

'How do you know who she is?'

'Had a parcel for the Brigadier—gramophone records, I think. Didn't know what do with it, him being dead an' all. Sorting office said deliver it anyway so I took it down to the house, thinking Christine would sign for it. Christine ain't there. It's this other woman with an accent even funnier than mine—English, lah-de-dah. When I ask for Christine she gives me a sniff and a stare and tells me Miss Summers is no longer resident. I ask her what I'm to do with the parcel. She says she'll sign for it. I ask her who she is and she says she's Mrs Crockett. I'd've asked for proof, like, but she's not the sort you argue with.'

342

'What sort is she?'

'Five feet dot, fat as a pig, about forty-five, fifty, I reckon.'

'What name did she sign?'

Les pulled out his log, flipped it open and held it up for Beatty to read.

'Mrs Irene Crockett,' he said. 'See, right here in black and white.'

'He had a wife, did he?' Beatty said. 'A wife nobody knew about. Unless she's his long-lost daughter. No, she wouldn't have his name, would she?'

Les leaned from the van window. 'Any roads, I've mail for the Doc, so up I go to Moss House and who opens the door but old Ma Summers. "Oh," she says, "we're living here now." And I say, "Will that be temporary, Mrs Summers?" And she says, "That remains to be seen." What do you make of it, Beatty?'

'I don't know what to make of it,' Beatty said, 'yet.'

'I'll keep my ear to the ground, like.'

'I'll go one better,' Beatty said. 'Give me two minutes to fetch my purse and you can drop me off.'

'Drop you off where?'

'Ottershaw Co-op, of course,' said Beatty.

*   *   *

The smell came out to greet him as soon as he parked the motorcar, a spicy odour so rich that it made his mouth water. He hung his overcoat and hat in the hall and headed for the kitchen which was wreathed in steam and as warm as an Indian

343

summer. Maude Summers darted between the stove and the electrical plate and seemed to have more arms than the goddess Kali. In a trim lace-fringed apron, Christine was calmly setting the kitchen table.

'What,' Alan said, 'is that delicious smell?'

'Lamb curry,' Christine told him. 'I do hope you'll like it?'

'I love curry. I haven't had one in years.'

'A favourite with the Brigadier,' Maude put in.

'It's almost ready,' Christine said. 'You'll just have time to wash.'

Alan cantered upstairs into the bathroom and half filled the washbasin. He caught sight of himself in the mirror above the sink: a tired, haggard face, every line deep-etched. The long afternoon at the table had taken its toll. He had worked until almost six. It was now half past seven. How, he wondered, had the women timed things so well? Then it dawned on him that he might be slipping into the pitfall that Josie had warned him about.

'Alan'—Christine's voice from downstairs—'you have visitors.'

'Damn!' he said, tossed the towel into the basket and went downstairs to see who had turned up to keep a hungry man from his meat.

*　　　*　　　*

'Mrs Mackintosh,' Alan said, 'won't you step into the drawing-room? I'm sure you and—ah—Mr Mackintosh will be more comfortable there.'

'The kitchen will suit us just fine, thank you.'

'Aye, just fine,' said the other half.

He was a small man, older than his wife, round-shouldered and sour. Quite clearly he wished he was elsewhere. Christine had given them each a chair which Mrs Mack had pulled away from the table so that they sat out of the way of the stove and the cook.

'We'll not be keepin' you, Doctor,' Mrs Mackintosh said. 'What I have to say will not take long.'

'Aye, not long.'

Alan nodded. 'You're handing in your notice, aren't you?'

'I am, and not a minute too soon.'

Christine and her mother discreetly turned their backs and if it hadn't been for the pots and saucepans bubbling on the stove, would have left the kitchen altogether. Alan experienced a moment of guilt. He was tempted to beg the woman to stay. Then he realised he did not want her to stay, that he had put up with her only because it was convenient and because he thought he owed it to Marion.

'I'm sorry you feel that way, Mrs Mackintosh.'

'You've no right to replace me without notice.'

'Without notice, aye.'

'Mrs Summers and her daughter aren't replacing you; they're my guests,' Alan told her. 'I'm not asking you to leave but if you feel you can't continue to work here . . .'

'With her? No.'

'Very well. If you wait just a moment I'll fetch my cheque book and pay what I owe you and a month—will a month be enough?—in lieu of notice.'

'I'm not needin' your money.

345

'But she'll take it,' her husband said.

Alan was disinclined to leave Mrs Mackintosh and Maude Summers together for one minute longer than necessary. He ran into the study, found his cheque book and fountain pen and hastened back to the kitchen. He placed the book on the table, filled out a cheque and signed it. He blew on it to dry it and handed it to the woman. She peered at it then handed it to her husband who peered at it in turn before folding it neatly and tucking it into his waistcoat pocket.

Nothing was said during the transaction, no thanks offered.

'I'll not be keepin' you from your dinner, then,' Mrs Mackintosh said.

She nudged her husband. The pair got to their feet.

Alan dived to the door to open it and usher them out through the hall.

He was overwhelmingly relieved to be rid of the woman. She had told him once that it was his house and he could do what he liked in it but she hadn't meant a word of it. She had set herself up as his moral guardian, which had been all very well when he had toed the Calvinistic line and had, by her lights, behaved himself.

The husband went out into the hall. It appeared that the woman was about to follow him. Then she turned. 'You're not the first, you know,' she said. 'He's had women here before. He's had them upstairs, trollops from Glasgow, an' that Beatty McCall from down the road at Picton. Don't think I don't know what goes on in this house. Harlots. You're all just harlots.'

Then, before anyone could react, she followed

her husband through the front door which Alan, rather belatedly, closed behind them.

He returned to the kitchen and seated himself at the table, unfolded his napkin and smoothed it over his lap. 'Well,' he said, 'now we know, don't we? Now we know.'

Maude Summers placed a bowl of rice upon the table and followed it with an ashet filled with curry. She carried the dishes in a folded tea-towel and set them down with great care. She put a serving spoon in each dish and, looking directly at Alan for the first time, said, 'Will you serve, Dr Kelso, or shall I?'

CHAPTER THIRTY-ONE

It was a little after nine. The sky was streaked with light from the setting sun. It gleamed on the west-facing windows and slanted into the sitting-room where Alan had taken refuge as soon as dinner was over. He was by the window, outlined against the light, a cigarette hanging from the corner of his mouth.

Chris put the tray of coffee things on the table by the hearth. She remembered the last time someone had served coffee in this room: the pony woman, Beatty McCall, who had taken charge not just of Alan but of everyone.

'Where's your mother?' Alan asked.

'Washing up.'

The cigarette bobbing on his lip made him seem careless.

'It's true,' he said, 'some of it.'

347

'You don't have to explain anything to me, Alan.'

'There were no women from Glasgow,' he said. 'No—what did she call them?—no trollops. But Beatty and I did have something more than a friendship.'

'You were lovers?'

'Yes.'

'Before or after your wife died?'

She was unsure whether naïveté or spite prompted the question. She saw him spin round, ash spilling from the tip of his cigarette.

'You don't really think that of me, Chris, do you?'

'I don't know what to think. What does she think of you?' Christine said. 'Is she in love with you?'

'No.'

'You seem very sure of that.'

'She—she understands.'

'What does she understand?'

'About us.'

'That's more than I do,' Christine said.

He went to the table and lifted the coffee pot.

'Will you have coffee with me?' he said.

'I don't think I should.'

'Why ever not?'

'Look,' she said, 'I've no idea what I am to you.'

'You're my—my guest, Christine.'

'Is that all I am?'

'No, but . . .'

She hated him for hesitating. She needed him to make everything clear. If he wanted her she would be ready for it, would put aside her fears and in spite of anything her mother might say, give herself to him. But if he said he loved her then she was entitled to negotiate.

He replaced the coffee pot and seated himself on the pouffe.

He looked silly in that position, as silly as she had felt that afternoon when Beatty McCall had tried to scare her off. He stretched out his legs and balanced on his hands. If that pouffe slips, Chris thought, he'll land on his backside and come an awful cropper. 'Get up,' she heard herself say. 'If you're going to lecture me I'd prefer it if you weren't sprawled on the floor while you're doing it.'

'I'm not going to lecture you.'

He got up and, folding his arms, looked down at her.

'Five thousand pounds, possibly more,' he said, 'that's what will come your way when this business is settled.'

'How do you know?'

'Harrison told me.'

'How does he know?' Christine said. 'There are bank accounts and bonds and shares and things and the house will fetch quite a bit. I'm not even sure the Brigadier knew what he was worth. It isn't the money, Alan. The money makes no difference to me.'

'Oh, but it will,' said Alan. 'Five thousand pounds will buy you a house anywhere you wish to live and leave a considerable sum to invest.'

'But it won't bring him back, will it?'

'No,' Alan said. 'What you had, it's gone.'

'And what will I put in its place?' Christine said.

'I can't answer that question, Christine,' he told her. 'The money may not matter to you but it matters to me.'

'Oh,' she said, 'don't tell me you're after my fortune too.'

'I'm not going to apologise for what happened with Beatty. It's over and done with. Nothing like that will ever happen again.'

'Because you'll have me?'

'I don't have you,' he said. 'That's the point.'

'Alan, you're talking in circles.'

'I want you to stay but I don't want you to be under any obligation—and that's what makes it difficult.'

'My mother will gladly cook and clean house.'

'That's not the sort of obligation I'm talking about.'

'I know what you're talking about,' Christine said. 'It's quite a scandalous situation you've created for all of us, isn't it? A widower and an unmarried woman sharing a house, even with a chaperone of sorts to keep everything above board. I wouldn't be surprised if I was asked to leave the teaching profession because of it.'

'Surely you don't mean that?'

'Perhaps not, but tongues will be wagging even now.'

'Do you care about that? I don't.'

'Doesn't it make you even the least bit uncomfortable?' Christine said.

'I imagine,' Alan said, 'we'll get used to it.'

'I'm not sure I want to get used to it,' Christine said. 'Moss House is your home, not mine. Mama and I will always be strangers here.'

'You can't have it both ways, Christine,' he said. 'Five thousand pounds is a great deal of money. It will give you independence. Something you're not used to. It's not the situation we find ourselves in that's bothering you but the realisation that in six months or a year, when Johnston squares the bill, you'll be in a position to choose. You won't have the Brigadier to lean on and make decisions for you. You'll be at liberty to make your own mistakes.'

'Isn't this a mistake?'

'I don't know,' Alan said. 'Is it?'

'It's all that woman's fault.'

'You can hardly blame Irene Crockett for the Brigadier's death,' Alan said. 'Look at it this way: if she hadn't popped up to stake her claim you'd be struggling with a fortune, a real fortune.'

'I don't like being cheated,' Christine said.

'Is that how you see it?'

'Deceived,' she said. 'Let down.'

'What do you mean? Let down by the Brigadier?'

She could not bring herself to answer. She knew he was right. She lifted the coffee pot and for a single violent moment was tempted to throw it at him and might have done so if the sound of a motorcar drawing up outside hadn't sent Alan hurrying to the window.

'Who is it now?' she asked in a nervous whisper.

'Ross Harrison,' Alan answered. 'What the devil can he want at this hour?'

She was suddenly afraid again. Everything that happened now took her back to the shock of that afternoon at the fete, one thing after another coming at her out of nowhere, cutting away her sense of self.

She followed Alan out into the hall.

Her mother stood in the mouth of the passageway that led to the kitchen. She wore an

351

apron and was drying her hands on a tea-towel. She too looked frightened as if some monstrous thing was about to lumber into the house, some force against which even Dr Kelso would be powerless.

Ross Harrison perched awkwardly on the doorstep, rocking from foot to foot, his hat politely in his hand.

'I brought you the dog,' he said. 'She doesn't want him. She only kept him out of spite. She's talking about having him put down. I assume you'll take him in?'

'I think,' Alan said, 'we might be inclined to do that. Where is he?'

'In the car.'

Ross stepped back and opened the rear door of the Wolseley.

Bruce bounded out, almost knocking the teacher down, and in four short scurrying strides gained enough momentum to leap straight into Christine's arms.

'You'll keep him?' Ross Harrison said.

'We'll keep him,' Alan said.

*   *   *

Moss House was airy and spacious, more modern than Preaching Friar, if you could call a building put up over half a century ago 'modern'. Rooms on the first floor mimicked in size and shape the public rooms below and the bedroom that Christine shared with her mother looked out on a panoramic view of the Kennart 'alps', the range of rolling hills whose protecting arms encircled three or four parishes.

The ceiling light was encased in an etched glass globe but the bedside lamp, in a parchment shade, was more than adequate to read by and shed sufficient light on the dressing-table for Maude to apply various creams and potions and screw in a battery of paper curlers.

Christine lowered the book she had borrowed from Alan's shelves and peered at her mother's reflection in the mirror of the dressing-table.

'Do you do that every night, Mama?'

'Certainly, I do.'

'May I ask why?'

'To keep my complexion fresh and youthful.'

'And the curlers?'

'Don't tell me you thought my curls were natural?'

Their lives in Preaching Friar had been so private and contained that Christine had never seen her mother in anything more revealing than a dressing-gown, let alone been made privy to what the French called her *toilette*.

'Where did you get all that—that stuff?'

'It isn't "stuff", dearest. These jars contain the best quality preparations made to the highest scientific standards.'

'From the Co-op?'

'Well, yes, but not the Co-op in Ottershaw.'

'Oh, that makes all the difference,' Christine said. 'Is that what you spend your allowance on?'

Her mother's busy fingers paused; a strip of heavy paper, torn from a magazine, sprang loose and released a curl of chestnut hair.

'What I spend my money on is my business,' she said. 'But, if you must know, the Brigadier paid for them.' She preened for a moment then leaning

353

forward, peered at her image in the mirror. 'He liked me to look . . .' She sighed. 'Much good it will do him—or me—now.'

'To look what?' Christine asked.

'Young and beautiful,' Maude answered.

'Mama!'

Maude whipped round. 'Oh, no, no, nothing like that. Nothing, no, ever. Sandy was a gentleman, always a gentleman but he—he . . .' Her voice broke a little. 'He told me once if he'd been thirty years younger I'd have been the girl for him.'

Christine picked up the book again and, scrunching round, punched the feather pillow into a more accommodating shape.

It had been flattery, of course, one of the charming compliments that the Brigadier threw out from time to time. He had always been, by nature if not intention, a ladies' man. It was on the tip of her tongue to tell her mother that Sandy had meant nothing by it, that he was merely being kind. But when Maude tied the last paper curler and, rubbing lotion into her hands, rose and came towards the bed, Christine realised with an embarrassing shock that her mother was still in the prime of life. She had married at eighteen, given birth a year and a half later and was, therefore, still shy of fifty; not much older than Allan, in fact.

Maude fitted a filmy net nightcap over her hair.

'What's wrong with you?' she said. 'You look as if you'd seen a ghost.'

'Nothing's wrong with me.' Christine fixed her eyes on the page without taking in a word. 'Which side of the bed do you want?'

'The left,' said Maude without hesitation. 'I always had the inside berth when your father and I

. . . Oh, well, that's just another bad habit best forgotten.' She pulled back the covers and slipped into bed. 'What are you reading?'

'Chekhov.'

'Is it a love story?'

'No, he's a Russian. I found it downstairs.'

'One of hers, I expect.'

Maude lowered herself on the pillow until her chin rested against the edge of the sheet. Her arms, smooth and strong, stuck down over the top of the quilt.

'You're not going to sleep like that, are you?' said Christine.

'I'm just doing my breathing exercises.'

'Of course you are.'

Her mother turned her head. 'Where's Bruce?'

'Believe it or not, I think he's curled up at the foot of Alan's bed.'

'Where you should be,' Maude said.

Christine dropped the book to the floor and, propped on to her elbow, frowned down at her mother whose eyes were now closed.

'I thought you didn't like Alan.'

'I've changed my mind.'

'How convenient.'

An eyelid fluttered, opened just wide enough to show a pupil. 'I'm not pushing you in a direction you don't want to go, dear,' Maude said. 'Sandy was keen on him, too. He thought you'd make an ideal couple.'

'We're not going to be here for ever, Mama.'

'I don't see why not?'

'For heaven's sake!' Christine said, falling back. 'I'm not going to—to give myself to a man just to keep a roof over our heads. In any case, Sandy didn't leave us penniless. We'll have money, quite a lot of money, when everything's settled.'

'Hmm,' said Maude.

'Then we can do anything we like, go where we like.'

'Hmm.'

'We could move back to Glasgow and buy a flat in the West End. Mother, are you listening to me?'

'Every word.'

Disturbed more than angered by Maude's indifference, Chris pulled herself upright against the pillow and shook her mother's arm.

Maude sat up. 'What is it? What's wrong now?'

'In the garden, at the funeral, I met a young man; a corporal.'

Maude stiffened and a wary look stole over her face. 'What corporal? What does he have to do with us?'

Christine placed an arm about her mother's shoulders and drew her close. 'He told me certain things, things we didn't know, about Daddy. The corporal's father fought at Neuve Chapelle. He told me all about it and—and other things too.'

'What other things?'

'About the Brigadier.'

'Not bad things?' Maude said.

'No, Mama, not bad things,' said Chris.

*   *   *

Bruce raised his head from the blanket and let out a drowsy growl. Alan lifted himself an inch or two from the pillow. Faint sounds came from the bedroom at the end of the corridor but whether it was sobbing, laughter or just one of the ladies

356

clearing her throat he could not be sure. He remained alert until the Scottie settled again then let his head sink back into the pillow.

Soon after that, about midnight, he and the dog fell asleep.

CHAPTER THIRTY-TWO

May gave way to a damp and dismal June. It was light until well after ten but the mountains were obscured by cloud and there was never much more than a blink of watery sunlight to remind the good folk of the parish that this was supposed to be summer. Life in Moss House settled into a routine. Alan went off every morning and returned every evening to gleaming furniture and floors, clean linen and a well-cooked meal. After dinner—sometimes before—Chris and he walked the dog and later, in the parlour with Maude, they listened to the wireless or played cards. More often than not, they wound up speculating on what Irene Crockett was up to and how she was adjusting to living alone in the rambling house of Preaching Friar.

Driving home from Glasgow in the evening Alan would detour past the gate of Preaching Friar and on more than one occasion saw the Wolseley parked outside. Once, to his surprise, he caught a glimpse of Mrs Mackintosh emerging from the kitchen door. That little mystery was soon solved when Maude encountered the woman in the Ottershaw Co-operative and was told, smugly, that she, Mrs Mackintosh, had taken over as part-time housekeeper to that very nice lady, Mrs Crockett, who was a model of respectability and an ideal employer; a judgement the occupants of Moss House took, quite naturally, with a pinch of salt. It was, however, safe to assume that if Irene Crockett had hired a housekeeper she did not intend to return to Eastbourne in the near future.

On a muggy Sunday afternoon ten days into the month Alan, Maude and Christine walked the short distance from Moss House to the new cemetery to inspect the stone that had been erected to mark the Brigadier's last resting place. Maude brought flowers that Mr McDonald, Alan's gardener, had cut for her and Christine carried a mat, fork and trowel with which to clear the weeds that the warm wet weather had brought out in profusion. Alan, for his part, did what he could to preserve the regimental wreath and the Brigadier's sodden old cap and make them last at least until summer's end.

When the tasks had been completed and a few tears shed, Christine asked delicately, 'Where does your wife lie, Alan?'

'There,' he said. 'Just there.'

Chris crossed to the marker. Alan wished now that he had brought flowers, too. He stood back a pace, not knowing what to do. He watched her spread the rubber mat, kneel and began to dig up weeds and drop them into her basket. The curve of her back and slope of her shoulders seemed submissive; her skirt tight across her bottom, knees squeezed together, calves, shaped by flat-heeled shoes, forming a vee that vanished beneath her thighs.

He experienced a sudden unwelcome surge of

sexual longing.

'Christine,' he said, 'that's enough.'

'I don't mind doing it, you know,' she said.

'I know, but next time we come here it's my turn.'

If they had been anywhere but the graveyard, and if Maude had not been with them, he would have pulled her into his arms and kissed her, let his hands slide over her body until she told him to stop or—the thought was jarring—did not.

'Come along,' he said gruffly. 'I think it's time we went home.'

*   *   *

Les had taken to bussing into Glasgow on Saturday afternoons. Now that the lambs needed less attention, Charley went with him. Not long ago travelling into Glasgow by bus would have been a noisy adventure, but they were grown men now, men with a purpose. They sat together at the back, smoking and chatting while lads and lassies, and a few old wives, clambered aboard, village by village, until the vehicle was crammed full and swayed alarmingly on the last run into the city.

Tramping round oily yards and rat-ridden scrapheaps was hardly Charley's idea of fun but he was almost, if not quite, as keen as Mr Woodcock to track down the elusive motorcycle parts. Later, leg-weary, they popped into a fish and chip shop and blew more of their wages on a belly-buster which, as Les pointed out, was a blessed sight better than pissing it away on booze.

If the haul of metal parts was light Les would stuff it into a canvas sack and carry it boldly into a picture house of Charley's choice, sit with it on his lap or tuck it under the seat while the stalls filled up and Charley, wreathed in cigarette smoke and reeking of wine gums, slumped lower and lower in his seat and went off into a black and white trance that Les was too considerate to disturb until the programme spun round again.

'Hey, Charley, this is where we came in.'

'Aye, aye, a minute or two more, eh.'

Les would fix his eye on the clock above the exit door or twist his wrist to allow his watch to catch the light and only at the last possible moment would rise, shoulder his swag and head for the street and the bus station with Charley lumbering after him.

'I don't think,' said Beatty, 'he's ever really had a pal before.'

'I'm not his pal,' Les said. 'I'm his sworn enemy.'

Beatty laughed. 'It doesn't look like that to me.'

'We're just keeping an eye on each other, that's all.'

'Am I supposed to fall for it and ask why?'

'Suit yourself,' Les said.

'Well, Charley's always been popular,' Beatty said. 'Everybody's friend, and nobody's chum, if you know what I mean? I think that's why he took such a notion to Christine Summers.'

The door of the hut was open but the evening was too wet to sit outside. Rain dripped mercilessly from the eaves and the windows were steamed over. After she'd cooked supper Beatty had raked the fire in the barrel stove but the coals had caught again and the glow in the stove's little porthole was comforting. Supper over, Beatty lay on the bed while Les, quite at home in Picton now, straddled a

360

kitchen chair and thoughtfully studied the flames.

Throughout his childhood and youth roving the streets of Liverpool it had never occurred to him that he would ever be anything other than a city boy. He had never hankered for the country life, hadn't gone out 'rambling' with one of the local clubs or bicycling up on the moors. Within a month of his arrival in Kennart, though, he had known that he had found his niche, his Eden, and had set about putting down roots.

'He told you about us, didn't he?' Beatty said.

'Yeah, but he doesn't remember much about it,' Les said.

'Oh, that's very flattering—I don't think,' Beatty said. 'Of course he was just a kid at the time.' She swung into a sitting position. 'Charley's always been a pal, but he got caught up thinking he was "in love" with Christine Summers. She was no more the right woman for him than I am. God knows what Charley really wants. I don't—and I'm not sure he knows himself.'

'Glamour,' Mr Woodcock told her.

'Glamour?' Beatty snorted. 'What does he mean by glamour?'

'He's a farmer who doesn't want to be married to a farmer's wife.'

It cheered Beatty to have the postman to talk to and to know he was just over the top of the hill if she ever needed him. He was young, but not as young as he looked, and there was something admirably mature in the way he organised himself. She was still put out, though, by his rejection that night on the hill—or, perhaps, by the fact that he'd seen right through her.

'I'm no saint, you know,' she said. 'I've had a lot

361

of men in my time; none of them worth tuppence.'

'Not even the Doc?'

'I think he's what you might call an aberration. I knew from the start it wouldn't go anywhere. Was that *my* brush with glamour? Maybe it was.' She cocked her head. 'Do you want to go to bed with me, Les?'

'Yep.'

'Why don't you?'

'I'm playing hard to get.'

'My, my! And I thought you were a man of the world.'

'I thought I was, too,' Les said. 'But we live and learn, like.'

He got up, not abruptly, swinging his leg over the chair back as if he were dismounting from a motorbike. He was everything that Charley was not, Beatty thought: quick-witted, perceptive, cocky without being vain. If only she could persuade him to shave off the daft moustache, he might do, might do at a pinch.

'Couple of weeks,' he said, 'my sister Pearl's coming up from Liverpool.'

'Really? What for? A holiday?'

'Nope—to give you the once-over.'

'Give *me* the once-over? Why, for God's sake?'

'To see if she approves.'

'Approves?'

'Of the woman I hope to marry,' the postman said. 'This old bird with nothing to offer but twenty-four ponies and a smile. Pearl thinks it's the ponies I'm after but it ain't.'

'What is it then?' said Beatty softly.

He shrugged. 'Must be the smile, I guess.'

June was a squandered month as far as the pupils of Greenhill Primary were concerned. Fine weather and long light evenings engendered feelings of resentment that they must waste the mid-summer trailing off to be educated when every instinct told them that this was the zenith of their youth.

The wet weather of 1932 dampened the fires of their antipathy, however. When it came time for the official, state-approved, end-of-term examinations the kiddies got their heads down with glum resolution and scrawled and scribbled over the papers or stumbled over long words like 'giraffe' and 'elephant' in spelling tests. In Freddy's class the cry 'Bring Back the Tick' rang out unspoken, a sentiment with which Freddy could not but agree.

Freddy's report to the Board of Rural Education had caused a bit of a furore in committee, so the inspector, Mr Warrender, informed him, but it hadn't been shot down in flames. While multiple-choice testing was regarded as a mite too advanced for the general run of scholars in the county, it had received vociferous support from the deputy convenor, Mr Harrison, who, Mr Warrender said—with a sniff—had got quite carried away with himself.

'In other words,' Freddy sighed, 'it's business as usual.'

'Did you expect anything else?' said Christine.

'At least they didn't throw me out on my ear.'

'I'm glad Ross changed his mind.'

'Didn't have much choice, did he,' Freddy said,

363

'given that you have him over a barrel? I hope old Warrender can snaffle me a copy of the minutes. I'd love to find out exactly what Harrison said. I take it he's stopped badgering you now you're no longer in line to inherit a fortune?'

'He brought back the Brigadier's dog. I haven't seen him since.'

'Pardon me for being nosy,' Freddy said, 'but just what the hell did Harrison think he was doing throwing himself at you in the first place?'

'I don't know,' Christine said. 'It's all very fishy. Ross and his stepfather seem to know more about Irene Crockett than either of them are letting on.'

'What about the will? Is it kosher?'

'Alan's sure it is. No, it's not the will,' Christine said, 'it's something else that doesn't smell right. Alan thinks Ross may have thrown himself at me as a form of insurance. Insurance isn't quite the right word, really, but I think we may assume Ross knew in advance just what the Brigadier might be worth and that if Irene Crockett dropped out of the picture . . .'

'Or the Brigadier changed lawyers and altered his will,' Freddy put in, 'then all that money would go a-begging or, rather, fall into the laps of a mere housekeeper and her daughter. Devious, my dear Watson, very devious.'

'She is his wife, or was, so I suppose she's entitled—'

'Rubbish!' Freddy interrupted. 'She abandoned the poor old beggar, didn't she? She didn't even have the decency to turn up for the funeral. She was obviously afraid she'd bump into one of the Brigadier's chums. Think how embarrassing that might have been.'

364

'That's what Alan said too.'

'You seem to set a lot of store by what the doctor says.' Freddy paused. 'I take it you know you've acquired the reputation of being a bit of a scarlet woman for living in the house of a guy who isn't your husband.'

'It doesn't bother Alan so why should it bother me?'

'Wouldn't you like to be his wife? Living in sin's all very well, but—'

'I am not living in sin.'

'Of course you're not,' said Freddy hastily. 'You are, nonetheless, perceived to be living in sin. Might as well go the whole hog, if you ask me.'

'I did not ask you.'

'I know, I know. I'm sorry,' Freddy said. 'I just wish there was something I could do to help.'

'Like what?'

But Freddy had no answer to that question.

*   *   *

Beatty would never forget the first time she'd been on a horse. Her father had lifted her up and put her on the back of one of the huge draught horses in the carrier's yard in Blairgowrie. She, aged three, had sat there too numb with fright to utter a word. He'd led the horse round the stable yard while walls and rooftops had gone past in a blur and the cobbles had seemed so far below that it had been all she could do not to faint, for she was not at all sure that if she fell her daddy would catch her.

Sometimes she wondered if that childhood experience was the origin of her affinity with

365

ponies which were so much closer to the ground than draught horses. She still didn't ride for pleasure. It had been a year or more since she'd put a bridle on Lavender and when she mounted the docile mare and set off for the hill pasture where Charley was counting sheep, she was not at ease.

The rain had ceased but the air was heavy and clouds of biting insects hovered over every bush. Charley had rolled down his shirt sleeves and pulled his cap over his ears to keep the midges at bay. Beatty had found an old straw hat to cover her hair but with her bare legs jutting over the pony's belly she was trailed by spirals of the voracious little insects.

'You picked a fine night to go for a ride, Beats. Blue murder, isn't it?' Charley said. 'Are you headin' for McCall's farm?'

'I am. But I need a word with you first.' She brought the mare to the tractor but did not dismount. 'What the devil have you been saying to Les about me?'

'Nothin', Beatty. Well, nothin' much.'

'I don't like being talked about behind my back.'

'He's really keen on you, you know.'

'Damn it, Charley. I know he is. He's fetching his sister up from Liverpool to check me over.'

Charley laughed. 'Bloody cheek!'

'I don't know that I want to marry a postman. I don't know that I want to marry anyone to tell you the truth. I mean, I hardly know the man. He's only been here about ten minutes and—'

'He isn't the Doc?'

'No,' Beatty agreed. 'He isn't the Doc.'

'On the other hand, not many guys would build

you a motorbike.'

'Is that what he thinks he's doing?' Beatty said.

'Les is the only person round here who really does knows what he's doin'.'

'Oh, and what's that?'

'Making a life for himself,' said Charley.

*　　　*　　　*

It all respects it looked like being a waste of Sunday afternoon. He picked his uncle up in the West End at half past one and whisked him down the coast in the Alvis, an hour's run through teeming rain towards the shrouded sea.

George was not happy. He was an old man, of course, well over eighty and had been a widower for the best part of ten years. He was looked after by a housekeeper and a day maid, for if there was one thing George was not it was short of cash. He was frail but still relatively healthy and it was only when you looked into his eyes that you realised to what degree the diffidence that prepared you for death had taken hold. He took no pleasure in the trip, no interest in the passing scene. He sat with his knees under a rug and stared at the raindrops on the windscreen as if each little droplet was another minute of his life trickling into oblivion.

There had been no children of the marriage. Lizzie, his wife, had been unable to conceive. Her barren state had made her bitter and had driven a wedge between George and his brother, Willie, whose wife, Flora, had dropped one healthy baby after another, just out of spite; ten in all, six boys and four girls, Alan's cousins, scattered, like some wandering tribe, far and wide across the globe,

367

each breeding with the same fantastic ease as Flora. She had followed Willie and Lizzie to the grave some years ago and Alan could barely remember her now.

His mother was not in the visitors' lounge or in the conservatory.

It frightened him to discover her in nightgown and bed-jacket propped up in bed all alone in her room.

He left George by the bedside on the room's solitary chair while he hurried off to find the matron who assured him there was nothing wrong with Mrs Kelso except a wee touch of the sniffles. For one irrational moment Alan was tempted to shout at the matron and accuse her of neglect but at heart he knew that his mother was no worse than she had been on his last visit and that bed was the best place for her on such a damp and dreary afternoon.

One day—perhaps soon, perhaps not—the chair in the lounge would be empty and the bed too. And she would be gone, the last mute remnant of her existence extinguished, and there would be nothing left for him to do but carry away her scant belongings and the few faded memories she had left behind.

'She doesn't know who I am,' George said.

'She's asleep, George,' Alan told him.

'No, she's awake. She just doesn't know me.' He looked up at Alan. 'Will I go like this too, do you think?'

'I doubt it,' Alan said.

'At least she's not afraid,' George said. 'That's one consolation.'

'Afraid of what?' said Alan.

'You know,' his uncle murmured. 'You know.'

The truth was that he did not know, not yet, though in that pale, square room, its walls freckled by the shadows of the summer rain, he had just an inkling of what his uncle meant.

They lingered for an hour, George seated, Alan standing by the window. His mother did not waken even when George, quite gently, shook her hand. There were several other visitors in the nursing home that afternoon and the noises from the lounge were loud enough to be bothersome: a general chatter, the scrape of chairs and a strange, low-pitched wailing that went on and on.

When Alan suggested it was time to go, George got to his feet at once.

He kissed his sister on the cheek and headed for the door.

Alan chose the coast road for the drive back to Glasgow. The sky had cleared out to the west and the islands in the firth were visible, brooding and dark against the milky band of light that linked sky and sea.

George shed no tears. He seemed, if anything, relieved that his sister had not been awake. He hunched in the passenger seat, the rug discarded, and when, after five or six miles on the road, Alan drew the Alvis to the kerb in front of a small tea shop, he looked up and said, hopefully, 'Toilets?'

A sagging awning covered the shop front. Beneath it, hung on hooks by the door were little spades and buckets, holiday paraphernalia waiting for summer to arrive. George shuffled off to relieve himself in the closet at the rear of the tea-room while Alan found a table close to the window which, like every other window in the land, it seemed, dripped with condensation.

He ordered coffee. George found what he was looking for on the stained menu card and seemed pleased that beef tea was available.

Alan watched his uncle sip the scalding black liquid, watched him break the crackers that came with it and shove the pieces into his mouth.

If his mother had been awake he would have told her his news. It would, of course, have been pointless, utterly, utterly pointless, but he would have told her anyway and, against all reason, have looked for her approval.

'George,' he said. 'Uncle George.'

He expected little or nothing. He was prepared for disappointment.

'What is it?' his uncle said. 'Is something wrong?'

'I'm thinking of getting married again.'

It was as if a switch had been thrown inside his uncle's head. The brows moved first, rising, then the eyes, buried in wrinkled flesh, widened and lit up.

'A doctor, is she?' George asked.

'A teacher, a school teacher.'

'Is she young?'

'Yes,' Alan said. 'Quite young.'

'Oh, that's good news, son,' his uncle said, beaming. 'Jolly good news,' and narrowly missing the Bovril cup, lunged across the table to shake his nephew's hand.

*   *   *

It was cooler now, with the hint of a breeze coming up from the loch. The smells of the garden wafted around him as he stepped from the car and, pausing to collect his thoughts, looked away to the hills.

There had been nothing complicated about it after all. He had committed himself that afternoon in the tea shop by telling his uncle of his intentions.

Now all he had to do was bide his time, a day or two at most, and out there on the ridge road, close to the spot where he'd first caught sight of her, go down on one knee and ask Christine to be his wife. He did not think she would refuse. She was his prisoner, his hostage.

Five thousand pounds was no small sum but would it be enough to change her life and Maude's for ever? Wasn't that what every young woman dreamed of, why she longed to be loved and to be married to the man she loved: to change her life for ever, to be happy ever after? He would do that for her. He would make a comfortable life for Christine and her mother here in Moss House. Over the past few months, he had come to realise what had been denied him—what he had denied himself—and thanked God and his lucky stars that he had bumped against Christine before it was too late.

Whistling to himself, he bounded up the steps into the house and, like the husband he soon would be, called out to announce that he was home.

CHAPTER THIRTY-THREE

'Here he is now,' Christine said. 'I'm sorry you've had to wait but I think it best if he hears it from you and not, as it were, second-hand.'

Freddy put down his glass and looked expectantly towards the sitting-room door. His wife, on the sofa by his side, continued to sip sherry as if nothing was happening, while Maude, who had been darting in and out for the past half-hour or so, was suddenly motionless.

'Here, we're in here,' Christine called.

A moment later Alan threw open the door and peeped round it.

'There you are, darling . . .' he began, then, checking himself, said, 'I'm sorry, I didn't realise you had guests.'

He was cheerful, almost gay. Christine wondered what had brought on his effervescent mood and why he had called her 'darling.' Before he'd left to collect his uncle for the drive down into Ayrshire he had been moody and depressed. What had changed him? Had his mother shown signs of recovery? If so what difference would that make to him, to all of them?

'Mrs McKay'—Alan offered his hand—'what an unexpected pleasure.'

Lucille held the sherry glass at arm's length, bit the finger of her best black Sunday glove and removed it before, skin to skin, she shook the doctor's hand.

'Mr McKay'—Alan politely detached himself from Lucille—'good to meet you again. Nice of you to drop by. I see you've been taken care of. May I freshen up your drink?'

'It isn't a social call, Alan,' Christine said, 'not exactly.'

Freddy wiped his hand across his mouth, got to his feet and dropped into teaching mode. 'We—look, what do I call you?'

'Alan. I think we know each other well enough to dispense with formality.'

'Well, Alan,' Freddy went on, 'something rather interesting has come to our attention or perhaps I should say to my dear lady wife's attention.'

Alan glanced at Maude who, with hands clasped at her breast, was as mute as marble. He glanced next at Christine who frowned and shook her head.

'And what,' Alan said guardedly, 'might that be?'

With a little flourish, Freddy said, 'Lucille,' and, sitting down, gave the floor over to his wife. She did not make a grand production out of it. She sank back into the cushions, crossed one leg over the other, took a sip of sherry and eased into her story as if it had no more weight than the usual village gossip.

'Do you know the little corner shop in Kennart?' she began.

'I know where it is,' said Alan.

'Today I go there. It opens on Sunday for three hours to sell the newspapers. I am there about one o'clock for cigarettes and the newspaper that we read, the *Post*. They do not sell drink on Sunday; a stupid bye-law, is it not?'

'Lucille,' said Freddy in an inoffensive sing-song. 'Move on.'

'Three or four people are buying newspapers and other items. I take myself into the queue, for the shop is not large. I see ahead of me a woman who is buying newspapers and cigarettes. She is not familiar to me, not really so, until she turns to pass by me out of the shop. She is there and I am here.' Lucille held up her hand, palm innermost, and pressed it to the tip of her nose. 'Like so.'

'Face to face,' said Freddy, nodding.

'Yes, face to face. And what a face I have to confront. It is a face from out of the fog of my past. She looks at me with hardness and I look at her.'

'Tell them what you said,' Freddy suggested.

'I said, "Gladys—Gladys Hobbs, what on earth are you doing here?" She looks at me with hardness, with loathing—is that the word, Freddy?'

'I imagine it probably is.'

'With—with hatred and loathing. She does not say, "Hello, Lucille, how are you?" She says nothing, not a word. She hits me with her arm, her shoulder and goes out into the street. I am hurt and I am confused.'

'Dear God,' Alan murmured. 'I see where this is going.'

'Oh, yes,' said Freddy. 'No flies on my Lucille.'

'It's two of them, I think,' Lucille McKay continued. 'I think, no, it cannot be that Gladys Hobbs has a double. I go to the counter and I ask the woman there, "Who is that rude woman?" And the woman at the counter, who knows everyone, says, "That is Mrs Crockett from Preaching Friar, the widow of the old Brigadier." I ask, "How do you know that?" She answers, "It is the name on her account."'

'A new account,' said Freddy. 'Brand spanking new.'

'Gladys,' Alan said. 'Gladys, not Irene.'

'Her sister,' Christine said. 'Tell him the rest of it, Lucille.'

'I knew them both when I lived in London some time before I went to be employed by the Royal Flying Corps, before I met . . .'

'Freddy,' said Freddy.

'Before I met Freddy, yes. Gladys was the small one, the fat one, though not so fat as she has now become,' Lucille said. 'Irene was the other one, the older. She was the looker. So attractive, tall, with blonde hair. All the officers were chasing after her, begging her to go with them.'

'Where did all this take place?' Alan asked.

'In London. In the places where officers meet: picnics, dancing clubs, the balls given by the regiments. She was there, Irene, always. She was famous for it.'

'I'll bet she was,' said Freddy. 'Perhaps, dearest, you'd better tell them what you were doing there. I mean, of course, what all the girls were after, not just you.'

Lucille waved the sherry glass. 'Men. We were after men. We were after a man to take care of us—or marry us if he did not already have a wife. It was a glorious opportunity for those of us who were young and pretty. There was the smell of war in the air to bring excitement to the soldiers, to make them . . .' Lucille rolled her eyes. 'To make them . . .'

'Say eager,' Freddy told her.

'To make them so eager, so—virile,' Lucille said. 'Irene had a boy from the Irish Guards, but he was only a second lieutenant. He was so mad for her he would have died for her.'

'Which he probably did,' said Freddy.

'Did you know the Brigadier?' Maude put in. 'Was he one of the officers?'

'I knew him to look at but I did not know who he was. He was too old for me, too whiskery. I had a man who said he would look after me and I left London to be with him before we went to the Royal Flying Corps. I did not see the old Brigadier with Irene Hobbs but I heard she had married him and it had all gone wrong.'

Christine had seated herself in an armchair while Lucille told her story. Alan rested on the arm of the chair and put an arm about her.

'What about Gladys?' he said.

'She was the clinging one, the . . .' Lucille hesitated.

'Hanger-on,' said Freddy.

'The hanger-on, yes. She married too, a younger man, I heard.'

'Leonard was his name,' Christine said. 'He was killed in France.'

'Which means?' Freddy said.

And Alan said, 'A pension.'

'That is all I know,' Lucille said. 'Is it enough for you?'

'Are you absolutely sure this woman is Gladys Hobbs?' Alan asked.

'I am sure,' Lucille answered. 'It is a face you cannot forget.'

'Then it's enough for us—for Christine and her mama,' Alan said. 'What do you think, darling?'

He had called her 'darling' again. She looked up at him, frowning.

If what Lucille McKay said was true Maude would inherit everything the Brigadier had willed to the woman who had once been his wife, but was not his wife at all. She should have been excited but she was not. She said, 'Can we be sure that Irene Crockett hasn't brought her sister to stay with her in Preaching Friar?'

'And sign her accounts as Irene Crockett?' Alan said. 'Highly unlikely.'

'Five feet tall and fat,' Freddy said. 'There can't be two like that, can there?'

Maude said, 'Her name wouldn't be Crockett, or even Hobbs, not if she was widowed in the Great War. She would be—what was it, dear?'

'Leonard,' Christine answered. 'If she's Gladys, where's Irene?'

'Dead for all we know,' Maude said.

'Or married again,' said Freddy. 'Oh, what a gift that would be.'

'If that is all I can do for you,' Lucille McKay said, 'we will go home.'

Alan sprang to his feet. 'Nonsense,' he said. 'Maude, can you put up supper for five with what's in the larder?'

'I certainly can,' Maude said chirpily.

Christine said, 'Alan, what are we going to do?'

'Eat, drink and be merry, of course.'

'But what about Geddes Johnston?'

'Leave Geddes Johnston to me.'

*   *   *

There had been a touch of thunder in the night. The morning was cool and pleasant. Mist carpeted the fields and smudged the outline of the hills. The platform at Ottershaw Halt was wet with either rain or dew.

Alan opened the door and stepped into the

carriage.

Geddes Johnston glanced up from his newspaper.

'Motorcar broken down, Kelso?' he said.

'No,' Alan said. 'I want a word with you, that's all.'

'A word. With me. About what?'

'Fraud,' Alan said. 'Bare-faced fraud.'

CHAPTER THIRTY-FOUR

Beatty lay back on the grassy bank that fronted the old McCall place. She took a mouthful of beer and passed the bottle to the postman who sat cross-legged beside her. She looked up at the sky, a brilliant blue, fading just a little into dusk.

'In such a night as this,' she said, 'when the sweet wind did gently kiss the trees, and they did make no noise, in such a night Troilus methinks mounted the Troyan walls, and sighed his soul toward the Grecian tents, where Cressid lay that night.'

'I wish you wouldn't do that,' Mr Woodcock said.

'Do what?'

'Spout poetry.'

'Why not? Nothing wrong with a bit of Shakespeare.'

'You make me feel ignorant.'

Beatty rolled on to her hip and elbow and put a hand on his knee.

'One thing you're not, Sunny Jim, is ignorant.'

'I never had no education, you know.'

'Neither did I,' said Beatty.

'How come you know so much then?'

'Don't kid yourself, Les, just because I can reel off a few verses from *The Merchant of Venice* doesn't make me smart. It all comes from a book, a book my daddy gave me because he thought I'd like the pictures. And I did like the pictures. But I liked the words better and I learned a lot of them by heart, even though I didn't know what they meant back then.'

'Still got it, have you?'

'The book? Yeah, still got it.'

'Bet you know what the words mean now?'

She smiled. 'Some of them, yes, some of them.'

He put the bottle down carefully, threw a leg over her and pressed her flat upon the grass. He fitted his thighs around her hips and planted an elbow on each side of her head.

'Give's a bit more then,' he said.

'A bit more what?'

'Shakespeare, of course.'

She thought for a moment. 'In such a night did young Lorenzo swear he loved her well, stealing her soul with many vows of faith—and ne'er a true one.'

'Like that, was it?'

'Like what?'

'This Lorenzo guy was a con man.'

'Pretty much, I suppose,' Beatty said.

'You don't think I'm a con man, Beatty, do you?'

'I just don't understand what you see in me.'

He grinned and let out a little howl.

'Now don't start anything you don't intend to finish,' Beatty told him. 'Anyhow, that's not an answer, not the answer I'm looking for.'

He sighed and unhitched himself. 'What do you expect me to say, like?' he asked. 'You know what you are and you know what I am. Ain't that good enough for you?'

She got on her knees and faced him, as if she were a child about to put a daisy chain around his neck. 'No,' she said, 'I want to hear you say it; just once I want to hear you say it.'

'Even if it isn't true?'

She put both hands on his shoulders and stared into his eyes. 'I have special powers, Mr Woodcock. I'll be able to tell if it's true or not.'

'Geeze,' he said. 'I hope not.'

'You wouldn't lie to me, Les, would you?'

'Nah,' he said nervously. 'I wouldn't lie to you.'

'Then say it. Just once—say it.'

'Okay, okay. Beatty—I love you.'

'Very nice. Would you like to try again?'

'I love you, Beatty McCall, I really and truly do.'

'Once more?'

'Don't push your luck,' the postman said.

*   *   *

The master of delay, the arch-prevaricator could move like lightning, it seemed, when his neck was on the block. The letter was delivered at Moss House by special courier late on Tuesday afternoon. It was headed with Geddes Johnston's name and the address of his office in Glasgow, and was couched in a style so convoluted that it read less like a confession than a government statute. It contained no admission of guilt, of malfeasance, deception, fraud or any wrong-doing whatsoever. There was no mention of Gladys Hobbs, Gladys

380

Leonard—or any other Gladys for that matter. It was as if Gladys, not Irene, had vanished from the face of the earth.

As sole executor of the estate of the late Alexander Crockett, it was incumbent upon Randolph Geddes Johnston to inform Maude Summers that prior to the will's advancement to proving and registration, the widow of said Alexander Crockett, namely Mrs Irene Hobbs Crockett, had elected to relinquish claim to the whole of the residue of the estate and within the terms of bequest the estate in its entirety would consequently fall to Maude Summers, pursuant to completion of inventory and settlements.

No reason was given for Mrs Crockett's decision. Under law, no reason was required. The typewritten copy of the Declaration of Disclaim was signed by Irene Crockett, witnessed and dated by Randolph Geddes Johnston; a final act of forgery on the lady's part and of wilful deceit on the part of the lawyer, who had probably decided that if he was going to swing it might as well be for a sheep as a lamb.

On Wednesday forenoon a second letter reached Maude at Moss House, together with a cheque drawn against the estate to cover out-of-pocket funeral expenses, plus a further sum of £200 to prevent further 'distress and disarray', a term that defied any legal definition and simply meant conscience money.

On Wednesday evening, soon after supper, Alan drove Maude and Christine down to Preaching Friar, together with their luggage and the dog.

The front door key had been left in the lock and the bunch of keys to the other locks in the house had been tossed on the hall table. Unwashed dishes were piled in the sink and the larder was almost empty. There was mud on the carpet in the sitting-room, cold ashes in the grate in the fireplace. The bed in the upstairs room, Maude's room, had not been made and throughout the house ashtrays were filled with the remains of cork-tipped cigarettes. The drawers in the Brigadier's roll-top desk had been hauled out and rammed roughly back in place but nothing appeared to have been taken—nothing, that is, but the bundle of greeting cards and the photograph of Irene in her wedding gown which, in Gladys Hobbs Leonard's view, might well be construed as evidence.

By half past nine Maude, Christine and the Scottie were installed in Preaching Friar as if they had never been away.

And by half past ten Alan was back in Moss House which seemed more empty, echoing and lonely than ever before.

*   *   *

'For someone who's just inherited wealth beyond the dreams of avarice,' Freddy said, 'you're looking rather down in the mouth.'

'I haven't inherited a penny,' Christine told him. 'My mother has.'

'So what! She's not going to kick you out, is she?'

'Of course not.'

'I reckon you'll be giving up the profession of teaching as soon as you can hand in your notice?'

'I—I'm not sure.'

'Well, I suppose you might need something to occupy the idle hours. Embroidery would be the better bet, though.' He paused. 'Like the Lady of Shalott.'

'What's that supposed to mean?'

'Come to think of it, that was weaving not embroidery,' Freddy said. 'I was never much taken with Tennyson.'

Christine lifted the corner of a sandwich and sniffed at the filling.

Freddy and she were seated on a bench at the front of the school. Giving them a wide berth, the children scampered about, enjoying the sunshine. Freddy drank soda pop from a brown glass bottle. He was a bit of clown, he knew that well enough, but he'd been through the mill in his day and was astute enough to realise what was bothering his dainty wee cohort.

'She did you no favours, my dear lady wife, did she?' he said.

'Of course she did. My mother's delighted to be back in Preaching Friar, although she misses Sandy more than she cares to let on. I do, too, to be honest. Oh, it's a lovely house and we're very comfortable there and when everything's finally settled . . .' She hesitated. 'It's an awful lot of money, Freddy, an awful lot.'

'If you feel like giving any of it away I'd be happy to take it off your hands,' Freddy said. 'He's backed off, hasn't he?'

Christine watched the little girls skipping rope in the corner where the playground gave on to the edge of Charley Noonan's potato field. There was no Charley Noonan, though, only the strong, straggling shoots of the spring planting.

383

'Yes, he's backed off,' Christine said. 'He thinks we don't need him.'

'But you do, don't you?'

'I need someone, that's certain.' She nibbled the edge of the sandwich. 'He'll go back to her, to the pony woman, I expect.'

'Then I think he'll be disappointed. That horse has already bolted.'

'What do you mean?'

'She doesn't need him either. From what I hear from little birdies Mrs McCall has practically moved in with our postman up at the old farm.'

'Mr Woodcock?'

'Flash Harry, yep; the very same.'

'Really?'

'Wedding bells or maybe baby booties are in the offing.'

'You really are a fount of knowledge, Freddy,' Christine said and took a great big bite of cheese and pickle and, when it was offered her, a hearty slug of soda pop to wash it down.

*   *   *

Dumpy little Mrs Mackintosh was too outraged to keep her mouth shut. She had no idea, of course, what had really happened, or why, in the course of a single afternoon, Monday, she had gone from being housekeeper to a respectable middle-aged English lady to being unemployed.

When news reached her, as news will, that Maude Summers and that daughter of hers had moved back into Preaching Friar and Dr Kelso was on his own again, she had stuffed her pride in her pocket, had gone stumping down to Moss House and had told him, though not in so many words, that she was willing to forgive and forget and if he needed her services she would be able to return to work immediately. He hadn't even asked her to step in, hadn't even been courteous enough to let her finish before he'd told her, in no uncertain terms, that he wouldn't employ her again if she was the last woman in Ottershaw. And not once did it dawn on little Mrs Mackintosh that she, not he, was in the wrong and that she, not he, had committed the unpardonable sin of indiscretion.

'Serves the old bitch right,' said Beatty. 'At least Alan didn't give in to her.'

'Come on, Beats,' Charley said. 'He's not the villain here.'

'No, I don't suppose he is,' Beatty conceded. 'I thought it was fixed, though. I thought once the teacher got her feet under his table that would be the end of it. I wonder what happened to change things?'

'Something about the old boy's will,' Charley said. 'Maybe it wasn't signed.'

'Maybe not,' Beatty said. 'But you'd think the Brigadier's lawyer would have sorted all that out before the widow came up from England.'

Charley was still seated on the tractor. He had made it clear that he didn't have much time to hang around and chat. He had several acres to manure and second plough and at the end of the month, the shearing. He said, 'Anyway, by the way Mrs Mack's carryin' on you'd think he'd jilted her at the steps o' the altar.'

'Jilted who? Who are we talking about, Charley?'

'Nobody really, just a figure o' speech.' He

385

leaned on the steering wheel. 'It's probably as well, though, that you an' our Les are spliced.'

'We're not spliced yet.'

Charley cleared his throat and tapped his fingers on the steering wheel. 'You wouldn't go givin' Les the heave-ho, would you, Beatty?'

'Now why would I do that?'

'If the Doc came by, cap in hand, say?'

'Did Les send you here to sound me out?'

'Geeze, no! He'd kill me if he thought I was meddling.'

Beatty rose from the step, sauntered over to the Wallis and tapped Charley's arm. 'Well, if my name does happen to come up in conversation you can assure "our Les" that if anybody's going to weasel out of our arrangement, such as it is, it isn't going to be me. Got that?'

'Got it loud and clear,' Charley said. 'When's his kid sister due to arrive?'

'Tomorrow sometime.'

'And then what? A beeline to the altar?'

'This isn't *Range Romances*, Charley. I'm not rushing into anything.'

'Now where have I heard that before?' said Charley. 'If Les does ask you to marry him what are you gonna say?'

'I'm going to say I'll think about it,' Beatty said.

'For how long?'

'Oh, ten minutes. Maybe fifteen.'

'And then what?' said Charley again.

'I'm going to say yes, of course.'

386

CHAPTER THIRTY-FIVE

It had been, as Josie put it, 'an absolute bugger of a day'. In the morning there had been an acute case of mastoiditis to deal with—gouge, mallet, sterile gauze, and not much chat over the table.

Then, just before lunch, with no warning at all, a ten-year-old boy had been rushed into the hospital in a police van suffering from what was swiftly diagnosed as a ruptured liver. He had, it appeared, being playing truant from school along with two pals and risking life and limb in the dangerous game of teasing the big dray horses at the foot of the West Nile Street hill. One kick from one hoof had sent him flying across the pavement and he had been dashed lucky that a police van had been passing along St Vincent Street at precisely that moment or shock and haemorrhage would have done for him on the spot.

As it was, he was barely conscious and his pulse was through the roof when he was rushed to the theatre wing where Alan, Josie and the crew were tidying up before going in search of lunch. He was on the table within minutes of arrival, his blood pressure soaring as Josie administered the ether, theatre nurses running hither and thither to fetch the large curved needles and thick catgut that Alan shouted for, and Hargreaves, half in and half out of his gown, already in position with the clamps that would be required to close off the hepatic artery and portal vein if the kid was to have any chance at all of pulling through.

Josie watched Alan angle the knife and, without

hesitation, draw the blade down the middle line above the umbilicus, and open the abdomen. There was blood everywhere. The child began to twitch and shake and at that moment she thought they'd lost him. She looked from the gauges to Alan Kelso's face and saw the sheer, fearless authority in his eyes, that commanding masculine confidence that marked the best surgeons from the also-rans. There was no thought in his head that this child might die, though the mortality rate in such severe cases was in excess of eighty per cent. He was engaged, totally engaged with the half-grown body before him, his fingers toying—for that's what it looked like—toying with the damaged organ that the knife had exposed.

She lay back against the leather and tried to relax. She was used to long shifts, to emergencies, to being on her feet and trading on her nerves but for some reason the afternoon had knocked the stuffing out of her.

When Alan had offered to drop her off at her flat, she hadn't refused.

The motorcar turned from the top of Byres Road and headed west.

It was still early. Yards and factories hadn't let out yet. There were children about, schoolchildren, a different breed from the ragamuffins whose idea of fun was to duck out of school and taunt the big dray horses that stood passively at the foot of the city centre hill waiting for trade. Children in neat uniforms, the boys in grey flannels, the girls in pleated skirts and blazers; if she'd ever had a child, Josie thought, they'd have been like that, clean and respectable and, most of all, safe.

She said, 'Do you think he'll pull through?'

'Hmm,' Alan said. 'Fair chance.'

'Did the police find the mother?'

'Yes.'

'Did you tell her he might not recover?'

'No, I told her he'll live to fight another day. And he will.'

She looked from the side window at the elegant terraces flying past.

'You're good, Kelso,' she said. 'You really are good. I've never told you so before and I'll never tell you again, but you—'

'All right,' he said. 'That's enough soft soap. It's all in the day's work.'

'The devil it is,' said Josie, with a sigh. 'Turn right at the next corner.'

Ashburn Gardens swung into view. The oval of grass was velvety in the sunlight, the trees in full leaf. Small children with nannies were out and about. Behind the trees the curved terrace of town houses towered into the blue sky, brass handles and polished doors gleaming.

Alan parked the Alvis at the kerb, leaned over and looked up.

'So this is where you live?' he said.

'Been here for ages,' Josie said. 'For ever, just about.'

'Very grand.'

'Not that grand,' she said. 'I'm right up there, top floor, in what used to be the servants' loft. I do have a balcony, though—well, a balustrade. If you don't mind climbing through the window, the view is magnificent. Come up for a drink. I'll show you the city as you've never seen it before.'

She expected him to refuse, concoct an excuse,

389

hustle her from the car, give her, as he always did, the brush-off.

'Yes,' he said. 'I'd like that.'

She led him though the gloomy hallway and up three flights, opened the door to her flat with her key and let him enter first. She had dreamed of this moment, but somehow it didn't mean as much as she'd thought it would.

She showed him into the living-room, pointed at the sideboard and told him to help himself to gin and tonic. She went into her bedroom, closed the door, and changed into a long-skirted print dress. She did up all the buttons, tidied her hair then went back into the living-room and took the glass from his hand. He had sliced up one of the lemons that nestled in a basket on the sideboard and her drink tasted sharp and refreshing.

The room seemed smaller with Alan in it. It hadn't occurred to her before just how bijou and 'one person' her flat really was.

He drank from the tall glass and licked his lower lip. 'Very welcome.'

They remained standing, as awkward as two strangers who had arrived early at a cocktail party. He took a pace towards the fireplace and looked up at the framed portrait that hung above the mantelpiece.

'Who is it?' he said.

'The painter? Nobody you've ever heard of—Oliver Slater. He was fond of muted colours. Beige was his trademark.'

'I mean the man, the subject.'

'That's Eric—in uniform.'

'And who's Eric?'

'Oh, just a fellow I used to know.'

Alan shook his glass and drank again.

After a moment, he said, 'I hadn't realised you'd lost someone in the war.'

She stood beside him, looking up at the portrait too. 'Oh, I didn't lose him,' she said. 'I know exactly where he is. He's in a bungalow in Eastwood with his wife and three daughters. Three daughters! Serves the bastard right. No, Eric didn't meet a sticky end. He just decided I wasn't the girl for him and scurried off in another direction.'

'I'm sorry.'

'He was probably right. I probably wasn't the girl for him,' she said. 'However, I promised you a view. Come, Mr Kelso, and be duly amazed.'

She opened the catch on the crescent-shaped window and pulled it upward. It swung open on two big oily hinges and admitted the sounds and smells of the city. She stepped on to a blanket chest positioned below the window and, dipping her head, carried her drink out on to a strip of roof protected by a carved stone balustrade. She took Alan's hand and helped him through the opening.

Behind him black slates sloped steeply to the roof ridge. Before him most of Glasgow was spread out like a three-dimensional map, east, south and west, and a straight half-mile away the hospital posed majestically on its hill. Josie put an arm about his shoulder and pointed out the landmarks, the chimneys, churches, parks, cranes and even the thoroughfares that climbed out of the smoky river basin.

'Impressed?' she asked.

'Very impressed,' he answered.

'All this could have been yours, my son, if only you'd married me.' She leaned into him, shoulder to shoulder. 'What are you doing here, Alan? I mean, why aren't you galloping home to your child of the wild wood, your teacher person—and her old mother, of course?'

'They've gone.'

'Gone? What does that mean? Left Ottershaw?'

'They've gone back to Preaching Friar.'

'Don't tell me you got fresh with her and she took fright?'

'Perhaps I should have—what is it?—"got fresh" with her but, as it happens, I didn't. The Brigadier's widow I told you about turned out to be an impostor. By a stroke of sheer good fortune she was recognised by someone who'd known her in London before the war. She wasn't Irene Crockett at all but her sister, Gladys. It was a fiddle, a swindle. When I confronted the lawyer with what we'd learned, he told me everything; just him and me sitting in the carriage of the local train at an early hour of the morning, two respectable gentlemen discreetly sharing secrets—and making a deal. That's why Chris and her mother are back in Preaching Friar and will soon be legal owners of the place.'

'You cut your own throat, didn't you?'

'I reached an agreement with the lawyer, that's all. It seems the Brigadier's widow, Irene, fell head over heels in love with a Canadian pilot. When the war ended, he asked her to go back to Canada and marry him there. Problem was that Irene was still married to the Brigadier who was not only rich but old and ailing—or so she thought.'

'I smell bigamy.'

'And greed,' Alan said. 'And mendacity. The little sister, Gladys, *had* been widowed in the war.

392

She was struggling along on a bit of money her husband left her plus her widow's pension and making ends meet by running a small boarding house in Eastbourne. Brigadier Crockett, generous fellow, had allocated a monthly sum to Irene in the hope that one day perhaps she might come back to him.'

'No fool like an old fool,' Josie put in.

She leaned her backside on the balustrade, the gin glass in both hands. Alan wasn't really telling her the tale. He seemed, rather, to be broadcasting it to the city of Glasgow, or maybe just to the empty air. A matter of hours ago she'd watched him slice boldly into the abdomen of a young boy and swiftly repair a lacerated liver. Now, though, he seemed bewildered, as if he were struggling to make sense of another man's life, another man's mistake.

'The sisters put their heads together and came up with a scheme,' Alan continued. 'Irene went off to Canada to wed her pilot, conveniently neglecting to mention that she was already married. Gladys, as far as Sandy Crockett was concerned, became Irene. She sent him Christmas cards, postcards in plain envelopes, greetings from time to time, just to let him know that he was still in her thoughts.'

'In other words,' Josie said, 'to keep the flame alive while cashing monthly cheques. That, I assume, was part of the agreement with her sister.'

'All very well and good until the Brigadier came to his senses and sent his lawyer, Johnston, to Eastbourne to negotiate a divorce.'

'How long ago?'

'Quite some time ago, I think. Johnston took his

393

stepson with him, presumably for a holiday, and, of course, tumbled to the deception immediately. He convinced the Brigadier that divorce was not advisable or tenable or some such thing and cut himself in for a share of the estate when the Brigadier eventually passed on.'

'Do you think he's sleeping with this woman, this Gladys?'

'The thought had crossed my mind. When it became clear that the Brigadier was about to press more strenuously for a divorce and leave everything to Maude and Christine Summers, young Harrison stepped in or, perhaps, was brought in—it hardly matters—to court and marry Christine as a precaution. The trouble was that he was too hasty, too clumsy to do it properly. And then, without warning, the Brigadier was no more.'

'I'm surprised the lawyer fellow told you all this.'

'He had very little choice,' Alan said. 'He knew we'd have no compunction in exposing him and the sisters and that if the will was challenged in court any lawyer worth his fee would dig deep and everything would come to the surface. Irene would be charged with bigamy, her sister with fraud, and Johnston's career would be wrecked. I gave Johnston my word I'd say nothing provided he made everything right in as short a time as possible. So far, he's kept his side of the bargain. The widow who wasn't has gone and Maude Summers should have her money by early autumn. Meanwhile Christine's back living in her beloved Preaching Friar—and I'm out in the cold.'

'Are you out in the cold?'

'Christine doesn't need me any more.'

'Is that your excuse? Feeble, old chum, feeble

isn't the word for it,' Josie said. 'Tell me, why *did* you come up here today? It wasn't for the gin and it certainly wasn't to lure me into bed.'

'I need advice, Josie, and you're the only friend I have.'

'Poor you,' she said. 'What about your pony farmer?'

'Talking to her about it would not be a good idea.'

'No, that much I can see,' Josie said. 'What do you expect from me, Alan?'

'Tell me what to do.'

'For God's sake, you're what—forty-two years old . . .'

'Forty-six. Christine's not quite thirty.'

'Do you think you'll wind up like the Brigadier and be taken advantage of?' Josie said. 'Hold on a minute. I've got it: you don't think you've enough to offer, do you? You were hoping to buy the girl's gratitude in case love wasn't enough. You're a devious beggar, Kelso; devious but stupid. You don't have a clue about women, do you? You don't understand us at all.'

'I was about to ask her to marry me when this happened. Everything changed overnight. I suppose you're right, Josie: I did rather cut my own throat.'

Josie drained her glass and put it down at her feet.

'Tell me,' she said, 'when you were planting sutures in that wee boy's liver this afternoon were you thinking about her?'

'Christine? Yes, as a matter of fact I was,' Alan admitted. 'She's always there in the back of my mind. I don't know what to do, Josie, truly I don't.

What can I offer her now? I've a big empty house and she has this place called Preaching Friar. How do you settle that sort of thing?'

'First of all you have to trust her,' Josie said. 'And then you have to compromise. It's as simple as that, Alan; compromise.'

'It's something I've never been much good at—compromise, I mean.'

'You should have taken lessons when you had the chance.'

'Lessons? Lessons from whom?'

'Marion,' Josie told him. 'Marion, your wife.'

*   *   *

It was a shade too early for the boozers to be heading for the Bull even on a warm June evening and the top end of Main Street was quiet. Charley had parked the tractor and trailer well clear of the bus stop and Les and he were seated on the wall at the end of the church grounds watching for the bus from Glasgow to nose round the corner and draw to a halt.

'I don't know what the heck I'm doin' here,' said Charley. 'I mean, is your sister crippled or somethin', she can't walk a couple o' miles over dry ground in broad daylight?'

'She's used to pavements, Charley.'

'Well, if she's stayin' with you for any length o' time she'd better get used to roughin' it. Have you done up a room for her?'

'Yep. The big bedroom upstairs.'

'Carved her a four-poster out o' a tree trunk at the weekend, I suppose.'

'Camp bed.'

'Silk sheets on a camp bed.' Charley shook his head. 'Tut-tut-tut!'

'She's me sister, Charley. She's not made of porcelain, like.'

'Porcelain or not,' Charley said, 'she's not gonna be too pleased at bein' dumped in a farm cart on her first visit to Scotland. What's she doin' up here, any roads? Have you really dragged her north just to give Beatty the once-over?'

'I didn't drag her anywhere,' Les said. 'One thing you don't do with our Pearl is make her do something she doesn't fancy. Matter of fact, she volunteered. She's pretty sick of Liverpool right now since she lost her job. Apart from that, she's curious, I guess.'

'Can't say I blame her,' Charley conceded. 'I'd be curious too if my brother was seriously thinkin' of gettin' hitched to—'

'Careful,' Les said pleasantly. 'You're talking of the woman I love.'

'Where is Beatty, anyway?'

'My place,' Les said. 'Cooking.'

'Cookin' what?'

'Whatever she can fit into the frying pan. By the by, you're invited to stick around for supper.'

'Won't that be awkward?'

'Beatty's idea. Three's a crowd, she says, and she needs moral support.'

'Me? Moral support? That'll be the day,' Charley said. 'Besides, I'm not dressed for company. Your sister's not expecting me to be togged out in a kilt, is she? I haven't worn a kilt since my auntie's weddin' when I was five year old.'

'You look fine, Charley. Dungarees suit you.'

'If I'd thought,' Charley said, 'I'd have put on my

397

blue suit.'

'Too late now, man,' Les told him as the single-decker from Glasgow hove into view, ground to a halt at the bus stop and the passengers began to alight.

'Where is she?' Charley said. 'Don't tell me she's missed it.'

'Nope. There she is. My very own kid sister.'

'That's her?' said Charley. 'You're kidding me!'

If the high-waisted, close-fitting dress with the skirt split to the knee had been bought off the peg Charley wasn't aware of it, nor did he care. It was the hat that really did the trick: the little hat pulled down over one eye, with just a strand of pure platinum blonde hair falling across her face. Garbo, he thought: no, Harlow: no, the other one, what's her name?

'Pearl, this is my friend Charley Noonan.'

'So *this* is Charley,' the girl said. 'I *am* pleased to meetcha.'

She had a husky voice and the strangely exotic Liverpool accent that Charley would never quite get used to or tired of over the years.

'An'—an'—I'm pleased to meet *you*,' he got out.

She gave her brother a hug. Why not me, why not me? Charley thought.

Taking the suitcase from her hand he threw it up on his shoulder then waving his arm like a wagon master, cried, 'This way, Miss Woodcock. This way,' and led her along the pavement to the tractor.

'Oooo,' she said, 'now this is classy, real classy. Do I get to drive?'

He couldn't refuse. He didn't have the gall, the gumption, the temerity, the willpower to refuse her

398

anything. 'There's only one seat, but,' was the best he could manage but that, he already knew, would not be enough to deter this girl.

'Leslie, in the back,' Pearl said and, hoisting up her skirt, climbed on to the Wallis and settled her delicate, heart-shaped bottom on the skinny metal seat. 'I like this. Oooo, I do like this. Charley, show me how it works, will yah?'

He glanced at Les who grinned, lobbed the suitcase into the trailer and scrambled up after it. It was up to him, Charley realised, all up to him. He drew in a great deep breath, deeper than any breath he had ever drawn before and, adopting his tough *Public Enemy* snarl, said, 'Yeah, sure thing.'

He hauled himself up and positioned himself behind her, his knees almost pinching her hips. He felt tall, very tall, ten feet tall as he looked down the collar of her dress and saw the white lace edge of her brassiere and the tops of her breasts and her slender legs, exposed beneath the skirt, and her feet in half-heeled shoes hovering over the big muddy pedals.

'Switch on,' he said. 'There.'

He felt the engine splutter and catch, the throb in the long tube of the exhaust pipe as it coughed out its usual gout of black smoke. He leaned forward, covered her left hand with his, transferred it to the knob of the gear lever and gave it a push.

'Right pedal,' he said laconically. 'Brake off.'

The trailer tipped. Les yelped. The Wallis trundled forward. Elbows flaring, fists loose on the worn old steering wheel, Pearl guided the Wallis into the top end of the Kennart Road as if she knew, even now, exactly where she was going.

'Straight on,' Charley told her. 'It's all downhill

399

from here.'

'Yah wanna bet,' Pearl said, and flashed him such a bold and glamorous look that Charley thought he might fall off the tractor, never to rise again.

*   *   *

Alan shortened his stride, smiled, and a step or two before their paths crossed, lifted his hat in casual greeting. 'Beautiful evening.'

'Quite beautiful.'

'Just enough breeze to keep the insects at bay.'

'South winds,' she said, 'are always soft. Which way are you headed?'

'I thought I might go as far as the crossroad before I turn for home.'

'Home?' she said. 'Now where might that be?'

'Actually,' he said, 'I'm not quite sure. Perhaps you can help me.'

'Perhaps I can,' she said.

In a flurry of leaves and grass the Scottie burst from the hedgerow and, with his stump of a tail wagging furiously, threw himself at Alan.

'Well, someone's pleased to see you,' Christine said.

He bent down, lifted the dog, held him on his chest and let him lick his face.

'He needs a bath, I'm afraid,' Chris said.

'He's not the only one,' said Alan.

He put the dog down, took her in his arms and kissed her.

'What is that taste?' she said. 'Is that gin?'

'I had a little noggin after work with my friend Josie.'

400

'How many friends do you have, Mr Kelso?'

'Far too few,' he said.

'I'm not sure I believe you,' said Christine. 'I think you've a secret life you keep all to yourself.'

'That, I'm afraid, is true.'

'I knew a man once who had a secret life.'

'Different sort of secret. Different generation.'

'Why do you never talk about your wife?'

He took her hand and they walked down the ridge road towards the crossroad. The fields on both sides swooped away. The hills above Kennart were dappled with sunlight. The mountains above the loch dozed in the summer heat.

'Didn't you love her?' Christine asked.

'I did—or I thought I did,' Alan answered.

'Surely you knew.'

'I think what I mean is that I didn't give it any thought at all.'

'You took her for granted, is that it?'

'Not exactly.' He paused. 'I just didn't give her enough.'

'Enough of what? Love?'

'Myself,' he said. 'I wish now I had given her more. But people change. Circumstances change them. I strolled into marriage and expected it all to be pie.'

'And it wasn't.'

'Nothing ever is,' he told her. 'Will you give up teaching?'

'I don't see why I should.'

'Because you'll be rich.'

'I don't really see what that's got to do with it.'

'Because you'll be married.'

'Will I?' said Chris. 'To whom?'

'Oh,' he said, 'I was rather hoping it wouldn't

401

come to this.'

He lowered himself carefully to one knee and took her hand.

Bruce watched, warily, from the shelter of the hedge.

'I have absolutely nothing to offer you,' Alan said. 'I'm a self-centred, somewhat obsessive member of the medical profession with a house that neither of us needs, and rather too many miles on the clock to hold this position for long. I'll come to the point, if I may?'

'I do wish you would,' said Christine.

'Miss Summers—Christine—would you do me the honour of—'

'Yes,' she said. 'Yes, you fool, of course I will.'